HAWKS

HAWKS

by

Joseph Amiel

G. P. Putnam's Sons
New York

Library of Congress Cataloging in Publication Data

Amiel, Joseph.
Hawks.

I. Title.
PZ4.A5164Haw 1979 [PS3551.M53] 813'.5'4 79–10989

ISBN 0–399–12312–1

PRINTED IN THE UNITED STATES OF AMERICA

In memory of my mother

HAWKS

1

"Mr. William Nye, please contact GUA Information. Mr. William Nye, please contact GUA Information."

Will's eyes rolled up toward the ceiling. Another few minutes and he would have been aloft and tilting south toward Mexico for the week's vacation he had shoehorned between the months of work just completed and the months of work to come.

The gate agent was holding the phone out to him. Will pushed himself out of the chair and crossed the crowded boarding lounge to take the call.

"This is Will Nye."

"Oh, Mr. Nye, I'm glad we caught you. The Old Man's office called. They want you over there right away."

Who else would it be but the Old Man? "Did they say why?"

"They think one of our planes may be down."

Will's breath caught. "Anything more than that?"

"No, sir."

"Thanks."

For a moment, Will stood immobile at the counter, walled off from his surroundings by a dark foreboding. But why had the Old Man sent for *him*? he wondered. He was a lawyer and could do little in this crisis.

Still, as he handed the phone back to the agent in the yellow GUA blazer, Will admitted that he was pleased; the Old Man had come to depend on him. In the half year he had been with the company, he had penetrated the inner circle.

"You'd better scratch me from this flight, Ed. Any other flights later tonight for somewhere warm?"

"Sorry, Mr. Nye." The agent reached below the counter for a schedule. "Would you like me to find you a morning flight?"

"No, thanks. The Thanksgiving rush will be over by then. I'll just come down and get on something."

Will returned to the chair for his suitcase. Automatically, he lifted it with his left hand, so that the good right leg would be under him when it swung forward at each stride. He would have to walk back out into the heavily falling snow to his car and drive around the perimeter of the field to reach the GUA building.

Will cast a final glance out of the wide boarding-lounge windows. The snow was blowing across them, partly obscuring the 707 parked at the mouth of the enclosed ramp. In the silvery blackness beyond, he could make out lights descending like a family of shooting stars—a small plane attempting to land. He watched until the wheels touched down and the craft began slowing along the runway. Then Will turned away. Somewhere else tonight another, larger plane might have failed to make it.

The Westwind taxied on, beyond the arms of the passenger terminal, which was proferring its last passengers to the few planes still drawn up at its ramps. Ben Buck kept the executive jet's nose wheel firmly on the center line of the taxiway. The GUA maintenance hangars and office building appeared luminous through the new snow ahead of him, as if viewed through a soft-focus lens. With his sweat and his vision, the huge white-haired man had built Global Universal Airlines. He was a living legend, the last of his kind. Like Lindbergh, Earhart and Rickenbacker, like Bill Boeing, Donald Douglas and Juan Trippe, the name Ben Buck conjured up bright images of a time when flight was a miracle wrought by the young and daring.

The ominous call from Keller had reached him in the air. No second call had come, so Buck supposed nothing more was known yet. He had notified his secretary, Eloise Cooper, from the cockpit and, after a moment's thought, had told her to track down Will.

The plane drew to a halt near the rear entrance to the GUA Building. Buck and a blond girl muffled to the nose against the cold in a wool scarf rushed out of the Westwind and across the windy tarmac, whitening with snow. The co-pilot would take care of the plane as he was instructed; it would be standing by, refueled, with a Presidential Service crew, ready to take off at a moment's notice.

Normally, Buck would have glanced at the maintenance hangars to make sure not too many planes were out of service at one time. But now he hurried into the rear entrance of the building, instructed a lobby guard to escort the young woman to his office to wait, and went directly to Operations Control.

The nerve center of any airline, at GUA Operations Control, occupied a good part of the second floor. At the center of the large room was a glass-walled area filled with computer terminals and Teletype and Telefax machines, sending and receiving messages from all of the company's offices. The ability to maintain administrative surveillance was why Buck had insisted on keeping the company's headquarters at the airport.

"Look at the successful airlines," he would say. "Delta's at the Atlanta airport. United's at O'Hare. Continental and Western at Los Angeles International. Braniff at Dallas–Fort Worth. People can sense problems early when they're right where the action is. They react quicker. The ones that have had the toughest times are administered from downtown office buildings."

Ordinarily Buck would have scanned the Teletypes for problems. Tonight a storm had diverted planes from New Delhi to Karachi, mechanical problems had delayed Flight 22 inbound from Brussels and London to JFK, and a flight engineer had been routed directly back home because of a family emergency. Chances were Buck would have sent a note to the man in the morning. But another, more urgent event not yet on the Teletype dominated his mind.

At Flight Dispatch, white boards with a strip to track each plane along its route covered one long wall. The information gathered in this center—weather reports, fuel burn rates, schedules, air traffic—would be fed to the computer programmed to prepare a flight plan for each trip that the captain could use or revise as he saw fit. Regional Flight Dispatch Centers operated twenty-four hours a day in New York, London and New Delhi, but Denver was the brain stem.

Buck didn't look up. Instead he quickened his pace, his own destination closer in view. Between Flight Dispatch and the Tech Center, which monitored on-line repairs, at the long table where the duty manager sat to oversee the airline's worldwide flight operations, Buck found Jim Keller, senior vice-president of Operations.

Short, his body muscled like a bulldog's, Keller's appearance reflected his tough, uncompromising nature. Only a couple of years earlier, Buck had lured him away from another airline. Keller's shirtsleeves were rolled up, exposing hamlike forearms. His hand tightly clenched the phone receiver. His eyes were fixed on the cathode-ray screen of the Telex machine beside him. The duty manager, a tall, composed man wearing glasses, leaned over his shoulder, his gaze also intent on the green screen. A third man, a controller responsible for GUA traffic in North America, stood at his side.

"Any more news?" Buck asked.

None of the men shifted their eyes from the screen.

"Nothing decisive," Keller said quietly. "But I'll fill you in. Flight 211 arrived at O'Hare from L.A. at ten-thirty-five local tonight and left the gate for New York at ten-fifty-five."

"Right on time."

"To the minute. It lifted off from O'Hare at eleven-thirteen. Four minutes later Departure Control handed the plane off to Chicago Center. Twenty minutes after that, at the Medum intersection, Chicago Center advised the pilot it was terminating radar service and to contact Cleveland Center for the next leg of the flight. But the plane never contacted Cleveland Center. It just disappeared."

Ben Buck watched the blank screen for a long moment. He seemed to be staring through it, trying to penetrate the solid walls and see through a thousand miles of night. Finally, he turned away to pick out the plane's route on the wall map. In the long gray overcoat, topped by his white mane, he looked like a massive, solitary mountain.

"Oh, God!" one of the men exclaimed.

The image on the screen had suddenly changed. Keller lowered the phone, then he rose and walked the few steps to where Buck stood.

"Chicago just confirmed. The plane is down."

A pent-up moan exploded from Buck's lips. "Where?"

"Northeastern part of Indiana, just west of the Ohio border. It was a 747 carrying three hundred and twenty-four passengers and a crew of fifteen."

"Three hundred and thirty-nine people! It had to be a holiday weekend!" Buck's hands were shaking. He gripped the back of the chair. "You know, Jimbo, it's been maybe eleven, twelve years since our last accident . . ." Then he took a deep breath, let it out, regaining his self-control. "Tell the switchboard to start on the call list," he ordered, and walked away.

Jim Keller picked up the phone again. He would give a short statement to the switchboard, which would then begin calling key personnel in the prescribed order. Then, once he had made sure a search party was on the way, with ambulances and medical personnel in case there were survivors, he would start contacting his top people. Before dawn, the National Transportation Safety Board's investigating Go-Team from Washington, Keller himself, and GUA and manufacturer experts in every aspect of flight would be in the air bound for northeastern Indiana.

Others in the company had other assigned tasks. An accurate passenger list had to be compiled, and there was the sad task of contacting the relatives of those on board. GUA officials would help with arrangements to bring them to the crash site, if they wished. System controllers would shift around equipment to cover the routes the downed plane would have flown in the next few days.

Buck stopped at the Tech Center desk. Highlighted on the wall before it were maintenance problems and inspection dates of particular aircraft. Buck recognized a man recently promoted from power plant supervisor. "Gino, Flight 211 has gone down. Pull a full maintenance log out of the computer. Give one to Mr. Keller right away. Send one up to my office when you have a chance."

Just beyond, at the Crew Tracking area, were charts detailing the crews for each flight. A tracker pointed out Flight 211.

Again, Buck felt a vast sadness. The downed plane had carried people he knew. He had always prided himself on a phenomenal memory that allowed him to recall the names and histories of an awesome number of GUA employees. Now that memory was a curse.

Benson and DeMarco! Jayson—he was in the group of flight engineers just rehired. And the flight attendants—he would know all of the older ones at the very least. He perused the list. It took some seconds before he could lift his eyes and say to the tracker, "Flight 211 is down between Chicago and New York. You'd better start shifting crews to cover flights."

The man blanched. "But that's a 747!"

Buck nodded sadly and moved toward the door. Others would take over the process of dealing with the million tasks of those rocked by the tragedy's wake, the grief of survivors and relatives, the investigations into the causes of the crash, the legal controversies and insurance claims. Buck's responsibility was to safeguard the company.

He went to his office and had Eloise telephone Maxwell Creighton, the airline's investment banker in New York.

Will Nye unwound his long body from the Porsche he had parked near the glass office building. The street lamps hazily defined his figure through the swirling flakes: blond locks falling haphazardly about a handsome face; the features punctuated by a scar-lifted eyebrow above unyielding eyes; and deftly tailored clothing even when, as now, the garb was casual—a brown turtleneck sweater, twill slacks and tweed sport jacket.

His suitcase was in the back seat, so he bent over to make certain the doors were locked, then straightened up and headed toward the building's entrance. His movements were slow and deliberate as, shifting from the good leg to the artificial one, he trod a line of footprints into the patina of new snow.

Will paused for a moment at the revolving door. The falling snow had endowed GUA's semiabstract raptor-in-flight symbol above the entrance with a greater verisimilitude than the sculptor had intended. With the construction of sharp, thin aluminum wedges forming the head and neck fluffed out feathery white, it now bore the more realistic likeness of an American eagle. But Will noticed another resemblance: the white hair, hunter's eye, boxer-bent nose reminded him of the man whose total creation Global Universal was.

Three parts of the large building were lit above the sculpture: "Reservations," where dozens of agents booked flights over the telephone for a good part of the nation; "Operations," where work had already begun and might continue for weeks and months to pin down the cause of the crash; and a corner of the top floor, familiarly called "the Control Tower," where Ben Buck awaited him.

The uniformed guard, as alert as if it had been midday, unlocked the glass doors to admit Will, then relocked them as the lawyer stopped to brush the snow off his hair and coat. Security and the Legal Department were under Will's management. Normally, upon his entering a patrolled area Will's eye would turn critical, but now he felt only relief because of the sense of solidity once more beneath his feet—and then chagrin for the moment of weakness.

The guard gestured that he would sign Will into the night visitors' register. Will quickened his pace toward the elevators.

Eloise Cooper stood near her desk filling the coffeemaker. Although she was past fifty, her small figure was still straight as the rifle that one of her Yankee forebears must have leveled at Concord or Lexington. She was Buck's eyes and ears and voice for all the things he was too busy to attend to personally.

Eloise greeted Will and then nodded toward the coffeemaker. "I'll bring a cup in to you as soon as it's ready." She remembered something. "I'm sorry about interrupting your vacation." The cadences of her voice still recalled the narrow cobblestone streets and busy whaling ports of New England.

"I'm sorry I ever told you when I was leaving. All I got from Information was that a plane was down. Have we heard anything more?"

"It's a 747. There's a rumor that survivors were spotted at the crash site by a search plane. Is Del going to be handling the crash for Legal?"

Will nodded. Del Moore had been watching over litigation and insurance matters for twenty years. Del's work would start later, when all the parties began haggling over liabilities and compensation. More immediate were the problems of Security. Will's Security director, Dan Pope, would be flying to the embarkation point of the flight to make certain there had been no slipups in security procedures.

Perhaps the Old Man is calling me in because a security breach is suspected on the flight, Will speculated.

"Please call the switchboard for me, Eloise, and make sure Del and Dan Pope were alerted."

She handed Will a copy of the passenger manifest. The photocopy machine had been off a hair in reproducing the list and, ironically, had placed a thin black border along the top of the copy and along one side.

Another small courtesy of the technological age, Will thought bleakly as his eye ran down the list of names, automatically seeking "Talbot, R." beside the designation "First Officer." A different name was there, and he felt himself breathing again. Among the crew he knew only Benson, the captain, who was head of the pilots' local and whom he liked very much. He knew none of the passengers.

Will's gaze lifted to the open doorway into Buck's office. A halo of ceiling lights cast a white island around the desk. The grayness seemed to lap placidly at the edge of the white, rolling outward in dimness to the wall of windows where the huge Old Man stood in his customary slacks and short-sleeved shirt, staring eastward across half a continent of flat plain. To the west, the dark mountains rose like brawny sentinels safeguarding the aerie city.

There was no denying that Ben Buck was larger than life in many ways. Well over six feet tall by age fourteen, Ben Buck had lied about his age to join the Flying Service in 1917, the same day he had seen his first biplane chug suddenly out from behind a hill and across the sky. He had chased it all the way to town. During the war he had gunned down his share of Fokkers and, swooping and wheeling like the cavalry he replaced, had had his share of fighter planes shot out from under him. He had barnstormed in the twenties—like so many who could not rid themselves of the addiction to air and skill and death—then had flown mail to South America. On the spindly backs of those mail routes, Ben Buck had built an airline, leaving it only to fight a second war, when he had helped put a worldwide air transport network together almost from scratch. After that he was "the General" to most of his employees, "Big Ben" to those who had known him longer, "Buckie" to a few old-timers still captaining Global Universal's flights around the world, and the "Old Man" to all. Until the early seventies, he could do no wrong. Global Universal grew to become America's premier air carrier. But in recent years higher fuel and operating costs and lower ticket sales had hurt airline revenues. Global Universal had been hard hit. Only last week *Financial World* had asked in its cover story, "Has Big Ben Finally Struck Out at Global Universal?" After what the company had undergone in recent months, Will wondered himself. Nobody could blame the Old Man if, at his age and with his impressive record of accomplishments, he threw in the towel.

The moonlight through the window, lambent on the Old Man's face, seemed to whisk away six decades and reveal the sky-struck youth staring at his first "aeroplane." Will had experienced the same sense of wonder at defying the natural forces. How many Saturdays had he hung around the little airport near the factory hoping Ed Bender would give him just one ride between lessons or let him come along on the tow for Mr. Cline's sail plane? Will hardened himself at the recollection; it had been the seductive precursor of his career as a war pilot and the impersonal killing six miles high over Vietnam. And yet, that early wonder tied him to Ben Buck in a way the earthbound would never understand; they were children of Icarus, at last attaining his ancient dream.

In the midst of Will's musing, Ben Buck suddenly spun around.

"Took you long enough."

It was always a mistake, Will reminded himself for the dozenth time, to consider Ben Buck in terms of the past. Buck himself lived in the most immediate present. Will was able to maintain an approximation of equality with him by returning crustiness in kind and because the Old Man believed Will would just as soon leave as stay.

"Bannister lives just down the road," Will retorted. "He could have been here half an hour ago."

"He's out somewhere in a goddamn Winnebago! The man

could have flown anywhere in the world for the weekend and he takes off in a goddamn house on wheels." Buck enjoyed teasing the flinty, conservative financial chief, but the Old Man was angry now at not being able to reach him. Aboard any jetliner in most parts of the world, Bannister could have been contacted within minutes.

Buck's voice softened. "Did you hear about 211?"

"Eloise said there may be survivors."

"Christ, let's hope so." A glint of light flickered across the hardscrabble landscape of Buck's face. "Remember the one in the Everglades, where a lot of people made it?"

"I remember."

Buck pivoted away from the window, his face tight with anguish. "What the hell happened out there? Flying's twice as safe as car travel. Eighty percent of all travel between cities is by plane. The 747's the safest form of transportation there is. Our pilots are put through constant hell to make sure they're the best, the safest. Our mechanics take every precaution that . . ." His voice trailed off. The statistics airline executives lived by and could rattle off instantly would not help now. His eyes shifted back to the window and the night sky. The obscuring snow made more graphic their distance from the crash site and their ignorance of what had occurred over a farm field a thousand or more miles away.

"I feel helpless," Buck said softly to himself. A few moments later, he turned to Will. "I've been thinking about what this crash will do to the company. Is the insurance in order?"

Will nodded. The airline and its investors were protected, he knew, by one Lloyd's of London syndicate that would make good on the liability to victims' families within rather high limits. A second syndicate insured the aircraft itself: GUA would be repaid its share of the plane's value, and the members of the public who had financed the rest of the transport's cost by buying loan certificates and leasing the plane to the airline would be similarly reimbursed.

"The stock market's been too skittish lately not to get terrified when something like this happens," the Old Man reflected aloud. "The average guy thinks we're in the hole for thirty-five million dollars' worth of aircraft. Or else he'll think passengers will stay away. Probably will, too, for a week or so. The truth is, recovering the cash value of a jetliner can be a damned blessing, although I'd rather have lost a 707—they're older and a hell of a lot less efficient. Damned stockholders and smart-ass analysts don't think that way. By noon tomorrow our stock should have dropped to eight or below." Buck's fist slammed against the desk. "That's just the opportunity that son of a bitch Girard has been waiting for!"

After quietly buying up Global Universal stock for months, utilizing brokers' names and bank nominees to conceal its growing ownership, Girard's huge conglomerate, Faranco Inc., had acquired five percent of the airline and was forced by law to reveal the fact to the appropriate government bodies—the Securities and Exchange Commission (SEC) and the Civil Aeronautics Board (CAB). That was a few months ago. Will guessed that by now Girard had pushed Faranco's ownership to six or seven percent. Buck owned nine percent or so and was borrowing to buy more. Thc Buck Foundation owned another five. The rest of the GUA shares were held by the public, including a substantial amount by company employees and financial institutions. Despite Girard's press release stating that Faranco was simply an investor, few doubted that a man who had built a billion-dollar business empire on similar acquisitions meant to stop before he had gained control of the airline or been forced to shift his sights to some other target.

Buck moved toward the bar. As he reached for his glass, his eye caught the dark rectangle that took up most of the adjacent wall. He flipped a switch, and a Mercator projection of the world was vividly illuminated. Global Universal's routes crisscrossed the map like arteries, through which flowed people and goods and communications to dozens of countries on every inhabited continent.

"Damn it, the bastard wants it!" Buck exclaimed. "He held off making a public tender offer for the stock, hoping I'd agree to sell my shares. He knows now I'd let him spit in my face first, but it bought a few months' more time."

Buck sought in Will's face a sign that he was an ally. He saw only the keen intelligence that drew him toward the young man and simultaneously kept him at bay. He could not guess that

Will Nye harbored as deep a dislike for J. Stephen Girard as his own—and for very much the same reason. Like Girard, Will Nye wanted to head GUA someday soon. But he was young, had too few years in the industry, and was not a line executive—all very good reasons to doubt that the Old Man would choose him as his successor. On the other hand, there was something in Buck's voice when he spoke to the young lawyer that Will did not hear when he spoke to the other executives. That softness, that affinity, gave Will hope and made J. Stephen Girard his natural enemy.

The Old Man leaned over the small white sofa and straightened a blanket of nearly the same color. For the first time Will noticed a fringe of blond hair. A young woman was cuddled into the corner of the sofa, asleep beneath the blanket.

"A hell of a weekend. She couldn't get enough." Buck winked. "The Old Man's still got it."

Just then the girl shifted, and Will saw her open childlike eyes for a moment, focus on the Old Man, then close them as she rolled back under the blanket.

"She's got a nice laugh," Buck murmured softly. Then he turned toward Will with a grin. "And a hell of a pair of knockers."

The two men chuckled, breaking the tension, before Buck returned to the problem at hand. "With the stock at ten bucks a share, would you listen to some fast-talker offering twelve for a company with assets alone worth sixteen? *But*—" and Buck emphasized the word as he dropped into his desk chair—"if the stock were at eight, twelve might sound like an invitation to the Inaugural Ball. Which brings us to the point of this meeting."

"I was wondering about that."

Buck leaned back and placed the soles of his shoes against the edge of the desk. "Will, I want Global Universal to borrow fifty million dollars."

"I thought the company's cash flow was beginning to ease," Will remarked with some concern.

"That's not what the loan's for. The money's ammunition to attack before Girard makes his move." Buck paused to sip his drink and to heighten the effect of what he was about to say. "Will, I want Global Universal to start buying in its own stock over the next couple of months. Fifty million dollars' worth. That kind of buying should keep the price of the stock up and out of Girard's range. I've already spoken to Max Creighton. He thinks he can pull off the loan. He's expecting you in his office in the morning to discuss the terms."

"That's a lot of extra debt for this company to carry right now."

Buck dismissed the notion with a wave of his hand. "The Westwind and a fresh crew should be ready at the hangar for you by now. I've known Max Creighton forty years, in good times and bad. When he gives his word, you've got a deal. As soon as he does, get on the phone with the financial guys at the wire services, the *Times*, the *Wall Street Journal*—I don't have to tell you who—and hammer home that it shows the faith we have in our future and that the banks have in us by supporting the stock."

"What I'll tell them is we're buying our own shares for investment, to use in possible corporate acquisitions and for other corporate purposes. End quote. Buying our own shares is illegal if we do it to keep the stock's price up."

Buck waved his hand broadly again; the legal niceties were Will's concern.

Will tried to fight off weariness by straightening his spine against the soft white womb chair. "If Creighton can put together the banks," he conceded, "it's quite a strategy." Even as he spoke, a tiny doubt about what Buck was up to tried to scratch its way into his brain.

"I sure as hell wasn't going to wait until Girard was on my tail and firing," declared Buck with a self-satisfied grin.

"Bannister or one of the other financial types around here would be a lot more logical to send. I was just about to take a couple of days off."

"You prepared to guarantee Bannister's ETA in a goddamn Winnebago in a snowstorm? We have to move fast. With the Westwind's range it'll have you in New York nonstop by the start of the business day." Characteristically, Buck switched subjects without a break. "Did you ever fly stunt planes?"

Will shook his head.

"When we were barnstorming, it was usually the tall, wiry

ones like you," said Buck, "who didn't give a shit about anything, that made it."

"That's a hell of a theory for running a company with forty thousand employees."

Buck leaned toward the younger man. "Besides, Will, God is always on the side of any poor fool dumb enough to think that all the machinery under him can really fly."

The comment brought to mind the recent tragedy, and both men fell silent. A few moments later, Eloise Cooper entered with coffee for Will.

"Anything new?" he asked her.

She shook her head as she handed him the cup. Buck raised his glass questioningly. She nodded and walked to the bar, never glancing at the form on the sofa. Except for occasional trips back East to visit married relatives and her nieces and nephews, for the past thirty years Eloise's life had been totally given over to Buck and to Global Universal, in which she owned an astonishingly large block of stock. She made herself a drink and sat down.

Suddenly, Lee Conway stepped into the room; his cheeks, which had begun to sag into middle-aged slackness, were now tight and red from the cold.

"I came as soon as I heard, General."

He moved toward the desk before the Old Man might gesture that the meeting was private.

Send *him* to New York, you old bastard, Will thought. He'd consider it an honor to be rocketed across the continent to convince lenders the most heavily overborrowed company in the industry needs fifty million dollars to buy stock—not planes or fuel or to pay bills, but stock. He'd be too inflated by the glory of it to notice he was rushing toward the edge of a precipice.

"One of the guys at the Tech Desk asked me to bring up the plane's maintenance log." Conway handed Buck a folded computer printout and took a seat. "I also thought you'd want to see the flight crew records. I've already been on the phone with our Chicago and New York people. We're doing everything we can for the families and friends. Not three months ago I had every airport office review the procedures in case something like this occurred, so you can be proud your people are on their toes."

"Jim Keller was here when it happened," said Buck acidly.

Conway smiled wanly, trying to fathom how he had suddenly lost points despite his promptness.

This place will be a barnyard within an hour, Will decided. All the top executives who can't help directly with the crash will be here to flatter and cluster around the aging Sun King.

Buck looked up from the paper. "Well, whatever caused it, the chances are pretty good it wasn't the plane."

He lifted the phone and pushed three buttons in succession. "Buck here. Any more news?" There was a pause. His eyelids dropped like weights, and he let the phone fall back to the cradle. Finally he muttered to the others, "No survivors! Three hundred and thirty-nine people on board, and no survivors!"

His fist slammed futilely against the desk top once more. "Benson and DeMarco were both topnotch. Topnotch! Hell, Benson's been piloting for us since DC-3s."

His huge hand enveloped the glass. "They say it's the worst single plane disaster in U.S. aviation. I guess once in a while God becomes a little forgetful," he whispered to no one in particular.

And then he did something that touched Will deeply. All the pilots lived in Denver. Buck left his office to drive to their homes and personally break the tragic news to their wives.

Donna Harney flashed her ID at the guard and directed the taxi driver through the wire fence between the hangars and onto the tarmac at Global Universal's sprawling complex. Positive she would not be needed, Donna had swapped flight for standby duty with another stewardess in order to decorate her new apartment.

Because as a child she had been shuttled back and forth among unwilling relatives with too little themselves and among a couple of foster homes as well, nothing else in the world was so important as this apartment, a home of her own. She had allowed herself few luxuries and saved every spare penny while rooming with several other girls. She had been so close to having enough a year and a half before, when the airline suddenly announced employee layoffs. Her seniority had been insufficient to protect her from the cut; she would work a couple of months, then be laid off. In between she would wait on tables. Jobs of any kind were hard to come by with so many Denver-based women in the same predicament. Several friends found their way eased by "helpful" men. Donna avoided them and kept looking for work. Finally, attrition of those with greater seniority had assured her of uninterrupted employment, and she had leased her own apartment.

The past day and night had been spent painting the large old rooms from ceiling to floor. Sometime after midnight she had finally dropped onto a sofa in exhausted sleep. The call from Crew Scheduling seemed to come only an instant later. A Presidential Service crew, which called for a flight attendant as well, was needed for one of the business jets usually rented out to corporations: "spur of the moment . . . V.I.P.s . . . get here as fast as you can." For a moment after the voice ceased and the line went dead, she was uncertain whether it had been a dream, but then she felt the receiver against her ear and shuffled toward the shower.

The last time Will had been in the Westwind was with a contingent of GUA executives traveling to Houston to hammer out a long-term jet-fuel arrangement with a large oil company. He had piloted the sleek plane then to build up hours. It was firm GUA policy that management personnel with operational skills maintain them sharply honed. Buck felt strongly that it kept his managers in touch with the nuts and bolts of running an airline.

The Westwind's cabin contained two rows of seats and a sitting/sleeping divan along one side of the cabin. Will hung up his jacket and loosened his tie. He was just about to stretch out and catch some sleep when he noticed headlights racing toward the plane. A slim girl clutching a small saffron-colored valise charged out of a taxi and up the stairs. For a moment she seemed confused by the sight that greeted her. Then disbelieving anger widened her eyes to blue floodlights.

"One person? You hired this plane and got us all out here in the middle of the night in a snowstorm for just one person?" The question was an indictment.

She had been in such a hurry to make the plane that the buttons on her saffron-and-violet uniform blouse had worked open a good way toward the top of her skirt. Will found himself staring at the slash of skin.

He lifted his eyes. "If it's any consolation, lady, it wasn't my idea either."

He turned away and put her out of his mind. Since returning to the Rockies, Will Nye had simplified his personal life in many ways. Most importantly, he had given up the illusion that he sought the one right woman to open his heart to: he enjoyed sex and good company immensely, but sharing himself beyond the natural boundary of the dawn's early light was out of the question. His one real commitment was to his career. That single passion consumed and drove him completely. All other pursuits were merely recreation. He sincerely believed that he needed no one.

Will pulled the small curtains across the window, belted himself in and closed his eyes. The last sound he heard was the hatch closing, and the plane began to roll.

He awoke to the sound of yawning. The girl was curled into a ball in one of the other seats. She had gone to sleep soon after him and was now waking up.

"You probably want breakfast, right?" Her tone had not acquired warmth in the intervening hours. A woman he barely knew was treating him like the husband in an unhappy marriage; it was a feeling he had once known only too well.

He removed the toiletry case and the fresh clothing from his valise and went to the lavatory, carefully reaching for a handhold before each step. His thoughts were hundreds of miles ahead of him in New York City, which for all its fiscal misfortunes was still the financial center of the world.

When Will was beginning to rebuild a life shattered by the Vietnam War and divorce, he chose a law school in New York, Columbia University. Only in a city of so many people could he be assured of the anonymity that would allow him to rehabilitate himself at his own pace. Later he found the intensity, the diversity of New York so heady that he stayed on and became one of the bright young men climbing the greased rungs of a Wall Street law-firm ladder. He had an instinct for life as commerce—giving in consideration for getting. He understood that the ritual dances were a game and that the purpose was to win. He thrived. Ben Buck picked him for that instinct, that understanding, just in time—when he had begun to lose interest in the game.

Coming to the airline had reinvigorated Will, offering a prize so dazzling that all other interests paled to invisibility. However far away it might be, however remote his chances of winning it, the merest hope that he might someday run Global Universal Airlines was worth every effort to which his will could exhort mind and body. Now J. Stephen Girard was threatening to knock over all the pieces and seize the board. . . .

Will silently reviewed the usual tender-offer technique. An announcement suddenly appears in the *Wall Street Journal*, and sometimes the *New York Times* and other papers, offering shareholders a premium above the market price for their stock in a usually unsuspecting and undervalued public company. The offering price is too good to refuse. Within a few short days, the target company is caught in the strong claws of the raider. Large companies like Avis Rent-A-Car, Armour Meat, Jones & Laughlin Steel and Reliance Insurance had been snatched up in such a way.

Global Universal was a good deal larger than most target companies and, as an airline, was under the protection of the CAB. That made hunting, even by the most persistent predator, a much more difficult undertaking. By carving out an investment position in GUA, Girard had relinquished the opportunity for surprise, but had also effectively discouraged other companies that might have had a similar scheme in mind.

Will sloshed the shaving cream off and dried his face. As he combed the mass of dark-blond hair, he caught a glimpse of himself in the mirror. Only during unprepared-for glances like this did he sense a truth about himself: the faint wrinkles at eye and forehead adding character to his good looks were a mere disguise, the fashionable adult clothes a ruse. Underneath, there was still a skinny eighteen-year-old from a small town who had carried an unused condom in his wallet for two years, a high-scoring basketball captain bright enough to know that winning the state championship was not the apex of his life but too dazzled by the adulation to acknowledge it. That was the hero Ben Buck was sending out on the attack.

When Will returned to his seat, the aroma of coffee filled the cabin. He stopped for a moment to gaze at the woman preparing the breakfast tray. Her coloring was vivid: chestnut hair; pale, nearly white skin; blue eyes. She was taller, her features sharper, more like a model's, than the Miss America types Global Universal almost invariably hired.

When she brought him the breakfast tray, he smiled politely. Civility? She was having none of it.

"Instead of renting this plane, you could have waited a few hours and taken the eight-o'clock nonstop." She seemed to be continuing the earlier conversation as if the intervening hours had never passed.

"I also could have walked. Are you this pleasant to your regular passengers?"

"Sorry," she said curtly. "I'll have to lay over in New York to pick up my flight to Europe and the Middle East on Tuesday. I won't be back in Denver till the end of the week." She glanced at her watch. "The carpets will be delivered in two hours and the movers arrive four hours later with my new furniture."

"Have someone else let them in."

"The only one who might have been able to do it took over my flight duty the last two days. She's probably in New York already."

Will felt a sudden vacuum in his stomach. "What flight?"

"Two Eleven," she replied. "L.A.–Chicago–New York."

His eyes flicked over to her name plate. "Donna," he began, feeling overwhelmed by the effort to meet her eyes, "you'd better sit down. Something has happened."

As dawn came up and the floodlights were turned off one by one, some of the drama seemed to evaporate. The landscape was gray now, nearly matching the color of the twisted metal. The blood splashes had turned brown, drab. Nearly all the bodies and parts of bodies found strewn on the earth in grotesque disarray had been covered with sheets. Many had already been tagged, placed in black plastic bags and hauled away to a local high-school gymnasium to await identification. In their place wooden stakes sprouted like barren saplings. At intervals a black plastic bag would emerge from a gaping hole in the tilted fuselage and be carried on a stretcher to a waiting truck.

The FBI Disaster Squad, victim identification experts, was on the scene, helping with the tagging and the loading. State police would also pitch in. For many days, both groups would aid local coroners trying to match bodies with names. Eventually, they would certify as deceased 339 people, in some cases on evidence as flimsy as the lone bent earring recognized by a daughter on a table of unidentified passenger belongings.

Local police had cordoned off the site to keep onlookers and the press at a distance—theft of strewn plane parts as grisly souvenirs could prevent discovery of the crash's cause. Gathered around the twisted debris were small groups of investigators from the National Transportation Safety Board (NTSB), the Federal Aviation Administration (FAA), Global Universal, the airframe and engine manufacturers, the airline pilots' union and the insurance company, as well as local authorities. Only the first, the NTSB, could be considered fully objective. They were government experts whose sole responsibility was to determine the probable cause of the crash. That determination would weigh heavily in recommending improved equipment and procedures and in the court cases that would surely follow. Those found responsible could become liable for millions of dollars in claims made by the families of those on board.

Slipping among the various investigators were photographers and surveyors whose task was to record accurately where objects had been found, an important tool in reconstructing the exact sequence of events. At what point did the plane hit the ground? Were some plane parts already detached before impact? How far were bodies thrown? How far did the fuselage skid?

Power plant specialists were trying to determine if birds had been ingested into the jet fans, cutting off the air intake, or if icing had occurred or fuel starvation or fire. Airframe experts, if metal fatigue had caused failure of a vital structural member. Systems people, whether the electrical, hydraulic or control systems had failed in some way. Only by such painstaking study could future crashes be prevented.

With a practiced eye, FBI agent Owen Clayton had spent hours traversing the crash site. Specializing in aircraft crimes, with a broad, trusting face that belied the wariness behind it, Clayton had quickly established in his own mind that the plane, apparently still in one piece, had dived sharply into the ground near a grove of trees, compressing and cracking apart the fuselage and scattering bodies, cargo and metal. The nose and the collapsed front end, as well as the wings and the engines, had dug deep craters in the earth.

Fire often follows crashes, but here only the trees were seared into charcoal. The wing tanks had burst upon impact, the force instantly vaporizing the fuel, which then rose as twin fireballs and continued forward into the trees. A moment later the flames were gone, leaving giant spent matchsticks behind.

Clayton found himself drawn to the plane's tail. Still whole but separated from the rest of the plane, it thrust upward like a huge dagger toward the rising sun. Unscratched, the golden GUA bird of prey on its surface still appeared to be soaring toward the heavens.

The night before, Owen Clayton had carried Edna up to the bedroom not long after dinner. She had been more tired than usual, because their daughter, Hannah, had brought the baby over to visit for the afternoon. A victim of muscular dystrophy, Edna had lain limply on the pillow trying to chat cheerfully with her husband, but her strength failed her, and her eyelids had soon closed. The rest of the evening, Clayton had been glad to be able to sit alone. After what the doctor had told him about the test results, he needed time to think.

Clayton had been with the FBI for over twenty years. His career had not turned out as he had hoped. Many of those who had begun with him at the Academy or were rookies when he was already a veteran had long since passed him by. As an investigator, his superiors had assured him, he was as good an agent as there was in the Bureau, with one of the best arrest records on the force. But he was a loner, they said, logical and relentless, lacking the temperament to supervise others who would do the actual investigating. Clayton suspected they were right. The paperwork atop which the Bureau floated bored him, as did the routine aid one agent often had to give another and the simple, quickly solved cases the law enforcement agency often undertook because they made for impressive statistics. He was happiest tracking down the missing pieces to a perplexing puzzle, living people who hid or evaded, or facts that might complete a pattern of clues. Nothing else had ever provided equivalent satisfaction.

He had been a small-plane charter pilot for a while after a tour of duty as an M.P. in Korea. One night, while watching an old film on TV in which "G-men" hunted "gangsters," he decided that was what he wanted to do in life. Twenty years later the compulsion that drove him on during a hunt could still overcome him so completely that it blocked out what he knew to be true every other waking moment of his life: that such satisfaction was the root cause of his failing Edna—and himself.

Owen Clayton made a decent living, to be sure, but hardly enough for what he had promised a younger, more vital Edna. Last night he had looked around the living room as if for the first time. The sofa needed reupholstering. The carpet was threadbare. The house itself was in a deteriorating part of Chicago, and now—with the heavy medical expenses and Hannah's husband having left her—on a salary too small for one household, let alone two, Clayton could not afford to move away. Edna had always yearned for land and enough sunlight in the back yard to plant a garden. She was too weak to do more than sit on the porch and feel the sun warm her bones through the continually wasting muscles. A few months before, he had played with the hope that he might be able to find her such a house in one of the more distant suburbs, where prices were still within reason. But the doctor's brutal frankness had aborted even that modest dream.

After midnight, he had finally roused himself from the armchair, determined to stop dwelling on his problems. If they were insoluble, he could do nothing. Otherwise, time would provide answers. He had emptied the ashtray into the downstairs toilet and flushed, then dug out a fresh pack of cigarettes. He had gone through a pack since dinner. For a moment he had considered taking out his stamp collection, but he was too agitated. Instead, he had flipped on the television set just as the grisly bulletin began running incongruously across the screen below Johnny Carson's smile. At about the same time, the phone had rung.

After his transfer to the Chicago field office, many aviation cases had been directed Clayton's way because of his flying background. The phone call had been from his supervisor, to give him the ticket on the plane crash he had just seen reported.

Clayton had then called his housekeeper, Mrs. Evans, to ask

her to spend the rest of the night with Edna. He had slipped back into the bedroom and stopped for a moment at Edna's side, his stockiness sadly bulking above his wife's skeletal shape. Half a minute passed before he had satisfied himself that her chest was regularly rising and falling. He had checked for his wallet with the FBI identification card, slipped on his holster and jacket, and put on his gray fedora. Then he had left the house, gotten into the car, and begun driving in the direction of Angola, Indiana.

Gorlick, the Special Agent-in-Charge of Clayton's Chicago office, had arrived just after him. They had toured the devastation together. The FBI administrator was known for his iron-hard manner, but he had never seen an air disaster's remains before; the carnage had left him stunned. Clayton had walked him back to his car in silence until, finally, the younger man had recovered and could speak.

"Indianapolis is sending a resident agent from Fort Wayne as a formality, but the Bureau has cleared Chicago as the office of origination. I fought to get it. That means I'm on the line, Clayton." Gorlick's tough-guy façade had returned. He had to prove wrong all those who thought him too young to be made SAC of an office as important as Chicago. If this crash were not an accident, but had been criminally caused, the case would have national importance and exposure, and finding the perpetrator could go a long way toward solidifying Gorlick's position. "Oliver says you're the best there is on these things. Drop everything else until there's no doubt about the cause one way or the other. I'll assign you a team to get started right away—following leads, checking out people, whatever you need. If you can use more people, let me know."

He had eyed the heavyset agent critically. "I'll be honest, Clayton. I'll be watching to see how you work with the other agents and run the investigation. With your experience, you should be supervising a squad. If it goes well, I'll recommend you."

Clayton had nodded and expressed appreciation for the opportunity, but he was struck by the irony that many aboard the doomed plane must have been relishing some similar piece of good news just a moment or two before they fell out of the sky.

* * *

Dwight Raeburn, head of the NTSB's Go-Team, looked up from the bright tangle of ripped wires at the sliced-open rear fuselage and spotted Clayton. They had worked together in the past, but on nothing of this immensity.

"It's a God-awful mess, isn't it?"

"When are the dogs expected?" Clayton asked.

"The FAA says they loaned the closest team out to you guys investigating a theft of explosives from an army base. Another's sniffing out a bomb in an office building. There's no longer an emergency here."

"What does it look like?"

"Can't be sure. The fuselage folded up like an accordion when it hit. Any evidence of explosive decompression in the fore section is hidden right now."

"But you've *got* to be suspicious. Items from the plane are turning up for miles around."

"Owen, I can't be sure of anything yet. This is one where we won't know definitely until we pull it out of the crater and piece it together."

The process of hauling every piece of the wreckage to an empty hangar and diligently reconstructing the mammoth airplane, like a great Chinese puzzle, could take months.

"I can't wait for that. The trail will be cold by then. Have you spoken to your guys checking out Operations and Air Traffic Control at O'Hare?"

The smaller man pulled the clipboard from under his arm. "Just before it went down, the plane was at an altitude of twenty-seven thousand feet and an airspeed of five hundred and forty miles per hour. Nothing near it. Weather clear. No turbulence, so far as we know. And then the plane just dived. It's not much, but, believe me, it's all we know right now."

"Dwight, I know you don't want to be put on the spot this early, but if you had my job, would you treat this like a potential criminal matter?"

This time Raeburn did not hesitate. "I'd bust my ass on it, if I were you. Look, any number of things could have caused this, and the clues are still buried in the wreckage. But right now it smells of sabotage. We'll know more when we find the recorders, but even they might not tell the whole story."

Heavily protected to survive a crash, the recorders monitor the flight and provide hard evidence for investigators after an accident. The flight data recorder chronologically registers takeoffs, altitudes, speeds, angles and other indicia of the flight by means of styluses impressing lines on foil. The voice recorder captures the voices of the cockpit crew on tape by means of three overhead microphones.

"You haven't found them yet?"

Raeburn shook his head. "We're cutting away metal at the place we think the *flight* recorder should be. We're just not sure yet where the *voice* recorder is buried. God, it's a horror!"

"Call me as soon as you know something more."

They separated. Clayton took a slow walk through the debris. This was a last search for any clue he might have missed that would spark an insight into what had suddenly happened on a clear night twenty-seven thousand feet above the unyielding ground.

Suddenly, Clayton paused, noticing first a glint in the sky and then the sound of an engine. A helicopter was swooping in low over the blackened trees. It circled twice over the crash site and then tipped to one side as it pulled away. At that moment Clayton caught sight of a photographer on the passenger side.

"Damned press. They're ghouls," he grumbled to himself, although he knew how restrained the news media were about showing truly gory photos. In this case the photos would never appear in the news for another reason. The photographer worked for Faranco Inc. The photographs would be on the desk of J. Stephen Girard before noon.

Clayton's eye was then caught by something on the ground, but when he realized what it was, he hurried on. As many times as he had walked a crash site and as tough as everyone thought he was, the sight of a child's effects was still too much for him to endure. A teddy bear was lying face down beneath a seat cushion. Ghostly white, it too appeared dead.

2

Although many may have speculated, only J. Stephen Girard himself truly understood the reason for his success. He was, he knew, an almost totally cynical man.

A bit below average height, thin, fit, athletic, hairline receding to accentuate a high forehead and an aquiline nose, Girard's appearance reflected his sober nature. His commitment to business was nearly total, his schedule practically undeviating. He awoke at six-fifteen in the morning and exercised for half an hour. Then a shower and a shave. At seven he watched the news on television, then dressed. While being driven to the office, he read the *New York Times*, the *Washington Post* and the *Wall Street Journal.* One of his secretaries would be waiting with coffee at his desk when he arrived at eight.

Like most people who worked for him, the secretary was, no doubt, capable, courteous and, at the core, terrified of J. Stephen Girard. To be effective, he believed, people must be driven by some force: self-interest, love, loyalty, hate or fear. Fear was the simplest. Some feared the humiliation of Girard's searing rebuke, some the revelation of a secret, and some the loss of a job at a salary just a bit too high for them to renounce without sacrifice. But Girard's own private life was closed off from the gaze of colleagues and the public alike. Although professionally accessible, he was a mystery man. Except for such bare facts as an excellent academic record, almost nothing was known about him; and although he occasionally appeared in public, he avoided the social scene. Girard was not naturally shy or oblivious to his public image. He simply believed that the less that was known to others, the less vulnerable he was to their attacks. And he acted accordingly, deliberately. Even a small detail, like the dark glasses he invariably wore, became a mystery. Did he wear them for medical reasons, or out of choice? No one was quite certain and no one could find out, because he granted no interviews.

When Girard awoke on Monday morning, he felt very good indeed. He had made Marie a promise many years before that he would be a millionaire by age thirty and be worth ten times that by thirty-five. As his fiftieth birthday approached, his wealth on paper was nearing two hundred million. Those who thought they knew Girard would not have recognized the tenderness in his eyes as he reached over and let his fingers brush against his sleeping wife's cheek. She was the only woman he had ever loved. Her face was still pretty—high cheekbones, skin firm, hair carefully touched up—but he was too much the realist to delude himself that the difference in their ages was not becoming ever more apparent.

Marie Girard was older than her husband. A few who knew them ascribed to an uncharacteristic vanity her efforts to appear the younger. The Girards' married life was very private; their pleasures were personal. They had no children. For the last few months, Jamie—she was the only one who called Girard that—had been playing with the idea of giving her a very unusual present for her birthday next year, one more lavish than any he had ever given her. That present was Global Universal Airlines.

The merits of the company were obvious. Air travel would increase in the long-term future. Fuel prices had at least stabilized. Airline profits were about to begin skyrocketing. And, despite setbacks in recent years, Global Universal was still a pearl among the airlines, a giant, a legend, a symbol of American air travel around the world. For Faranco that was important; the conglomerate lacked a vivid identity among investors. Heavy equipment, machine tools, oil drilling hardware, roofing materials, valves, specialty steels, a small helicopter charter service and a bank holding company were highly profitable but not very glamorous. Even the new joint venture with Kalex Metallurgy to exploit mineral resources in West Africa was still two years away from production.

As he shaved, occasionally glancing over at the built-in TV for the first view of the news portion of the *Today* show—his signal to turn up the volume—Girard reviewed his strategy. All the early forays had been and would be made by others, with nothing traceable to him, no matter what suspicions others might have. As each sally was fired at GUA, he need only sit back and wait. Only when and if *he* felt the time was right need he risk an overt act—and then it would be a full-scale assault.

Familiar faces appeared on the screen, smiling, bright-eyed faces possible at that hour only on men and women being paid a good deal of money to wake up. Girard increased the volume. The news report commenced with the Global Universal plane crash. Girard already knew about it, of course. Now he listened for details.

The list of crash victims had been verified. Among the more notable were three members of the U.S. water polo team, an Assistant Treasury Secretary, and the chief of the SEC's Enforcement Division, who had only recently been nominated by the President to be the head of the Securities and Exchange Commission. The merest suggestion of a smile lifted the corners of Girard's mouth. The week was starting off auspiciously. He reached for the telephone and dialed a number at Faranco.

"Colonel Merrill should have arrived in New York by now. Track him down. I want him in my office at nine-thirty."

Will got out of the cab in front of the tall iron gates of Creighton, Cromwell & Co. Great rusticated stone blocks, edges smoothly rounded, sealed off the ground floor from public view. Fifteen feet above his head, the first iron-barred windows emerged from the granite. The architecture evoked banking's beginnings, the fortresslike palaces of Renaissance Italy, where finance first became a high art so prosperous it could finance other arts.

Not nearly so old, Creighton, Cromwell & Co. had grown out of the nineteenth-century enterprise of two merchant families, one British, the other American. Although it provided very little financing itself, this international investment banking partnership was the catalyst for public and private underwritings and bank loans totaling billions each year.

Once inside the building, Will remembered how traditional and predictable was the décor in such firms, as if bright colors and modern furniture might signify insubstantiality. Firms like Creighton, Cromwell rose or fell on their reputations for solidity.

At the end of a green carpet, just past a middle-aged secretary seated at a large simple desk, was Maxwell Creighton IV. Slight of build, wearing a modestly tailored dark suit and old-fashioned clear-plastic-framed spectacles, he was almost indistinguishable from those departed Maxwell Creightons I, II, and III whose sober portraits hung like sentinels from facing walls of the reception room. Presumably, consecutively numbered Cromwells were hung at some equally key checkpoint. Presumably, they too had bland eyes and constricted, cautious mouths.

Will Nye shook hands with this fourth Maxwell Creighton, and sat down in a chair opposite the desk.

A slim manila file was the only paperwork in sight. It contained material on Global Universal. Creighton had been considering Ben Buck's plan to borrow fifty million dollars to buy up its own stock, but he appeared unenthusiastic.

"That would make, let me see . . ." He found the figure on the paper before him. "A quarter of a billion dollars of unsecured debt. When you add in the secured debt and the financing for the airplanes, that would come to over one billion, two hundred million dollars owed in total by Global Universal Airlines, Inc."

Creighton's brow wrinkled. "I doubt the public is willing to invest the same confidence in Global Universal that management has. I doubt the banks will, either." A thought struck him. "Let's get an idea what the public is thinking." He lifted the phone and pushed the intercom button. "Mrs. Welles, please find out what Global Universal's stock and bonds opened at, then telephone Jim Kean at Willoughby Securities and ask what the loan certificates are trading at."

A few minutes later the report came back. The stock opened at 8¾, down 1¼. GUA's bond issues were down as well. Kean was not in his office yet, but the previous day's reports showed that the certificates could be bought for less than two thirds of face value.

Will tried to screen the defensiveness from his voice. "Those stock and bond prices don't really represent GUA's future prospects."

"On the whole, it isn't too forceful a performance, I'm afraid. Losing that aircraft only aggravated a difficult situation."

"What you seem to be saying is that a company can obtain financing if it's strong enough not to need it."

"Oh, I'm not saying that it's impossible, Mr. Nye. No, no, I'm not saying that at all. But it won't be easy. I can assure you that the banks we approach will view Global Universal even more harshly than the marketplace. I think we need a little time to ponder the problem."

"Mr. Creighton, time is exactly what we do not have. That stock will be half a point lower next time you check. We have to give the public a demonstration of strength, and fast."

Will plucked a report from his briefcase. "This was completed by Bannister's people late Friday night on the most confidential basis. It shows our economists' best estimate for airlines in the coming year and for our company in particular. We expect twelve percent traffic growth during the next fiscal year and income to increase nearly thirty percent. Those levels should be even higher the year after."

The investment banker took the report. "I'll look this over right away, meet with my people, and be back to you before the end of the day. Where can you be reached?"

"We all stay at the Dennison; it's part of Global Universal Hotels."

"Yes, of course." Creighton made a note of it.

"You'll see from the report that the hotels have been strong, but we expect hotel revenue to increase substantially as well."

Creighton rose. "Well, this sounds a bit more hopeful, although of course it's only the company's own projection."

They shook hands. Will nodded toward Creighton's secretary as he walked from the outer office. He rounded the corner and halted. Something troubled him. Creighton had been encouraging last night on the phone with Buck. He had known the general range of the figures then. So what had changed?

Will counted to thirty, then stepped back into Creighton's outer office. Mrs. Welles was turned away from him. She was pushing buttons on her phone, unaware of his return. Over her shoulder he could see the open Rolodex card. It read: "GIRARD, J. STEPHEN, Faranco Inc."

Will strode by her just as she was advising her employer that his party was on the line. She half rose out of her chair to stop the intruder's progress, but Will was already through the door.

Creighton's gaze fell on Will at the same moment that he reached for the phone and only an instant before Will spoke.

"On second thought, I'd better keep that report, Mr. Creighton."

Creighton's hand hung above the phone as if palsied. Will swept the open report off the desk. His eyes bored through the other man's.

"If you lift that phone, my lawsuit will smear your reputation so black that people will think this firm started out as a minstrel show."

"This is a completely different matter, Mr. Nye, I assure you." His voice was still soft and sincere.

Slipping the report into his briefcase, Will stepped to the door. There he stopped, turned around and said in a voice as gentle as the banker's, "I'm reminded of another business a lot like yours, Mr. Creighton. Their clothing and cars are a lot flashier, but they also make a living arranging for customers to get fucked."

Smiling pleasantly at the shocked face of the very proper Mrs. Welles, Will walked jauntily toward the elevator.

Craig Merrill's gaze fell on the newspaper rack only an instant after the hotel elevator doors opened and he stepped into the lobby. "GUA 747 CRASH KILLS 339 IN INDIANA." The others at the airline hadn't listened to him, he remembered bitterly. He had tried to warn them, and they had refused to take him seriously. Now Benson and De Marco were dead. So many more as well. It was a horrible but inevitable lesson.

Merrill bought a paper and began to read. Even those passersby who could not remember the astronaut's name halted for a moment in recognition. Bright eyes, pale-blond lashes and eyebrows, a corrugated forehead, and thin wisps of blond-white hair. They had seen that face for heart-stopping hours as he and two others had rocketed to the moon and back.

An Air Force test pilot and aeronautical engineer for nearly ten years, Craig Merrill had led a life that revolved completely around the NASA moon project. There was no doubt in anyone's mind that this capable, self-effacing man with the smiling wife and the Norman Rockwell children would eventually be chosen for a moon flight. A few years ago his turn had come, and he had finally set foot on the moon, planted a flag, collected rocks, returned home, and spoken to the President on the phone. After the last debriefing was over, it suddenly occurred to Craig Merrill that he had nothing left to do. His life began to fall apart.

He managed one of the NASA programs for a while, but the work seemed anticlimactic after his own great adventure, and he couldn't shake the awful perception that had overpowered him when viewing Earth from the moon, that our planet and people and life were irrelevant against the backdrop of a universe limitless in breadth and blackness and eternity. Merrill quit NASA and tried to fill his life with the wife and children he had relegated to odd moments for so long. But the novelty of domesticity soon palled, the great thoughts he had planned to explore somehow evaded him, and he began to drink. Without income, he soon fell into debt. Finally, his wife was forced to take a job as a cocktail waitress fifteen miles up the coast from Los Angeles. It was one of the few jobs that paid enough and also permitted her to care for the children during the day. She never complained. That only made Merrill's drinking worse. Money was running out, money and time.

Craig Merrill finally took hold of his life after receiving an offer from Global Universal to head up Sales and Service for the airline. At Global Universal the S and S Department was located in Los Angeles and encompassed all relations of GUA personnel with the public, including to some degree areas as diverse as flight attendants' uniforms, ticket-counter etiquette, marketing and labor relations. Increasingly, Merrill had found himself concerned about passenger safety. Eventually he mounted an internal campaign, aimed at top-echelon GUA executives, to shift the company's operational and marketing emphasis from "food and frills" to greater safety precautions: greater use of projectile-resistant materials, more frequent pilot reexaminations, frisking all passengers just before boarding (like El Al and some European airlines) and armed guards on board.

"Given a real choice, I'd rather fly the safest airline than the prettiest," he maintained.

Merrill had brought the issue to a head at a senior staff meeting. It turned into a shouting match. Lee Conway had argued vehemently that glamour, service and punctuality sold seats, not gaudy precautions and fear. Security was part of Will's division, and Will objected to Merrill's savage characterizations.

Ben Buck had sided with Nye and Conway in no uncertain terms. "Airplanes are the safest way to travel. And our planes are the safest in the world. Where do you stop? Parachutes strapped on every passenger? Let's not put any crazy ideas in the public's head. This matter is closed."

Bannister, who had flirted with Merrill's ideas on the basis of lowered cost, quickly came over to Buck's opinion.

Merrill accused Buck and the others of callously putting profits before lives. He threatened to resign if the decision went against him. The others denounced his fanaticism. He predicted terrible crashes and hijackings for which they would bear full responsibility. Then he resigned and stormed out.

Many weeks of bitter resentment had festered within Craig Merrill by the time Girard called him. Girard seemed well informed about the dispute at Global Universal. He said some kind things about Merrill's insistence on safety and the work he had done at the airline. He asked Merrill to come to New York to discuss an important position with Faranco. Merrill had flown in from his home in Los Angeles late the night before, and now, folding the newspaper and tucking it under his arm, he briskly strode onto the bright sidewalk in the direction of the Faranco Building. This meeting with J. Stephen Girard could very well be a new start for him.

Will Nye might not have been so vigilant about protecting the confidentiality of the airline's revenue projections if he had known that a copy was already waiting on Girard's desk when the industrialist arrived at his office that morning. He had already read it before the astronaut appeared.

"For a man who flew into the city during the wee hours of the morning, you look quite fresh, Colonel," Girard commented as they shook hands.

"Clean living, Mr. Girard."

The two had spoken on the phone but never met in person. Merrill had seen one of the few photos of Girard the newspapers possessed (and so kept reusing). His impression had been of someone trying to affect more personality with dark glasses than a bookkeeper face and smallish body might otherwise provide. Girard had seen newspaper photos of Merrill too, as well as the TV coverage of the astronaut walking on the moon.

The men sat on opposing twin Louis XVI settees that were ornately carved and upholstered in patterned silk brocade. J. Stephen Girard's office was traditional in a way the French monarchy might have envied. Besides the settees, two exquisite commodes adorned with gold rococo scrollwork stood against the walls. Girard's desk was a large Boulle writing table, trimmed with bronze mounts; it was at least two hundred and fifty years old.

All this was lost on the astronaut, however. He was a scientist, most comfortable with quantities and mechanics, things as they were in the most basic measurable sense. Despite the mystery that surrounded Girard, Craig Merrill's first impression of the industrialist was quite unintimidating. He seemed to be the familiar sort of wealthy man who could command the presence of sports figures or movie stars or astronauts and then attempted to ingratiate himself with them. But in the next moment a brutal reappraisal forced itself on Merrill.

"Colonel, I will come to the point," Girard intoned. "Your personal finances are in disarray, and you have no present prospect of employment. As I understand it, all your debts, including the twenty-five thousand dollars loaned to you by Western Shore Savings Bank, now come to about forty-five thousand dollars."

Merrill sat bolt upright. "My debts are my own business."

"As a matter of fact they are mine as well," Girard responded with a half-smile. "One of our subsidiaries controls that bank."

Merrill's hand moved unconsciously to smooth his thinning hair. "If you want your money back, it might take me a few days until I put out the word for some job offers, but you can be sure that—"

Girard answered quietly, but his words cut like a razor. "People would check into your credit rating, the controversy you instigated at Global Universal, the personal problems you have had, and what might be termed your present stability!"

Merrill stood up, his face flushed.

"Just a moment, Colonel. Before you make up your mind, let me tell you what I am prepared to offer." The invitation now infusing Girard's soft tone was as clear as the threat had been a moment before. "One hundred thousand dollars a year to represent Faranco in TV commercials. My advertising people tell me we need a specific host personality in order to focus public attention on the overall company, not merely on individual products. You'll do fine."

The hundred-thousand-dollar figure had a visible effect on Merrill, who fell back slightly against the settee.

"But that's secondary, Colonel," Girard continued. "Despite your . . . eccentricities, I believe you are capable, and you understand airplanes and airlines. That will prove helpful to both of us. If my plans work out, you could be president of Global Universal within a few months. At times you will be called upon to do some little thing toward that end."

"Like what?" Merrill asked, but he was unable to mask his desire with wariness.

"Today we will announce at a press conference your association with Faranco and mention that you are also advising us on our investment in GUA. We own a good deal of its stock, and so that would be understandable."

"Sure, that's fine."

Girard leaned forward slightly for emphasis. "Then you'll mention how concerned you are about the safety of passengers riding GUA planes, and that you want to get to the bottom of the crash to find out why passenger safety is being jeopardized."

Merrill tried to object. "I fought for a lot of things in private, but we were arguing then about a matter of degree, not outright negligence. How can I—"

"The stock's price will go down. When we finally make our

move, dissatisfied or frightened GUA stockholders will welcome us with open arms—if they haven't sold out long before that point." Girard leaned back. "Those are my terms." The words carried the finality of a steel vault slamming shut.

"I won't lie," Merrill said at last.

"Lies are usually a mistake. They can be refuted by facts." Girard stood up. "My public-relations people will brief you. They've called the press conference for noon. You and I will talk more about Global Universal this afternoon."

The meeting was over.

Dwarfed on all sides by shoulder-to-shoulder skyscrapers, Will Nye stood on the narrow pavement that had once been a wall around New Amsterdam—now Wall Street—perplexed about what to do next. He had tried to reach Arnold Bannister, but Bannister's Winnebago had not yet returned. Will had only one idea. If that did not work, he would have no choice but to call Denver again and admit his failure to the Old Man. His own failure was what he feared most—and could forgive least.

He turned in a direction he had trod hundreds of times in the three years he had labored in the area as a lawyer. Two blocks later along the paved canyon floors that pass for streets in the financial district Will came to the black slab office tower in which the law firm of Masefield, Bevin & Parkhurst occupied three floors. Will Nye had been an associate at the prestigious firm, which was still Global Universal's "outside" legal arm.

He walked across the familiar lobby, entered an elevator, and pushed the button for the fifteenth floor.

Headly T. Parkhurst's secretary regretfully informed him that Mr. Parkhurst was attending a meeting in the conference room. Will replied that the matter was urgent, and took a seat in one of the deep armchairs. As he waited for the senior partner to arrive, he reflected on his career with the firm.

Having seen military service, Will had been a few years older than other law school graduates hired by the firm. Perhaps because of that, Parkhurst had given him more responsibility earlier. He had worked with Parkhurst on GUA's legal matters and finally took on the airline as his own client after Ben Buck, having learned he had been a fighter pilot in Vietnam, insisted that

Will do all of the company's legal work. When GUA's general counsel retired, Buck offered Will a vice-presidency, stock options and a high salary. That offer had come at an opportune time. Will saw his imminent partnership in the law firm as a prize not worth the continued tedium, and the New York City living he had loved so much in the beginning had become oppressive; each time he stepped into the firm's long corridors, lawyers filed away in offices along either side, he was more content with his decision to accept Buck's offer.

Looking back now, Will realized that those factors had really been secondary. He had been close enough to the excitement of airline operations as GUA's outside lawyer to taste it and want it for himself. And he had been close enough to the power Ben Buck wielded to taste and want that for himself, too.

Parkhurst left his meeting as soon as he received the message that Will was waiting. He felt a fondness and respect for the younger man. As they greeted each other and Parkhurst expressed his sympathies for the recent crash, he was struck as always by the disparity between Will's appearance and the substance lurking beneath; the natty dress and devil-may-care façade concealed white-hot competitive desire and a penetrating mind.

In Parkhurst's office, the two men took seats across a coffee table. Will described Ben Buck's plan, while Parkhurst sat back, fingertips touching, and listened. He peered over his half-glasses, never letting his gaze stray until Will had finished recounting what had occurred at his meeting with Creighton. Then Parkhurst leaned back and closed his eyes for a moment in thought.

The Wall Street lawyer and the investment banker were both members of that powerful inner circle composed of family and prep-school connections that is the real Establishment. The behavior of which Will had accused Creighton was unthinkable among this elite. Yet, Parkhurst trusted Will Nye. And now, he realized, he would never fully trust Maxwell Creighton again. He began to think aloud.

"As you know all too well, Girard is involved in several big takeover efforts each year. Being represented by Creighton, Cromwell in the GUA matter gives him a lot of clout. Creighton, Cromwell, for its part, ends up with a lot more cash and warrants to purchase stock if the price goes up than it could ever make on an underwriting to raise capital for GUA. And if Girard is successful in taking over the company, they haven't even lost that."

Satisfied with his own explanation, Parkhurst looked over his fingertips at Will. "What can I do for you?"

"The largest bank loan we have outstanding is with Metrobank, a hundred million. Do you know anyone there?"

"Winstead, the president, and I are both on the Board of our yacht club."

"What's he like?"

"Capable, honest, bright, good family, tough."

"I'd like to meet with him."

"When?"

"Now."

The thick eyebrows lifted only slightly as Parkhurst reached for the phone and told his secretary to ring Bob Winstead. After some social conversation, Will had his appointment. For two-thirty. Winstead would push back the OPEC representative an hour.

Will smiled wryly at Parkhurst. "For that indignity, a certain Middle Eastern country will plant a tree in your honor."

Parkhurst laughed, then his face grew sober again. "Winstead says there's still a lot of concern about the airlines among lenders. I wouldn't want to be the one asking Metrobank for fifty million dollars. They might just decide to let Girard have a go at running the shop. Incidentally, have you tied up Eli Teicher on a retainer, as I suggested?"

Will nodded. The older lawyer was pleased. "Faranco always uses Samuel Friedman. Teicher's the only other takeover lawyer in his class, and, for my money, a shade more imaginative. One of them should be in our corner when Faranco makes its move. I'll call him for a conference later so our firms can coordinate."

Parkhurst had something more on his mind. "One more piece of advice, Will. Start now to find out everything you can about Girard and his company."

"My files on Faranco go back a long way. I've got every piece of financial information there is on the company and its—"

"Everything," Parkhurst broke in, "on Faranco and on Girard

himself! Bill McCormick used to be with the FBI before he went with the U.S. Attorney's office and then with us. He knows some top ex-FBI men now on their own. I'll have him put a detective on it right now."

"Don't tell me this hallowed firm hires detectives!"

"You know better than that." Parkhurst smiled. "This firm hires other firms that hire detectives. In this case you saved us the bother. The detectives will be on Teicher's bill."

3

Belinda waited patiently at the door as Marcie raced around the guest room looking frantically for her other shoe and then her makeup case (Belinda pointed it out on the dresser) and then her wristwatch (in her open suitcase). Marcie Manning had spent the night in Belinda's SoHo loft after flying into New York for a meeting with her lawyer about what his letter had rather ominously characterized as the "corpus" of her late parents' estates. Marcie had moved back to Phoenix two years earlier to care for her ailing mother, and then stayed on after her mother died, drifting purposelessly. But through all this, she had maintained her friendship with Belinda by phone and by letter.

Belinda was an artist, whose seemingly boundless talents and passions were focused by the very faculty for organization Marcie lacked. In the last two years Belinda's career had skyrocketed. First, recognition as a serious painter, then commissions as a textile designer and more recently as a dress designer. Her flair for publicizing herself and her accomplishments had broadcast her name to an ever-widening public. Blessed with extraordinary good looks that forced one to take notice of her, a quick mind, and a clever tongue, Belinda had managed to attract many powerful friends and open many doors.

"How do I look?" Marcie asked tentatively, showing off her red suit.

"Like all the millions they're going to hand over to you. Come on, the taxi should be waiting downstairs by now. Do you have the address of the law firm?"

Marcie looked desperate for an instant and began scurrying around the room once more, searching for her handbag.

"Try the suitcase again," Belinda said.

"I've looked there twice already." Suddenly Marcie stopped, her gaze fixed on the open suitcase. "Oh, God, how did I ever miss it?"

"It was hiding," Belinda said gently.

Marcie and Belinda were ten minutes late when they hurried into the large black office building and rushed toward the elevator doors that were just opening. Marcie's eyes were on the green light above the doors. Will Nye was just stepping out of the elevator, and they collided.

"Damn it," Marcie muttered to Will, "can't you watch where you're going?"

He bent toward the terrazzo floor to retrieve her handbag. She was short and attractive, he noticed, but a bit frantic, her blond hair a little unkempt. "I tried to," he answered sharply, and as he turned he thought he recognized the taller woman. She spoke first.

"I think we've met . . . at Carla Ruggieri's."

Of course. Chic in a flamboyant style, high boots, green skirt, bold scarf, Cossack coat, very black hair. He remembered having met her at Carla's dinner party the night he broke up with Carla.

"I'm Belinda," the black-haired woman said.

"Oh, yes." Will remembered the large dark eyes. "You're the one with only one name. Painter."

She smiled.

Will noticed that the small blond girl with the not-quite-cheerleader looks was impatient. She implored Belinda, "I don't want to be any later than we already are."

"Will Nye, Marcie Manning," Belinda said, then went on, "I thought you had left New York."

"Yes, I moved to Colorado. I'm here on business."

"Belinda . . ." Marcie urged.

Belinda did not want to be hurried. "If you're free tonight, there's a private party for my show at the Stoller Gallery any time after seven."

"Thanks, I'll keep it in mind."

They parted. Belinda watched as Will went through the revolving door, and then the two women entered the elevator. As the doors closed, Belinda remarked, "Carla dropped Rickie the moment she met him. She was absolutely insane about Will Nye. To hear her talk you'd have thought she personally invented the orgasm."

But Marcie could think of Will only as an annoying interruption. She was intent on her appointment at Masefield, Bevin & Parkhurst. Absently, as she watched the numbers light consecutively overhead, she asked, "Will Carla be there tonight?"

"I'm sure he's not going to care one way or another," Belinda replied, "but it might be interesting. She's engaged now, you know, to Davey Delauney, the one whose father left him one third of the world's supply of some mineral or other but only half the customary supply of brains."

The numbers stopped changing. The elevator door opened. And Marcie informed a woman at the desk she wished to speak to Mr. Mundy.

Algernon Mundy was an eminence in that branch of the law known as "trusts and estates," mostly by reason of his apparently infinite capacity to endure, and even to take pleasure in, minutiae of phraseology that would bore a more normal man insane. His desk was piled high with files, and more were piled on the floor. He rambled on in legal terms Marcie could not comprehend, until finally she interrupted him with a question.

"Mr. Mundy, just tell me, how much am I getting?"

He lifted his eyes from the file it had taken him several minutes to extract from the stack protecting his left flank and peered at Marcie through the gap in the stacks.

"But, Miss Manning, that is exactly what I have been trying to explain. The principal of your father's trust is composed entirely of stock in Global Universal Airlines."

He consulted the file again. "What with stock splits and stock dividends over the years, it now amounts to eight hundred three thousand, seven hundred and seventeen shares."

"How much is that worth?" She gripped Belinda's hand.

"At one time the stock sold for twenty-three dollars per share. Knowing you would be here today, I telephoned a stock exchange firm on Friday and was told the stock was at ten. I telephoned again a few minutes ago and was informed the stock is now selling at eight and a quarter. It seems there was a most unfortunate accident to one of their planes and as a consequence—"

"I'm not really interested in their air crashes, Mr. Mundy," Marcie interjected, trying to restrain her impatience at this fussy, fusty, impossible man who could not get to the point. "As I understand it, right this minute my stock is worth about eight dollars a share."

He nodded.

"And I have about eight hundred thousand shares."

He nodded again.

"Then right this minute I am worth between six and . . . seven million dollars." Marcie's voice cracked with excitement.

"In a manner of speaking, yes," Mundy replied.

Marcie's voice rose. "Either I am or I'm not!"

"You are," he said thoughtfully, "and then again you are not."

She clenched her teeth as he slowly explained. "You own the stock and are entitled to the dividends, of course, but you do not control it. You cannot sell it, for example."

Marcie's good spirits seemed to be slowly evaporating.

"Our firm handled all of your father's legal work and introduced him to another client, Global Universal Airlines, when he wanted to sell his own small airline. It was not particularly profitable, but it did have several routes that were advantageous to Global Universal. The man who headed that company would not pay cash, only stock, but was afraid of that much stock finding its way into unfriendly hands. Thus, part of the arrangement was that the stock could not be sold for ten years." He glanced down at the file and then up. "Until next April thirtieth."

"That's only five months from now!" exclaimed Belinda.

"How much cash is in the account?" Marcie inquired. When she was growing up, even after her father's death, it seemed a bottomless chest able to meet any family expense, no matter how lavish.

"Well, the dividends were more or less exhausted by your mother's long illness. She received the income during her lifetime, as you know. When our firm's final bill is rendered, I'm afraid there will not be more than one or two thousand dollars, if that much. Of course we will first have to receive the court's final order regarding the accounting and distribution."

Mundy handed her a long page with a column of numbers on it. Marcie's shoulders sagged as she read it.

"Are any more dividends expected soon?"

"The airline hasn't paid any dividends in several years, I'm afraid."

She threw the paper toward him. "Worth millions and months behind in my rent! If it weren't for that damned agreement . . ."

Mundy carefully retrieved the accounting and placed it in its proper position in the file.

"Miss Manning, may I offer a comment?" He cleared his throat, blowing the straggly mustache hair outward. "If it weren't for that agreement, I hazard the guess that your father could well have died a pauper and left you and the late Mrs. Manning nothing. He made a good deal of money in his lifetime and spent it recklessly. In his last years I gathered that he was most grateful for the Global Universal dividends. As executor of his estate, I can assure you it allowed your mother to live in a rather affluent life style and you to attend college, then spend a year in Europe, then come to New York and attend college again and then . . ."

This stuffy old man, it seemed to her, had become acquainted with the most intimate details of her life as he doled out the trust income and checked the bills that came in. The weight of Marcie's indecision settled heavily onto her shoulders. Pampered by a dashing, generous father and a sweet but vague mother, she was finding it difficult to deal with problems in the absence of money as the wonder drug.

Belinda was a far more practical person. "Marcie, why not give up your Phoenix apartment, sell the furniture and move in with me? My apartment is practically endless."

"But I can't pay my own way."

"We'll keep a list of expenses, and you can pay me when you have the money. It'll be great fun to have your company."

Marcie relaxed. Belinda lived an exciting life and knew all the most exciting people in an exciting city, while her own life in Phoenix had become a grubby rat race among desperate relationships. She objected weakly one more time for form's sake, then said yes and thanked her friend.

Belinda gave Algernon Mundy her address. He carefully filed it in the proper place.

Before leaving for Chicago, Owen Clayton interviewed the three eyewitnesses to the crash. Their stories agreed. A cop driving along the main country road saw lights in the sky ahead of him, which floated all the way to the ground. He first thought it was a UFO, or maybe several, and might have been too embarrassed to call in a report if he had not then heard the plane strike the earth. He was the first person to reach the scene and radioed for aid. The other two witnesses were a girl and a boy walking home from a date. They had given nearly the same description except that, being closer, they had guessed it was a plane. They ran to her house to telephone for help.

To avoid unnecessary delay, Clayton drove to a local airport and hopped a plane to O'Hare. Someone else would drive his car out later.

Working through the night, GUA O'Hare personnel had made the passenger list as accurate as they could, obtaining addresses from computer records, travel agents roused from sleep, and credit-card companies. By dawn the Chicago regional vice-president had assembled his managerial staff and sent them out in pairs to break the news personally to the families and friends of 211's passengers residing in the area. Many would later remember that act of thoughtfulness with gratitude.

By the time Clayton arrived at O'Hare, FBI agents assigned by Gorlick had already passed on the names of passengers from Los Angeles and New York to those offices for immediate checking, and they had begun the process in their own areas. Many of the passengers had come into those hubs from smaller cities, and they too would be investigated. Security personnel had been assembled to relate their recollections of the people passing between ten and eleven o'clock through the checkpoint into the corridor containing 211's gate.

After quickly reviewing what the other agents were doing, Clayton asked to see the GUA ticket agents on duty the previous night. He had one specific question: Had anyone paid cash for a ticket? Buying an airplane ticket with cash makes a person immediately suspect. The ticket agent looks him or her over closely for any of the telltale signs listed in the FAA's tightly guarded psychological behavior profile of potential skyjackers and saboteurs. But no one who paid cash the night before had come close to fitting the profile, none had behaved unusually, and all had been aboard the plane when it left O'Hare. Clayton was assured that similar efforts were being made in New York and Los Angeles.

Later in the morning, he called his colleagues together to trade information. The FBI's airport office was too small, so they sat on boxes and crates in a large storeroom. A few possible leads had come to light.

One local passenger, Harold Markowitz, had bought a hundred thousand dollars of insurance from the airport insurance sales agent and named his wife as beneficiary.

A Mrs. Evelyn Flein, age fifty-six, also from the area, was insured by her son for three hundred thousand dollars. She was on the plane. He was not.

That's a possible, Clayton thought, and made a note of both items.

A cursory review of 211's passenger list had turned up some interesting and prominent names. Vito Manfredi had been a passenger. Under the protection of the federal government since agreeing to testify against his former Mafia colleagues and bosses, Manfredi had been traveling to New York under an assumed name in the company of three U.S. marshals. The FBI agents at O'Hare had been privy to the reason for his trip, despite its extreme secrecy: Aldo Lozzallo, a Mafia kingpin, was about to be tried in New Jersey after a four-year investigation, and without Manfredi the government had no case.

"I notified New York," Jeff Wolf reported. "They've put a team on looking for a connection with Lozzallo."

"The best lead is whether there was a secrecy leak in Manfredi's travel plans," Clayton told him. "Take over that part of it, Jeff."

Edward Landover had been a first-class passenger on 211. Head of Landover Minerals, and very rich, he had been in the midst of a bitter divorce fight that had dominated the headlines for weeks. His wife had seemed certain to win a large settlement until Landover revealed he possessed proof of her adultery with several influential men. That would have reduced the expected alimony drastically. But now his death assured her of a large share of his estate.

"Well, the price was right," Clayton remarked. He lit a cigarette with the butt end of the old one. "Anyone else prominent?"

"An Assistant Secretary of the Treasury no one seems to have disliked, probably because he didn't have much responsibility. And Guerin, the head of the SEC's Enforcement Division, but also the President's nominee as chairman of the Commission."

"We sure can't accuse *him* of having no enemies. The Senate confirmation hearings have been dragging on for weeks."

Wolf nodded. "I did some of the background checks on him. Business screamed bloody murder when the President decided to up Guerin from the staff to the chairmanship. All the consumer-shareholder types loved it. We're trying to find out who he spent yesterday with."

"Have the Bureau get a list from the SEC of the people and companies Guerin was ripping into." Clayton gestured for Wolf to go on.

"A banker and his wife and a vice-president of Jennings Machines. The banker did a lot of business in the Middle East."

"Follow up in the usual way. Anything else?"

A small man in wireframe glasses nodded and tapped the note in his hand. "Two anonymous calls—one to us, one to police headquarters—claiming responsibility for the crash. Both said their motives were political."

"What time they come in?"

"One at seven-fifteen A.M. and the other seven-thirty-four A.M."

"*After* it appeared on the news. The ones to pay attention to come in before word gets out or can give you some detail that wasn't on the news. The group to check out is GUA personnel. Ballman, follow up on that. It's a tough one. Airlines laid off people left and right for a couple of years. A lot of people might have held a grudge. To begin with, concentrate on the most recent terminations, then any flight personnel who were scheduled for the flight but missed it."

Clayton felt fatigue beginning to hang on his body and dull his faculties. In a couple of hours, he would be moving and thinking in painful slow motion. He decided that after this he would go home for a few hours' sleep and a look-in on Edna. En route he would stop off at the homes of some of the suspects. Only a few more items to cover.

"What about cargo?"

"Nothing so far," a man in the corner reported. "The cargo shipping orders didn't show any explosives or dangerous substances."

Clayton restrained the retort that came to mind and explained what should have been obvious. "Al, once in a while shippers put prohibited substances aboard under false labels and they get by even though the airlines try to keep an eye out for that kind of thing. The suppliers figure nothing will go wrong. Track each and every cargo shipment back to the point of origin."

A bright rookie Clayton knew slightly had been going through the records of the "Personal Package Service" items shipped in the plane's cabin. Three packages had been carried aboard the plane by flight attendants, each paid for by a separate person. The addressees presumably would have picked up the packages upon arrival at JFK.

"That last one," the young agent pointed out to Clayton. "We checked it out pretty carefully, but it seems to be from a phony sender to a phony party on the other end."

"It figures," Clayton remarked glumly and slid down from the edge of the table. "We probably won't find the package either."

He adjourned the meeting with a nod, ground his lit butt underfoot and began lumbering out.

"What if something comes up?" one of the agents called after him.

"I should be back by the end of the day, but you can call me at home. Don't get your hopes up. This one will probably take months."

"Uh, sir," another young agent offered, "I have an idea of what caused it."

Patiently Clayton explained, "We all do, son. But the thing that's going to break our asses is figuring out *who.*"

"Bannister will be fit to be tied when he learns the Old Man sent someone else to New York and not him," Lee Conway gloated. His wife placed a glass of orange juice on the table before him and turned back to the stove. "Bannister's supposed to be the financial genius."

Lee Conway had returned home well after Helen had gotten the children off to school. He had spent the night on the phone, directing his airport people in the sad tasks of notifying the victims' families and of arranging to fly free to the crash scene those who wished to come. Helen had waited for him to wake before leaving for the day. Despite having been a bachelor for years prior to meeting her, he was incapable of frying an egg.

She was younger than Lee and still attractive, or so the occasional man she had sneaked into bed with had told her. But there was no other man in her life now, and she was bored.

"Who did Buck send?"

"Your friend Nye."

"Which one is Nye?" She remembered him very well.

"The one you chatted with for so long at the Davidsons'."

Helen thought of him often: tall and good-looking, with the same clean-cut college-boy look they all seemed to have at the company. Except for the eyes. They had put her off. His eyes were very dark, nearly black—unusual for someone with fair hair—and they never left hers in conversation. The intensity of his self-possession had been disconcerting. Unlike the others near the top of the corporate pyramid, Nye did not seem to care whether anyone liked him or not.

The day after the party, Lee had left for the Asian offices. On a pretext she had called Nye, driven to his home that night and bedded him. She could not remember a more exciting lover. Yet his mind had seemed so far away that she felt demeaned by the very depths of the frenzy that had seized her body. She never called him again.

"What was Nye sent to New York for?"

"No one knows for sure. When the Old Man's not meddling with every decision you make, he's got you up there playing some guessing game. He did mention it involved some oddball financial scheme that could help fend off Girard."

"Why did he send Nye and not you?"

Conway's eyes flicked up to hers, seeking the criticism in the question. Only curiosity was apparent in her expression.

"Nye's a lawyer—smug son of a bitch! Bannister was away. Marketing doesn't get involved in the financial stuff."

Helen slid the eggs out of the pan and onto the plate between the toast wedges and set the breakfast down in front of her husband.

"Is there really a chance Girard could take over Global Universal?" she asked. "It seems impossible."

Conway looked up at her. For the first time in months her tone imparted real concern, instead of that amiable accommodation they had both slipped into. He shrugged his shoulders and reached for his fork. "You going to United Fund today?"

She nodded and poured his coffee from the electric pot. She wondered whether he would call later to make sure she was there. "I'm late for a meeting. You set?"

He nodded. She kissed his cheek perfunctorily and started toward the hall. A thought stopped her. "By the way, what about the plane?"

"Which plane?"

"The one that crashed last night."

"All dead. No explanation."

Anxiety showed briefly in her eyes. "Lee, if they don't find the reason by the time we're supposed to leave for Hawaii, I'm taking the kids on another airline."

"These things happen, Helen. We still have the best safety record of any American carrier."

"I mean it, Lee."

Walking down the hotel corridor, Will Nye heard a voice call to him from inside a room as he passed. The door was open. He looked inside. The stewardess on the Westwind, in a cream-colored pants suit, sat crosslegged on the red carpet, newspapers headlining the crash scattered around her. She had not cried on the plane; it was a point of pride, he realized. But the sorrow was now evident in the limpness of her spine and the glazed look of shock in her eyes at the miracle of her own escape. She lifted a newspaper.

"It was horrible. Bodies all over the place. They never had a chance."

He did not reach for the paper.

A phone began to ring in the next room.

"That's your room," she told him.

Will had gone directly from the airport to Creighton, Cromwell. The crew had put his valise in the room for him.

Will unlocked the door and picked up the phone. Ben Buck's voice boomed out at him.

"Is that you, Will?"

"Yes, General."

"Where the hell have you been all morning?"

"I was just about to phone you."

"Max Creighton called. His exact words were you were 'difficult' and 'offensive' and you 'cursed' at him."

"What else did he say?"

"That he wanted me to appoint Bannister or Greer to handle this thing, someone on a higher level than you."

"What did you tell him?"

"That if he wants someone on a higher level I'd give you a promotion."

"Thanks for the confidence."

"The truth is I'm ready to string you up by the balls. You're not in New York one hour and you fuck up everything. What the hell are you trying to do?"

"Creighton is working with Girard. But I guess you figured that," Will retorted contemptuously.

There was a momentary hesitation before Buck exploded. "That's bullshit! I've known Max Creighton . . . I had half a dozen single-engine planes and one hangar when he put together that first financing for me! Global Universal has made a lot of money for him over the years."

"He found someone who could make more." Will briefly recounted the morning's events.

"What it amounts to, Will, is you're asking me to take your word over Max Creighton's."

Silence emptied out the wire.

"I was a damned fool to send a boy on a man's mission," Buck fumed. "It was a simple job."

"Global Universal's borrowed up to its throat. For two years every cent you could wheedle out of the banks went to pay debt service on the rest of the money that's owed."

"Creighton said . . ." Buck began, then halted. "I hope you've got some other ideas."

"Just one, General. I figure Metrobank has loaned the company so much they might be willing to protect their investment with one more loan. Do you know Winstead there?"

"Met him once, I think, but the fellow I know well there is Gorman."

"Gorman retired five years ago."

"Shit!" Ben Buck was unaccustomed to feeling powerless. "Hold on. I'm going to check with Arnold."

Will heard a click and waited for Buck to reach Bannister. A minute or so later he came back on. "He says he deals with a Don Cavanaugh there, a senior V.P. in Commercial Lending. If Bannister leaves now, he can be in New York by five."

"My meeting with Winstead is at two-thirty."

"Can you put it off?"

"He's the president."

There was a long silence. "Call me as soon as the meeting with Metrobank is over."

Will hung up. The play was all his now. Donna was standing in the doorway.

"Can I speak to you?" she asked.

He nodded.

She closed the door behind her. The blue eyes were anxious.

"You were kind before . . . and I have to tell someone."

The words seemed to hang back, like outnumbered soldiers. "Now that I know you're with the company, maybe you can tell them for me."

She was leaning against the wall, relying on it. "I've never been afraid to fly. I never really thought about anything happening up there. The evacuation drills, the oxygen masks and life vests were just something you did as part of the job, not because you might need them." She paused to refocus her thoughts. A hint of her fear was beginning to quicken her words. "I should have been on that plane last night. Jeanne would be alive. I barely knew her. Jeanne was just a stew who happened to live in my new building and was willing to switch trips with me."

She turned on her listener. "You can't understand what it's like knowing you've caused another person's death, and this isn't the end of it. Every day I'd have to wake up to a job of flying in something that can kill me and hundreds of other people in an instant."

"Whether I understand or not isn't the point," Will responded. "If you want to quit, I'll call Personnel for you and advise them. Do you have another way to pay for your apartment?"

"We're talking about my life!"

"Your home seemed awfully important a few hours ago."

"A lot has happened since then. I'll just have to get another job. With a normal schedule maybe I can go to college."

"How are you getting back to Denver?"

"What difference does that make? Train. Bus."

"They take a long time. If you wait a few hours or so and can bring yourself to fly one more time, I'll be able to tell you when the Westwind is heading back."

"You really are an annoying bastard," she said, anger beginning to replace the fear and the sorrow. "I was right about you last night, I really was."

"I gather then you don't want a lift back to Denver."

Unexpectedly, she laughed. "I hoped you would at least give me the satisfaction of talking me out of quitting."

The laugh had been warm, her distress genuine. Will was caught offguard by the unanticipated intimacy. His own tone softened.

"If it's cheap advice you want, I'll give it to you. But let's get some lunch. I've got a two-thirty appointment I can't be late for."

He held the door for her. She did not move.

"You know," she said, not bothering to mask the surprise in

her voice, "it just occurred to me that you're probably important enough to get me fired, the way I talked to you last night."

"You just said you were quitting."

With a smile she allowed the surprise to burst on her features again. "I knew I heard that somewhere."

While Donna washed up, Will read newspaper accounts of the crash. With a sinking feeling Will realized that the intimations of a criminal cause could lay the blame for failing to prevent the mass deaths at his own door.

"Accidents don't just happen on airplanes. They're caused . . . by negligence and mismanagement. And that starts at the top. I owe it to those who died, to those who fly Global Universal, to the stockholders of that company and this one, and to my conscience, to get to the bottom of that terrible tragedy.

"I believed I was serving the American people when I took that journey to the moon. I'm honored to be given the opportunity by Faranco to continue to serve."

Girard watched Merrill's press conference on a television screen in his office. He never sat in at a conference himself but watched those of interest on a concealed closed-circuit hookup originating from the main conference room. Standing between the vice-presidents of Public Relations and Finance, Merrill exuded the small-town appeal that seemed to have been a job qualification for American astronauts. On an easel beside them was an aerial photo of the crash site.

The phone buzzed. Girard listened to his secretary, then took the call that had just come in. He waited silently for the speaker to finish before responding.

"Tell your people that I don't want to buy a single share right now, no matter *how* low it drops, Max. Any buying will only raise the stock's price, or at least support it. We want it to drop. You're close to the specialists making the market in it, aren't you?" He paused for a reply before he declared, "Then let it sink through the floor!"

Donna had done most of the talking during lunch, compulsively recounting every detail of the newspaper reports. Will could have recited all the safety statistics, but he soon realized she needed to verbalize her grief and guilt. He lapsed into silence, ruminating on those facts which had evaded Security that might point away from pilot error or mechanical failure and toward sabotage.

But whenever he started to get caught up in his own thoughts, Donna's eyes pulled him back. In the subdued restaurant light, they seemed grayer than he remembered, like the winter moon. They compelled his attention. And as he listened Will began to be intrigued by her character as well. She seemed to have a sense of herself and her values; there wasn't a millimeter of space between the soles of her feet and the ground below them.

When the conversation shifted away from the crash, Will felt her words resonating a responsive, like chord within him. She was cautious about people, and so was he. Like himself, Donna had been raised in small-town America, where hard work disciplines most of the illusion and the self-importance out of one. But her youth had been harsh, or so he gathered. Arkansas and Oklahoma were in her voice, rocky farms and dusty main streets. They had made her tough and resilient. Will's youth had been much easier. His father, an austere, remote man, was a doctor and his mother a nurse in a small Midwest town. He found himself disclosing that his mother had opposed his decision to study at the Air Force Academy in Colorado, despite his love of flying, but his father had not, remarking simply, "Some men need mountains and sky when they're young. Will more than most." Will kept from Donna his recollection of the shock he felt on discovering that the man understood his feelings. It was the closest his father ever came to complimenting him.

When the menu arrived, Donna realized she had not eaten since breakfast the previous day, and she did not bother to conceal her hunger. She had early learned that one could never be sure where the next square meal would come from. Will was not hungry and gave her the rest of his steak when hers was eaten to the bone. At that point she suddenly remembered where she had first heard Will Nye's name.

"Aren't you the one we negotiated with for a new contract?"

He nodded.

The blue fire again lit her eyes. "Is it true that when Mitzi Carpenter accused management of hiring stewardesses as sex objects, you agreed?"

Now he was management. Being with her was like riding blindfolded on a rollercoaster.

"Off the record, so it wouldn't be usable as part of the arbitration record, I told your negotiating team I agreed. They immediately called a press conference."

"Your opinion of women isn't very high."

"We're in the business of selling a product to a customer who can choose at least one or two other companies on every major route. So we need every edge. We hire pretty, pleasant girls, not ugly ones. We serve the best food we can for the price and under the conditions of flight . . ."

Her eyes rolled upward. He ignored her silent critique.

". . . and we make TV commercials telling everyone how friendly we are. If some businessman interprets that to mean a more intimate friendliness than other airlines are offering, that's a point in our favor."

"We're there for safety. The FAA says so," Donna countered. "We're trained to evacuate the aircraft in case of emergencies."

"How much evacuation was needed last night?"

That brought the conversation back to the depressing subject of air crashes. They were both silent for a while. Donna was thinking.

"What time will the plane go back to Denver?" she asked.

"If things go well, this afternoon. If they don't, I may have to hide out in Timbuktu."

"I still don't want to be a stew, but the law of averages should be with me for one last trip back."

Will smiled; her slightest yielding was grudging, reluctant. "I'll get you posted to desk duty for a couple of weeks," he said. "See what you want to do."

Her eyes flashed with hostility again. "Why would you do that for me?"

"The truth?"

"Yes."

He briefly considered a platitude, then realized he would have to disclose a small part of himself. It was difficult for him. "Nobody understands wanting to give up flying better than I do. I went to law school because I had grown to loathe it. I stuck with it after Vietnam only long enough to earn all my civilian licenses."

"But if you hated flying . . ."

"I hated more the feeling that one leg less made a difference."

Why had he mentioned his handicap, he wondered, to someone he barely knew? A play for pity? Or to make it easier to undress if something developed between them? He silently castigated himself.

"I thought you had a slight limp." Her tone was factual, conveying neither pity nor revulsion. "You're sure you didn't leave the Air Force because they wouldn't let you fly anymore?"

He nodded. "I had a long time to think about it." He paused. "Will you have dinner with me tonight?"

"Why?"

Will was unused to women who were so frontally frank.

"I think I like you," he said finally.

Untold seasons of weather seemed to sweep across her face in an instant. Then she smiled. "Sex object?"

"Yes."

"Fair enough. More than that?"

"Yes."

She attacked her half-finished salad. He waited for her to speak. When the bottom of the salad bowl finally appeared, she glanced up at him again.

"Okay, but I'm not sure about you yet."

After coffee Donna walked Will to the glass Metrobank Building. They shared opinions on the people and shops they passed. Neither one wished to break off the conversation when they arrived at Metrobank, and so, being early, Will asked her to keep him company while he waited in Winstead's reception area.

Comfortable in the deep tweed-covered armchairs, Donna described her apartment and Will the large, snug cabin he had renovated in the woods above Denver. It was nearly two-forty before the banker arrived.

Tall and slim, perhaps fifty, Bob Winstead cut a quietly impressive figure as he entered, a courteous apology on his lips. His lunch meeting in the dining room upstairs had run a few minutes late.

"I wish I had taken your flight to London last week," Winstead remarked upon greeting Will and Donna.

"What airline did you fly?" Will asked.

"Can't really remember, to tell you the truth, but the British authorities are so worried about terrorists they held the plane up for nearly an hour and a half at the end of the runway. I should have flown Global Universal." He smiled. "They have the prettiest stewardesses."

Will caught Donna's eye for an instant before saying, "And we owe you a lot of money, so all the business helps."

Donna sat down again as Winstead ushered Will into his office.

Winstead gestured for Will to take a seat at a long teak table near the window. He lowered a blind to block the afternoon sun and then said matter-of-factly, "No problem with our loan, is there?"

"Not if you let us borrow more," Will replied.

As he began to explain his mission, Will tried to read Winstead's character from the clothing he wore, the nod of his head as Will spoke, the books and photographs in the wall unit. The only unusual item was a photo on the top shelf of a much younger Winstead at the helm of a sailboat. A beard covered the square jaw, and he was bare to the waist. An island was hazily outlined in the background. Beneath the dark suit before him, Will conjectured, was probably a well-disguised individualist. That would have to do for an approach.

"To put it more simply, Mr. Winstead, you don't abandon a proven captain just because a storm has come up. That's exactly when you need someone who knows how to guide the ship. Ben Buck is no youngster and he's not a typical executive, but he built an airline single-handedly because he was smart and decisive. Times have been bad for *all* airlines, and that's why the vultures are out there circling. But we're convinced that GUA and the entire industry are at the turnaround point. The best investment we can make is in our own future, and that's really what the fifty million dollars is for."

Will took a deep breath. Here was the right moment for the point he had been waiting all morning to make. "If I were a banker with a hundred million dollars already in the company, I'd want to be sure that experienced management remained firmly in place, without having to waste energy fighting off the vultures."

Will pulled the folder from his briefcase. It contained the most up-to-date operating statements, as well as future projections. "For one thing, our productivity is now at the point where we break even on a half-empty plane and . . ."

The banker held up his hand. Deep creases lengthened from cheekbone to chin. He went to the door and asked his secretary for the airline study the bank's transportation industry economists had recently completed. He was about to close the door again when a question sprang to mind.

"Miss Harney, may I ask your opinion on something?"

Donna looked up from a magazine.

"If you weren't with GUA, would you fly more?"

"This morning I had just about decided never to fly again—you know, the crash last night and all." She paused for an instant. Watching Donna in thought through the open doorway, Will felt the ball game slipping through his fingers. "But . . . business is more spread out. People's lives are more hectic, so they need more vacations. The economy seems a little better, so people can afford them. Yes," she concluded, "I'd travel more. I think everyone will."

Winstead thanked her, closed the door again and returned to his chair. He opened his economists' report and scanned the tables and the text. After several minutes he looked up. "You've got a time problem, so I can poll our Executive Committee by phone if your company's own figures make sense."

Will opened to the unaudited last quarter statement. The banker drew his chair closer, and Will began to explain.

At precisely three-thirty, Bob Winstead put down the phone after the final call. "You have five million now," he announced. "The other forty-five will be put to the Executive Committee on Thursday. But their reaction on the phone was quite positive."

Initially, Will felt only relief at not having failed. Happiness followed a long moment later.

"Our lawyers can start on the documentation right away," continued Winstead, reaching for the phone again.

Will rose. "That can wait a few minutes. I'd like to call our public-relations people and some of the wire services and papers right away."

Winstead led him to an empty office with a telephone, and just after four o'clock, news of the loan transaction was released to Dow Jones, UPI, AP, Reuters, and prominent newspapers.

By a quarter after four, the price of GUA stock had jumped a point and a half on the Pacific Exchange. Investors understood that the loan to GUA would put a powerful buyer into the marketplace. An up-to-fifty-million-dollar stake and carefully timed purchases would keep the price of GUA stock high enough for management to feel relatively safe. Barring unforeseen catastrophes, the loan had bought them time.

By four-thirty, the Old Man had been notified; he was expansive. "That Winstead is one son of a bitch who talks my language. Hah, I knew you could do it, Will Nye! I knew it! If anyone deserved a bonus . . . One of the troubles with you is you work too hard, don't know how to relax. Take a week off! Go anywhere and charge it to the company."

"What about the crash? The morning paper said the FBI was investigating for possible—"

"Shit, Will, if Dan Pope, with all his experience, can't hold the fort in Security till you get back, then we're all in trouble."

"But if there was a security breach, and the plane was sabotaged in some way . . ."

"Will, this is an order: Get off somewhere and relax. I'll call you if I need you. Just keep Eloise up to date on where you are."

By five o'clock, Global Universal had climbed back over nine.

4

"Mr. Girard, it's so good of you and Marie to come. You too, Colonel. And you, Senator."

The woman on the end had not been introduced. Belinda assumed she was the Senator's wife: clothes with modest lines, a bit outdated; anxious eyes.

"This is my wife, Kathy," the Senator volunteered, almost as an afterthought. The woman smiled and took Belinda's outstretched hand.

Belinda's pleasure at their arrival had not been a matter of courtesy. She had labored for two months to have a guest list newsworthy enough to insure that her party would be talked about and written up in all the papers. But at the last minute, the Governor, who Belinda was hoping would bring one of his celebrity escorts (lately he had been dating the *"Fortune* 500" Index of Catholic Womanhood), had called to cancel. Immediately after came an apologetic call from Bitsy Von Salter, who had promised to fly back from her home in Barbados after the Thanksgiving weekend, but had chosen to stay on instead. Half her house guests had decided to stay on as well, and every one of them had been on Belinda's "A" list. Marie Girard's call a few hours ago had broken the streak of bad news. Out of courtesy Belinda had extended an invitation to the Girards, certain that they would not attend. But Marie Girard's fondness for Belinda had prompted her to convince her husband, as well as their dinner guests, to make this one of their rare appearances.

Belinda escorted them into the gallery area. So normally reclusive were the Girards that Belinda thought it possible they might escape recognition by the press entirely, and she would respect their desire for privacy. But their guests were another matter. Craig Merrill was a certified red-white-and-blue American hero, still nationally revered. And Senator Crockett Avery was a rising political star, having been widely considered a Vice-Presidential possibility until Carter settled on Mondale.

Girard stood apart from the others, scrutinizing the paintings on the gallery walls.

"You're a good painter," he said. The words were a statement, not a pleasantry. "Marie bought one of your paintings last year."

"If Marie hadn't liked it so much, I doubt if I'd have parted with it. She promised I could come up occasionally to visit it."

Belinda and Marie Girard had met at their hairdresser's. At the time Belinda could hardly afford such a periodic extravagance, but the owner was a good friend. The paintings she had given him were now worth dozens of times what his services would have cost her in cash. Belinda had invited Marie Girard for lunch at her studio, where she had seen the painting that so captivated her. Belinda had tried to divert her to other canvases, but the woman's mind was made up. She insisted on buying it right then and there.

Simple, with very little knowledge of art, Marie had made a choice that surprised Belinda. Apparently abstract, the painting had captured perfectly, Belinda knew—or as perfectly as crystalline memory petrified into paint ever could—her cherished recollection of swiftly racing water spraying across bright round stones. She had played by a brook during those few precious summer weeks during her girlhood when her whole family had driven up to a rented bungalow in the Catskills they had saved all year for.

"Yes, you're good," Girard stated again with finality. Belinda was about to thank him when she realized that the slight industrialist in the strange dark glasses was merely confirming for himself the value of one of his assets.

"If you'd like to buy any of the paintings in the show, please see me, Mr. Girard. I think I can talk the gallery owner into a special price."

He nodded, excused himself and strolled off.

No one liked a bargain better than the rich, Belinda knew, particularly the rich in business. Later on, she would steer her group of distinguished guests past Mory Schactman. He would be impressed. And that was really the point of this extravaganza. The money for it had come from Schactman, a dress manufacturer who believed that her growing reputation could sell dresses. This opening-night party was planned partly to announce the new dress line and partly to assure her new partner that he was wise to invest in it.

Belinda took the opportunity of a free moment to slip into the small office on one side of the gallery. Her manager and one-third partner, Ron Bailey, was curled around the phone receiver, but he beckoned her to stay until he could finish the call. She checked herself in the mirror.

Belinda was well aware that her striking beauty relied on contrast, not subtlety. The large dark eyes were arresting; the nose had a slight bump at the bridge, but it seemed right because it was not ordinary; the high cheekbones widened the face a touch, making it appear vaguely Asian. She had designed a dress to show off her looks. Several layers of thin rose-gray chiffon were softly draped from swanlike throat to waist, then again to the floor. This first design was a preview of the new line.

Ron dropped the phone onto its cradle. "The TV news crew we were promised is tied up at a fire in Brownsville, but the Mayor was there, too. When they heard he was leaving to come here, they agreed to stop off on the way back to the station. When they arrive you'll have ten minutes, tops, to make the presentation. If you can do it, we make the news at eleven."

Ron stopped to review the schedule on his clipboard. "Sorry, *five* minutes. They need the first five minutes to get shots of the celebrities. I promised them Faye Dunaway and Craig Merrill."

Belinda was flabbergasted. "Faye Dunaway wasn't even invited!"

Ron shrugged. "I'll tell them she just left. Or maybe that she's in the crapper. Move up whoever we do have to the front of the gallery so the crew can shoot them fast."

Ron was a hungry kid from a poor family who had parlayed good looks and a hustler's wits into a career. He sported a thin blond mustache, and his blond hair was sprayed into a stylish helmet. Belinda had taken him on to find new outlets for her design activities. The partnership seemed to be paying off so far. He had induced Schactman to back the dress line, and, a few days ago, a cosmetics company that manufactured on contract for others had agreed to consider extending credit for a line of Belinda cosmetics.

"Ron?" Belinda began with unaccustomed timidity. He was straightening his powder-blue velvet bow tie in the mirror. His tuxedo was the same color. The shirt front billowed outward in great cumulus puffs of lace. "Do you have any idea what a show like this would have meant to me ten years ago?" Nearly all the paintings she had left were here. Now that all her time would be devoted to the dress line, it might be a couple of years before she would have time to paint again.

"It's a hell of a vehicle, isn't it?" Ron replied, his eyes intent on the tie. The party had been his idea. "Stoller is sure he can sell your whole inventory for maybe twice what you've been getting."

Vexed by Ron's shallowness, Belinda twirled around and reached for the door handle. "Ron, if somebody asks where you bought your outfit, don't let on it came as a bonus with *Liberace's Greatest Hits.*"

Ron's forehead wrinkled in puzzlement.

"Never mind. You've done a great job."

She strode back out into the gallery. The DiBiases were still in front of "Still Life and Face"—that might be a sale. The *Times* had sent its top fashion reporter. Melanie Arbuthnot and her crowd had arrived—she would have to greet them in a minute. Senator Avery had managed to lose his wife and latch onto the new model *Vogue* had discovered, the one with the impossibly long legs and the pretensions of intellect. Belinda fastidiously refrained from looking at the walls.

Will had spent several hours with Metrobank's lawyers after Winstead approved the loan. An information statement would be filed with the SEC and a letter published to notify shareholders of the loan and the stock purchase agreement. Only then would GUA actually begin to buy the stock. If, as expected, the bank's Executive Committee increased the size of the loan to fifty million dollars, the papers would be amended.

The business at hand was to hammer out a short interim letter agreement concerning the loan until a full set of documents was ready. To facilitate any changes GUA might wish to make in the arrangements later on, Will had insisted that the bank and the airline both utilize subsidiary corporations for the loan. It was nearly eight o'clock when he finally signed on behalf of Global Universal and a vice-president did the same for Metrobank.

Donna was still waiting. Will had told her the process might take time and had suggested she return to the hotel, but, fascinated by the language and the procedures, she had stayed.

Will had expected a barrage of questions from her as they left the building, but she was silent. Exhilaration over his accomplishment lifted Will like helium, but he held off speaking until they were out on the street.

"You cold?"

She shook her head.

"Hungry?"

She did not bother to answer.

"Okay, what is it, then?"

"You people really run the show. There's a secret world where people like you and those others really manage things. The rest of us don't know it's even there. We kid ourselves into thinking we understand what's going on. But that just shows our ignorance."

"Lawyers aren't witches or medieval sorcerers. We just know the law and try to avoid problems before they happen."

"It's not being a lawyer I'm talking about, but the power people like you and Winstead have to do things. One 'yes' and millions of dollars suddenly move to your side of the table. No one came out with a suitcase full of cash and put it into your hands. You just called up newspeople and said you had it. They believed you and told everyone else. And people started paying more for your stock. It might not be magic, but don't try to tell me ordinary folks even dream that a few people they never heard of have that kind of power."

Donna was wound up now. "You can't know how much I hated all you important, protected people in that glass office building when I was laid off. I waited six months to be hired, spent a month at that finishing school for idiots, was finally making a living and then they fired me."

"You and a lot of other people, including executives."

"How could they play with people's lives like that?"

"Everybody thought prosperity would last forever. Some of the same executives who planned with that in mind were the first to go."

"Not the great Ben Buck. God, how I hate that man. Fire a thousand pilots. Chop off two thousand flight attendants and anyone else who wasn't around forty years ago. We got a mimeographed letter of sympathy some P.R. guy probably wrote for him." The passage of time had not lessened her anger. "Do you know what kind of sacrifice Buck made? He cut his own salary by twelve thousand dollars a year, all the way back to two hundred thousand dollars."

"Did you ever meet him?"

"Once. At training-school graduation he came around to pin on our wings and see what the new crop of eligible 'chicks' looked like. If he ever flew on one of my flights, I'd probably pour a pitcher of hot coffee in his lap."

"Wouldn't work. When was the last time anybody got hot coffee on an airline?"

She didn't laugh. "When was the last time you were fired because people you never had anything to do with were incompetent?"

They crossed the avenue and were halfway into the next block before Will spoke again, and then it was only to ask once more whether Donna was cold.

Until they happened upon the onlookers gathered outside the art gallery, Will had forgotten the chance meeting in the elevator that morning and Belinda's invitation. Security guards stood at the entrance, holding back a crowd that pushed as close as possible in order to peer into the brightly lit room behind the shop window.

"You in a mood for a party? I'll bet you can eat them out of hors d'oeuvres in half an hour."

Before Donna could respond, he was talking to the guards. In amazement, she watched the taller one scan a list and nod to Will. A moment later he ushered them inside the gallery. Wide draperies of Belinda's textile designs swept in great arcs above their heads. Hanging on the white walls were her large expanses of canvas: complex color patterns with sudden moments of realism lurking among them, occasionally a self-portrait barely visible or else suddenly exposed.

Belinda stood in the center of the main exhibition room. She was just finishing her speech as Will and Donna made their way through the guests to a spot where they could see.

She was smiling as she gestured toward a balding, stout man in a three-button tuxedo, whose hand sported a long cigar as a woman's might an oversized diamond ring. A moment later, Belinda spun around to show off the dress she wore, then again to allow the cameras to get a closeup. Flashbulbs popped. A moment later she finished speaking. The glaring TV lights died out as if an artificial dusk had suddenly fallen. The TV crew and reporters hurriedly retreated single file, cutting a path through the crowd, followed by the newspaper reporters.

The hors d'oeuvres were at the back of the gallery. Donna led the way. Too late, Will realized that Craig Merrill stood in his path, conversing with a man whose back was toward him. Merrill looked up. For an instant he was disoriented.

"Hey, it's . . . Hey, Will! This is a surprise. I figured I had left all you GUA people back in Denver."

Will shook his hand. They had not become close while Merrill had been with the airline, despite their common military background. Will found Merrill too doctrinaire in his beliefs, too humorless about himself, too self-righteous.

"What are you doing in New York?" Merrill asked.

"Company business."

The other man had turned around, and now Merrill introduced them.

"Will Nye, J. Stephen Girard."

Will was startled. It was one thing to view his photo, to read about him, to toss his name about with a familiarity grounded in anger rather than knowledge. It was another to see the name made flesh, standing before him.

"You've had a busy day, Mr. Nye."

"A successful one as well."

"Or perhaps merely expensive. Only time will tell."

Now that the initial surprise had passed, Will rapidly took in as much of Girard as he could. Small, straight-backed, sure of himself, so sure he felt no need to hide that he knew who Will was and what he had been doing. But there was something else in his manner.

"Is it significant that you two are here together?" asked Will.

"The Colonel has agreed to join us at Faranco. We announced it earlier today."

"Congratulations, Craig. What will you be doing for them?"

A touch of embarrassment was evident for a moment, quickly replaced by belligerence. "Oh, I'll do lots of things. One of them is to keep an eye on Faranco's investment in Global Universal."

A smile flickered across Will's mouth as he turned back to the industrialist. "That doesn't really seem necessary, Mr. Girard. We're doing a very good job of watching it for you right now. Unless, of course, you're seeking more than just an investment."

"If I do, Mr. Nye, you and the SEC will be the first to know."

Superb self-control. That was it, Will thought, that was what set the man apart. Craig Merrill, for all his training under stress conditions, could not completely hide his emotions on first encountering Will. But J. Stephen Girard could have been discussing the weather. What was beneath that self-mastery? Will asked himself. Could it be emotions so strong, so demanding, that only such exquisite self-control could handle them?

The bantering tone left Will's voice. A question had been on his mind for months and he decided to ask it. "Why do you want to invest in an airline? The costs of running one today are astronomical and the return is about the lowest of any industry going. Some years only a single passenger on each flight is the margin between profit and loss. Airlines are going to need seventy billion dollars' worth of new planes by 1990. And they're not producing the kind of income to fund such an enormous investment."

"For the moment you may be right." Girard nodded toward Crockett Avery, who was still deep in conversation with the model and hurriedly scribbling something on a scrap of paper. "Senator Avery there and others, like Kennedy and Cannon, believe that lifting government restraints on competition will lower fares and put so many more people on planes that the airlines will soon be prospering."

"Do you?"

Girard shrugged his shoulders. "Some will and some won't. I think Global Universal can. Using your own logic, a few *more* percentage points higher in passenger load would produce immense profits."

"But on the surface, there seem to be so many more profitable investments you could make."

"Mr. Nye," Girard replied, and this time the suggestion of a smile seemed to materialize at the corners of his mouth, "there's always another reason for everything."

Will decided to push him further. "Perhaps you've held off because you're afraid to take on Ben Buck."

Will had hoped the jab would draw a retort laden with disclosure. Instead, it drew contempt.

"Your Mr. Buck is an anachronism. If the federal government hadn't protected the airlines from outside competition for so many years, the industry's loose financial controls and mediocre talent would long since have been upgraded. Buck and the few other pioneers still hanging on would be safely away in old-age homes building model planes instead of sending office boys like you on desperate errands. The companies they ran would now be thriving."

"If run by people like you."

"Particularly if run by people like me. Companies that don't make money die. Most people say they want to make money but haven't the stomach for it. I make money."

Without a word of leavetaking, Girard turned his back on Will and resumed his conversation with Merrill. Will felt demeaned by the rudeness but, strangely, reassured by the intense dislike that Girard had aroused in him. He knew now that if the battle for control were ever joined, the memory of that bloodless, insatiable face would sustain the fervor of his effort.

As soon as Will began picking his way among the small knots of people to locate Donna, his high spirits returned. The day's work had been a triumph. The party and the excitement of New York had buoyed him.

"Oh, my God! Will!"

He turned toward the voice. "Hello, Carla."

He had broken off with Carla the same night she asked him to move in with her, as he guessed she would; she had timed every move with exasperating precision. Will had told her he did not intend to be squeezed and bent to fit the empty places in someone else's life.

"You're . . . you're in New York."

"Only for the night. How have you been?"

"I've been well, Will." She had regained her poise. "I'm into self-actualization now and it's given me a great deal of confidence."

"The new hair style, is that part of it?"

"The hair style, the clothes—I think they express a freer, more open me. The best part is that I've been able to come to grips with my father's role in my life—you remember me telling you about my father—and accept him and understand that he acted out of love. I can say all those things openly to him now."

"Isn't your father dead?"

"That really isn't the point."

A hand slipped through Will's arm. "I see you two have found each other again. What do old lovers say to each other?"

Belinda had joined them. Her face was lit by a mischievous grin. Will refused to be drawn in.

"The really old ones talk about their grandchildren, lumbago and hospital costs. Belinda, this is a spectacular show. I had no idea you were so accomplished."

"Thank you. I'm glad you could come." She turned to Carla. "We literally bumped into each other on an elevator this morning. I was with Marcie." She turned back to Will. "Carla is engaged, you know."

"Congratulations. Do I know him?"

Will's interest seemed merely courteous, Belinda noted.

"Dave Delauney. He's gone to fetch me a drink."

"The way you say that bodes well for a satisfying life together."

Belinda said, "I hope you don't mind, Carla, if I introduce Will to some people here."

"It was good to see you, Will. Perhaps we could have dinner."

"Perhaps on some other trip."

Belinda guided Will toward a large canvas. Gloomy colors formed a faint profile of the painter.

"That's what I look like in the morning," she remarked lightly.

"I apologize for the way my compliment before may have sounded," Will said. "It's just that so many of Carla's friends did nothing with their lives, and they all called themselves interior decorators or jewelry designers . . ."

"Or painters?"

"Or painters. Why do you paint your self-portrait so often? Narcissism?"

"Cheap model." She eyed him wryly. "People who dislike me say it's a clever way to promote myself. Now, what about you? You live in Colorado, you said. What kind of work do you do there?"

"Legal work, for Global Universal Airlines."

"That's interesting."

"Every time I tell people who I work for, they insist on telling me how they were bumped off a flight or lost their luggage. What have you lost?"

"Absolutely nothing. In fact, I'm still a virgin with my first set of teeth."

Will laughed unreservedly. With friends, Belinda's funny, outrageous lines snapped the air around her like firecrackers. But with new people, especially men, enjoyment of them was a kind of test—one that Will had just passed. Particularly now, Belinda would have liked to stay with him, but she had other commitments.

"I've got to greet all my guests. I hope we'll have time to chat later. You should really talk to Marcie. That's why I said where you work is interesting. After meeting you this morning, she learned she had inherited a lot of Global Universal stock."

An older couple approached them.

"Belinda, the show is just marvelous. Isn't it, George?" the woman gushed. "We must have one of your marvelous paintings for our summer house, something with a lot of blue in it, I think. What would you suggest?"

Belinda smiled a warm goodbye to Will and took the woman's arm.

"There's *just* the painting in the other room, Adelaide, one of the best things I've ever done. The blues in it are bewitching, like lapis lazuli from the tomb of an ancient empress."

Will watched Belinda sweep the older couple into the next room, then began to search the gallery for Donna. Five minutes later he was certain she had gone. And Will was suddenly, uncomfortably aware that finding her was important to him.

Will found her at the hotel. She was packing.

"Why did you leave?" he asked. "You didn't say a word to me."

She lifted a pair of shoes from the floor and placed them in the small valise.

"I think I deserve an explanation," Will continued. "Or at least a goodbye."

Finally she straightened up. As she transferred clothing from the closet to the valise, she spoke.

"Look, I'm not like those people. My needs are very basic, Will. Food, clothing, shelter and a little love. We'd never hit it off."

"When I first came to New York, parties like that terrified me. Everyone seemed so quick and clever. And they knew all kinds of people and topics."

"But I'll bet you soon fitted right in there."

"Yes, and I'm proud of it. I worked hard at it."

For the first time, she looked straight at Will. "Why the hell should something so silly be so worthwhile?"

"For me it was a form of survival, an affirmation of life, a proof that I could thrive and even shine among other people."

"Pure bullshit!"

She bent over the valise again. Will's gaze was held by the graceful line of her back, by her hands seemingly incapable of wasted motion. Impulsively, he reached for her hands and drew her to a chair.

She stared at him without speaking. He looked away, struggling to decide whether telling her was the only way to regain the affinity that had become nearly palpable only a few hours before.

"I've never told this to anyone," he began. He started to pace, then halted. "When I got back from Vietnam, I was sent to a V.A. hospital for rehabilitation. They hadn't gotten around yet to fixing me up with a prosthetic leg when my wife came to visit me. She knew I had been wounded in the leg, but she had no idea it was gone.

"She called from the lobby, and when the elevator doors opened, I was waiting for her at the end of the corridor on my crutches, only one foot on the floor . . . like a dying stork. As she walked toward me, she never smiled or said a word. I could see the revulsion in her eyes. An incident half a world away had trapped her with a cripple for the rest of her life. I made up my mind that no matter what, I wasn't going to beg her to stay. She left a few minutes later, and I never saw or spoke to her again. The divorce was handled through lawyers.

"The leg wasn't the only reason for the divorce, but after a year-and-a-half separation, it was the final blow. At twenty-five, she was young enough to start over again."

"And you?"

His stare turned hard. "Me? I learned you can't depend on other people. Ever! I was accepted at Columbia Law School and worked my tail off for three years to win a job with a top law firm. I worked just as hard to rebuild the rest of my life that had been buried for so long."

"Parties."

"And people. And them wanting my company and wanting me to like them. And I don't have to depend on anybody." He paused. "Where were you going?"

"Back to Denver."

"Do you have any plans?"

"Not yet. Just to have the furniture delivered."

"I thought I'd fly to the Caribbean for a few days of vacation. Maybe you'd like to come. My secretary could arrange for your furniture."

"Which island?"

"I thought we'd send the Westwind back to Denver and just go out to the airport and catch a plane somewhere."

A child's concentration gripped her face.

"You assuming anything?" she asked warily.

Will shook his head. "I'm not assuming anything."

Donna stood up, walked to her valise and snapped it shut. Lifting it, she turned around.

"I'll give it a try."

Owen Clayton made some stops on his way home. The first was at the home of Harold Markowitz.

The Markowitz family had gathered together in shock upon hearing about the plane crash. Soon neighbors had joined them. By the time Clayton arrived, Hillary Markowitz was charging through the house, desperately playing hostess with time out only for comforting the kids. Clayton gently led her to a corner of the tasteful beige living room. No, he didn't want a bite to eat or a piece of fruit or a glass of soda or a cup of coffee. With no action to crowd out the reality of her sorrow, with a stranger before whom she had no need to maintain an attitude of gritty indomitability, she began to cry. Harold was dead, and tomorrow he would still be dead, and the day after, and the day after that, and all the days of her life to come.

Later Clayton was able to question her. Their home life had been happy. They were high-school sweethearts married for fifteen years, the envy of divorced and dissatisfied friends. He had been a thoughtful, loving father, respected in the community, on the Board of their synagogue. No obstacles had arisen in Harold's career. In fact, he had just received a raise. Why had he purchased a hundred-thousand-dollar insurance policy? He always bought one when he traveled (she nonetheless seemed relieved to be told that he had done so this time).

Clayton spoke with others at the house who confirmed Hillary's statement with a consistency that could not be ascribed merely to people speaking well of the dead.

He then called the family doctor. Harold Markowitz had undergone his annual medical examination the previous week. Except for being five pounds overweight, he had been in good health—particularly since he had recently given up smoking. No leads there. Thanking the doctor for his time, Clayton hung up and slipped out of the house.

The beneficiary of another sizable insurance policy lived in a nearby upper-income suburb. The large Tudor-style house was empty. Clayton noticed a huge square greenhouse behind it.

Condensation had obscured the glass. He found the door. The structure housed an artificial ice rink. A young man, perhaps nineteen or twenty, dressed in tight black pants and a black silk shirt, was gliding listlessly across it.

"Mr. Flein?"

The young man did not notice the intruder for several seconds. When he finally did, he skated over.

"Randolph Flein?"

The young man nodded.

"Sorry to disturb you," Clayton began. "I know this isn't an easy time for you. I'm Owen Clayton, with the FBI. Could I ask you a few questions?"

Clayton observed that their breath was white smoke. The young man's subdued "Yes" was more visible than audible.

"We want to find out about the insurance you took out on your mother's life."

"Mother insisted on it." He gripped the wood railing. "She was afraid something might happen to her."

"Had there been any threat, any . . ."

"Oh, no, nothing like that. But she hated to fly. She was always afraid of planes. Not afraid for herself, you understand, but that I would be left alone."

He dropped his eyes. Clayton waited patiently for him to begin speaking again.

"You see, my mother is . . . *was* an important advertising executive and made a good deal of money at it. Several times a year she flew to New York. She was afraid that if anything happened to her I'd have no income and would have to give up skating."

"Aren't there professional skaters?"

A horrified expression appeared on the young man's face. "Mother would never forgive me if I skated for money. I skate only for the beauty I can bring to it, like she did. I'm fourth nationally. With my new coach I could pull it all together by next year."

"Your mother was a skater?"

"She broke an ankle during the Olympic tryouts and had to give it up. She taught me everything, built me this rink. She is the most important person in the . . ."

And then he remembered she was dead. He let his skates carry him off to a side. Several minutes passed before he returned.

"The insurance. If you check, Mr. . . ."

"Clayton."

". . . Mr. Clayton, you'll find that my mother paid for the insurance herself. She was late for the plane and had me fill out the form. She buys insurance every time she flies . . . *flew*."

Clayton asked a few more questions for the 302s, the standard FBI interview report forms, but he had become certain Flein's story would check out.

As Clayton left, Flein glided back onto the ice in a long, flowing arabesque, his free leg held elegantly aloft and his arms extended as if trying to reach the other skater, who was no longer there.

Clayton's last stop was at the home of Sandra Guerin, the wife of the late SEC official. Grief was slowly evolving into resentment at having been left behind to cope with raising children, paying the mortgage and the taxes, not having enough insurance money to stay in graduate school and, worst of all, having to live out every day, from rising till sleeping, alone.

They had spent Thanksgiving weekend with her mother. She and the kids had planned to spend the rest of the week at Grandma's before returning to Washington on Friday. He had left for the airport at eight, attended a meeting there and caught a later plane than he had originally planned to take.

Charles Guerin had received a telephone call that morning, his wife explained. She had overheard snatches of a conversation that seemed to deal with the Senate confirmation hearings. He appeared to be angry after he hung up, and said only that he had agreed to an airport meeting and would have to change his reservation.

No, she didn't have any idea whom the appointment was with. No, she didn't have the name of anyone else who might know.

Clayton's colleagues had already questioned dozens of people who had been at O'Hare the night before. They had all been shown a photograph of Guerin, but none could recall having seen him. Clayton held out little hope that more information would be uncovered.

Occasionally Owen was struck by the realization of how

superficially even the most intense investigation scanned a person's life. Markowitz might have been hated by a mistress no one would ever know about. Evelyn Flein might have had a secret suicide compulsion. Charles Guerin might have had a shoebox full of thousand-dollar bills stashed in a closet. And there were three hundred and thirty-six other passengers and crew members whose lives would ultimately remain as much a mystery as these. Clayton knew that his best chance was to stumble after motives and hope he bumped into the real one, like a grown man playing blindman's buff.

As Clayton was about to leave Guerin's house, Sandra Guerin added to the mystery by remarking she was sure that when Charles left the house that night he told her he was flying to Washington, not New York.

At home Clayton was unable to sleep. He chatted with Edna for a while. Then when she fell asleep he showered, changed his clothes, and drove straight back to the airport. A phone message from Dwight Raeburn was waiting on his desk. Clayton sank down heavily into a chair, hoping Dwight had uncovered some leads. The clerk dialed as Owen glanced at the reports on his desk. They were as disappointing as his afternoon had been.

The path of the investigation he had considered hottest was rapidly cooling off. According to the reports, Vito Manfredi had randomly plucked the GUA flight's tickets out of a marshal's hat only ten minutes before its scheduled departure. In order to prevent information leaks about his itinerary, tickets had been purchased in false names for three flights leaving at almost the same time. Choosing one of the other carriers would have put them on a nonstop to Newark or Philadelphia. A further precaution had been Manfredi's decision not to fly from his Minneapolis hideout directly to New York, but rather by way of Chicago.

Clayton flipped the page face down and skimmed the next report.

Laura Landover, involved in an acrimonious divorce fight with her husband, certainly had a good reason for doing away with him. But at the time of the crash and for hours before it, she had been at a small dinner party in New York City (confirmed by three guests). Upon hearing of her husband's death, she had made immediate plans to throw a *real* Thanksgiving party. Suspicious, but understandable. She would be checked out further.

"Mr. Raeburn? One moment, please."

Clayton lifted the extension.

"Hello, Dwight? How's it going?"

"We just cut the flight recorder out of the fuselage with acetylene torches. We think the voice recorder is buried in the wreckage that cratered. We're trying to bring in heavy cranes to lift the fuselage."

"Fort Wayne?"

"Probably. But I'm not as impatient to get at it as I was this morning."

"Why's that?"

"Your dogs finally showed up. They started yapping like they were doing a dog-food commercial as soon as they got near the front end."

"At least we know."

"That's not proof."

"But it's a damned good reason for us to keep at it. Thanks, Dwight."

They said goodbye and hung up.

Clayton's first impressions at the crash site had begun to prove out. Once the wreckage was lifted out of the hole and pieces were rushed to the FBI lab in Washington for analysis, the investigators might have some hard facts to go on.

The door opened, and one of the investigators, Mark Ballman, hurried in.

"We're still checking out crank letters and grudges held by ex-employees, but one interesting fact did pop up," he said. "A stewardess named Donna Harney was supposed to have been on 211 but switched trips with another stewardess . . ." He stopped to scan his notebook. ". . . Jeanne Scott, two days before. Scott was aboard when the plane was lost. Harney had been furloughed for several extended periods the year before."

"So she might have had a grudge?"

Ballman shrugged. "Don't know. I'll have Denver check her out."

"If they can find her."

Ballman looked puzzled. "Do you really think this stewardess is a possible?"

"Right now, *everyone's* a possible."

5

The terminal buildings at JFK, linked to the road circling just inland of them, glowed in the night like luminous charms on a huge bracelet. Airline personnel could be seen moving brightly in and around them like colorful nocturnal birds: blues and reds at Eastern and Delta and Northwest; lighter blue heading for the elegant, umbrella-roofed Pan Am Worldport; a rainbow of plumage through the glass façade along the twin International Arrivals Buildings. Behind the windows enclosing the soaring wings of Saarinen's TWA terminal, the color was red; pastels at National; blues at British; and then the exotic purple and gold within the GUA glass dome. Next to GUA was American. Will and Donna had booked reservations on American's last plane that night to a Caribbean island neither had visited before.

Donna had hesitated at the door of the DC-10, eyeing the sleek skin nervously before plunging inside and seating herself with fatalistic resignation. Yet the wide-body had not swung off the tarmac before her eyes closed. Now the plane floated on the night, high above clouds that the moon had turned spun silver.

On some airlines, Will and Donna would have had to pay a small amount for tickets, but American and GUA allowed each other's employees free passage on their routes. If the plane had been crowded, Donna's reservation would have been chancy, her pass entitling her only to the equivalent of stand-by. Will was an airline corporate officer, so his reservation was "space positive," assuring him a free seat on the same basis as a paying passenger.

And yet, an implicit courtesy prevailed during these straitened times if someone suddenly bought that last seat. Will would be expected to yield his seat even if he had already taken it. If the class in which he was seated were full, he would be moved to the other section. Once, when no seats remained, a 727 captain had invited Will to ride the cockpit jump seat, delighted to have found a fellow flyer whom he could instruct in the wonders of that wonderful machine.

Will shifted to look at Donna. Asleep in the reclined seat, she had somehow managed to tuck her long legs under her and still buckle the seat belt tightly to prevent being awakened by a conscientious flight attendant if turbulence occurred. Her face appeared softer now with the overhead lights extinguished. He wondered what would happen if he leaned over and kissed her lips—sexy and inviting now because partly open in a secret, dream-caused smile. She was such a raw mixture of trust and self-protection, he thought, at one moment suddenly bristling with anger, the next full of trust—but like a too-wise doe, still tremulous with suspicion. He had the feeling that if trust were ever to predominate, her loyalty and giving would be overwhelming. And then, he wondered, would his habitual ennui set in? Perhaps her unpredictability was the attraction.

Too much to think about, with too little to go on, he told himself, as he settled back into the seat and closed his own eyes.

Like coffee in shades ranging from very light to black, the natives poured through the open sides of the sprawling wooden structure that served as the island's main market. Some were hauling in fruits, vegetables and meats from outlying farms. Others were there to buy. Will and Donna had parked the rented pink Jeep with the candy-striped surrey near enough to keep an eye on their luggage and had stopped off to buy breakfast at the market before visiting the Tourist Bureau to inquire about a hotel. The voices were as colorful as the clothing and the produce.

"Mangos! I got mangos big as melons and twice as . . ."

"Fresh coconut here . . . fresh coconut . . ." The voices rose like a song.

A wizened ebony-skinned man sliced the pineapple Will chose and proffered the first slice to Donna on the end of his machete.

"We're looking for a hotel," Will said as he accepted his slice.

"Plenty of rooms," the old vendor began in the island's calypso cadence, " 'cept Merriwether's Plantation House, of course. Try de Hilton, jus' de other side de city."

"What about the Plantation House? What's so special about it?"

"It's pretty, mon," the old man said with smiling finality.

"Will the Tourist Bureau be able to tell us if they have rooms?"

"Emerald Merriwether can tell you faster." He pointed to a plump woman pinching tomatoes. "But if she don't like you," he warned, "she don't have no rooms."

Will turned to Donna. "How does it sound?"

"I guess there's got to be a reason why it's so popular."

They strolled over to the middle-aged woman and asked for reservations. She straightened up, eyed both of them critically and told them she had a cottage available.

"Two bedrooms?" asked Donna.

"One bedroom and a pullout couch in the living room."

Will and Donna exchanged a questioning glance, shrugged and then turned to Mrs. Merriwether with nods of acceptance.

She handed one overflowing basket to Will and a second to Donna. "Now give me a hand," she ordered.

Emerald Merriwether had rented her newest guests accommodations farthest from the main building. The white cottage sat among stoop-shouldered palms and squat palmettos at the edge of the beach encircling the lagoon. It contained a bedroom and bath, a living room and a front porch with wicker chairs facing the sea.

Donna had bought a blue bikini in town and quickly changed into it in the bedroom. When she emerged ready for a swim, Will had not yet gone to the bathroom to slip into his swim trunks.

"I think I'll read awhile," he said, and added, "By the way, you look good in a bathing suit."

Donna glanced shrewdly at the open suitcase and then at the slacks Will wore. "You've already told me about the artificial leg," she reminded him. "Sooner or later you're going to want to swim."

"Well, if you're looking for company, maybe I will," he replied, after only the merest hesitation.

Donna was calf-deep in the mild surf when she caught sight of Will, now in bathing trunks, walking onto the beach. The vinyl skin of the artificial leg was a grayish pink. At each step, the hinges bent at the ball of the foot and the knee, where the strong spring straightened the leg as Will's weight shifted back to the good one. Donna made no effort to avert her eyes as he unstrapped the belt from around his body and let his thigh stump slip out of the soft leather pocket in which it rested. Will hopped down to the water on the powerfully muscled other leg. His eyes met hers defiantly.

"You look good in a bathing suit, too," she said.

She dived into the next wave, arced upward into the air like a porpoise behind its crest, and swam with strong, graceful strokes toward the open end of the lagoon. Will followed a moment later. As he pulled alongside of where she treaded water effortlessly, a happy smile on her face, he noticed that her eyes seemed to have changed color; like mirrors they now matched perfectly the translucent turquoise patches of the sea around them. Only then did he realize how wide and relaxed was his own smile.

They sunbathed the rest of the morning and spent the afternoon sightseeing in the pink Jeep.

Donna coaxed the parrot at the game farm for long, patient minutes until it finally rewarded them with a string of nautical curses taught by some sailor long ago. Donna was delighted.

When Will borrowed a machete from a worker, split the thin trunk of a sapling palm down the center and handed her the sweet white heart to eat, her face lit with pleasure.

Will observed that she seemed to delight in everything, as if each experience were a new discovery.

At sunset they strolled up from the cottage to the hotel's main building, once the center of a huge sugarcane plantation. The British owners had built their home as a replica of a large English country mansion. More than a hundred years later, the native white limestone still glistened.

Three great crystal chandeliers and white-coated waiters lent an atmosphere of genteel elegance to the polished wood dining room, as if nothing had changed in the intervening century. The widowed proprietress took great care that it should be so, and it gave her a great deal of amusement as well. Emerald Merriwether was a mulatto, and the matriarchs in her ancestry would have been allowed into great houses like these only to serve their "betters." "That," she occasionally explained to shock her stiffer guests, "was how our skins grew so light by my generation. And how I inherited the property."

After dinner Will and Donna alternately danced on the patio to the steel band and retreated to chairs overlooking the water to talk. It was nearly midnight when they walked back down the path to their cottage. The sofa had been converted into a bed, which was made up.

Donna kissed Will goodnight lightly on the cheek and walked toward the bedroom. At the bedroom door something occurred to her and she turned around.

"You know," she said, "you're not half bad when you're not trying to get your own way about everything."

Then she closed the door for the night.

The next morning they rode horses to a distant point along a cool, dark path cut through heavy foliage. Will found himself captured by the look of her as she allowed her horse to lope freely on ahead of his. A pair of thin jeans separated strong legs and lean hips from the chestnut's back. Except for the blue bikini top, she was bare from the waist up. Her own chestnut hair streamed out behind her. Her broad smile reflected the near-ecstasy on her face.

Only children ever shine with that pure happiness, he thought. There's nothing cerebral or considered about it. I don't think I will ever feel as happy about anything, as unself-consciously happy, as she feels right now about the simple pleasures of motion and wind.

At a brook near a country school, they dismounted to let the horses drink and take a breather. The children, in class, could be seen through the windows of the low thatched-roof building. A basketball had been left behind on the packed earth near the single backboard and hoop fastened to a palm tree. Will tossed it to Donna, who flipped it back. Without thinking, Will jumped and shot for the basket with the automatic grace of one for whom the game had been the religion of his youth.

The ball arced high and true toward the rim. Will landed stumbling and off balance, trying to right himself with the strength of one leg. He ended up sprawled face down in the dust. He rolled over and scrambled back to his feet. Ashamed to look at Donna, he brushed himself off while hurrying to his horse. Foot in stirrup, balancing on the artificial leg, he hauled himself into the saddle. Only when their horses were side by side, ambling once more along the road, did Donna speak.

"You made the shot," she said.

The path wound up the mountain. At the top they gazed downward as their mounts stood quietly beside each other. The island slid away from them like the back of a lazy green sea turtle. The beaches glistened in narrow crescents between peninsulas paddling through ocean that stretched forever.

"I'm glad you came here with me," Will said, and leaned toward Donna. It seemed very natural not to speak but to kiss. After a moment Donna tipped her head back and searched Will's face. Finally, she drew it to hers and kissed him again, this time with a deep, undisguised passion that caught both of them by surprise.

They rode back to the Plantation House in silence. Mrs. Merriwether eyed them with amusement as they approached.

Much later, when they returned to their cottage after dinner that night, they found that the sofa had been replaced by two armchairs.

"I suppose we'll just have to make do," Will said gently.

There was no reticence when he kissed her this time.

"I guess we have no choice," she replied with a smile. She walked ahead of him into the bedroom.

As they moved to embrace on the bed, the moonlight falling across their naked bodies made each look to the other like a silver statue come to life. But the touch was warm and thrilling and, in a moment, evoked a primal frenzy that blocked all thought.

* * *

To Donna and Will, in the days that followed, time became a discreet friend gone off to visit busier places. The days were warm and the nights clear. Sunlight, hunger, sex and sleep—these were the only clocks. They were discovering each other and reluctant, disorienting, compelling feelings they could not explain . . . and were happy not to.

On Friday morning a cable arrived. Metrobank's Executive Committee had approved the rest of the fifty-million-dollar loan, and drafts of the loan documents would be arriving by plane at four that afternoon. In order to close early, Will would have to read them over the weekend.

The plane was circling when Will and Donna arrived at the little airport. They intended to pick up the package, then visit an old church a local buccaneer was said to have built so that God would look the other way when he killed and looted. After that, they would have a quiet dinner at a restaurant in an old fort above the harbor.

Their plans were suddenly changed. What dropped out of the bright sky and pulled up to the gate was the GUA Westwind. Out of the graceful white missile stepped a huge man, clad in the wildest sport shirt the island had ever seen. Spotting Will, he boomed out, "With all these funny little islands, damned if we didn't find the right one!"

General Ben Buck had arrived!

He carried a very thick manila envelope. "Didn't want the company to waste money on postage, so I brought these loan papers down myself." He hefted the package. "Probably cost less."

A second figure emerged from the plane—Preston Frey, the corporate secretary. Buck gestured toward the open door. "You know old Pres, don't you?"

Will was furious. Life had been play again and fun. He and Donna wanted no intruders. Buck had exhorted him to take a vacation, then, like a meddling in-law, had come along. And Will knew that if *he* were angry at these uninvited guests, Donna must be about to explode. She had made the depth of her hatred for Ben Buck quite clear.

Will never got the chance to introduce her. Buck put his arm around her, his eyes fixed on the scant halter top. "Have you ever given a thought to a career as a stewardess for the world's greatest airline?"

"I guess you can't be expected to remember *all* the cute little Barbie dolls who work for Global Universal."

Buck's expression grew serious. "I apologize. It didn't occur to me . . . Wait a minute." His eyebrows drew together in concentration. "Donna. An Oklahoma girl. You joined the company about three years ago. Furloughing must have given you a rough time of it for a while."

Donna stared at Buck in speechless confusion. He turned to Will. "Now, where do you suggest some thirsty people find themselves a drink?"

Donna slipped her arm around Buck's ample waist. "You let me handle that, General. They make a rum drink on this island that will knock you on your ear."

The last person off the business jet was Rick Talbot, or Tal, as everyone called him. He and Will had flown in the same unit in Vietnam and had become fast friends. Huck Finn reborn and raised up in a technological age, Talbot had gone to GUA as a flight engineer, earned seniority enough to co-pilot executive jets and, because Will had pulled strings for him, was due to be upped in the coming week to the right-hand seat on a jetliner, much earlier than seniority should have entitled him. Perhaps to buy Will's hospitality, Buck had selected Talbot as his co-pilot for the trip. Will tried in vain to restrain a welcoming smile.

Customs and Immigration took only a minute. Buck strode to the car-rental booths. One look at Will and Donna's pink Jeep, and Buck insisted on renting a mate for it in blue.

As they waited for the vehicle to be brought to the terminal entrance, Will tried to convince Buck the Hilton would be the most comfortable place to stay, but Buck would not hear of it.

"How's your hotel?"

"Okay."

"On the beach?"

"Sure, but it isn't as modern as—"

"It'll do fine, just as long as it's restful. We just came from Indiana." The pain of recollection registered on Buck's face for a long moment before he went on. "The Safety Board will play the tape in Washington on Monday. I'd like you there with me."

Will nodded.

"Sometime in the next day or two," Buck continued, "I want us to have a chance to talk."

"About the crash?"

"A bunch of things."

A horn honked. A dark-skinned young man bounced out of a blue Jeep. Buck insisted Donna join him in it. As she climbed in beside him and the attendant loaded the luggage in the back seat, Buck roared to the others, "Just watch out. I'm liable to pull up into your tailpipe and start trying to make little Jeeps!"

Will clambered glumly into the other vehicle, Tal beside him, Frey in the rear seat. Not only had their arrival disrupted his and Donna's idyll here, but the concerns the others had hauled here with them—fear and mortality—had no place in Paradise. His only consolation was Pres Frey's despondency at having to yield his customary place within patting distance of the Old Man's back.

Will led the little caravan over thc mountains, twice being jounced when his rear bumper was nudged by a horn-tooting Ben Buck. And each time, Frey cackled, "This is like the good old days. Isn't this just like the good old days?" For Will, the good old days had ended half an hour ago.

Mrs. Merriwether not only had rooms in the main building but, to Will's even greater displeasure, was charmed by Buck and insisted the entire party join her for drinks. Seated behind the white limestone balustrade guarding the wide terrace, they watched the day slowly expire in a thousand shades of glory.

Higher than the pink cherubim clouds, a jet trail extended northward across the sunset like a chalk line drawn across a fantasy blackboard. The sun's fingers seemed to clutch at the vapor, widening and diffusing it into a candy cane. A shower of copper coins tossed across the sea sparkled at the spectators.

Rick Talbot whispered into Will's ear almost too softly for Will to hear, "Sometimes when it looks like that up there, I want to point straight up and climb till you couldn't tell me from the sunset." And then he quickly glanced at the others to be certain they had not heard.

"I'm glad you came, Tal," Will admitted gently.

"I tried to have Dee take the weekend off, but she couldn't find a switch, so she'll be flying all weekend. Gee, it would have been great, the four of us. Maybe next weekend we'll all get together in Denver."

Will glanced over at Donna. Her face was turned up to the sky. Her lightly tanned skin glowed. Wonder filled the wide eyes, now nearly violet in the late-afternoon light. Her mouth hung open till she noticed him, and then she smiled and squeezed his hand, the pressure growing stronger as, unconsciously, she tried to hold back the night.

Dinner was a noisy affair, laced with half a century of anecdotes about airplanes and the characters who flew them.

Danny Morell, who had a mail route in the twenties. He was too farsighted to read the compass and too vain to wear glasses, so he followed the railroad tracks below him from one city to the next. One day fog rolled in unexpectedly, and when he finally landed at what he thought was Baltimore, it turned out to be Washington, D.C. "Take me to the Postmaster General," he demanded. "I want to bid on a new mail route to Baltimore I just discovered."

Then there was the time Buck agreed to publicize GUA's new jets, just delivered to replace piston craft. The plan called for him and a planeful of reporters to have breakfast in New York and lunch in Los Angeles; they'd be back in New York for a late dinner that night. It was an eye-catching stunt for a nation only three decades from biplanes and wire wing supports. Unfortunately, a new employee at Los Angeles Airport mistook a football team for the planeload of newsmen; lunch was gone when the jet touched down.

"You know," the GUA man finally admitted after the shock wore off, "I thought they were kind of big for reporters, but I couldn't be sure. I've never been East."

Frey remembered the times during the war when the General, dog-tired from months of unceasing work to build an air transport system capable of supporting the war effort, would disappear for a few days of R and R. Frey was his driver then—that was how they met—and the one who shared the roistering hours when Buck let off steam.

"We were known in every whorehouse in every two-bit town that had an air base. Only the General never gave his real name. He called himself General Benjamin," the small man recalled, with a wink at Buck. "Remember Annette, with the business cards? She had business cards printed to advertise her house, with a line at the bottom of the card saying General Benjamin recommended it."

The table exploded in laughter, Buck's loudest of all. Frey's head bobbed up and down. "Know what he did when he found out? Know what he did? He insisted on a month of free visits or else he would have his own cards printed up taking back the endorsement." The laughter burst forth again. "Annette's cards started turning up all over Washington, and two General Benjamins nearly ended up court-martialed."

Frey waited for the laughter to subside. "But any girl with a hard-luck story, he was the softest touch in America—"

Buck cut him off. "Nobody wants to hear about that. Tell them about that time in New Orleans. Remember New Orleans, Pres?"

Frey remembered. "New Orleans was the best. Everywhere we turned there was puss—pardon me, ma'am . . . there were girls. You know what that big stud over there did? He rented the grandest whorehouse you ever saw for one solid week just for the two of us. The War Department and Western Union were three days tracking us down to get a message to the General. The lucky son of a B who delivered the message spent the next two days there with us. Western Union had to send out a search party for *him.*"

The Old Man's eyes were dancing as he picked up the story. "One of the councilmen got so damned horny waiting all that time for the house to reopen, he had the police break in and arrest us. They didn't want to say prostitution was going on, so they accused us of 'illegal entry.'"

As the laughter died down, Frey said, with a faraway look in his eyes, "There was one city where a little girl was so sweet on the General whenever we were there we lived right in the whorehouse, like kings. And me, I never had less than two or three girls there with me at a time. They don't make wars like that anymore."

It was very late when the group stood up from the table, several among them happily wobbly from Planter's Punches and Singapore Slings and Frozen Banana Daiquiris and Merriwether Hurricanes that each had insisted the others try.

Will and Donna wove unsteadily down the path to their beach bungalow and laughingly woke people in two others before finding their own. When they made love, it was fumbling and affectionate and joyous.

The next morning Will woke first and sauntered out to the porch. Pres Frey was forty yards away. Clothed in a white dress shirt, suit pants and brown laced oxfords, he was sitting on the trunk of an overturned palm. Thick fronds above him protected the pink skin on his bald head and face from burning. He was patiently awaiting the return of the lone swimmer far out in the lagoon.

Will slipped on a pair of slacks and walked over to where Frey sat. Small, so thin the skin seemed too tight to enclose the bones protruding sharply at the joints, Pres Frey perched upon the bleached gray log like a dragonfly. His eyes left the swimmer only for an instant as Will approached.

"Something happens to him, what the hell can I do? He's no kid anymore. But try telling that to him. He thinks he's a kid. Nearly seventy-five and he tries to act like a kid."

"Did you go to work for him right after the war, Pres?"

"Ten minutes after the Japs surrendered we were in the car and cannonballing it to the airport. He pulled me into this little two-seater plane and took off before I knew what was happening. I'm only a sergeant, I told him. They can court-martial me for this. So he tells me, As of an hour ago you became a civilian and you're working for my airline. What's my job? I ask. Whatever I tell you, he says. I always had a good head for details, so after a while I drifted into the corporate secretary's job and went to law school at night. Years later he let me be in charge of the gift catalogue we put on the planes." Frey half rose from the log. "Shit, he's out there a long way."

"When are you going to give me the information on the nominees holding our stock?"

"We'll get to it."

"It's been a month."

Frey's head spun around toward Will. "I said we'll get to it."

"That analysis is essential in figuring out who the banks and brokerage houses are really holding their stock for."

Frey's eyes narrowed. His voice became sharp. "I don't need a Johnny-come-lately to teach me and my people their jobs. The letters informing the shareholders about the bank loan and stock purchases are a priority, right? The General's been buying stock. That has to go to the SEC on time too, right?"

Will nodded, but was unconvinced.

"You'll get the analysis when it's ready," Frey said, and then forced a smile. "Hell, this is a vacation, right?" He winked at Will. "You got yourself a hell of a cute tour package in that cottage, Counselor. Coffee, tea or you-know-what."

Will stood up. Ben Buck was emerging from the water like a great albino sea mammal. Despite his age and bulk, the muscles were still surprisingly hard, the flesh solid.

"God, it was great. You been out yct today, Will?" Hc glanced at Will's leg and his brow puckered. "You don't wear that thing when you swim, do you?"

Will shook his head.

"It's none of my business," said Buck awkwardly, "but what about when you're in the hay?"

"Depends on how much of a hurry I'm in."

"I'm the same way about shoes and socks." Buck took the towel Frey held out to him. "Pres, could you give me a few minutes with Will? Some legal matters."

"I was just going off to reserve a tee-off time at the golf course. You still want a match later?"

"Fine. How about you, Will?"

"No, thanks. Donna, Tal and I were planning on sailing to one of the little islands out there for a picnic and snorkeling."

Buck paused and then blurted out, "You've got a hell of a good gal there. Maybe this'll sound funny, but she's one of the boys, know what I mean? No airs or standing on politeness."

"I know what you mean."

Buck dropped onto the log as Frey hurried off. "I wanted to talk about J. Stephen Girard. Have you seen the paper? Our stock closed just under ten yesterday. We're timing those purchases very carefully, trying to make sure we'll have a reserve if we need it."

"That's not going to stop him."

"What will?"

"He's not ready yet."

"How can you be sure?"

"I met him at a party Monday night."

Buck eyed Will warily. "First Max Creighton, now you."

"You're implying something I don't like."

"He's some kind of eccentric who doesn't meet many people, everybody kept telling me. You just *happen* to run into him at a party."

"Don't feel hurt," retorted Will sharply. "He sent you his regards."

"He must have been setting me up with Creighton right from the beginning. This whole business is what I wanted to talk to you about, Will. It really hit home when you told me Max was on Girard's side. Now that you've met Girard, what's your opinion?"

"The man hasn't a nerve in his body. Cold. Impersonal. A computer. I haven't the slightest idea what makes him tick."

"You said you thought he wasn't ready to tender for our stock yet."

Will nodded. "Nothing he said, just a feeling I had. But I don't know what he's waiting for."

"Well, at least we're ready for him now."

"He'll roll over you like a tank," Will answered disdainfully.

"Shit! You were hired to stop him. Maybe I should have hired somebody else, somebody with more experience who believed in Global Universal!"

Buck's unwanted arrival in the midst of a hard-earned vacation had only intensified Will's resentment over the older man's deceit.

"You lied to me," Will retorted, his voice a lash. "Creighton never told you on the phone Sunday night that he was prepared to set up a loan for the company; he was too unenthusiastic when I saw him the next morning. Creighton's too smart to obligate himself to a loan that will benefit his opponent. Sending me to New York to raise money was the longest kind of shot, but at worst I could test your own suspicions about Creighton without involving you. If I failed you could blame me. If I somehow pulled it off, you had a fifty-million-dollar miracle. And both ways you were playing *me* off against Bannister, just in case he might be feeling complacent . . . or think his strength with lenders might give him the clout for a stab at your job."

"I don't have to explain my orders to people who work for me."

"In the last couple of minutes, you've taken two shots at me. One more and you'd better start looking to replace me. Other people may play ball in the dark. I won't!"

Will's hard stare was as unyielding as Buck's, each man taking the measure of the other. After a very long time, Ben Buck slowly tipped his head.

"You have my word, Will."

An unspoken barrier had been leveled. Will felt that another chunk of respect had been won, and his indignation was assuaged. Ben Buck had been reluctant to allow Will to institute measures designed to protect against takeovers. Whenever Buck did take action, it was usually a shrewd, impulsive stroke—like the loan strategy—that protected a potentially vulnerable flank but failed to reinforce fundamental gaps in their defense. Now Will had an opportunity to make his case.

"I've been telling you for six months that we aren't prepared. You just didn't want to hear. Otis Elevator, Air West, Piper Aircraft, Carborundum, J. J. Newberry—the list of companies knocked off by raiders is as long as your arm. Girard has the initiative: he can pick the time when he's strongest and we're weakest. It will take every bit of strength to beat off his attack."

"You make it sound like some kind of war," countered the Old Man.

"There's not much difference. And unless we arm now, we won't be ready when the fighting starts." Will decided that this was the time to be frank with Buck. "For one thing, Girard is now breathing down our necks so closely that we've already lost the opportunity to have the shareholders vote to require that a raider must buy up, say, eighty percent of the stock for a takeover. For another thing, your directors have to vote on any offer Girard makes, but some of those characters could end up killing you."

"They're as loyal as you are."

"A few moments ago you weren't too sure about me. What about Dresser? Half the time he doesn't understand what it is he's voting on. And Landy? He'd agree to sell his mother for an extra buck in his pocket."

Buck was suddenly eyeing Will with respectful interest. The lawyer plunged on. "Right now we can't even legally call the Board together for a meeting on less than a week's notice. Nobody in the company has the slightest idea what he's supposed to do when a tender is announced. We'll look like the Keystone Kops. We've hired a takeover lawyer, but we need a top investment banking firm and a good financial P.R. firm on our side, too."

Will watched Buck weighing the threat on the one hand against his instinctive aversion to relinquishing personal authority on the other. The threat was too large, too final, to go away.

"Pick the best people," said Buck at last. "Do whatever you have to do to get us ready. I'll handle Bannister on the matter of the investment banker. Is there anyone else you want to hire?"

"A professional solicitation firm to help get the word to the stockholders. If we wait too long, Faranco might hire all three top firms just to keep us without one of them. It's been done before."

"Whatever you have to do, Will," repeated Buck resignedly. He picked up a handful of sand and flung it toward the surf. "Shit, just when we were coming back."

"If we were still in trouble," Will pointed out, "he wouldn't be interested. But if you let him provoke us into mistrusting each other, we'll become divided and confused. I'm not the enemy, he is."

Buck smiled slyly. "Will, I had to be sure. If I sometimes act devious, understand that's how I survived all these years and most of the others didn't. And that's why GUA survived."

The sailboat bobbed quietly a few yards from the beach. Donna swam slowly near the boat, a red plastic snorkel tube following her submerged head like a drifting buoy. Will and Tal lay sunbathing on beach towels, talking desultorily. The large island they had come from was painted sketchily along the horizon like an idea. Donna was fishing for their lunch.

"Will," asked Tal, "did you ever think when we were in Vietnam that we'd be together on a beach somewhere ten years later, working for the same company?"

"I didn't think about anything much at the time, Tal," said Will, although he knew that was true only at the beginning. "And I didn't suppose you did, either."

"Lately I have. We suffered fifty percent casualties from ground fire for a while." His eyes flicked up to Will's. "I guess you know that. After you nearly bought it, I realized for the first time something could get at me. One day you were gone, and another guy was in your bunk. Baldwin, his name was, from Paducah, Kentucky. That could happen to me, I said to myself. I could disappear without a trace except for the new name plates."

"What started you thinking about it lately?"

Tal turned over and sat up, his arms around his drawn-up knees. He looked out at the water. His voice was shy when he spoke.

"Dee and I are getting married Christmastime, when we visit her folks."

"Congratulations! That's wonderful, Tal!"

"I thought I'd be scared shitless getting married, but I can't wait. I really want to be part of a family and have kids and watch them grow up. You know what I mean?"

Will nodded.

"And then I started thinking about how those kids would never have been born if a SAM had been aimed just a fraction more right or left when I was coming in. And *their* kids. And their *kids'* kids. It would have ended with me."

"*I* would have, too."

"Shoot," Tal said, reddening. "I'm sorry I brought it up. I didn't mean it like it came out."

"Don't be sorry. I owe very little to anyone in this world, Tal, but I owe you my life."

Will's and Tal's planes had been the last two in the fighter-bomber formation to go in over the target. The rocket launchers had zeroed in by the time they came over. One of the blasts had rocked Will's fighter, shattering his left leg and crippling the plane. But Tal refused to race off after dropping his bombs; he rolled back and drew the ground fire until Will could limp out of range. Only Tal's superb flying skill made his plane too elusive a target for the electronic hunters below.

Tal's glance shot up at Will and then down again. "I used to want to be like you. You knew that, I guess. And after you were gone, I really got to think I *was* like you. Then I visited you at your law school, and you showed me where you studied in that library, with thousands of books around you and a pile more on your desk, all the size of concrete blocks. That night we went drinking like we used to—remember?—but we had trouble finding things to talk about."

"It did take a long time," Will concurred.

"How do you stick it out at a desk all day long? Don't you miss flying?"

Will thought a moment. "To be truthful, even if I had come home with both legs, I'd still hate flying planes . . . all the killing they can do. . . . I used to think the world began and ended with flying. Now just one plane doesn't seem important enough."

"Everybody at GUA says you're really a comer, that you've got the big guys worried. I want you to know how much your getting me into the jetliners means to me." Will did not answer; Tal did not expect him to. "So we're different is what I'm saying. I'm not one of the Musketeers, like you used to call us. I want a family and the good suburban life."

"It's tough to be a Musketeer over thirty."

"The Old Man, he's still a Musketeer."

"He's still a Musketeer," Will agreed.

Tal caught his eye. "And you are, too, you know, Will."

"No, I'm just ambitious."

Donna was close to shore when she suddenly dove. She seemed to be under for much too long a time. At last she swooped up out of the shallow water, a large fish clutched in her strong fingers; the back of the hand holding the unused spear gun pushed up the face mask as she raced toward them in smiling triumph. Sunlight twinkled off the water droplets that flew from her feet.

"I have our lunch," she was yelling.

She dropped the fish into Will's lap. It flopped and wriggled wildly, cold and slippery against his sun-warmed skin.

"Oh, shit! Come on, Donna. Shit, get this thing off me!"

Her hand closed deftly around the thin part of the body near the tail. She pulled a knife from the canvas bag they had brought.

"I don't suppose you want to help clean it," said Donna, the corner of her mouth twisted in mock disdain.

"No, thanks. I'd probably mess it up."

As she walked back to the water's edge to begin, she called loudly over her shoulder, "Probably can't butcher a hog worth a damn either."

Will and Donna spent all of Sunday away from the others. Late Sunday night they sat on the hill that formed one side of the lagoon and watched the waves roll in and break to gentleness over the submerged coral reef stretching to the far point. A campfire had been built on the beach for a hotel party. The two of them had left it, meandered up the hill and then watched the little match fire grow even smaller until it was only a glow and the tiny people gathered around it had gradually trickled away.

Later, they saw some toy figures move toward their cottage—a white-haired man and lightly clad women clustering behind. The General had gone to a local nightclub for the evening. With him, they guessed, was the chorus line brought back by the General to entertain them. He knocked on their door. After a few moments, receiving no answer, the small figures turned away from the cottage and filed into the dark vegetation in the direction of the hotel.

Much later Will and Donna went down to the water and swam one last time. As they floated amid cream spilled by the full moon, he took her face between his hands and gazed into her eyes. They were so blue they made his insides tremble, and he wondered why that should be so.

6

"That's the last voice communication."

Dwight Raeburn pressed the off button. Silence replaced the roar of the slipstream. The listeners flinched as if, against all reason, they believed that Raeburn's act had cruelly cut off the lives of 211's disembodied voices. The room was filled with the horror of 211's last minutes.

Raeburn waited a few moments for them to compose themselves. Then he spoke.

"We think that after the explosion Captain Benson was able to get his oxygen mask on. Our supposition—based on increased noise from the slipstream—is that a hole was opened up in the fuselage, but we won't know for certain till the wreckage can be examined in detail. "

"Then you're sure that sound we heard was an explosion?"

Raeburn nodded. "Captain Benson obviously thought so, too. The word 'explosion' was fairly clear on the tape. Mr. Clayton of the FBI will be speaking in a moment about that, but all of the evidence we have so far points to an explosion. The information on the flight data recorder corroborates it—perfectly normal flight till that moment." He flipped a page.

"Our Human Factors group reports that all of the autopsies performed on the cockpit crew turned up metal fragments. The flight crew was dead on impact. The shrapnel produced by the plane's structure during the explosion was the cause of death—vital organs, vessels, nerves were punctured. Jayson, the flight engineer, was closest to the blast and was killed immediately. DeMarco died shortly thereafter. Our conclusion is that Captain Benson, the last one alive on the flight deck, tried to regain control of the plane but was unable to obtain a response from the systems. The flight recorder reveals that the plane had gone into a steep dive. When Benson died, he was trying to turn the transponder dial to the seventy-seven-hundred radar code to alert Air Traffic Control that the plane was experiencing an emergency."

A cautious head poked into the room.

"Yes, Eunice?"

"Call for Mr. Clayton. They said it was important."

Owen Clayton hurried out the door as Raeburn picked up the thread of his speech.

"The passengers probably never felt the final impact. The autopsies show oxygen insufficiency. As near as we can figure it, the air inside the plane, pressurized at the equivalent of eight thousand feet, rushed out the hole torn in the fuselage into the lower pressure outside the plane at twenty-seven thousand feet. The explosion was a large one, so the plane itself must have been rocked, and then it began to dive. The oxygen masks were released, but chances are few people had the presence of mind to put them on. Without them they would have passed out within fifteen seconds. Even though the dive brought the plane into denser atmosphere, we don't believe many could have regained consciousness before impact. That turned out to be a blessing. There was no chance the aircraft could have survived the explosion."

"Because the pilots were already dead?" Keller interjected.

"That and the physical damage done to the plane. We think the control cables were severed by the explosion, making control of the tail surfaces impossible. Benson couldn't recover from the dive."

Clayton slipped back into the room and regained his seat at the conference table.

"Damn it," Jim Keller burst out, "there's nothing in that area that could explode!"

"Which, I guess, is as good a place as any to turn the meeting over to Mr. Clayton here. Let me remind you that what we're discussing, what you hear today, is confidential for the time being."

Owen Clayton stubbed out his cigarette. He had flown in from Chicago early that morning. The few hours of sleep he had managed the night before had failed to erase a week of fatigue. He started to speak, but a sudden cigarette cough stopped him and he had to begin again. He lifted a cutaway diagram of the 747.

"This shows where everything is in the plane. These are the first-class lavatories in the main cabin, lower level. The explosion probably took place around there somewhere. We won't be sure till the section is pieced together—the reconstruction will be directed to that area."

"Are you saying someone deliberately blew up the plane?" Will asked.

Clayton nodded.

Murmurs of shock escaped from the listeners.

Dan Pope, head of Security under Will, immediately pointed out the implication. "Unless we figure out how they did it and plug the security gap, they can do it again."

Clayton nodded. "So far we know only that someone got through the security precautions and placed a bomb in a vulnerable place in or near the first-class section."

"Suicide maybe," countered Pope. The black former police chief wasn't about to have the blame laid without hard evidence.

"Maybe. Or murder. Or a political act." Clayton shrugged. "That call I just got was from headquarters with the lab report I was waiting for. The FAA's dogs sniffed some sort of explosive, but we weren't sure which one until now. We found traces of Composition C-4." Clayton noticed that all eyes were riveted on him, but he directed his words toward Pope. "You probably know it as 'plastique' or plastic explosive. International terrorists use it a lot because it's high-velocity when it's activated but stable until it's detonated. It's pliable and you can mold it to just about any shape. But in this country plastic explosive is tough to get hold of. In fact, it's only available to the military."

Now Clayton shifted his gaze to Will. "Some of the leads to potential perpetrators point inside the company. GUA might need to institute tougher security measures to protect other planes. If this new suspect we've got in custody doesn't pan out, we're going to need a lot of cooperation from your company."

Will spoke up. "Our security is as good as any in the industry. But we can't do the FAA's job for them. *They* inspect hand luggage and scan the passengers for weapons, not us. And as for cooperation, we're just as interested in finding the killer as you are."

Buck interposed himself decisively. "We'll cooperate. But you said something about a suspect. Maybe this whole thing is already solved."

"As a matter of fact, it's a GUA employee." Clayton's tone conveyed no satisfaction. "The suspect withdrew from a scheduled duty assignment at the last moment and has been undercover since the crash, out of the country. The arrest was made here in Washington. The suspect was attempting to board a plane for Denver."

Buck was gripped by a terrible fury. "I promise you, Mr. Clayton, we'll give you all the cooperation you need to crucify the son of a bitch. Who is he?"

"A woman, a stewardess." Clayton pulled out a slip of paper. "Donna Harney's her name."

"Mr. Clayton," Will said with a chuckle, "I have a feeling you're going to have to go back to the drawing board."

After the meeting, Owen and Will were just leaving for the airport to arrange Donna's release when a call that had been a step behind Clayton all morning reached him. Peering absent-mindedly over the FBI man's shoulder as the latter scribbled a note, Will was suddenly jarred to attention as Clayton wrote down "Senator Crockett Avery" and "Carl Raymond." Carl Raymond was executive vice-president of Faranco Inc., and Girard's closest aide. Clayton concluded the phone call by arranging to meet both men at the airport and then walked out to the elevators with Will.

When Will asked about the call, Clayton told him it was confidential.

"Mr. Nye, is it true that GUA Flight 211 was sabotaged?"

The sunlight was intense for December. As Will stepped out of the building, he raised his hand in a limp salute to shield his eyes. In front of him, barring his way, he saw a boyish face with a nose like a long peg. The collar and necktie were open.

"Who are you?" asked Will.

"Desmond. *Newsweek*. There's a report circulating that the plane crashed because of an explosion on board. Any truth to that, Mr. Nye?"

"Where'd the report come from?"

"FBI."

Will glared reproachfully at Clayton for an instant, then back at the reporter. "This fellow here is the man you want to speak to," said Will with sincerity.

"Who is he?" the young reporter asked Will, as if Clayton were deaf and blind.

"His name's Mitty, Walter Mitty. He's in charge of GUA's press relations."

Will moved to the curb and hailed a cab. Clayton dove into the cab after Will, shouting "No comment!" over his shoulder.

"National Airport, driver." Clayton settled back into the seat.

Will stared at the buildings. After a few moments, he remarked casually, "You said something about cooperation."

"A couple of our Denver agents have had trouble getting to see your company's personnel records. Even your airport people have been less than open. You hiding something?"

"Dan Pope began to get the idea the FBI was looking for an easy scapegoat to make big headlines with—some poor GUA dummy who just happened to be in the wrong place at the wrong time."

"I don't operate that way."

"Tell that to Donna."

"Sorry." Clayton's tone was weighted with sincerity.

"The FBI's also been known to leak stuff they told everyone else was confidential, just to look like they were on top of things." Clayton shrugged his shoulders helplessly in reply. Will went on. "But if you're serious about cooperation, it'll have to work both ways. Our only interest is catching whoever blew up our 747."

Their eyes met for an instant.

"I'm serious," Clayton replied.

Will's gaze shifted to the passing scenery. "Who are we going to meet at the airport?"

"Your friend Donna."
"Anyone else?"
"Senator Avery and a friend of his."
"Who?"
"A man named Raymond, with Faranco."
Will was about to go on when Clayton interjected, "I don't know what it's about."
"Beautiful city, Washington," Will commented in the same nonchalant tone.

Dour, tall and round-shouldered, with a face like a white saucer, Carl Raymond, age thirty-six, stood outside the terminal at National Airport. He always wore black three-piece suits—heavy ones in winter and lighter ones in summer—so that up close he had the air of a nineteenth-century undertaker. From afar he resembled an ebony bishop's crook with an ivory knob at the end.

The cold had accentuated the red veins that passed for rosiness in his cheeks. The sandy hair blew in front of tiny blue eyes, which did not blink or waver, but sat like pits on the saucer face. He was awaiting a limousine transporting General Balu Odalu, President of Gomala, to the airport. He would greet the black West African leader as if for the first time in a long time and then escort him to New York City aboard one of Faranco's private jets, ostensibly just a courtesy gesture extended to the ruler of a nation in which the American conglomerate had vast, but unproven, mining concessions about to be developed with a Swiss partner.

But the truth was Raymond and Odalu had already spent several hours at sharp trading that morning, before Odalu's meeting with the American President. Several hours more this afternoon would be spent at Girard's office, where final deal terms would be set between Odalu and Girard, absolute rulers respectively of Gomala and Faranco. Gomala's rich natural resources would soon explode with economic development. One of Faranco's safe and untraceable corporations would be granted exclusive air rights into Gomala, as well as Odalu's aid in obtaining the same rights from four neighboring nations. Despite the complications caused by the most convenient death of a very disagreeable public official, Charles W. Guerin, Girard, for his part, would guarantee a large deposit placed in one of Odalu's many safe and untraceable bank accounts—the expression of political allegiance that the "Marxist" leader had always insisted, in previous transactions, was the most meaningful. Then, tonight, Raymond would fly to West Africa and work out the final details of this very lucrative air rights deal.

The first limousine to come into view was Crockett Avery's. The plastic daisy atop the antenna was practically a heraldic flag, a signal to young women that the handsome young Senator was fun-loving and spontaneous, despite his national prestige. The daisy's symbolism seemed rather inappropriate today; Avery's face was drawn, his hands spun small distraught circles. Distressing information had come his way: Charles Guerin's briefcase had just been found, intact and still locked, when the wreckage of 211 was pulled apart. It had been quickly claimed by Sandra Guerin's lawyer and whisked away from the crash site. Raymond had agreed with the Senator that a reassuring chat with the FBI might now be in order, preferably directly with the agent in charge of the case; going higher would only arouse suspicion.

"I'll do the talking," said Raymond with an air of natural command. At last Avery could relax.

Will waited with Clayton in the Eastern Airlines section of the airport concourse, listening noncommittally while the FBI man listed matters on which the airline's cooperation was needed. As he spoke, Clayton watched a colorful group of Africans enter the terminal and stop to chat. At the edge of the group was the highly recognizable face of Crockett Avery. Clayton assumed the tall, hard-mouthed man beside him was Carl Raymond. He cut short his conversation with Will and headed toward the two Americans.

Out of earshot of the Africans, Raymond did most of the talking, explaining that he had just happened to be with Senator Avery the night the Senator met with Charles Guerin in a car at O'Hare. As Girard Foundation trustees, Raymond and Avery had attended a University of Chicago cocktail party in appreciation for a research grant made by the Foundation. Avery utilized the occasion of the Chicago visit to question Guerin about his views on SEC policy in a more open way than was possible at the confirmation hearings. There was nothing "unusual" involved, of course, so Raymond had gone along.

Rather than risk the displeasure of his superiors by probing too deeply into so powerful a Senate force as Crockett Avery, Clayton asked instead what was the key question for him: "Why did Guerin take a New York-bound plane when he had told his wife and his aides that he would be returning to Washington?"

Both men shrugged their ignorance. A few more questions were asked that elicited little more information, and then the conversation ended.

Clayton headed back across the wide concourse. Will had observed the group intently during the several minutes of discussion.

"Learn anything?" he asked once he and Clayton were walking toward the airport's Security quarters.

"They wouldn't talk to me."

"I'm sure they gave you a lot more than name, rank and serial number."

"Not a thing."

"All in a day's work, I guess," said Will sardonically.

"I want to finish the conversation you and I started in the taxi."

"About cooperation and two-way streets? Clayton, you sound to me like a man who was just caught driving the wrong way on a one-way street."

Donna had dawdled behind Will and Buck after the Westwind had touched down that morning in Washington. Once inside the terminal, her name was barely out of her mouth before the FBI and other agencies descended on her.

Owen Clayton's apology did little to soothe her anger. She was still furious at GUA's slipup when he and Will arrived to secure her release from custody. Briefly she reconsidered her decision to request assignment. In the end she telephoned GUA and was immediately given a hedgehopping flight leaving that night for Mexico City by way of half a dozen small hot cities.

She and Will sat sipping coffee in the Crew Lounge, chatting before Donna would have to deadhead to Houston and Will take the Eastern shuttle to New York.

"I guess everything in life is a risk and a trap," she mused.

"Going back to flying, you mean?"
"That and the kind of week we just had. That's probably the biggest trap."
Will was a bit miffed. "You sound like it wasn't fun."
"It was wonderful fun, which is why it's such a trap. The truth is we've just had the best of each other. All of the good. None of the bad. Real life isn't like that."
"Are you trying to tell me that it's over between us?"
She brushed his cheek gently with her hand. "I hope not, but be honest: the experience was a fairy tale, Will. It had nothing to do with people who go to work every day and get angry at the dry cleaner or the boss or the burnt dinner. Let's face it, what do we have in common that would keep us interested in each other back in the everyday world? You read books all the time and have ideas that would never occur to me and are wrapped up in making a name for yourself and . . ."
"And you aren't, right?"
"The only thing we have in common is that neither of us wants to get tied down."
Will nodded with some chagrin. "You have a talent for saying all the blunt, honest things most people only think. But now that I hear them, I'm not so sure they're completely true."
"What does that mean?" she inquired warily.
His smile was open and candid. "Nothing awesome. Just that I would miss you a lot if I thought we'd never see each other again."
"I'd miss you too."
"Maybe we might even be able to stand each other in Denver. I'd expect some groveling now and then, but nothing extravagant." His voice became serious. "Will you be back by the weekend?"
"Friday."
"Then let's spend the weekend together and see how it goes."
She smiled broadly. "While I grovel, you can move my furniture into place."
They finished their coffee. Donna's plane was about to begin loading. The surroundings were too public a place to kiss goodbye, and shaking hands seemed inappropriate. Donna just hurried away after promising to telephone on Thursday.

Will walked slowly back to the Eastern counters. From a distance he recognized the *Newsweek* reporter who had cornered him outside the offices of the NTSB. The man was interviewing someone near the telephones. As they separated, Will recognized the other man as well: Carl Raymond of Faranco. Will would have given a lot to know the substance of that interview.

Lee Conway, Marketing chief, grunted a barely civil greeting at Will as they passed in the corridor of the GUA Building early Thursday morning. He had had a long argument with Helen the night before, and it still rankled. Now she was saying that the problem with their marriage was that she needed to "fulfill herself." Some do-good woman lawyer with some activist group had filled Helen's head at a lecture with talk about "personal achievement" and "doing one's part to better the world."

Running into Will Nye, the boy wonder, only added to his discontent. The Old Man had had upstart favorites before, Conway reminded himself. But all the bright comets had burned out fast and disappeared. Some on their own. Some with a little boost from helpful vice-presidents.

For his part, Will had avoided one-to-one meetings with Conway since the episode with the man's wife. He felt no guilt, rather the desire to stay away from a man he had no particular liking for and who had—if only the man knew it—a very good reason to dislike him. Will side-stepped Conway in the hall and hurried into his office to catch up on a week's worth of mail. He had barely seated himself behind his desk when a figure in a dark three-piece suit suddenly appeared in the doorway.

"I've got something to say to you, Nye."

Although articulate and capable of expressing himself tactfully when the occasion demanded, Arnold Bannister was a blunt and uncompromising man. About six feet tall, forty-nine years of age, with dark hair cut 1960s short and regular features that might have been considered handsome if they were not so purposefully unexpressive, he looked so average as to be ignored in a room full of strangers. But once he spoke, he was memorable indeed.

He had come to the company from a top post with another airline when the financial crisis was beginning to accelerate at

GUA. His goal was to cut expenses and manage the company's finances better. His first act had been to call a meeting of his division in the company's auditorium. He began with a sentence characteristically to the point: "If your name does not appear on the blackboard behind me, go upstairs and pack your things. You are redundant."

Bannister closed the door and turned back to Will. His eyes were smoldering.

"The Old Man says this company has you to thank for destroying our relationship with Creighton, Cromwell."

"Did he explain the circumstances?"

"What he explained and what I believe are very different."

"Did he tell you that Max Creighton was working with Faranco?"

"We are talking about Max Creighton, one of the most respected men in American finance, not one of your twist-the-facts-to-suit-their-pocket lawyer friends, Nye. Maxwell Creighton singlehandedly kept our credibility alive in the financial community when our losses were staggering."

"His relationship with GUA was already long gone when I arrived in New York," said Will.

Bannister parted his suit jacket and stuck his thumbs into the vest pockets belligerently. "And you made sure you would be the only one we can rely on for that opinion. The Old Man may be fooled by your power play, but I'm not."

"I was ordered to go to New York by the Old Man. The idea was his, and the order was his."

"And going behind my back to Metrobank was yours. We can't afford to let you use this company to further your personal ambitions. Now I have to pick up the pieces with our lenders and find a new investment banker for the company."

"We already have one. The General authorized me to hire Bergheim, Mack."

"You sneaking low-life! Finances are *my* concern!"

"Right now they're everybody's concern. We're faced with a takeover threat here that could knock all of us off. This is no time for egos."

Bannister stared at Will for several seconds before speaking. "I will see you fired and both Legal and Security part of my division if it's the last thing I do."

His eyes held Will's for several seconds more, and then he wheeled and left the room.

Ben Buck, you son of a bitch, Will found himself thinking. You did that on purpose. You deliberately failed to clear the investment banker choice with Bannister as you promised. "Divide and conquer." "Competition keeps them on their toes." You son of a bitch!

The phone buzzed. Will picked up the receiver.

"A Miss Harney is calling collect on five-one. She says you're waiting for her call."

His dark mood lifted like a curtain. "I sure am."

Will pressed the lighted button. "I'll accept the charges, Operator. Donna?"

"Hi, Will."

"Where are you?"

"Guadalajara. I've got to get right back to the plane. It's about to board. I'll be back in Denver tomorrow and then I'm off for the weekend."

"What's the Denver ETA?"

"Twelve-oh-five."

"I'll meet you at the gate. I can't wait to see you."

"It's wonderful to hear you say that. These last few days I've had a terrible feeling we'd never see each other again."

"We have the whole weekend together, but I promised Tal we'd have dinner with him and Dee tomorrow night. His plane should be getting in around the same time as yours."

"Great."

"I'll see you tomorrow."

"Tomorrow."

Accustomed to making public presentations, Al Goetz, lawyer and lobbyist of thirty years as well as a GUA senior vice-president and member of the Board, stood comfortably behind the easel outlining his analysis of what form the new CAB Act might take. New legislation was likely to present the airline industry with the terrifying dichotomy of trying to maintain the quality of its service to the public while fare and route competition raged among them for the first time. The odds were that only the biggest and strongest carriers would survive, because they could dominate the routes they went after with more planes and could withstand cutthroat price-slashing.

The other five men in the Board Room listened intently as Goetz concluded.

"My crystal ball is a little cloudier on the last points. Eventually you'll be able to freely add and drop routes. But no one is yet certain whether there'll be total freedom to set fares or whether, to begin with, there will be specific zones within which prices can fluctuate."

"Everyone will go after the lucrative routes like the charters do!" Keller broke in hotly. "Doesn't the government understand that our job is to transport people quickly from any place in the country to any other, whenever they want?"

Buck bent forward and pounded the table with his fist. "Our job *now* is to plan how to survive! We fought off a potential threat from Girard after the crash. And now the threat is from the government. The future of Global Universal rests on how we handle that new threat in the coming months!" He straightened up. "I'll be long gone from GUA when the new age comes. The guy who'll have to lead the company into it ought to have a say in the direction GUA takes."

"I didn't know you had picked a successor yet, General." Goetz's voice was strained.

Buck had always acted as if the inexorable laws of time did not exist for him. He had long since passed the age when nearly all other chief executives had yielded their places to younger men. But, so far, Buck had not even hinted at who his choice might be.

"I haven't and the Board hasn't," he said, "but there are only a few guys who could handle it. I'm forming a Future Planning Committee made up of the four of you." He eyed the senior vice-presidents in turn: Bannister, Conway, Keller and Goetz. "I want each of you to develop your own game plan for GUA's future. The next time the Committee meets, you each present your ideas, and we argue out the merits. Then I'll choose the plan to go to the company's directors.

"Keep Will informed of how things are going. He'll coordinate.

It's also a hell of a good opportunity for him to learn the nitty-gritty details of how an airline operates." Buck turned to Will. "Speak to anyone you want in the company—pilots, Scheduling, Aircraft Procurement—so you really understand what goes into the thinking."

Silence gripped the room, not the barest rustle of movement from anyone. Bannister, Conway, Goetz and Keller each understood that the first hurdle had at last been vaulted: the choice to succeed Ben Buck had narrowed down to the four of them.

Will understood something, too. He had been placed at the most advantageous point possible, by luck or design. He was going to be made privy to the formative thinking of the other four and would have an edge if he could come up with a plan of his own.

Will observed the senior vice-presidents. A row of sweat beads had broken out on Goetz's forehead. Conway was full of pride, unconsciously shooting his French cuffs and smoothing out the creases in his suit. Keller displayed no emotion. A basic man, he took each day as it came, matter-of-factly. And he was taking this in the same way. Bannister—he was the cleverest one, Will thought, and the hardest to outwit: Bannister was motivated to succeed by hate, and he would drive himself to crush the others by every means at hand.

Buck too had been circling the assemblage with his gaze. Now, for an instant, his eyes met Will's, and then he looked away. Will could not discern in that briefest of encounters whether Buck's placing him at the center and yet outside was designed to include him in the running. But he was determined to make it count for that.

Buck's thumb and forefinger reached up momentarily for the corners of his mouth. When he spoke, his voice was reflective. "You all know what aviation and this company mean to me. I loved it too much probably . . . never could allow room for a special woman in my life, for getting married. I consider you my family. Particularly in the last few years, we've been through a lot of hard times together. When I leave this company—and I know I'm getting on in years; the damned shaving mirror tells me every morning—I know I'll be leaving it in good hands and headed for a happy future." His expression hardened. "And no outsider is going to grab it out of our hands and ruin that future."

Buck stood up. "Arnold, I'm ready to go through next year's final budget if you've got some time now."

Bannister scooped up his files and followed Buck out of the Board Room.

When the door had closed, Lee Conway got to his feet, turned to the others and declared, "Gentlemen, if my count is correct, that's the fourth time in ten years he's treated us to the now celebrated 'getting on in years' speech."

They all laughed self-consciously.

Keller spoke up. "You've got me beat. That's only my third."

"We'll all be deep underground," Goetz added, "and he'll still be running this company. What do you think, Will?"

"Don't look at *me*, guys," Will countered. "I'm just here to hold your coats."

After the others had left, Keller came up to Will. "How soon can I replace the 747 we lost?"

"The insurance papers don't permit it."

"Damn it, our share of the plane's value has got to be seven, eight million."

"Just about. The public originally put up eighty percent of the plane's cost to buy our guaranteed loan certificates, and GUA put up twenty. So the public should get around twenty-four million dollars in insurance payments and GUA around eight."

"Shit!" Keller turned away to pick up the notes he had taken. "Will, the equipment we fly is critical in any future plans. As part of your schooling, you ought to be at the presentation Boeing's giving here tomorrow morning. They've got two new midsize jetliners on the drawing board to replace the 707s and DC-8s, with a lot better fuel and noise efficiency."

"Two?"

"One's a larger wide-body, around two hundred passengers. This is a hell of an opportunity for us to standardize with a single manufacturer. The Old Man is behind the basic concept. The maintenance savings will be enormous."

"I'll be there."

Keller looked Will in the eye. "Don't underestimate your part as the referee on this Future Planning Committee, Will. The General knows what a bloodbath it could turn into and figures you'll keep the rest of us honest. At least *I'm* counting on you for that. I don't have the time or the stomach for politics."

Will admired Jim Keller's straightforwardness—as well as his astuteness in realizing he needed someone to watch his back before he could safely turn it on the others.

"Okay. I'll do what I can to keep the low blows to a minimum."

"Do that and some guys around here lose their best punches!"

The next day Will slipped out of the Boeing presentation during the question-and-answer period in order to be at the terminal when Donna's plane arrived. The nearer he got to the gate, the happier he felt. He stopped short when he noticed a familiar figure peering out the boarding-lounge window at the runways. Dee Ullman was still in her flight attendant's uniform, her small yellow valise beside her. Not until he approached did he sense the tension gripping her small frame. She glanced up, her face suddenly pale when she recognized Will.

"Oh, God, have you heard something about Tal's plane?"

"No, I'm here to meet a girl friend. Actually, we were going to have dinner tonight with you and Tal. What's wrong?"

The young woman with the turned-up nose and open features, which always struck Will as being very like Tal's, tried to speak calmly, but her voice trembled. "I just heard a rumor one of our planes is down."

Will's spine turned to ice. He looked from her face to the liquid-mercury skies outside. "Does anyone know which flight?"

She shook her head. "I tried to call. No one would tell me."

"What flight was Tal on?"

"Five Nineteen from L.A. Your friend?"

"One Twenty Two."

She nodded. "Mexico." She waited for Will to continue.

"Her name's Donna Harney."

"I've flown with her. She's terrific."

They stood silently for a moment, watching for a speck to appear in the drab sky over the mountains. Finally, Will broke away and went to the gate phone.

"Let me have Operations Control. This is Will Nye."

He heard a ring, and waited for someone to pick up. Then he

saw Dee's body suddenly stiffen—a plane had appeared. Will's eyes sought out the TV screen announcing gates and arrival times. The word "Landing" was flashing on and off—beside "Flight 122." Relief swept over him, but it was immediately replaced by anxiety about Tal.

"Operations Control. Porter here."

"Fred, this is Will Nye. I've heard a plane may be down."

The voice paused. "Another 747. It's down in Utah. Wiped out. Same story as the last one."

"Which flight?"

"Five Nineteen."

As he moved toward the window where Dee stood watching, Will felt grief clawing at his breast, the kind of pain that had not ripped him open in a decade. But back then his youth and the sheer numbers dying all around him in Vietnam had helped immunize him. Miraculously, he and Tal had managed to survive. The skies could not have been waiting all this time to play so terrible a trick. And then Will remembered it was he who had manipulated matters so that Tal could leapfrog over others on the list for promotion and move into that right-hand seat. Guilt spread over him like a mantle.

The loudspeaker called tensely, "Will those people awaiting the arrival of Flight 519 from Los Angeles please come to the GUA ticket counter."

A rattling moan broke from Dee's throat as Will reached out and let her collapse against him. There was nothing he could say or do. Over her head, through the glass, he numbly watched the GUA 707 bring Donna safely down to earth.

With Donna following in Dee's car, Will drove Dee to the garden apartment she had shared with Tal. Several times they had invited Will there for dinner, but he had been unable to make it or had talked them into going to a restaurant instead. Now the hominess of the three rooms, of their belongings neatly placed, stabbed at him.

Will telephoned Tal's mother, who, like all of them, wanted so much not to believe the words. Later a doctor came by and gave Dee pills to help her sleep. When she finally did, Will stepped out on the second-floor balcony to think.

Winter usually comes early in Denver and leaves late. The

ground had frozen into brown rock. Only the pines were still green, but the gray afternoon was dying quickly, leaching out what little vividness remained.

"Coffee?" Donna held a steaming mug in each hand.

Will muttered his thanks.

"Strange," she said quietly, the smoke from her speech intermingled with the steam from the coffee. "This is how we first started talking . . . what was it? . . . ten days ago. A plane down. One of us touched personally by it."

Will's voice was tight with tension. "But you weren't responsible for causing that death."

"Will, it makes no sense to blame yourself. You were the one who showed me that after Jeanne died in the first crash."

"I *am* responsible—for the deaths of Tal and your friend and nearly five hundred others. My people were supposed to stop those bombs before they could ever get aboard."

"What could you have done?"

"I knew they were ruthless. I should have known they were maniacs."

"You sound like you have an idea who did it."

"We . . . *I* took them too lightly. I figured Faranco could be stopped with financial and legal maneuvering and that the first plane crash had nothing to do with them. Sure, we intensified security at the airports, but I just didn't realize how brutal they are."

"How can you be so sure it's Girard? It could be anyone. Craig Merrill, for instance—you told me how angry he was when he left GUA."

Will shrugged his shoulders. "One or the other. Maybe both. Someone is after this airline. I'm going after him."

The cold luster of Will's eyes scared her. "But that's the FBI's job."

"If they're willing to work with me, fine. If not, I'll do it on my own. Security for GUA is my responsibility. If Girard is behind it all, then it's doubly mine."

"It could be someone out there you don't know, with a motive you haven't thought of."

Will did not reply but watched unseeing as the city emerged in the distance in thousands of points of light.

"Stay here with Dee," Will said at last. "I've got a few things to take care of."

Will was turning to leave when Donna's question stopped him. "Will, could a person want to own something so much he would murder nearly five hundred people for it?"

The question hung before them on the sad twilight like a lone billboard on a desert highway.

"I'll call you later," Will said, and left.

First he drove back to his office and scribbled a memo Lorna would type and send out on Monday: Farber and Pope would take over more of the routine matters in their departments. His company was in jeopardy. He would concentrate on stopping the bombings and any takeover assault.

Then Will returned to the Porsche. He drove deliberately, containing himself until he reached the isolated cabin in the foothills. Then he stepped from the car and made his way slowly to the center of the clearing. Finally—with the black, empty sky alone to hear—he moaned out his pent-up sorrow and pain. Until only guilt was left . . . and rage. Someone would pay, he vowed. Someone would pay.

Every newscast that night led off with the crash of GUA's Flight 519 near Zion National Park in southern Utah. All one hundred twenty-seven passengers and a crew of fifteen had been killed. The wreckage and the bodies of the victims were being found spread out over an area of several square miles. It was a grisly spectacle, as the film clips revealed. In addition, the networks featured an on-the-spot interview with Craig Merrill, who had rushed to the site from his Los Angeles home. He expressed outrage that such a catastrophe could be allowed to occur twice in less than two weeks on one of the world's largest airlines. He urged that authorities undertake a full-scale investigation of Global Universal's operations and safety procedures. A few of the TV reporters pressed GUA people for a rebuttal, but their response—that the airline was careful and that no one yet knew the cause of the crash—and even their long list of additional security precautions seemed inadequate against the vivid horror of the disaster.

Owen Clayton had cooled his heels at O'Hare for nearly two

hours waiting for clearance from the Bureau to fly to Los Angeles. Although the aircraft had crashed in Utah, putting it under the Salt Lake City office's jurisdiction, and had taken off from Los Angeles, which gave that office a call on the case, Gorlick, his SAC, was trying to get Clayton assigned to the new investigation. In the end it was Clayton's reputation on aviation cases and the similarity to the Indiana crash that convinced the Bureau.

Will Nye's telephone call reached Clayton at his hotel room late Friday night, after Clayton had visited the Zion crash site, confirmed his suspicions and flown on to Los Angeles. Will was determined to join Clayton in the investigation.

"In Washington I wasn't willing to open wide the doors because I didn't trust you or your organization, Clayton," Will began. "I gave you an opportunity to be forthcoming with me and you held back."

"My job is to catch people, not to give confessions."

"I'm in charge of stopping people from bringing bombs on planes. I didn't stop them. And you didn't catch them."

A long moment of silence underscored the irrevocable nature of what had occurred, sobering both men.

"What can I do for you, Will?" Clayton asked quietly.

"Whether you agree with it or not, I'm going to get involved in the investigation. I'd like to work along with you, Owen—give you whatever aid I can—but if I have to do it on my own, I'm prepared to."

For a moment Will was apprehensive that Clayton's silence meant refusal. The latter's voice was low with distress when he responded.

"I saw on the list that the first officer, Talbot . . . he gave your name as the one to contact in case of emergencies. I'm sorry. He must have been a good friend of yours."

It was all Will could do to force the words out. "For a long time."

"Can you be at Los Angeles International around nine tomorrow? We'll be speaking to witnesses."

"Nine o'clock," Will confirmed, and he hung up.

Clayton hung up at his end, swung his swollen feet up onto the bed and leaned back against the pillows, content simply to relax. For months he had looked forward to an L.A. trip to see a friend's collection of early airmails, but other concerns would not permit it now. His mind kept returning to the various names that comprised his private list of suspects.

He had spent a good part of his week trying to reconstruct the last few hours of Charles Guerin's life. At forty-two, Guerin had been known as a controversial enforcer of the federal laws governing securities and publicly traded companies. He was an activist who rarely compromised. For days Clayton had conjectured about such a man's attitudes and motivations. Then two things happened: Guerin's briefcase was found at the crash site, and Avery and Raymond admitted meeting the Enforcement chief just before he left on the fatal trip.

Sandra Guerin had seemed shaken by the revelation that her husband had flown to New York after telling her he was leaving for Washington. Fearing that she might seek to protect his memory either by placing the briefcase in a bank vault or, worse, by destroying it, the FBI agent decided to act fast. When she, her mother and the children left the house to go to dinner early Wednesday evening, Clayton moved in with a squad of specialists for a "bag job." The usual technique was to break into the unoccupied premises and look around discreetly to be sure no hindrance existed to a full operation. The second break-in was to obtain the actual information. But this time, they had to fan out and find it on the first try; there might not be a second opportunity.

First a phone call to verify that no one was left in the house. Then simultaneous phone calls to divert the two neighbors who had views of the rear door, through which the squad would enter. Then, because all the windows were latched, a fast pick of the door lock, and they were inside. Maintaining radio contact with a lookout, they moved quickly. They found the briefcase in a locked closet. The briefcase too was locked, but it presented little problem for the deft fingers of the lock man. Within five minutes everything had been photographed, the briefcase and the closet relocked, and they were out of the house.

Breaking into homes to gather information without a valid search warrant was an unconstitutional invasion of a citizen's privacy, and any evidence gathered on such a break-in could not be used in a court of law. The real reason for the search was to obtain leads on what to look for and where. In this case, Clayton had found his lead carefully written into Guerin's appointment book next to a note reminding Guerin of his nine o'clock airport meeting with Avery and Raymond. That in itself was interesting, Clayton thought: Raymond had contended he was at the meeting only because he happened to be with Avery at the time. Then on the next page, in the space for 10 A.M., Guerin had written the following reminder: "J. Stephen Girard at Friedman, Potter and Green, 375 Park Avenue, New York City." Now he knew why Guerin had changed his plans and suddenly decided to fly to New York instead of Washington.

Clayton lay on the hotel bed trying to fit the pieces together. He guessed that some potentially damaging allegations about Faranco were being studied by the SEC; knowing how much Guerin wanted his nomination confirmed, Raymond had probably asked the powerful Senator Avery to arrange a meeting with Guerin, and, as a result of that talk, Guerin had agreed to meet with Girard in New York the following day. Nothing criminal in any of that, Clayton thought, unless Avery and Raymond had convinced Guerin to fly to New York, not for a meeting, but rather to insure he was aboard an airplane on which a bomb would go off.

One point did not fit. Raymond had said the meeting with Guerin had lasted half an hour or so—until nine-thirty. Flight 211 had boarded an hour later. And yet Guerin, a careful man, had not bought a ticket until after ten. What had happened in the intervening half hour? Clayton had no answer.

7

Marie Girard invariably woke earlier when she and Jamie were on vacation, to keep him company. While he sipped a second cup of coffee and began to leaf through the *Times,* she rose from the breakfast table set out on the aft deck and stretched out face down on a chaise. Although it was early and a breeze was blowing across the inland waterway, the sun already felt hot. This was their first weekend of the winter in Palm Beach, but she had little concern about exposing her skin to the sun. She had a tan all year round—renewed by a sun lamp in colder climates. That and careful attention to her diet enabled her to maintain the appearance of being younger than she actually was.

They had flown in the night before on one of the company jets. Marie could feel her spirits lifting with the plane as it rose through the grayness. While dressing for dinner, Jamie had noticed that she had neglected to pack any of the exquisite jewelry he had bought her over the years, only the gold wedding ring she always wore. Without telling her, he had sent Vincenzo, their private secretary, to a Palm Beach jeweler, and by the time dessert was served, the gift had arrived: turquoise and diamonds mounted in gold, a necklace and earrings. She had smiled with grateful surprise and put them on. She saw he was pleased with what he had bought her—the dazzling lavishness of it.

He thought she loved him for the opulence he unstintingly bestowed on her. But the truth was she felt foolish wearing the jewels, as if she were a child again, trying on grownup clothes pulled from an attic trunk. Not foolish really, because only Jamie was there to see it, and she was most comfortably herself around Jamie. But all the gifts and possessions were really unimportant to her. What was important was how dear Jamie looked when she opened the gift-wrapped box—expectant, smiling unsurely (he who was always so sure). And how happy and expansive when she smiled and thanked him! That made it worthwhile, every time.

The huge white yacht was the one possession of any importance to Marie Girard. During the early, difficult years, she had watched large ships floating toward the horizon and imagined that they carried rich people to the places pictured in magazines. This small ocean liner was the incarnation of that dream, and its insularity the protector of their privacy.

"Listen to this, Marie," Girard directed, spreading the newspaper on the breakfast table. "The *Times* is going to run a three-part series on airline safety starting Monday. They say it's in response to Senator Avery's 'timely call for a national exploration of the issue.' Well, what do you know?" He chuckled softly. Things were going well indeed. Crockett's latest speech was featured on the front page, right next to two columns on the previous day's air crash.

He turned to the page on which both stories were continued. "Oh, and look at this: 'The African nation of Gomala announced today that it has entered into discussions with several other West African nations that are considering a federation for the purpose of joint air transport development and future regional transportation projects.'"

"Very well indeed," he said with some satisfaction.

Marie raised her head and smiled appreciatively at her husband. Despite an occasional indulgent response, she absorbed little of his conversation. Business and politics did not interest her, nor did she easily comprehend their subtleties. On the rare occasions she did bother to pick up a newspaper, she seldom ventured beyond the fashion and beauty pages. But she knew Jamie enjoyed sharing his business concerns with her, so she always made a dutiful pretense of listening.

She was about to lower her head once more to the chaise when she noticed the launch setting out from the dock. Business people, she remembered, were coming aboard to speak with Jamie this morning. As the launch neared the yacht, she could make out two visitors behind the crew member at the wheel, a gray-haired man and a tall figure in a black suit—Carl Raymond. She disliked her husband's adjutant. Jamie said he was very helpful, so she endured his occasional visits, but she found his calculating manner intolerable. His frigid blue eyes, like scalpel tips lying on the pallid tray of a face, seemed to probe for secrets encapsulated like cysts in her soul.

She rose, adjusted the elastic edge of her bikini, retrieved her moisturizing cream, and moved off to the bow deck. Two crew members stepped aside on the outer walkway as she passed, then continued on to the davits that lowered the gangladder to the water level.

Girard put down the newspaper, greeted his visitors and guided them to armchairs on the fantail. A steward appeared with a tray of sweet rolls and fresh coffee. As the three men chatted, Girard rapidly read through the material Raymond had carried down on the plane that morning. Possessing the enviable gift of assimilating anything his eye fell upon, Girard could read whole pages at a glance. The visitors had just taken their first sips when their host slipped the file into the space between him and the arm of the chair and turned cordially to the gray-haired man.

"Would you care to go for a short cruise this morning?"

Max Creighton raised his hand in declination. He was dressed in tennis whites. "No, thank you, Stephen, I promised my wife I'd make our noon tennis date. As a matter of fact, Jane wanted me to raise something with you. She saw a picture of this ship in the Palm Beach paper this morning—it *is* overwhelming—and wanted me to ask a favor of you. Each year the Hospital Fund gives a party for three hundred very carefully chosen guests. This year Jane is chairman, and she's taken with the idea of having the party on your ship. Would you be willing to . . . ?"

Girard was amused. Only Marie could appreciate the irony of the rich and powerful clamoring to be among those invited to pay a lot of money for the privilege of visiting the Girards at home. Perhaps the irony was worth allowing those people to use the ship for the night.

"Have Jane let us know the date. We intend to dock here all winter, and perhaps we would be able to make the ship available."

"How very generous. You'd be the Fund's honored guests, of course, and anyone you wished to invite."

Using the ship was one thing. Using him was quite another, even though these last few months—after a lifetime of the security of seclusion—they had risked lowering the wall just a bit on rare occasions. There was little chance they would attend; it served no purpose.

Girard turned the conversation to the point of the meeting: Global Universal Airlines, Inc. "I gather you've all seen the news of the crash. I would have thought the price of the stock would be lower than eight and three quarters by now."

"The airline itself supported it," Creighton said, "but I imagine the closing price isn't far from where it would have recovered to in a few days."

"I'd be willing to offer thirteen for it—although perhaps not at the start."

"With all due respect, Stephen, that's fifty percent above the market—too generous a premium. You'd be offering nearly seven and a half times present earnings. The market would accept a lot lower than that."

"With all due respect, Max," the industrialist repeated with a touch too much courtesy, "they will earn a dollar-ninety this year and two-seventy next. So my offer is less than five times next year's earnings."

Creighton appeared incredulous. Girard tapped the manila folder at his side.

"The figures are those of their Finance V.P., Bannister. He gave them to GUA's president at a private meeting two days ago. Their revenue is increasing at a much higher rate than anyone predicted even a few weeks before. I understand the other copies of this report are safely locked in the airline's vault." He passed the envelope across, remarking lightly but with an edge of sarcasm, "Don't forget, Max, the SEC takes a dim view of anyone who trades on inside information he doesn't first reveal—not that the Commission's much of a worry anymore."

"Those are Bannister's initials, all right," Creighton noted in disbelief. "But how did you get hold of it?"

Behind the large sunglasses Girard's face relaxed its characteristic gravity for an instant. "As a boy, I played hard poker against grown men. I learned to go into a pot only when I was almost certain what the other players held. That's what made me a winner. Now let's get to the big question. Whose hands is the stock in?"

Creighton opened the manila envelope he carried and handed copies of the list to the other men.

"To the best of our knowledge, these are the major blocks, but they're only a small part of the entire list, and only GUA has that."

"Please run through them, Max."

"You own seven percent. Buck controls fifteen percent. The other seventy-eight percent is split among much smaller holders. The largest blocks are held by the Monroe Trust, Harrington Guaranty Bank, members of the Harrington family—Ephraim Harrington took a liking to Ben Buck when the company was starting up—and a woman named Marcie Manning, but her stock is controlled by Buck. There's a Brazilian conglomerate and a mutual fund."

"What about employees?"

"About twenty percent."

"Won't they be loyal to Buck and the old crowd?"

"I have a feeling the layoffs opened a lot of eyes. They can be sold."

"Tell me about this Marcie Manning."

"Father left her nearly two percent of the company, but Buck has an agreement that allows him to vote it."

"Forever?" Raymond asked.

"I don't know."

Girard turned toward his aide. "Check into it, Carl." Then his gaze returned to Creighton. "Tell me about the banks."

"They'll sell at fourteen, which would get their own shares and most of their clients' out without a loss. The Harrington family is willing to sell as well. Of course, they'll all want a most-favored-nation clause: if the ultimate tender price ends up above fourteen, you guarantee they'll get the higher price."

Both men knew that Faranco would finalize these purchases just before the tender offer was announced, for two reasons: the law prohibited private purchases afterward, and word of them would not have time to leak out.

Creighton had already tallied up the shares. "Calculating in only the stock we're certain of, you start out with thirteen percent. Have you made up your mind about the takeover? The hundred-and-fifty-million borrowing from the pension funds is assured."

"Max, nothing is assured."

Creighton looked at his wristwatch and stood up. "I get the point, Stephen. I'll call you personally as soon as the debentures are sold to the pension funds. Now, if you will excuse me, I have a date to get beaten at tennis by Jane for the three thousand and fourth consecutive time. Are you going back with me, Carl?"

"No, I have a few things to discuss with Stephen. About my recent trip."

The three men strolled to the gangladder.

"Where did you go?"

"Unusual place, as a matter of fact."

"Jane and I are always on the lookout for out-of-the-way places. Where were you?"

"West Africa."

"That's a bit *too* out of the way, I'm afraid. Well, we'll be in touch."

Girard and Raymond watched Creighton step into the launch and settle back for the short trip to the dock. Then they resumed their seats and began the real business of the day.

At the bow of the ship, over two hundred feet away, Marie Girard lay on a chaise and squinted into the sun at a hawk circling indolently over islands in the middle of the waterway. It looked like a red-tail, the kind she remembered watching for hours as a child. Seemingly motionless, it appeared to be the sole possessor of the vast blue sky. The underside of the spread wings were phantom white, imbuing the hawk with a fragile otherworldliness, as if it might be a spectral messenger to those below.

A break had opened in the fog over Los Angeles International Airport. GUA Flight 860 had been circling slowly at the bottom of the stack. Suddenly given clearance to land, it wheeled into the glide path, the landing gear grasping the runway only seconds before the fog rolled back over it.

Will Nye was first off the violet-and-gold 727. Clayton was waiting at the gate; he was anxious to pay a visit to Darlene Valentine. GUA gate personnel had reported that the famous film actress had refused to board Flight 519 just before takeoff, insisting the plane would crash. She had hysterically implored the airline people to cancel the flight, but with only her intuition to go on, they had refused, suggesting she and her husband take a later flight. He had refused to yield to another of what he called his wife's "tantrums"—he had an appointment to keep. He walked down the ramp to the first-class section, leaving her behind, sobbing. An hour later everyone on board the flight was dead.

Ten minutes from Los Angeles International, Will and Clayton had passed out of the fog surrounding the airport and into the bright sunshine in Beverly Hills. Now, driving between the open iron gates of "Valentine's Way" and along the winding road, the men had the same sensation of passage into a different dimension of existence. On the left was a white-fenced paddock where palominos were grazing. On the right, the lawn was as formal as a royal park. In the center stood a huge red-brick mansion.

Clayton braked the rented Chevy in the circular driveway, and the two men strode underneath the pillar-supported portico to the tall white door.

It was opened by a woman in her forties with the waspish air of a displeased schoolteacher. Horn-rimmed glasses hung from her neck on a thin gold chain. Her sweater and skirt were both of heavy brown wool.

Clayton and Will introduced themselves. In a clipped English accent, she informed them that her name was Haverwell; she was secretary to Mrs. Courtney.

"Mrs. Courtney?" Will repeated blankly.

"Darlene Valentine. Although I suppose she won't want me to call her Mrs. Courtney very much longer, now that Mr. Courtney is dead."

"You don't sound too broken up by his passing," Clayton commented.

Miss Haverwell turned out to be far more talkative than her pinched face had suggested. "I might as well be truthful, although one is supposed to speak well of the dead. I didn't like him very much, no. No one did, including Mrs. Courtney, if one were to judge by the yelling from that end of the house at night."

She started to lead the way to her employer, but Clayton stopped her.

"What sort of things did they yell about?"

"They didn't really need a topic, but in the last few months they were at each other night and day about the property settlement."

"They weren't happy together?"

One of Miss Haverwell's eyebrows rose. "Perhaps my own view is jaundiced. Until two weeks ago I worked for both the Courtneys." Her voice rose archly. "That was when they agreed in the property settlement that Mrs. Courtney would get me, and Mr. Courtney the mahogany credenza."

She turned and clomped with uncoordinated vigor ahead of them across the white marble foyer and down the hallway to the end of the east wing. The door to the sunroom was slightly ajar. Through the opening the men could see the back of a blond-haired woman in a black leotard sitting crosslegged on the floor. The French doors beyond her were open, and the sun's rays streamed through them and around her like a rectangular spotlight. A murmuring sound emanated from the room as if she were speaking to someone.

Miss Haverwell knocked softly on the doorframe and they waited to be acknowledged. When the seated woman failed to respond, her secretary knocked more loudly. With that, she slowly turned. Off the screen and without makeup, the famous seductress's face seemed fresh and wholesome, her large eyes clear. She rose gracefully and approached them. The sex-symbol promotion upon which her early career had been built left her visitors unprepared for the intelligence in her voice.

"I usually meditate in the nude, so I thank you for telephoning first."

Clayton wondered how much more there could be to see. The deep V-neck of her leotard exposed large expanses of breast, and the nipples pressed visibly through the taut material.

"You were talking to someone?"

"To Rolf."

Both men looked stunned.

"Or trying to," she continued in explanation. "But he's probably holding off contacting me out of pure spite."

"You've heard from him since the crash?" asked Clayton sharply.

"No, have you?"

Clayton was confused. "Why would he contact me?"

"He was rather an admirer of the Bureau." Darlene gestured toward the large pillows spilled randomly about the floor. "Why don't you sit down?"

Clayton dropped clumsily onto a pillow after great exertion. Will followed.

"I have a feeling we're not speaking the same language," Clayton said.

"His spirit must be quite confused. They often are, after an accident. It's difficult for them to make the transition when they've had so sudden and violent a passing."

Clayton took a deep breath. "Let's start again, Miss Valentine. Is your husband dead?"

"That's what your people told me. They found his physical body."

"Then who were you talking with before we came in?"

"I was trying to contact his spirit. He's probably wandering around out there."

"In Utah?"

"In confusion. Space and time don't exist in the spirit world. He's having difficulty making the transition, I just know it."

"Please, Miss Valentine, let's keep the conversation to *this* world. Was your marriage unhappy?"

She nodded.

"Unhappy enough for you to place a bomb aboard his plane?"

Her eyes snapped wide open in apparent astonishment. "Why would you think that?"

"Witnesses at the airport reported hearing you tell people the plane would crash."

"Yes, I knew it would happen. Oh, not the way you're thinking. I suddenly had a vision in my mind of the plane bursting into flames. It was terrible!"

Will spoke up for the first time, sarcasm edging into his voice. "You seem quite composed for someone who has just lost her husband so 'terribly.' "

"Once I could no longer stop him or all those others, it was clear to me that they were all meant to make the transition."

"Miss Valentine," Clayton interjected harshly, "the ramp agent told us that your husband walked aboard the plane with a large attache case. Do you happen to know what was in it?"

"Of course, promotional materials for the interviews. *Greater Good*—the picture we just made together—opens around the country tomorrow, and we had a string of TV and newspaper interviews coming up. Denver was the first. We thought announcing the divorce right now would hurt the film."

Will bent forward, the prosecutorial training surfacing. "So you continued to live together—and hate each other."

"Mr. . . . ?"

"Nye, Will Nye."

"Mr. Nye, neither Rolf nor I took a cent in salary for the film. He worked a year and a half to get it produced. I spent four months on location. It was the best work I've ever done, the best picture either of us ever made. But unless it's successful at the box office, we earn nothing from our share of the profits."

She dropped her eyes. "Rolf was a poor husband, but a great producer."

"Then perhaps it was to your benefit to have him dead: more profits, no worry about dividing up community property."

Darlene stood up and went to the door.

"Henrietta?" she called out.

Footsteps approached, and Miss Haverwell came into the room.

"Henrietta, you kept Mr. Courtney's checkbook at the time he died—how much was he worth?"

"Perhaps two hundred thousand dollars."

"And I?"

"With all the investments, it's difficult to say."

"Three million?"

"At least that."

"Henrietta, where did you and I and Mr. Courtney go two days ago?"

"To lunch, and before that to your lawyer's office."

"Did you sign anything there?"

"Yes. I witnessed the separation agreement between you and Mr. Courtney."

"Did my lawyer mention what the agreement generally dealt with?"

"He said it concerned a division of property when you became divorced. And that the divorce would take place six months from then. You made me promise not to say anything about it."

"Did Mr. Courtney and I sleep together during the last few months?"

The woman was silent.

"Didn't he sleep in his own bedroom?"

"On your birthday last month you both came out of his bedroom together the next morning."

Darlene's face turned red. "For auld lang syne," she murmured in explanation, and, recovering, looked back at Henrietta. "Any other time?"

"Not that I know of."

"Thank you, Henrietta."

The Englishwoman nodded and retreated. Darlene turned back to Will and Clayton.

"Before you leave, I'll give you my lawyer's name and number. You can check for yourself."

Will looked doubtful. "You'll pardon my skepticism, Miss Valentine, but your so-called psychic vision seems rather convenient."

"And you believe only in the here and now. Correct, Mr. Nye?"

"Absolutely correct."

"Do you mind letting me have a personal article of yours for a moment? Something you usually have on your person. That watch will do fine."

Darlene took the watch between her palms and rubbed it gently. Her eyes closed, and her facial expression grew blank. Will became restless after thirty or forty seconds and was about to speak, when she lifted the watch and placed it against her forehead. Her face grew very sorrowful and then began to twist in anguish.

"I'm so sad for you, Mr. Nye. I'm so sad for everyone who lost a loved one on the plane. You have so few real friends. You trust so few that each is particularly precious."

Her eyelids lifted. "I'm sorry. I really am."

Will realized that his fingernails were digging into his thighs and that he could not speak.

"Perhaps if your friend had been psychic," Darlene added, "he'd have been alive today."

"I don't know how you know about him," Will finally blurted out, and then he took control of himself again. "But I'm not gullible enough to believe such nonsense. I'm not taken in by one word of your story."

Her voice was soft and rueful when she answered him. "What you resent is the possibility that the intangible can possibly exist. My innocence would force you to think very hard about that possibility."

"If you *do* have this nonphysical gift," Will demanded with feigned courtesy, "Mr. Clayton and I would both appreciate your finding out for us who the murderer is."

Her chin dropped, and her gaze swung to a red maple beyond the French doors. Her voice was barely audible.

"I've tried to several times. I get . . . nothing."

After corroborating Darlene Valentine's story with her lawyer, Will and Clayton returned to the airport to be briefed by local FBI agents.

The "747 Bombings" had become a priority matter, and hundreds of agents around the country had spent the last twenty-four hours investigating the victims of the Zion crash. However, none of the early leads had panned out.

Will had been reluctant to voice his thoughts in the presence of top-flight professionals. But now that they were running out of leads, he ventured an opinion that the bomb might have been placed on the plane by someone en route from Seattle.

Clayton and two other agents, Bragen and Conklin, admitted

the possibility, but first wanted to be sure no clue had been missed relating to those killed in the crash. They were well into a detailed review of the victims' names and backgrounds when the phone rang. Clayton took the call, listened for a few minutes and then hung up.

"Well, now we know," he said to the others. "The fellows putting the first plane back together found something buried in the metal structure. They think the blast pounded it in. It's part of a pocket watch. They're pretty sure it was the timer on the bomb; a wire was fused to it by the heat of the blast." He nodded graciously toward Will. "That means the second bomb could very well have been put in place by someone who boarded in Seattle and got off here."

"Or while it was on the tarmac in Seattle," commented Bragen, a small, tough man whose belligerence often seemed as much directed at his FBI colleagues as at the criminal world.

Clayton glanced over at Will for an answer.

"That would have been a lot tougher this week," Will declared, more confident now about voicing an opinion. "We put on extra security guards in every city we service to protect our aircraft between flights."

"But someone authorized to board the plane could have done it," Bragen stubbornly insisted, "like a cabin cleaner."

"Sure, but the guards are under strict orders to inspect every package and piece of hand luggage going aboard. If they followed orders, they would have intercepted the explosives."

Bragen headed for the door. "I'll wire Seattle to check on it right away."

Will and Clayton sat back and tried to digest the new information. The second air crash had provided an additional clue for cross-checking the passenger lists. The bomb had been placed in the rear of the coach section, inside a rear lavatory probably. The most vulnerable area on an airplane, the tail is the point at which control cables and hydraulic systems come together. If the killer had put the bomb in place while each plane was in the air, he must have sat in first class on 211 and in coach on 519. And he would have had to be off both planes before they embarked on their fatal legs. Matt Conklin first made a quick review of potential suspects who got off 519 in Los Angeles. A rock group, a Watergate defendant, and a businessman who had once been acquitted of murdering his partner had all been searched before the plane left Seattle.

Clayton sighed. "Maybe we're looking at it the wrong way. Maybe we should be looking for—I don't know—people who had demolitions training in the military or maybe a history of belonging to radical organizations."

"No Green Berets, if that's the sort of thing you're aiming at."

"Let's go through the unaccounted-fors," said Clayton. "They paid cash, so we can't trace them through the credit-card companies. We have no addresses for them. Not even a description for some."

Conklin reached for a pencil. "Let's see. On GUA 519 coach, a Ms. E. Carter. Paid cash in Seattle, was ticketed to Los Angeles and disembarked there. Same for a Mr. J. Connally. No one at either airport remembered the Carter woman. But we do have a couple of pieces of information on the man: old, glasses, hearing aid. The agent said he was the quiet, withdrawn type. Reminded her of her grandfather who died last year."

"Maybe we should dig up the grandfather and bring him in for questioning," one of the young agents muttered in frustration.

"At least we'd know where to find the grandfather," Clayton retorted. "Connally made the reservation from a phone booth at the Beverly Wilshire, which he gave as his telephone number. He wasn't registered at the hotel."

Clayton's thick fingers held the page a moment or two, staring at the names as if intensity could bring out something more. Then he dropped it and lifted another.

"Four passengers unaccounted for on 211. *All* first class. Coach was filled by reservations three days before takeoff. Because of the demand, the airline called the reserveds to be sure. So if a person wanted a last-minute ticket, he had to shell out for first class. Four of them haven't been traceable: a Mr. S. Wojelski, a Mr. A. Tanak, a Mr. P. Pearse, and a Ms. B. LaVigne."

"The ticket agent remembered LaVigne," Conklin said, and opened a manila file. "He gave us a description: 'Short, dark hair, backpack, great boobs.' "

Will spoke up. "What business does a girl have with a backpack in winter, especially one who can afford to pay cash for a first-class seat?"

No one had an answer. Clayton assigned a man to check her out.

Attention turned to Wojelski, but the name had drawn a blank. No information to go on.

A female passenger and a gate agent both remembered Pearse, a stevedore type with a beer belly, dark hair, a Fu Manchu mustache and a tattoo on his hand. Conklin summarized their statements. "The passenger asked Pearse to hold her fur coat for a second at the gate counter while she rummaged in her handbag for her ticket. The ticket agent said she was kind of arrogant about it. Pearse said, 'Shove it, lady.' When she objected to the remark, he said something like 'If you're rich enough to buy it, you're rich enough to hire someone to hold it.' "

"Was he angry when he said it?" Clayton asked.

"No, just not helpful. He was polite to the gate agent who took his ticket, but wanted to make sure his seat assignment was apart from the woman."

"Did the FBI agent who interviewed the woman form any opinion of her?"

Conklin looked up from the paper. "She was a pain-in-the-neck scatterbrain. The gate agent was right about her arrogance. Husband made money in car dealerships and suddenly she's Queen Victoria in mink. She also claimed she saw Pearse drinking whiskey from a bottle in the boarding lounge. Nobody else did."

Clayton knew the type of witness she was. You had to take her testimony with a grain of salt. Anyone poorer or differently colored was a hooligan, and her imagination became inseparable from her memory. He glanced down at the file again. "Here's my favorite. Swarthy Middle-Eastern type, about five feet eight, named Tanak. No luggage. Paid cash."

"Did Security go over him?"

"Inch by inch."

"How much cash was he carrying?"

"Enough to choke a horse. Said he was a student at UCLA and that his father's a cousin of the Saudi King."

"Naturally," said Clayton, with a skepticism born of experience, "no one by that name is registered at UCLA."

Conklin nodded. "And the Saudi Embassy and Immigration had never heard of him. Naturally."

For a moment Will had a notion that a couple of the names sounded familiar, but he could not bring anything more to mind and turned his thinking to a more fruitful avenue of investigation: the material to make the bomb.

"You said plastic explosive was tough to come by, Owen. Whoever is blowing up the planes seems to have found the mother lode."

"We're pretty sure we know where it came from, although explosives don't have chemical tracers. After the first crash we tracked down all known military depositories of the stuff in the U.S. Damned good thing we did. All the time the Army kept insisting none was missing. But an ordnance center in Missouri turned out to have enough weaponry missing for a do-it-yourself army."

Conklin read from Clayton's last weekly report on the Indiana crash. "'Four thousand M-16s, thirty-five hundred sidearms, two hundred thousand rounds of ammunition, three dozen cases of grenades, twenty-five bazookas, eight cases of shells for same . . .' Here it is: 'One thousand pounds of plastic explosive (Composition C-4 type), one dozen cases of electric blasting caps for same.'"

Conklin lowered the report. "I left out miscellaneous items like claymore mines and those top-secret binoculars that let you see in the dark."

"The plastic explosive . . . is a thousand pounds a lot?" Will asked.

"Put it in the San Andreas Fault and we'd all be standing on the world's longest island."

"Seriously."

"It's enough to wipe out half a hundred planes."

"That's what makes us believe it might be a radical group," Clayton said as he lit a fresh cigarette. "Your average everyday bomber doesn't need four thousand rifles."

"Any suspects at the base?" Will asked.

"A dead end so far. It could have happened any time in the past year or two. My own guess is that the stuff was probably taken while being trucked in or moved from one base to another. Try to find the one or two army truck drivers. Or the clerk who doctored the papers. Everybody in the Army is either a truck driver or a clerk."

"Have you been able to come up with any suspects inside the company?"

"Getting the names from Pope is like pulling teeth."

Will's face tightened. "You'll have a complete list and unqualified access as of this moment. But I'm sure you've checked out Craig Merrill by now. He lives in L.A. and he could have been here that night and again yesterday morning."

Conklin's brow wrinkled. His gaze dropped to the lists. "He's not on any of the passenger manifests."

"He probably wouldn't be," Will explained. "Corporate officers just show their passes to get on planes."

Clayton stood up quickly. "Let's talk to the gate agent."

Conklin looked at his notes, made a phone call, and then turned to the others. "His name's Dawkins. If we hurry we can catch him before his break."

F. J. Dawkins had been on duty the night 211 lifted into the night toward Chicago for the last time, and he remembered that Craig Merrill had been there, too. Merrill had shown up early, asked if Captain Benson had gone aboard yet. Then he walked onto the plane to join him and was on board when the plane took off.

"Why didn't you tell us that before?" Conklin demanded hotly.

"You never asked about anybody but the names on the list," the uniformed agent replied. "Supervisors are always getting on planes."

Conklin spun toward Will. "But you said Merrill quit before then."

"Not officially. He had certain deferred salary rights that would be coming into effect in a couple of weeks, and there were certain projects he had to finish off. We also figured it might be easier for him to get a new job if people thought he was still with GUA."

"So the employees still considered him an officer of the airline," Clayton said, "and he still had his pass."

"One thing you ought to be aware of: Merrill was in New York only a few hours after the crash. He gave a press conference in the morning, and I saw him there with my own eyes that night."

The conclusion was obvious: If Merrill had left on 211 and

was still alive, that meant he had disembarked in Chicago and switched to another airline before flying on to New York. Why?

Clayton and Will decided to drive to Merrill's house. Meanwhile, Conklin would question people who were on duty yesterday and find out whether Craig Merrill had ever set foot on 519.

A small boy in a red-and-blue-striped rugby shirt swiveled his yellow skateboard down the gentle incline between the garage and the street. He dutifully kicked the front end up and about at the curb line, lifted the board and returned to the garage door for another run.

Clayton turned off the ignition.

A woman next door was gardening. Across the street, two children astride bikes had stopped to chat. At the end of the block, a man was washing his car. A typical Saturday afternoon. Well-kept, expensive houses in a good neighborhood on a typical street. Many of the crash victims probably lived on streets like these. It seemed preposterous that a plane could suddenly fall from the sky and destroy this sort of tranquility irrevocably.

Will opened the car door, straightened up and, as the boy on the skateboard reached the curb once more, asked if this was Craig Merrill's house. The boy was Craig Merrill's youngest child. He said his mother was inside.

Janet Merrill was drying her hands on a paper towel as she opened the door for the visitors. Brushing a wisp of blond hair with the back of her hand, she ushered them in. She had just started to make herself coffee and invited them to join her.

Will had seen her from a distance at a couple of company functions, but now he found himself studying her as she moved about the kitchen. She answered their questions at the same time. The movements were economical, as if she was not bored by the daily repetition of small tasks, but comfortable because of it. She reminded Will of so many military officers' wives. Sweet fresh looks, showing age a little earlier than more classic features might. A sense of duty to her role. Certainty as to what it was.

She poured the coffee into the cups and brought them to the table.

"I was telling you about Craig's schedule. He was able to fly back and join us for a couple of days this week, but the new job keeps him in New York so much of the time. You know about the plane crash yesterday. He had to go there as soon as we heard about it."

"Was he here all morning?" Clayton asked.

"Except for a couple of hours when he went fishing."

"Alone?"

She nodded. "The kids had school. His being away so much is especially tough on our boy. The part of Craig's being an astronaut I hated was the long training missions. The moon shot was exciting, because I could speak to him from Mission Control and see him on TV, but the training missions really separated us." She brushed back the wisp of hair again, this time self-consciously, as if not used to speaking of private matters. "Craig and I are very close."

She jumped up. "I just remembered, I bought a pound cake."

She brought it to the table and began slicing rectangles off the end. "Well, Craig thinks it shouldn't be too much longer. After the takeover, we'll probably all move to Denver. Or maybe they'll transfer the headquarters here, like Continental did." An instant later her face was filled with apology. "I'm sorry, Mr. Nye. I didn't mean that to sound as cold-blooded as it came out. It's just that Craig says they're all very confident about it at Faranco."

Will had another matter on his mind. "Mrs. Merrill, do you know why your husband didn't fly nonstop to New York Thanksgiving weekend, but changed planes in Chicago?"

She looked puzzled. "I didn't know he had."

Will was silent on the ride back to the airport. Speaking with Janet Merrill had produced no answers. At every turn Will found himself frustrated in venting his need for vengeance, at assuaging the guilt and sorrow raging within him; the doors that opened seemed to lead solely to more doors.

"Why did we fly all the way to Chicago to stand in this airport parking lot at nine-thirty on a freezing-cold night?"

"Around this time on a Sunday, Charles Guerin got out of a

car parked in this lot and walked into the terminal," Clayton told Will, and then he headed back toward the terminal himself. Will fell into step beside him.

"He was a methodical man," Clayton continued. "A cautious man despite that slightly radical outlook. He decided sometime Sunday to fly to New York City and not Washington, but he made no reservation to New York."

"What time did he change his plans?"

They stepped into the brightly lit building.

"For argument's sake let's say just about now."

"That gave him a long time to buy a ticket on the plane."

"But he didn't. That's the funny thing. He bought the ticket on 211 at the gate more than half an hour later."

Hands now on hips, Clayton stood in the center of the floor gazing around him. To one side was United. To the other side was Global Universal.

"What made him buy a ticket on the GUA flight and not United?"

"Give me the answer to that, I'll put every other airline out of business."

"No, seriously. The United counter was nearer, and both airlines had New York flights leaving at about the same time."

"Better service," replied Will drily. "On-time dependability. We give you the sky."

Clayton snorted derisively.

"Maybe he was with someone who already had a reservation on our plane," Will suggested.

"The people he met with in the parking lot swear he was alone when he left them. But they could be lying. They flew East without him on a private jet."

"Maybe he met someone else in the terminal afterward. Where was he sitting in 211?"

Clayton, with a labored grunt, dropped to a squat beside his briefcase and opened it. He spread papers from it on the terrazzo. A few seconds later he looked up.

"Next to Gladmeyer, the Assistant Treasury Secretary."

"That fits."

"But how can we be sure they met first and *then* Guerin decided to fly with him on your plane?"

"You're going around in circles."

Clayton stuffed the papers back into the briefcase. Strange noises issued from his knees as he strained to rise. "How can I be sure that he wasn't maneuvered onto a plane that was set to kill him?"

"You're bothered by the fact that he didn't buy a ticket as soon as he got inside the terminal?"

Clayton nodded.

Will thought for a moment. "You've checked with United?"

"Guerin had no reservation on either plane. He had one only on United's Washington flight that he made in the afternoon, right after he agreed to go to that parking lot meeting."

"I'll make you a deal," offered Will. "Tell me whom he met with in the parking lot, and I might be able to come up with a way to check whether he reserved a seat on the United plane to New York."

"I just told you he didn't."

"Would you be breaking a law if you told me?"

Clayton hesitated, then capitulated. "Senator Avery and Carl Raymond. Now how the hell can we check with United?"

"Try his mother's and his wife's maiden names or his first name as a last name. People often use them when their plans aren't certain and they already have a reservation with that airline."

Clayton's eyes lit up. "Let's go to my office."

Fifteen minutes later they had the answer. "Deltraub, C." had a reservation on United's New York flight, which he never honored. Deltraub was Guerin's mother's maiden name.

"The lines were probably long at United Thanksgiving weekend," Will theorized, "so he telephoned a reservation right from inside the terminal. He intended to buy the ticket at the gate."

"But he met Gladmeyer," finished Clayton. "And he would be alive today if he hadn't."

Clayton leaned forward over 211's passenger list. He drew a pencil line through Guerin's name.

"What about Craig Merrill?" inquired Will. "He's looking more and more suspicious, especially since your people found out from his secretary that he's out of the country and she has no idea where."

"He didn't fly into New York on United that night—United was able to check that out just now. TWA, American and the rest will let us know by morning. Five hundred bodies," Clayton muttered. "One murderer somewhere." An ironic thought occurred to him. "You know, the time might come when we'll be tearing our hair out to narrow it down to only *one* murderer."

That night Will checked in at an airport hotel where he could get a good night's sleep before meeting Clayton for a flight out very early in the morning. As soon as they parted, Will telephoned Al Goetz's home in Washington. A recording device answered with a jocular greeting; Will's mouth turned downward at the ends with distaste. Will's message was for Goetz to find out whether Guerin and the SEC had been evaluating allegations against Faranco Inc. and what those allegations were.

Then Will called Donna. There was no answer at either her apartment or Dee's. They had already left for Kansas with Tal's body.

Sunday morning in Fort Wayne, Indiana, is for church or sleeping late. For Will and Clayton, the morning was for viewing a reconstructed section of a 747 in a drafty hangar at the edge of an airfield.

Hunks of debris from 211 were marked with chalk or tags and scattered about the floor, while the tail, still miraculously whole, towered high into the joists, emphasizing the devastation of the rest.

Tal's plane would look like this one, Will realized with a start. As a boy dragged along to church each week, he had pictured the Apocalypse like this—cemeteries littered with the broken toys of the forever departed.

"It's the most perfect flying machine ever built," Bill Ewing said softly as he led them around the twisted metal wired on wooden scaffolding into the rough configuration of what used to be the front end of a 747. "So perfect it can take off, guide itself across country, land and end up within twenty feet of the gates, with the flight crew playing gin rummy all the way. Every system has a backup. It can fly routinely on three engines and land on two. It has even made it safely down on one. It flew two billion miles without a fatal accident."

Ewing pointed to the far end of the empty hangar. "Those engines can lift over three quarters of a million pounds of fully loaded plane forty-five thousand feet into the sky and fly six hundred miles an hour carrying between four and five hundred people. But if only ten or twenty pounds of that load is high explosive, this is what you have left."

Bill Ewing had spent half of his sixty years designing and building ever larger, more sophisticated airliners, and the last ten years putting bits and pieces back together.

"Where exactly was the bomb placed?" Clayton asked.

"Right about there. Above the left lavatory in first class. Whoever put it there unscrewed a ceiling panel that shields the light fixture, placed the bomb inside and put back the panel."

"How could he be sure it would fit?" Will inquired.

"The material can be molded into any shape."

Ewing indicated a badly bent rectangle on the floor. "That's the lavatory door. It contained some of the downward force of the blast and helped direct more of it upward toward the control cables, where the bomber wanted it to go."

After several minutes of inspecting the wreckage, Clayton turned back to Ewing. "I'm eager to see the bomb."

"You called it 'Composition Something-or-other,'" Will said to Clayton.

"Composition C-4. There are two types of plastic explosive: C-4's an improved version of C-3. It's dirty white to tan. They're both like putty, come in bricks and consist of wax, as the plasticizer, and TNT and RDX, two of the highest explosives known." He paused. "I guess I don't have to tell you that." He turned back to Ewing. "Did you find the detonator or the power source for it?"

"No."

"Could he have used the wiring to the lavatory lights?"

"Maybe, but probably not. Leaving the lavatory turns out the lights—you cut off the power when you shoot back the lock bolt."

They filed carefully out of the infernal labyrinth to a workbench against the side wall. Ewing showed them a flattened piece of pocket watch.

"The flight deck is on the level above the main cabin, and the control cables run back from there below the second-level floor. The explosion shot up and out above the first-level lavatory, cutting through all the cables. Then it sliced through the two hydraulic lines and the plane's aluminum skin on the right side. Either one of the hydraulic systems on the left could have operated the plane if the control cables hadn't been knocked out. The whole thing probably took a couple of thousandths of a second."

"You only found the one hand on the watch and no pieces of the crystal?"

Ewing peered disbelievingly at Clayton over the top of the reading glasses he had slipped on. Clayton was too absorbed in studying the miraculously preserved watch-face remnant to notice.

"It's silver. That's odd. Most pocket watches are gold. Silver is a good conductor, but gold is better. Look at the hour hand. That's silver, too." Clayton glanced at Will. "Did you ever see the hands on an old watch? They're usually black and thin. This one is silver and thick."

He caught his bottom lip between his teeth and fell silent. Finally he indicated the remnant of wire wrapped around the hour hand and fused by the blast to it.

"I would guess the other wire, the missing one, was taped to the face with the crystal removed. When the wired hour hand came around and touched the exposed end of that second wire, the circuit was completed and the juice could flow to the detonator."

Ewing nodded. "Using the hour hand gave the bomber up to twelve hours' lead time."

Clayton's body sagged in discouragement. "Then he could have set it that morning, while the plane was on its way west to California before the turnaround back to Chicago."

"I don't think that necessarily follows," Will said slowly. "Too long a time delay could mean the plane wouldn't be in the air when the bomb exploded—more chance of bad weather coming up or mechanical delay."

"I see your point," Clayton agreed.

"Would the plane be demolished if it exploded on the ground?"

Ewing looked back at the debris and shook his head. "No.

Look, if the charge hadn't been placed just right, this plane would probably have made it."

Clayton agreed. "The real damage happened when the plane hit the ground at five hundred miles an hour."

Will suddenly looked up and said, "Is there a phone here?"

Ewing pointed to the opposite wall.

A few minutes later Will returned to the workbench. "The last passengers to Seattle got off the plane that became Flight 519 at maybe eight o'clock last Thursday night, and guards were posted immediately. That second plane crashed at eleven o'clock the next morning. That's a fifteen-hour time lapse. His watch could give him only twelve."

Clayton smiled for the first time in days. "Which means our bomber placed the bomb during the second plane's run to L.A. Friday morning. If we're dealing with the same bomber on both planes, then his M.O. is to blow them up with a bomb placed on the leg just before the fatal one."

He slipped the watch into his briefcase and began writing out a receipt. "Next problem, Will: How did it get through Security?"

"The magnetometer detects only ferrous metal. Plastic explosive isn't metal. How big is the detonator?"

"Small. The size of a firecracker, half a pencil. Electricity heats a coil that sets off a charge in the blasting cap. That detonates the plastic material."

"You could put it in a metal pen, hide it in the takeup reel of a camera, anywhere. If the materials were X-rayed, nothing suspicious would show up. The system is designed to stop skyjackings by screening out weapons. But change the rules of the game and it's helpless." Will found himself echoing Craig Merrill's warning. "We're preventing last year's catastrophe, not tomorrow's."

As the three men began moving toward the entrance, Will turned to Clayton again. "Is it always like this?"

"Like what?"

"Oh, like trying to grab minnows in your bare hands."

After a moment of incomprehension, Clayton's clouded expression lifted, replaced by a soft smile. "Only the really good ones."

* * *

Several hours later Will Nye arrived in Kansas for Tal's funeral. He rented a car at the airport and drove to the small city where Tal grew up.

The funeral parlor sat at the far end of the street, the city hall at the near. They were the largest buildings downtown, and both were of solid brick—the only structures for miles that a tornado might not be able to blow away.

Will recognized Rick Talbot's mother at once, a worn woman with endurance scored into lines on her brow and cheeks, a tight mouth, uncompromising eyes and carefully disciplined hair. He had spoken to her twice on the phone, once several years ago when Tal had called on her birthday and insisted she speak to his friend. The conversation had been strained and awkward for both of them. The second time was after Tal's death.

She sat on a folding chair to one side, a woman friend or relative beside and half turned toward her. The coffin, closed and sealed shut, rested on sawhorses in the center of the gloomily lit room. Dee and Donna sat on folding chairs placed against the wall on the other side.

Mrs. Talbot's hand was cold when Will shook it. She murmured her thanks for Will's condolence and dropped her eyes. Will tried to extend the moment, to impress on her how much the friendship with her son had meant to him—and to soften his distress that Tal's death had been his doing. But when she glanced back up at him, Will saw antagonism in the look, and resentment. So he broke off and crossed to take a seat beside his friends, the pain he was feeling intensified.

Donna's rueful little smile communicated that she too had tried and failed to break through to the woman, that her own past was full of such people for whom love was a wall one built around feelings, and grief the price one paid for having them. She held Dee's hand. Dee had hoped to share her sorrow with the mother who had loved Tal as much as she. When they met at the small airport and waited for the coffin to be pulled from the plane's belly like a stillborn child, Dee finally broke the silence by telling the woman how much Tal had meant to her and that they had planned to marry. No answer, not even a look, came back in response. The men in Mrs. Talbot's life might have been taken from her, but they were taken *only* from her.

The coffin was carried out of the funeral home to a small

church. The service was short. The pastor was at a convention in Atlanta, so the assistant, a kindly, incapable man who worked in the hardware store, filled in. He had not known Richard Talbot, he said, because he had moved there long after the young man had gone off to war. But the deceased must have been a brave young man; he was a war hero, after all. And his mother was a fine woman, active in the church. The speaker hesitated, groping for something more to say, then settled for a mumbled Lord's Prayer.

The coffin was placed in the hearse, and the abbreviated funeral cortege, three vehicles in all, rolled slowly out of town to the cemetery.

Only half listening to the hardware clerk's uncertain drone of liturgy, Will stared at the coffin suspended above the grave by green nylon straps. What did Tal look like now? Will wondered. Was he lying peacefully within the closed coffin as if asleep? Perhaps inside there were only unclaimed parts of a person, randomly dealt out among those coffins for which no whole body could be identified.

Will fought back the stinging in his eyes and felt fingers threading between his. Donna was peering at him with soft-eyed compassion. She was so unself-conscious and natural. A lot like Tal. Her presence consoled him. He squeezed Donna's hand and turned to look at Dee. She was white, her mouth half open, tears falling freely from desperate comprehension that this was the final ritual. Will did as Donna had done with him, placed his hand in hers.

The speaker's voice intoned the Twenty-third Psalm, then dwindled to a halt. The gravediggers leaning against their shovels took that as their signal. They stepped up to the grave, pulled a handle, and the green nylon straps slowly unrolled, lowering the coffin into the cavity. A few more words were said. Handfuls of dirt were thrown into the hole by the mourners, who then began to file back to the cars.

Later in the day Will put Dee on a plane that, with a change or two, would bring her to Clovis, New Mexico, and her family. Will and Donna flew back to Denver.

That night he stayed with her in her apartment, but they lay beside each other with the celibacy of those so recently shaken by death as to be incapable of any act that celebrated life. When

Will was certain Donna was asleep, he rose, dressed, slipped from the apartment and drove up to his cabin.

J. Stephen Girard had come to North Africa at the request of President Balu Odalu. Heads of state from all over Africa were holding a conference there, and Odalu felt it a propitious opportunity to seal the arrangement with those from his own region of the continent for the West African Air Federation. Craig Merrill was present, as was newly appointed David Johnson, a black aviation executive Raymond had hired to direct the local airline Faranco had secretly bought. But so far the conference had dragged on two days longer than expected and the issue of the Federation had not yet come up.

"Tonight," Odalu assured Girard. "It is all a formality. They are ready to agree." And then, resplendent in his colorful robes, he glided away like an exotic sailboat, leaving the three Americans waiting in the hotel lobby for Odalu's friend, Prince Abdul al Sakr, who was going to entertain them with an afternoon of hunting with falcons.

The prince and his Scottish falconer arrived in separate Land-Rovers to take the men out of the white city, along the seacoast highway. Girard and Merrill rode with the prince, a soft-spoken man in traditional kaffiyeh headgear that flowed behind him in the open vehicle.

"The sport is much more romantic on horseback, I assure you, but modern life does not permit us the time." The crisp English accent indicated a British education.

"Hunting with birds of prey has been traced back thousands of years in Asia. Alexander the Great hunted with them. Caesar used them to bring down enemy messenger pigeons. The Crusaders returning to Europe brought trained birds and falconers from the East. Everyone who could afford it kept a bird of prey. Even nuns at prayer often had their hunting birds resting on their fists. For seven hundred years its popularity was as great as, for example, your baseball is in America."

Girard paid no more attention to his host's remarks than was required to be polite. His mind was completely absorbed with examining the intricacies of a takeover fight for Global Universal.

Carl Raymond had called early that morning to confirm that

Faranco's funding was assured: the $150-million debenture issue was substantially sold out and the $100-million bank loan arranged so that it could be taken down at any time over the next year at a favorable rate of interest. The price of Global Universal stock had been depressed since the second crash. Tonight a memorandum of agreement almost certainly would be signed by the leaders of the five member nations of the new Air Federation. Exclusive air rights to the region would soon look like gold and, handed over to GUA (once the takeover had been accomplished), would make the airline look like platinum. Girard had reason to be pleased. All of the carefully managed pieces of the plot seemed to be falling into place.

But he had to be sure. Once the attack was launched, the cost of defeat or even retreat could be great. His reputation for invincibility might be irreparably crippled.

The vehicles had veered off the highway and were bouncing along a dirt road. At the top of a low hill, the road abruptly ended, and the Rovers halted. The prince turned off the ignition and concluded his thought: "In the West, only a few still know the pleasure of hunting with birds of prey. A few clubs still exist for the sport. In America I believe the heartland of hawking is Colorado."

His words had accidentally brushed against the edge of Girard's thoughts. Startled by the coincidence, the industrialist's attention was suddenly caught by the hunt.

The prince allowed the largest of the birds to step atop the oversized leather glove he had slipped on. He led the party to a low rise in the terrain. The hooded hawk sat quietly. The bells tied to its legs made hardly a sound.

"The eye of the hawk is a fierce hunter's eye, ten times sharper than a man's," said the prince. "Only when its eyes are covered is the hawk in repose. In fact, the hawk is born with its eyes open."

The Arab's own eyes narrowed to slits against the sun. He searched the sky as he spoke. "This bird is a peregrine falcon that was trapped during her first migration. Like all falcons she has the long, pointed wing that sets her apart from other hawks. Like all females she is a third larger than the male. Like all peregrines she is an extraordinary hunter. When you see her dive, you will be watching a living creature flying at one hundred and sixty to two hundred miles an hour."

The prince ceased speaking. Staring intently at the northern sky, he slipped off the hood. The hawk's eyes instantly fixed on twin specks high above. A moment later the others too saw the prey.

"Pigeons?" the prince asked. His free hand stroked the black-barred brown feathers.

"Aye, late migrators," the Scot said, his voice rolling like the ocean across the *rs*. "Europe's had it warm so far."

"Watch this, gentlemen." The prince rotated the hawk's body nearly ninety degrees, but the bird's gaze never left the quarry.

Finally the Arab extended his gloved hand, held it there long enough for the falcon to gain her balance, and then cast her upward. Her jesses released, the falcon leaped forward, and with one beat of her powerful wings she was airborne and climbing. Higher and higher she ascended, spiraling upward until she was only a speck herself. Then she hovered motionless, the sun behind her, awaiting the inevitable moment when the guileless pigeons' flight would carry them beneath her.

Girard had sensed the excitement mounting within him as the peregrine sped upward. He felt a kinship with the soaring predator. Every part of her body had been designed by nature for her single purpose in life, the hunt. Success at the hunt meant survival.

The falcon had already chosen which was to be her victim and the point in the sky where they would meet. She seemed to wait forever, as if, hypnotized by the magic of flight, she had forgotten the kill. Then, almost too late, the wings snapping tight against her body, she suddenly plummeted. Faster she dove, until she was no more than a streaking blur. At the last instant, wings and tail spread, talons clenched, she swooped sharply upward into her prey, knocking the pigeon senseless. Helplessly, it fluttered downward like a pinwheel. Within seconds the falcon's claws clenched the stunned bird, and she was returning to earth. There she would mantle the pigeon with her wide wings before taking its neck within her beak and breaking it.

At that moment J. Stephen Girard decided it was time to bid for control of Global Universal Airlines.

8

Access to the cordoned-off wing of the Friedman, Potter law firm was restricted to trusted lawyers and secretaries directly involved in preparing the tender-offer documents. Samuel Friedman was a feared name to any incumbent management when he was leading a raid. His income now totaled over a million dollars a year. Still young and slim despite the years of prominence, with a graying ball of steel-wool hair above gold-rimmed glasses, he was as elegant and dangerous as a python. A believer in the all-out blitzkrieg offensive, the "Saturday-night special," he had chosen to file and publish the documents just before the weekend in order to slow the other side's response time. The demoralized target's Board members might even be so paralyzed with fear that they would yield without a fight at all.

That Friday morning three young lawyers, one woman and two men, snapped oversized briefcases closed and rushed out of the law firm's offices and down to the waiting limousine for a hurried ride to La Guardia. Each took a different plane.

The Eastern shuttle carried the woman to Washington and the offices of the Securities and Exchange Commission. At exactly 3:58 P.M., just after she saw the messenger sent by GUA's law firm leave after checking for filings, she removed the manila envelope from her briefcase and extracted from it and filed material required by the SEC under the Williams Act. The act's purposes are to force full and honest disclosure to stockholders by both the bidder and management when a tender offer is made and to allow stockholders sufficient time—at least ten days—to decide whether to sell to the bidder. From now until the fight for control of GUA ended, the Commission's lawyers would scrutinize every document produced and public statement made and attack every transgression of the act.

The second Friedman, Potter lawyer was standing by at the Civil Aeronautics Board. At exactly 3:59 P.M., he filed papers requesting Board approval of the takeover by Faranco. Then he hurried to the office of one of the most powerful lawyers in Washington and left a package of documents. The former Cabinet officer under several Democratic administrations was a key figure in the take over. Not coincidentally, he had dropped by the CAB the previous day just to renew old acquaintances.

The third lawyer's plane took him to the capital of the state where Global Universal was incorporated. Before the close of the business day, he had filed papers called for by the State Division of Securities, and he had left a package of them at GUA's local office. Fearing that the Williams Act's requirements were too lenient and could rush shareholders to a hasty decision before management had an opportunity to present its case, many states had recently passed laws familiarly known as "shark repellent," requiring longer notice periods before a tender offer could go into effect. Many critics claimed they were simply a bald attempt to protect local industry. But until a federal court ruled them unconstitutional, they were a fact of life Faranco would have to deal with.

Two other couriers left Friedman, Potter's offices with packages of documents. One went to the New York Stock Exchange. Another raced to the post office to mail a package to Global Universal's Denver headquarters, as well as to every other exchange on which the airline's stock was traded.

At four o'clock, after the stock market had closed, messengers were telephoned who had been waiting at Dow Jones (which owned the *Wall Street Journal*), at the *New York Times* and at the wire services; they were instructed to hand their envelopes to the financial editors. The news was now public: Faranco Inc. was offering Global Universal Airlines, Inc.'s, shareholders thirteen dollars a share if they tendered enough outstanding stock to raise Faranco's ownership interest to fifty-one percent.

The *Times*'s financial reporter's call found Ben Buck in San Francisco at a dinner for Western governors. He had just finished delivering a speech on regional transportation. The reporter had said it was urgent, so Buck returned the call.

"Faranco Inc. has just announced a thirteen-dollar-a-share cash takeover bid for your company. Do you have any comment?" the reporter wanted to know.

"Girard can go fuck himself!"

Buck slammed the phone down. But in the next moment, he picked it up again and alerted the GUA switchboard to begin calling people on the sealed list that had been left with them. Will had given the switchboard the phone number of a restaurant where he and a date would be dining. Buck called him there, then rushed to the airport for a flight back to Denver.

As soon as he received Buck's call, Will set out to locate lawyers Eli Teicher and Headly Parkhurst, the investment banker Serge Bergheim, publicist Bill Tait and solicitation expert Cole Glidden. It took him half an hour. By eleven o'clock New York time, they and their associates participating in the takeover defense were streaking toward Denver on a spare GUA 727. By midnight Denver time, most of the airline's top officials and three of its outside directors had made their way to the GUA Board Room.

Will was already there, reading the tender documents that had been Telefaxed to Denver. Most of the terms were standard. One was extraordinary: the stock Faranco purchased would be placed in a voting trust until the CAB approved Faranco's acquisition. The voting trustee would be Alton A. Atwater, former Secretary of the Treasury and of Commerce, former Undersecretary of State, former director of a major U.S. airline and presently the senior partner in one of the great Washington law firms. The object of the arrangement was to keep a court from claiming that no one would be running the airline if Faranco obtained majority control before the CAB approved its right to exercise that control. Will shook his head. He could imagine Faranco's rebuttal: "Is plaintiff trying to maintain that Mr. Atwater is capable of running the economy of the United States of America, but not its company?"

Ben Buck arrived, started the meeting and proceeded to impose chaos as if it were order. Everyone with an idea was heard—except those experienced in takeover fights. The advisers sat silently to one side, ignored by Buck, who seemed to regard them as a fifth column in his nation's bosom; he made a special point of ignoring Will Nye, as if his loyalty too were in question.

Will gazed around the room. Lee Conway, Arnold Bannister, Jim Keller—they all seemed dazed. Here were men called to the forefront of an exacting, dynamic industry, but nothing in their experience had prepared them for this form of competition. They were leaders with no idea where the battle was. This foe had neither planes nor routes to compete with. Its weapon was a financial concept, and its soldiers were lawyers.

With each new scheme Ben Buck's face lit up. He seemed to be desperately clutching the hope that now, as always in the past, he could devise a successful tactic that would also serve to maintain him in a position of command. Will soon gave up listening to the succession of unworkable and unlikely defenses. He picked up the tender offer and began to peruse it again.

Finally Walt Greer stood up. He was a tall, scholarly-looking man whose post of treasurer was nominally separated from Bannister's division, but whose main function was to supply a second signature on large checks. "The CAB surely won't allow some carpetbagger whose only credential is its bank balance to come in and rape one of the largest airlines in the world."

"Walt's right," Jim Keller chimed in. "They've got the public to consider here."

"You both make a lot of sense," Buck declared, with a new rush of zeal. The others quieted as he began to speak. "We've allowed ourselves to get stampeded here and charge off in a hundred directions. The CAB is on the airline's side. These Faranco people just bit off more than they can chew. They don't know the ropes, that's all." He turned to the consultants with a confident expression. "We've dealt with the CAB for forty years. The matter will end right there. But perhaps as a precaution, we might send a lawyer down to observe at the CAB hearings. You agree, Will?"

Will Nye stared at Ben Buck. After the disorder of the past minutes, the few seconds seemed endless. When he spoke his voice was low and steady.

"I don't think I've ever before heard such a load of horse shit."

Silence instantly spread outward in a shock wave. Will shifted his gaze from the stunned chief executive officer to Eli Teicher and nodded. Teicher stood up.

"Now that Mr. Nye here has managed to get your attention, I think you fellows ought to be told a few facts before you commit suicide."

Balding, overweight and short, clothes terminally nondescript, machine-gun speech delivered in a hard-voweled New York nasality exacerbated by a nasty cold, Eli Teicher seemed out of place.

"Usually, having to obtain a regulatory agency's approval is considered a 'showstopper' in takeovers. Raiders back away. But I think you're going to lose at the CAB. Samuel Friedman and I have locked horns too often for me to believe he would do anything so patently stupid as to pick a fight he'll lose in the first round. As I understand it, Congress is after the CAB right now for excluding newcomers from the airline industry for so long. The CAB statute says only that the person holding a route certificate must be fit, willing and able. Any half-ass qualifies if the CAB follows the rules for a change. And now they might have to. The problem here is trying to suspend the tender offer until the CAB acts. That buys us time."

Buck swung around to Will Nye. "What do you think? Is there a chance this thing could go beyond the CAB?"

"Congress is charging that the CAB squashed new carrier applications for three decades and the public suffered from the absence of route and fare competition. Faranco's application comes at the perfect time: by approving, the Board demonstrates it's not in business to protect entrenched airline management, and at the same time gets Congress off its back."

Bannister was on his feet. "We don't need your scare stories, Nye. You've got a way of making everything fit into your conspiracy theories. Max Creighton is a spy. The CAB will do things it's never done before. Damn it all, the public looks to us for levelheaded, responsible leadership. We shouldn't be railroaded into giving credibility to Faranco by overreacting like fools."

Will pointed to a copy of the tender offer. "Did you see the name at the bottom of the tender offer? 'Creighton, Cromwell and Company, Dealer-Manager.' "

"You forced them into Faranco's camp!"

"Did you see the fee they can earn if Faranco wins? One million, seven hundred fifty thousand dollars. The offer spells out in detail every private approach Girard made to the General through Creighton . . . and the purchase of large blocks by Faranco in the last few days. Here, look at the part about our future-earnings estimate. Are the figures accurate?"

Bannister nodded.

"Are they confidential?" Will asked.

Reluctantly, Bannister nodded again.

"Arnold, this thing was as well worked out as D-Day. We're playing ball against guys who know the game inside and out. They're experts. And they want this company enough to put more than two hundred million dollars on the line."

Teicher concurred. "Those guys *are* experts. That's why you hired me. *I'm* an expert. I'm also a dirty street fighter who'll do anything he can to win, even come to . . ." He looked around him and shook his head. "God help me, Denver, Colorado, on a weekend I have theater tickets, to listen to this garbage at . . ." He glanced at his watch. "Two in the morning—four in the morning civilized time."

Teicher blew his nose. "I'm the wrong religion for you. From the wrong part of the country. And I've gotten too rich doing this to know my place. But if I win, you'll be kissing the pavement I walk on. Instead of being out pounding it, looking for other jobs."

"Look here, you," Bannister interrupted sharply. "Your rough-guy talk isn't going to scare us into taking a back seat so you can run up enormous fees for yourself. Your job is to go to court when *we* decide it's necessary."

Teicher turned to Headly Parkhurst. "Who is this shmuck?"

"Bannister. Financial."

Teicher shot a glance over at Bannister. "You can stay, Bannister, but don't waste our time with that organizational shit. This isn't potsy. They're trying to rip your balls off. If I leave, you haven't got a cup jock."

"All right," Buck said belligerently. "What do you propose we do? Where are the ideas we're paying you for?"

Teicher was not intimidated. "First clear out the ribbon clerks, and then the rest of us can start talking this thing over."

Buck was about to counter with equal rudeness, then seemed to think better of it. He let out a long exhalation before he finally spoke, and then it was to ask those people to leave who were not outside directors, officer-directors or, like Will, responsible for functions associated with the defense.

Just as the doors were about to be closed behind those who had left, Al Goetz, briefcase in one hand and overnight case in the other, scurried into the room.

"Operators said they had a hard time tracking you down, Al," Lee Conway called out as Goetz took a seat.

"You in the saddle, old buddy?" Buck boomed. "Sorry we couldn't pick a more convenient time."

A volley of guffaws broke the tension.

Goetz reddened and said something about a dinner party. Will Nye tapped a pencil sharply on the edge of the conference table, then pointed it at Teicher. The voices stilled.

"Let's get down to business," Teicher said. He took a sip of coffee. "We'll work with your people to stop Faranco at the CAB. But at the same time we go for an injunction in federal court. I can think of three different causes of action right off the bat. We'll have to tie it up in state court also. Which law firm do you use where you're incorporated, Becker and Deane?"

Will nodded.

"They're fine. In both courts we'll argue that the offer's inadequate. For one thing, it's below asset value." He thought a moment. "Where do you have substantial physical assets located? Maybe you can give me a list of cities where you land. Some states will interfere if the target has assets located there. For others maybe we can claim that every state you land in is entitled to interfere because transportation and commerce will be hurt."

"Can we possibly win any of these?" asked Conway.

Teicher shrugged. "We're buying time. B. F. Goodrich tried everything. They lost every case, but they kept the offer from going into effect. After nine months Northwest Industries finally gave up. You're always trying to buy more time. If we fight Faranco every inch of the way, a lot of things can happen, and not only in court. The price of GUA's stock could drop and scare them away. Girard could die, and with him no longer dominating the company, its Board might pull out. The worst that can come out of this takeover fight is that either Faranco will end up paying more for the stock than their first bid or Prince Charming will come along."

Teicher noticed the puzzled expressions and chuckled.

"Prince Charming or the White Knight are what we call a new company that steps in and offers better terms to merge with the target. They're Mr. Right who saves Sleeping Beauty—that's you—from a fate worse than death with the raider."

"What the hell good does that do us?" demanded Buck sourly.

Teicher stood up and slipped his hands into his rear pants pockets. "I think it's important you all realize that the stockholders own this company, not management. When people buy a share of stock, they're buying a share, however small, of the ownership. Put a majority of those shares in one set of hands or group of hands, or get them to vote the same way, and they run the company. Stockholders have a right to sell their shares to anyone offering an acceptable price, even if the buyer ends up controlling the company. And remember, GUA's stockholders haven't had a price this high for their stock in years."

Teicher paused. This next point was vital. "You know, your Board of Directors will have to decide whether the tender offer is adequate and whether to recommend that the shareholders accept it. If they do, then the fight is over."

"They'll do that over my dead body!" Buck bellowed. His fierce gaze circled the room, fixing first on each officer-director—Conway, Goetz, and Bannister—and then on the outside directors present: the steel man Fuller; Dillingham, a banker; and Clarkson, an aging former college president. Finally Buck's eyes returned to Teicher.

"A quorum of the Board has just met. We vote no! It was unanimous. I'll speak to the others by phone in the morning."

A painstaking search for potential defenses followed—this

time without the frantic haste to take action for its own sake. At one point during the early-morning hours, Al Goetz caught Will's eye and indicated he wanted to meet privately. Together, the two lawyers headed for Will's office.

Will had been brought into Global Universal by Buck in anticipation of the retirement of the company's general counsel. The scuttlebut reaching Will's ears had been that Goetz felt Legal should have gone to him. Unpredictably, obstinately, Buck had gone outside the company and hired Will Nye, twenty-five years Goetz's junior. Not only that, Will had demanded and won direct access to Buck himself. Will was aware of Goetz's resentment, and he was sorry about it. He admired the man's style and ability in successfully steering Global Universal through the government shoals.

"This office looks like something out of Charles Dickens," Goetz commented as he removed a stack of folders from a chair and sat down.

"What's up?" Will asked, clasping his hands behind his head and leaning back in his desk chair. His shirt was open at the collar and the shirtsleeves were rolled up.

"You asked me to find out what the SEC had on Faranco." Goetz broke into a wide smile. "I don't know where you came up with the hunch, but it was a beaut. They've been treating this thing as hush-hush as you can get. Only two people in the SEC outside the actual commissioners were told about it: Guerin and the agency's general counsel. Guerin's dead, and the four commissioners who are left have locked all the papers in a vault. Word is they're waiting for the President to pick a new head and leaving the decision up to whoever's chosen."

"That leaves the general counsel. What's his name?"

"Ex-general counsel now. His name's Graham. He's well-connected at the White House and in his home state, and he thought he should have been chosen to head the Commission after Guerin's death. He wasn't, so he left to join a private law firm in Washington."

"Who's been picked?"

"My grapevine tell me it's a dark horse, a woman lawyer at the Justice Department no one figured on. Jenabelle Draper."

"Is there any line on her?"

"You mean about takeovers?"

"Or going after big business or anything else."

"Tough to say. I've gotten to know her a little since the rumors began to fly about her for the SEC, but she won't say much—anything, as a matter of fact—until the appointment is official. She's smart. About forty-five. Married to a country doctor. My bet is she's smart enough not to let anyone get much of a line on her till the Senate confirms. And that won't be a problem. This is the year of the woman, laddie."

Will grinned. He was considering something else. "What this firm needs is to be represented by one more Washington law firm."

The grin was contagious. "I thought you might say that."

"So you've already hired Graham."

"Five-thousand-dollar retainer."

Will shrugged. "My budget went out the window the minute Faranco tendered. What does he say?"

"Nobody knows any of the details, but he does know one thing for sure. Faranco's made over thirty million dollars' worth of what they keep calling 'sensitive foreign payments.' Faranco won't give names or countries because they say that would put their foreign executives in danger."

"Yahoo!" Will wailed at the top of his lungs. "Charles W. Guerin, you did not die in vain. We've got them with their hand in the cookie jar!"

A lot of companies had admitted paying foreign bribes, but Will knew that if Faranco wanted majority control of GUA, a judge could easily insist that the issue of its integrity was of paramount importance to the stockholders. Faranco would be caught in a dilemma: determined to keep the details of the payments secret, its tender offer might be placed in jeopardy unless those details were revealed.

"Graham was worth every penny of his fee, Al. We might even find some legal work for him to do."

Later, in the Board Room, the strategy against Faranco began to take shape. Besides the "sensitive foreign payments" issue Goetz and Teicher were working on, there was the matter of Creighton, Cromwell's collusion with Faranco. Nowhere in the tender-offer statement was it mentioned that Creighton, Cromwell still held warrants, obtained years earlier in a financing for GUA, to purchase GUA stock. But this was a bombshell that had to be kept in reserve until the time was right. Then, because the law prohibited GUA from voting any of its own stock, Will suggested Headly Parkhurst approach Winstead of Metrobank on the subject of taking custody of the stock GUA had bought with the Metrobank loan. The purpose was to place it in friendly hands that could vote it and to increase the number of shares Faranco would have to buy to gain voting control. Will had had the foresight to provide for this maneuver in the loan documents.

A press release was drafted, asserting that the bidder, Faranco, was trying to snatch Global Universal before the stock market could reflect its vastly improved prospects or the dividend that management had planned to declare. The takeover's potential injury to revenue was summed up by asking whether the public would risk flying in planes controlled by an unscrupulous mystery man responsible only to his own avarice. In conclusion, the statement declared that the Board of Directors had rejected Faranco's offer on the grounds that it was inadequate and not in the best interests of the company's shareholders. The Board had directed management to fight the takeover attempt.

Ben Buck's anger had begun to wear away during the long hours. Despondency had seeped into the places left empty. As he watched the lawyers—Will, Teicher, Goetz, Parkhurst and Tait—communicating last-minute details, he could not help feeling that control was slipping from his fingers after all. His destiny and the destiny of his company were in the hands of these—these jugglers! If only one of the dozen arcane abstractions whirling above their heads happened to fall, so might he.

9

"YOU SON OF A BITCH!" read the note affixed to the cabin door. And then Will remembered. Donna's plane got in Saturday afternoon—yesterday. The moon was now falling through the darkness like an old silver dollar. Dawn would soon rise to snatch it. He and Donna were supposed to have had dinner together—he looked at his watch—nine hours ago.

He let himself in, set the alarm and went to sleep for a few hours.

At nine in the morning he arrived at Donna's apartment with an armload of groceries. There was no answer when he rang her doorbell. Will left the groceries by the door and was walking down the street to find a phone booth when she suddenly rounded the corner at a brisk trot. She wore layers of old clothes. Running beside her was a black man the size of the building they had just passed. Despite the cold, only a T-shirt and shorts covered arms and legs that extended like huge, oiled ramrods.

Will stepped in front of the two, who continued to jog in place, Donna waiting with a disdainful expression for Will to say his piece and step out of their way. He eyed the man beside her distractedly, then forced himself to focus on Donna.

"I . . . I thought we might have breakfast and I could explain what happened. I brought a lot of groceries . . ."

She weighed his words for a moment and then turned to her companion. "You want breakfast?"

"Sure."

They jogged past Will into the apartment house.

While the groceries were put away, introductions were made. The black man, who filled the kitchen with his bulk, was Luke Malone. He played offensive line for the Denver Broncos.

Probably the whole offensive line, Will thought gloomily.

At the table Donna buttered her toast and then smiled blandly at Will. "You wanted to talk."

"It might be more appropriate if we were alone."

"Do you mind, Luke?"

He shook his head without shifting attention from his half-dozen scrambled eggs.

"Luke doesn't mind," she reported obtusely. She took a bite of her toast.

Will considered a moment, then asked, "Did he spend the night with you?"

"Luke, did you spend the night with me? "

He shook his head. "With the Kowalski twins."

"If you'll remember," Donna pointed out to Will, "I was forced to spend the night alone."

"That's what I wanted to talk to you about. An emergency came up. Faranco finally made a bid for the airline's stock on Friday. We've been in meetings since then. I just didn't have time to call you."

Suspicion arched her eyebrows. "Who is 'we'?"

"Directors, lawyers, bankers . . ."

"You found time to call *them*."

"Damn it, I didn't know where to reach you."

"Funny, there were no messages at the airport Crew Operations Room or with our supervisor or at the GUA switchboard when I called your number. I was here waiting all night. See, there were a lot of places *I* thought to call."

"Please pass the scrambled eggs," requested Malone. Will handed him the platter.

"I'm sorry," Will found himself saying.

Donna shrugged. "Live and learn."
Will's voice rose. "Try to understand. Faranco is threatening to take over GUA. It's a crisis."
"Good company," Malone commented, as he poured more milk. "I've got a thousand shares of Faranco in my portfolio."
"Shit," Will muttered.
"Look, Will," Donna declared, "it would have been important to know you cared enough to call and tell me."
"We had been up all Friday night and Saturday trying to come up with ways to stop the takeover. That was all we could think about."
Malone stood up, blocking the window light. "I've got to get to practice. We play the Rams tomorrow night on TV. Thanks for the breakfast." He nodded at Donna. "You going to jog on Wednesday?"
"No, I'll be away the middle of the week."
"Well, maybe I'll see you in the park on the weekend."
He waved a casual farewell to Will and headed for the door.
"Hey," Will called out as the door closed. "Remember me to the Kowalskis."
Donna's tone, flat and sharp as shale, was a rebuke. "He's got a Ph.D. in some kind of engineering." She leaned forward. "Will, anyone can forget to make a call. If that was the first time something like that happened . . ."
Will was incredulous. "What the hell are you talking about?"
Donna's voice was very firm and very quiet. "I spent all of last weekend comforting and traveling with a woman I barely knew and burying a friend of yours a thousand miles from here that I'd met only a week before. It never occurred to you to thank me."
"Come on. You know how grateful I was."
"No, I didn't know. I spend most of my flight time serving meals, and all this week I got to spend a lot of my free time cooking meals that usually ended up being eaten so late they were dried out or burned or thrown out. You just took for granted that I'd be standing by to see you, with no plans of my own, until you no longer had anything more interesting to do. Just like you took for granted you could safely forget about leaving a message for me yesterday."
"Now, that's not—"

"The first time you became concerned," she continued, ignoring his protest, "was when you saw me with Luke. And after you found out he's just a friend I jog with, you started preening like a rooster."

"Look, I'm trying to apologize. But I'm not the kind of person who makes commitments."

"I'm not looking to get or give commitments. I'm talking about consideration. Things were great on the island. You were attentive and thoughtful. Now I have trouble just arranging for some time with you—business seems to occupy every moment of your life and squeeze everything else out. When we *are* alone either your thoughts are some other place or you're all wit and gaiety. You're never willing to open up and really talk to me. Will, there are a lot of things more important than getting ahead by screwing the shirt off the other guy's back with a clever clause he didn't understand. There are people, Will, and consideration."

She rose and began to remove the plates. For a moment Will sat and watched her, then he too began clearing.

"I just want you to know," she said after a minute, "if you had sat there maybe two seconds longer, you'd have come to on the sidewalk."

When the dishes were washed and sitting on the drainboard, Will kissed her and asked whether he was forgiven. Without a word she led him into the bedroom.

Confident of the effect he was having on her, he drew her into his arms. She pushed straight forward, hard. He toppled backward onto the bed, a surprised look on his face. On hers was determination. She unzipped his slacks, yanked them and his jockey shorts down around his thighs, quickly located appropriate music on the radio, then stepped back to the center of the throw rug. Slowly she allowed the music to course through her body and direct its undulations. Finally, she began her striptease out of the sloppy, oversized gym clothes.

The movements were fluid, and her sense of her own grace was certain. Outer layers of clothing fell away, and the shapeless, pillowy mass began to narrow with promise. The music's beat became more insistent and so did her sensuality. Dance for its own sake gave way to ever bolder eroticism. To Will's astonishment, her eyes were fixed on his penis, and the performance was beginning to have an effect. A smile spread over Donna's face as she gripped the bottom of her T-shirt cross-handed and slowly pulled it up her rotating torso. For a long moment her face was covered. As the T-shirt cleared her head, her eyes were closed and her face was beginning to light with the rapture that sprang from deep within her cells.

Her eyelids opened lazily. Her gaze was still focused with accuracy. And his penis, now semihard, was lengthening, rising upward. With exquisite, teasing, sure lassitude, she slipped off her bra and let her breasts come free. Last were the panties. She rolled them into a rope across her hips, and then, finally naked, she pushed them down to join her gym shorts on the floor.

Will was hard and erect now, bulging with arousal. At last her eyes moved slowly up to join his. "Try to forget me now!" they seemed to be saying. "Just try to forget me now!"

At that moment, in New York, two men were just finishing lunch in the Urban Club, famous for its Tiepolo ceiling that had been brought over from an Italian palazzo at the turn of the century. One of the men was a very tired Headly Parkhurst, who had slept fitfully aboard the plane back from Denver. His guest was Bob Winstead of Metrobank. Parkhurst had proposed Will's plan to have Metrobank hold as security the shares GUA had purchased with the bank's loan. But Winstead had stubbornly resisted the idea.

"The *Post* is outraged. The *L.A. Times* has had half a dozen articles on the crashes. This is what's in the latest *Time* magazine." The banker lifted the magazine, already open to the appropriate page. He read:

> Sources close to the investigation refused to confirm rumors that bombs had been placed aboard both planes. But former astronaut Craig Merrill, reached for comment yesterday on a tour of West Africa, released a statement blaming lax security at Global Universal for the accessibility of its aircraft to potential bombers. He pointed out that Faranco Inc., the conglomerate seeking control of the airline, had listed among its reasons for the takeover a desire to protect both public safety and its investment by instituting new and modern attitudes, methods and management.

He lowered the paper. "Bombs or just plain accidents, the public is worried about the company. And I don't mind telling you,

Headly, that the bank is becoming anxious about its loan."

"You've seen the new earnings projections."

"The climate is improving for all the airlines. But what if things really get bad at Global Universal in particular? If word got out that we had taken possession of the stock to prop up management, how would the bank look then?" He shook his head discouragingly. "I'll take it under advisement, but don't hold out much hope for a positive answer from us."

He stood up to leave. "That's the best I can do."

As the two men passed the lounge, they noticed Senator Avery Crockett's face on the television screen. They stopped for a moment. Reporters were questioning the legislator on the upcoming aviation hearings. He was making very clear that his views about reforming the CAB might well hinge on how it responded to Faranco's application to acquire control of Global Universal Airlines.

"Aviation has been a closed little club for too long. Maybe we're better off without a CAB. I and a lot of my colleagues are watching to see how quickly and how positively the Board acts on the application of Faranco Inc. to acquire Global Universal."

Winstead glanced grimly at Parkhurst and continued toward the exit to the street.

His office seemed to have grown warmer. Al Goetz rose from his desk and opened the window a crack. Avery Crockett's face looked like a cartoon on the TV screen behind him—too bright and off color—because no one had bothered to reduce the excessive color saturation.

Goetz's CAB liaison and lawyer, John Rosenthal, nodded slowly and bit into his sandwich, his gaze not wavering from the set. "Do you think the CAB will move this thing to the top of its calendar?"

"You can bet your *cojones* on it," Madeline Naybaugh sang out as she strolled into Goetz's office. The typewriters were clattering behind her, and she closed the door for quiet. "An unofficial telephone poll by a certain charming airline lobbyist—excuse me, liaison—whose long-overdue raise has not yet come through . . ." She paused and glared at Goetz for the barest fraction of a second. ". . . produced the equally unofficial, but highly reliable, conclusion that they'll hear the case as fast as lightning."

She threw her coat on one end of the sofa and flounced down on the other. Madeline Naybaugh was one of the legion of smart, aggressive women who decide to give Washington a whirl after college and then stay on, addicted to the proximity to power. Fifteen years later Naybaugh could assure herself that she had stayed on by choice. Two other airlines and four trade associations had offered a considerable increase in salary if she would come work for them.

Although Goetz did not really feel comfortable with her, he respected her and he knew her worth as a congressional liaison. He would push hard for her raise.

"Who'd you speak to?" he asked.

"People associated with the CAB."

"Thanks," Rosenthal said tartly, his eyes still on the screen. A red-bearded young man who resembled a smallish Viking, he was out of sorts. Since being roused from bed at dawn by Goetz's call, he had been working hard to prepare a rough-draft brief to cripple Faranco's application at the Board. The brief had to be on Goetz's desk and Telefaxed to Will in Denver and to their Washington and New York law firms for rewrites before he could start lobbying at the CAB.

"You guys want to hear why they'll let Faranco try the tender offer?" Naybaugh chirped.

Both heads instantly turned.

"God, I love an audience. Okay, the reason is the obvious one that they want to show it's not the same old shit going on there. But it's also because GUA is an international carrier. They can approve and then send it over to the White House and dump it in the President's lap. It involves international routes, so he has the final decision and they're off the hook."

"Did you see your 'friend,' Senator Avery Crockett?" Goetz gestured toward the television. "He just about said he'd sponsor a bill to fire nukes at the CAB if the Board didn't approve Faranco's application."

For a short time Goetz had harbored the hope that Naybaugh's friendship with Crockett would blossom into something more intimate and thus more useful, but the woman never seemed to conduct her personal life as he would wish.

She lit a cigarette. "Even if he is friendly with Girard, Avery won't be alone on this. If you had been in town last night, you'd know. I hit four parties. Probably spoke to eight senators, twenty representatives, four to five White House types, a couple of undersecretaries, thirty to forty legislative aides, maybe a—"

"We get the picture, Maddy. Were they aware of the issue?"

An eyebrow arched. "Each one had gotten a copy of all the Faranco tender material in his morning mail, with a little flyer about how it was the American way to let the shareholders, and not a government agency, decide the issue."

Al Goetz felt his palms moistening. "We didn't know about that. Get hold of a copy. My secretary's been Telefaxing stuff to Denver and New York. Have her send it right out."

He stared at the view from the window. The day was crisp and sunny, and the Capitol dome glistened.

"That's crazy," he said, with a fervor that appeared intended more to convince himself than Naybaugh. "Do they think the CAB and Congress will believe that pure image once we reveal the SEC is investigating all kinds of foreign bribes by Faranco?"

"Thank God we've got something on them." Naybaugh was delighted. "The odds on us around this town are about the same as they are when Harold Stassen announces for the Presidency."

"You're getting carried away," Goetz warned her. "Our own campaign will bring in businessmen and officials who can influence each congressman to explain how disastrous new management at GUA could be to air service in their own part of the country. Build up congressional pressure on the CAB. Did you speak to anyone at the other airlines to get their lobbying help, maybe file petitions at the CAB supporting us?"

She nodded.

"What did they tell you?"

"To jump off before it sinks."

A dull pain in his arm woke Will. Donna's tawny head was resting on his shoulder; her limbs wound around him like ivy. The clock on the bureau read a little past one in the afternoon. He slid backward gently. She frowned in her sleep, then tried to cuddle against him. Not finding his body, she contracted into a ball and drifted back to deeper sleep.

Will dressed and then went into the living room, closing the door behind him. He dialed the GUA switchboard for messages. Dan Pope wanted to speak to him. It was urgent. The switchboard signaled the Security chief's beeper; shortly after, he was on the line. A demonstration calling for an investigation of the airline's management had suddenly materialized in front of the GUA Building. Reporters and photographers were everywhere.

Will could feel his blood quicken as Dan Pope spoke. "I'm on my way," he said. He was nearly out the door when he remembered to scribble a quick note to Donna.

Will could hear the demonstrators long before he could see them. More than a hundred people were marching in a long narrow oval past the front entrance, apparently for the edification of the press, whose members were eagerly seeking interviews and photos. Two TV crews were filming the action.

Leading the endless parade was Sally Emerson, professional consumer advocate and lawyer who had built a strong grassroots organization. She carried a sign denouncing GUA management for not ceasing operations until the cause of the crashes was determined and corrected. Will had tangled with her once in the past, during an antinoise suit. Although she was young and possessed the face of an innocent adolescent, Will knew how effective she was; treating her lightly was a mistake.

"He's with the airline!" Sally shouted when she saw Will crossing toward Dan Pope, who, with his men, barred the GUA doors. Then she stepped in front of Will, asking, "Is it true that bombs were placed on board both 747s that crashed, and you've done nothing to stop future sabotage?"

Will stood his ground. "The matter of determining cause is in the hands of the National Transportation Safety Board," he explained. "They haven't had a hearing yet. If there was sabotage, that's the FBI's province. Our security measures were adequate, but because of the increased threat we've tightened them even further."

Will began listing the new procedures slowly enough for the reporters to write them down. Sally interrupted.

"Isn't it true that Faranco's offering price is fair and they would bring in more modern and responsive management methods? You've decided to fight Faranco's tender offer only in order to hang on to your own power."

Trust that sweet-faced little killer to go right for the jugular, Will thought, and he wondered what or who had provoked her outrage.

"That's a matter for the stockholders to decide—" Will began to answer.

"It affects public safety and so it's a matter for every potential passenger and every citizen."

"Are there any stockholders present?" Will called out. "If there are, I'll be glad to discuss the matter."

No hands rose. Will was about to break off the dialogue and enter the building when a small group of women at the rear of the crowd began to chant, "We want an answer! We want an answer!"

"He's one of the reporters!" Pope exclaimed suddenly, staring at a man standing beside the chanters, egging them on.

Will's bad leg slowed his pace, yet he was only a few yards behind Pope as they moved around the crowd. The reporter noticed them almost immediately and broke into a run toward a car in the parking lot. As Pope grabbed the handle of the car door, he heard the click—it was locked. He banged on the side window. The car roared off. All Pope could do was note the license plate number.

But Will had recognized the slight young man.

"His name's Desmond," he said. "He says he's with *Newsweek*. I met him in Washington."

Pope shook his head in disagreement. "I'm sure I know him from somewhere. Maybe he worked here at one time. I can look it up. But I bet you he works for Faranco now." Pope started to say something more, then fell silent, deep in thought.

The two men walked back toward the building. As they neared the demonstrators, Pope finally made up his mind to speak.

"I noticed an envelope on the car seat," he said in a low voice. "It had Bannster's name on the return address."

When they phoned *Newsweek*, the magazine said no one

named Mat Desmond worked there. Then a call came in from a friend of Pope's who worked with the State Police. He had traced the license plate to a car rented in the name of Robert Jones and to a Pennsylvania driver's license that was probably false. By three o'clock Pope's memory of the interloper's face had been substantiated by employee records bearing the man's photo. His name was Ralph Coburn. He had worked in Accounting and had been terminated during an economy squeeze. Personnel had offered to rehire him seven months later, but the letter was returned "Addressee unknown."

"You'd better inform the FBI," directed Will.

"He'll go underground now," Pope observed ruefully. "That's the last we'll see of him. Faranco will put him to work somewhere else." His voice became scornful. "The FBI will only catch him if he's dumb enough to show up at his family's home."

Will put into words what both were thinking. "Unless, of course, he's not working for Faranco at all. He could be our bomber, looking for revenge."

Pope slammed fist to palm with frustration at having come so close to getting a hand on the man. The sound was like a rifle shot.

"But I don't think so," Will reasoned aloud. "A bomber working on his own wouldn't spend his time trying to stir up unfavorable press. And he wouldn't have that envelope you saw."

"Maybe that's why we haven't been able to stop the leaks out of here." Pope considered carefully before voicing an ultimate suspicion. "One person I never figured was Arnold Bannister himself."

The idea was not new to Will, because so much of the information leaking out had been financial and so much of it had originated with Bannister himself. Then there was the latter's friendship with Max Creighton, his anger at Will for having severed that tie, and J. Stephen Girard's pattern of giving control of his divisions to financially oriented executives.

Will briefed Pope on a plan he had formulated. He would write a short memo to Buck full of misinformation on the takeover defense. Another version would be routed to Bannister. It would differ in several important but barely noticeable ways, so that surveillance could determine whether the leak was from Bannister or from someone with access to Buck's office.

Pope agreed and left Will to draft the memo. As he wrote, Will wondered whether he would be so zealous if the suspect were not a rival for the top spot at GUA.

Will had one more task that evening before he could leave to pick up Donna for dinner—a meeting with Ben Buck.

She's like a loyal wife, Will thought as he greeted Eloise Cooper. Past nine o'clock on a Sunday night, she was busily typing.

"He's over at the airport," Eloise said. She rolled the page out of the typewriter and slipped it into a folder with some others. Then she stood up and reached for her coat. "I'll go with you." Buck was visiting the cargo hangar.

They found him standing on the brightly lit tarmac beside the newest plane in the fleet, a 747 Freighter. The transport's nose was swung up on a hinge just in front of the flight deck, and containers full of cargo were being loaded aboard through the opening.

Despite the cold, Buck wore no coat over his sport shirt. Catching the expression of disapproval on Eloise's face, he avoided her eyes.

"Inside," she said firmly. "We have things for you to sign."

They commandeered the cargo manager's office. Buck began reading the material. Will and the other lawyers had painstakingly chosen every word of the documents that would be released to the public. The SEC and the other side would deal harshly with any misstatements or omissions of fact.

The letter attacked takeover laws that permitted a rich or devious raider to gobble up a target company, no matter how well the target was run. It decried the loss of independent middle-sized companies to less efficient, less responsible giants, the hurtful impact on air transportation in general, and the plight of minority shareholders who suddenly find their stocks delisted from an exchange. It pointed out that the two hundred largest U.S. corporations now controlled two thirds of the nation's industrial production. The letter concluded by asking the reader to write and speak out against this "desecration of American values by a rapacious predator."

Buck looked up from the page. "What the hell does 'rapacious' mean, Will? Let's just say they're trying to rape us and we don't intend to bend over."

" 'Rapacious' isn't quite the same thing as 'rape.' "

"How about if we use both?"

" 'Rapacious' is enough," Will said and leaned wearily against the chair back.

"The letter's fine," said Buck grumpily, "but I wish we didn't have to be so polite."

"We can be impolite. We can't be inaccurate."

Buck signed the letter and handed it to Eloise. Will then apprised Buck of his flight to New York late tomorrow. He wanted to be present the following day when the airline's case would be argued for a preliminary injunction to stop the takeover.

"The trip's a good opportunity to talk with the Manning girl about extending the voting trust," the Old Man pointed out. "It's got five months to go, but you never know. What does she look like?"

"Cute enough, I guess."

"How's the body?"

Will shrugged.

"That's not like you," jeered Buck. "You usually file away their statistics like a computer."

Will chuckled. "She's got a friend—the one I met her with—who's a knockout. *Her* I remember."

Eloise stood up with an exaggerated motion, advertising her distaste for such conversation.

"Her friend doesn't own eight hundred thousand shares of GUA stock," the Old Man observed pragmatically. "That's a hell of a reason to be obliging. With a buck and a half worth of the charm that's given wet pants to every woman at headquarters, you could tie up her two percent of GUA stock for the next few years."

Eloise stalked out of the room with a glare.

"Present company excepted!" called Buck after her.

But Eloise preferred to wait in the hall. Even so, she lingered close enough to the open door to take in any of Buck's booming talk that related to her job.

Will agreed to call Marcie Manning that night and was about to ask Buck to sign the rest of the material he had brought, so it could be put aboard a plane to New York, when the older man's eyes abruptly caught his.

"Does anybody know when Merrill is expected back in the country?"

Will's face hardened. "Clayton tells me the FBI is still trying to find out."

"When he left Global Universal, I wondered whether he'd be lucky enough to find another job fast. It turned out the job he found was mine, and in a hell of a hurry."

"Maybe he makes his own luck."

Will pointed to the signature line. Buck scanned and signed the papers and, at the same time, continued to speak.

"Girard is the guy I've got suspicions of for these crashes," Buck rasped. "*There's* a guy who makes his own luck. Two planes go down and the price of our stock drops with them, just when he's looking to buy us. If that's luck it's real convenient luck."

Buck stood up and strolled to the window. "I've already gotten half a dozen calls from the heads of large corporations that figure I'd settle for a friendly takeover as a defensive move. Serge Bergheim warned me I'd get them."

Buck paused to watch a jetliner angle down toward the runway. The landing lights slowed to a stop at the edge of the airport. Violet-and-gold color scheme visible now, the GUA 727 turned and rolled back toward the terminal.

"Maybe it's wrong—I know it's a public company and all that—but I never stop thinking of Global Universal as *my* company. Not like I own every last plane and spare part. But like I would feel, I guess, if I had ever had children. I can still remember when it was just struggling to walk. The pride I feel looking at it now!"

He watched the 727 until the plane halted at a gate. "I'm wasting your time with all this bull. It's just that I wanted you to know—like I told you before . . . You know," he finally blurted out, "how much hanging on to this company means to me. And how grateful I am to you for the fight you're putting up."

A few minutes later Will and Eloise waited in the car for Buck to join them for the short drive around the field to the GUA Building.

"He didn't have to do that Wallace Beery imitation back there," Will commented quietly.

"I imagine he just wanted to be sure," replied the small, erect woman. Then she smiled slyly as if she had just told herself a wonderful joke. "Of course," she added, "there's always a chance that he's being sincere."

Will offered to take Donna to dinner, but she asked instead to see the cabin. They picked up a pizza and drove up winding roads into the foothills above Denver.

The cabin was exactly that: a roomy log structure in a clearing in the woods. Upon entering, Will turned on the lights and the heat and lit a fire in the fireplace. He laid the pizza on the rough-hewn table, went for plates and glasses and was about to call Donna, when he noticed she was absorbed in studying the books on the shelves that lined the cabin wall.

"Have you really read all of these?" she exclaimed.

"All except the ones by the bedroom door. When I read one I shift it from there to the main shelves."

"There's a lot here on knights and the Middle Ages."

"Nights can be fun no matter what age you are."

"You don't have to make a joke about it. It's impressive."

"What grabs me about those days," Will admitted, "is that everybody seemed to have faith in something . . . a mission."

"That sounds revealing about you. Would you pick one of the books for me to read?"

Will did. "I warn you, it might be a little dry."

"You're trying to tell me it's not a best seller."

"Not for six or seven hundred years. Want to change your mind?"

"I'll get through it," she said with determination, and crossed the room to take a seat at the table. "All the way up here you were telling me about the takeover fight. A lot of it went over my head. Now I understand you better, I think. You're like those knights, running around after dragons and crusades and women. Looking to score and make a name for yourself—or maybe I just don't understand at all."

"Sausage or plain?" Will replied.

"Sausage. How's the Old Man reacting?"

"Blustering around in the beginning, a lot more subdued now. He's acting like someone's trying to run off with *his* woman."

"Was he ever married?"

"Never even close. According to him he was too wrapped up in building GUA to get serious about a woman."

Donna sat silently for a few moments, her gaze unfocused in thought.

"Why did you ask?" Will inquired.

"Because he's a lot like you—or what you could turn into."

"A lot of people would consider Ben Buck a very successful man."

"Why? Because he can afford to bring a different hooker home every night? It's pretty sad when you can only relax with women you're paying."

"He's had a lot of women who weren't hookers."

"But they knew he didn't need them. You can't love someone who doesn't need you."

Will was scowling. "And needing ends up as a hard kick to the crotch."

Donna engaged his eyes. "You probably don't realize what really makes you attractive. The cleverness and the toughness are only good for openers, you know. It's the softness that sneaks under my skin—when you're not quite sure and you're tender."

Will groaned.

"You wear three-hundred-dollar suits and drive a twenty-thousand-dollar car," she continued, "but you live in a simple house in the mountains."

"Close enough for the power and telephone lines to reach," he added in a cynical tone.

She gestured toward the wide living-room window. "With the woods all around you. Why?"

Will's scowl softened into a reluctant smile. "You know the answer. I can relax here, renew myself," he admitted. "Away from here too long I feel like Ishmael when he's been away from the sea."

"Abraham's son?"

Will fetched a battered copy of *Moby Dick* and handed it to Donna.

"It's a thick one," she said warily, and reached for another slice of pizza. "I saw you on TV this evening. The news."

"The demonstration?"

Donna nodded. "That woman with the big glasses—she likes you. And you used it, whether or not you realized it."

"She'd cut my heart into sandwich meat if she could."

"She doesn't have to. You do it to yourself."

"I thought I made some good points!"

"Like a lawyer trying a case. If you had sounded like you do now, people would have believed you no matter what you said." Donna's eyes were on the last of the pizza. "Want any more?"

Will shook his head. She pulled the remaining pie wedges toward her, her face bright with anticipation.

"You know what I find attractive about *you*?" Will asked.

"I've got a good body, but otherwise I'm very ordinary. I like the ordinary things in life."

"It's the *way* you like them that's so fascinating. They're always new and interesting to you. You make me see them that way, too."

Will bent the pizza box in half and placed it in the fireplace. He stood watching the flames lick the edges and finally begin to consume it.

"Something on your mind?" Donna had taken a seat on the rug in front of the fireplace, her plate before her, as she finished the last pizza slice.

"The tender offer. Girard. There has to be a way to stop him."

"Will, you could get hurt because you're taking this whole thing so personally. A good lawyer will always be able to make a living."

"Shit!" Will exploded. "Is that all a job means to you—a good living?"

"Be realistic, Will. There are a lot of airlines and a lot of big companies. One's pretty much like the next. You're a hired hand—worse, a hired gun."

"You're depressing the hell out of me, Donna. I'm pretty close to the inner circle here, with a chance to move even higher. But even if I weren't, I'd still fight tooth and nail to stop Girard. If we give in to people like that, one more little piece of the things we value gets snatched away, and we have less purpose, less meaning, in life."

"No wonder you ended up in Vietnam. You turn everything into us against them. You can't kick the habit."

Will took a deep breath. "When life stops being an adventure, you might as well be dead. New thoughts, new activities, new people, new challenges."

"And that includes, I suppose, a constant turnover of new women. Carol—our supervisor—says you're a one-man shooting gallery. Bang! Bang! Bang!"

"Ah hah, that's what's really at the bottom of your insistence on my telephoning and performing the little courtesies like taking off your coat and pushing in your chair at a restaurant. You're afraid I consider you just another chick to be knocked off."

"Well, don't you? 'New people! New challenges!' I'm surprised you haven't got the notches carved on your wooden leg!"

"Donna, don't cheapen what's happening between us."

"And just exactly what is?"

"We're happy when we're together. We trust each other. We stimulate each other. You're not just another girl I date or sleep with. You're important to me."

"Then how about giving this relationship more of a chance to take root? Are you willing to stop seeing other women?"

Will scowled. "And play house? I'm very happy with my life just the way it is."

"Bang! Bang! Bang!"

10

GUA opened at 11⅜ on the New York Stock Exchange, tried to rise and was met by a barrage of sell orders. Serge Bergheim's telephone network and early selling pressure (starting first that morning on the Zurich Exchange) took effect. The pace in GUA trading on the floor of the Exchange slowed perceptibly. Risk arbitrageurs, professional investors who jump in to buy stock on the gamble the takeover will succeed, raising the price, seemed to be holding back out of wariness about regulatory-agency intercession. That was a good sign for management; after many takeover fights ended, more than half the stock turned up in the hands of arbitrageurs—and *their* only interest was in selling to the raider.

Al Goetz spent several hours with an old friend, the senior Senator from the state where GUA was incorporated. A member of the Banking Committee and a populist by temperament, Senator Cleary was moved by the emotional issue of bigness consuming everything in sight. He agreed to exert pressure on the SEC, the banking regulatory agencies and his colleagues to be energetic in demanding that Faranco comply with the regulations down to the tiniest details. Goetz's best hope in the House was the powerful Congresswoman Antoinette Munson, but her husband was gravely ill and she had not left his side for the entire week.

Bill Tait, public-relations specialist and a lawyer by training, had convinced an editor at *New York* magazine to come out with a strong muckraking article ripping into the greed and ruthlessness of "J. Stephen Girard: Mystery Tycoon Who's a Glutton for Companies." *Newsday* did a piece on the same theme.

Because Global Universal was carefully guarding its stockholder list from Faranco and would fight disclosure moves in the courts, the calls made by professional telephone solicitors and GUA's reservation agents were the only direct communication the average stockholder was getting. The personal touch was apparently having an effect. Many shareholders reported being impressed with GUA's responses in the press and with the announcement of a dividend. And few were in a rush to take advantage of the higher stock price.

Will hurried into the terminal Monday afternoon only a few minutes before takeoff, late for his plane because he and Pope had been in the mailroom, seeking among the pile of outgoing mail from Bannister a synopsis or, even better, a copy of the memo Will had delivered. There had been nothing.

Will was glad to be off for New York, even if this visit was a fast one, with little time to take in a show or a concert or visit a museum. He and Donna had tried to put the argument out of their thoughts after it happened but had each felt somewhat ill at ease with the other for a long while. Donna's priorities so diverged from his that their ground of common interest seemed painfully narrow. About to get on a plane alone, Will felt free as a stallion that has just cleared the corral fence.

If Will had not stopped to adjust his grip on the heavy briefcase, he might not have noticed the woman who rushed up to the GUA ticket counter and handed the agent a manila envelope. The woman was Bannister's secretary. Obviously in great haste, she must have been trying to take advantage of the company's Personal Package Service.

Will followed the agent carrying the envelope through the gate area and then onto the plane to New York. When the agent left, Will identified himself to the senior flight attendant and asked to see the envelope that had been left with her. A brief consultation with the captain confirmed Will as head of the Legal and Security Division, and the envelope was turned over to him.

Once the plane was aloft, Will steamed it open in the galley. To make sure there were witnesses, Will requested that two crew members watch this procedure as well as view the envelope's contents. Inside was Bannister's copy of the false memo. Carefully, Will resealed the flap. In New York he would take the package to the pickup room, and then he would wait for whoever came to pick it up. He strapped himself into an empty seat to get some sleep.

Will peered through the crack in the doorway. A young man of nineteen or twenty with pimples and a soiled red parka lounged against the counter. He had come for the manila envelope. He signed the receipt and left with the envelope under his arm.

Will followed him out of the La Guardia departure area. Airport Security had arranged for Will to park his rented Ford at the entrance. He waited for the messenger's blue pickup truck to pass him and then nosed out into the traffic just behind.

The truck had New York plates. Will made a note of the number as he wove through Queens, tailing it. The early-morning sun was at his back, painting a gold wash across the Manhattan skyscrapers that sprouted like a stand of autumn saplings.

A few blocks farther on the truck parked, and the driver entered an industrial building. The sign over the door read "Basehart Abrasives."

Will parked and waited. Not more than half an hour later a black Cadillac limousine stopped at the building's entrance. The driver was a very muscular white man in a dark suit. He looked more like a bouncer than a chauffeur—Will could make out the thickened brow ridges of an ex-boxer. The chauffeur was soon strolling back to the limousine with the envelope.

What Will didn't see was the man in a second-floor window who happened to notice the red Ford pull away from the curb just after the limousine. The observer picked up the telephone and dialed.

The limousine crossed the Queensboro Bridge into Manhattan's midtown area and parked in front of the Faranco Building.

Will followed the driver across the slate plaza and into the glass skyscraper.

He entered the polished-aluminum elevator just behind the chauffeur and a group of others. As the doors met, an unseen orchestra could suddenly be heard playing "Zing Went the Strings of My Heart." Each time the doors opened the orchestra would politely halt in midnote, more passengers would leave, and then, when the doors met again, the faithful orchestra would be heard once more.

At the top floor, the fiftieth, the driver stepped out. Will followed. The name FARANCO was written on the ebony wall behind the receptionist, each letter perfectly machined out of high-gloss stainless steel. The young woman behind the glass desk smiled a greeting.

"I have something for Mr. Trobard," the boxer said.

The young woman dialed her phone. "Eddie has something for Mr. Trobard." Hanging up, she spoke to the boxer again. "You can take it in yourself."

He turned away and headed down the corridor to the left. Now the receptionist addressed Will. "Can I help you?"

"I'd like to see Mr. Merrill."

"I'm sorry, he's away. Would you like to leave a message?"

"When is he expected back?"

"Around the end of the month."

"I'll be back."

Outside, Will removed the parking ticket that had been tucked under the left windshield wiper and slipped it into his pocket. He peered about cautiously before getting into the red Ford, but with all the pedestrian traffic moving along the sidewalk he failed to note a tall rugged man standing beside one of the pillars at the entrance to the building he had just left. The man was speaking into a walkie-talkie.

As Will eased into the flow of morning traffic, a black Plymouth did, too. And when Will stopped at the Dennison Hotel on Central Park South, leaving the doorman to watch the car, the Plymouth stopped as well. There were two men in the front seat.

Will checked into his room, hung up his extra suit, and made some local calls. It was too early to call Denver. A little while later he drove off again. So did the Plymouth.

He parked in a lot near the court building and then entered a drugstore to place a collect call to Dan Pope. Pope's office transferred the call to the president's office, where the Security chief was meeting with Buck. Eloise put Will through immediately.

"Dan, the reason we couldn't find the memo being sent out of Bannister's office was that it was placed on a plane to New York."

Pope's voice echoed; he was talking into a speaker phone. "I know. The police arrested her as soon as she left the terminal."

"She?"

"Barbara Cutler, Mr. Bannister's secretary. We've been watching her for a week."

Then Arnold Bannister's voice came on the line. "A week ago I did some calculations on a yellow pad and put it into my briefcase. An hour later it was gone. Two hours later it was back. I notified Dan, and we started following her."

"You ought to see the bitch's bank account," Buck's voice exploded.

"She's banked twenty thousand dollars in the last four months," Pope continued. "Five thousand of it went in yesterday. Pretty good for someone making twelve thousand dollars a year."

"Has she admitted anything?"

"A guy we can't trace proposed the deal to her. His description sounds like that fellow Coburn we chased yesterday. She dated him but says he traveled a lot. Every few weeks she'd see him and he'd give her a cash payment. She usually mailed photocopies of important papers to a post-office box in New York. If the information seemed particularly valuable, she'd put it on a plane directly, addressed to a John Fox. She'd call collect to a number in New York that wouldn't accept the call. That was the tipoff to expect the package. That's all she knew. The number turned out to be a candy-store pay phone; they say they never heard of her. Ditto the P.O. box holder."

"Fox was the name on the envelope I trailed this morning to a company in Queens called Basehart Abrasives. Someone picked it up and delivered it there." Will read off the license plate number. "A limousine driver came out with the envelope and delivered it to Faranco's finance V.P., Trobard."

"We know all that," roared Buck, who seemed to have the idea the speaker device was a megaphone. "Dan had someone following you and the package in New York—that detective agency we hired to investigate Girard."

Will's anger was immediate, but he refused Buck the satisfaction of a heated reply.

"You still there, Will?"

"Dan, she must have known where her boyfriend was living." Will's voice was even and unruffled.

"A motel near here. He had checked out by the time we got there. The rented car he had was found last night downtown. He probably abandoned it as soon as he was away from here. The FBI is staking out the airport, terminals, the bus and train stations. But Faranco will send someone to pick him up and we'll never see him again."

Buck's voice boomed out of the receiver again. "I'll bet you were beginning to think Arnold here was the culprit. Come on, now, admit it!"

"No, of course not," Will lied. Then he added acidly, "We're all one big, happy family at GUA."

"Well, *I* sure as hell was starting to," Buck admitted.

"Dan, why wasn't I told you suspected the girl?" Will asked.

"Same reason I didn't tell Mr. Bannister about the memo," Pope replied without hesitation. "Mr. Buck told me not to. He said this was one time when he couldn't trust *anyone.*"

Will said softly, more to himself than to anyone else, "Whatever it is this fight with Faranco is doing to us . . . I don't like it."

"For the first time in a long time I agree with a sentiment of yours, Nye," Bannister offered. But there was no warmth in the words.

A small, disheveled figure hurried through the halls of federal court in Manhattan. One hand was trying to shove the remains of a tunafish sandwich into his mouth. The other held a brief on the motion he was about to argue. Behind him, long legs taking one step to every two of Teicher's, Chris Flynn would have moved faster than her colleague (over whom the blond, blue-eyed woman lawyer towered) were it not for the armful of law books that she came close to dropping at each step.

Teicher suddenly stopped, nearly causing Flynn to crash into him. His gaze was transfixed by a large color poster. A jet bomber streaked upward over the closeup of a pilot's head, to intercept words that invited the reader to join the Air Force.

"Take my word for it, Eli, this country is in big trouble if Uncle Sam needs *you*," Chris Flynn remarked caustically.

Teicher did not react. The brief he carried argued, first, that the law required CAB approval *before* the takeover could commence; and, second, that Faranco had failed to divulge over thirty million dollars in questionable "sensitive payments" abroad. Teicher raced to the courtroom to find Will Nye already there. He had only one question to ask.

"Does Global Universal supply planes to the government in time of war?"

Will nodded, but before he could speak Teicher had hurried away.

Two minutes later Teicher was on the phone dictating a third point to the brief. Within half an hour, just as Judge Metucci was stepping to the bench, Eli Teicher's secretary arrived in the courtroom with the new last pages.

For two hours, Eli Teicher and Sam Friedman slashed at each other's contentions. The question of "sensitive payments" drew blood from Faranco. Teicher pressed hard on the issue. Friedman's responses were vague—so much so that the judge began to question Friedman himself. The lawyer asked for a short recess. Fifteen minutes later he was back with an aggressive defense. Yes, he admitted, the foreign payments had been made, but Faranco's only legal obligation was to admit the figure to the SEC and that had been done. Neither the names of recipients nor the specifics of any transaction were required. In fact, their release could endanger the lives of Faranco employees abroad and potential Faranco business. He concluded by insisting that the transactions were a trade secret and not the affair of GUA or the court.

Teicher's final point was the issue of national security. With absolute seriousness he conjured up an image of the armed Communist nations advancing against freedom-loving America. "In whose hands should we leave our national security: those of a great war hero or those of a mercenary multinational corporation, whose divided loyalties—profit versus patriotism—may well threaten us all in time of ultimate crisis?"

In rebuttal Friedman invoked the cry of "peace in our time" and made a plea for "industrial statesmen to be heard now and heeded, so that men might disarm and beat their swords into plowshares and their spears into pruning hooks."

As expected, Judge Metucci reserved decision.

The front-desk clerk at the Dennison Hotel was surprised when Will Nye telephoned for his messages. A man who said he worked for Will had just been by to pick them up. But the clerk remembered there had been only one—from a Mr. Dan Pope.

Will immediately telephoned Pope in a fury.

"Whoever that detective son of a bitch is you've got tailing me, get him off!"

"Look, Will, I'm sorry Mr. Buck wouldn't let me tell you about the investigation, but no one was ever put onto you personally. He was following the package pickup. I have some more information. Basehart Abrasives is a Faranco subsidiary. The pickup truck is registered in Basehart's name. The limousine is Faranco's, too."

"Which only tells us what we already know," Will fumed.

"The envelope was returned to the airport by someone from Basehart a couple of hours ago. He said there had been a mistake, that they had been given the wrong package. Late today a package with a similar addressee will probably be flown in using our service as a cover-up."

"They must have spotted me behind the truck or the limousine. Somebody picked up my phone messages at the Dennison a little while ago. Why don't you put that detective of ours to good use and have him look into it? Tell him to meet me in my hotel room at three."

Will hung up the phone receiver. He walked outside and looked in all directions. A man was lounging against the court building seemingly engrossed in a newspaper, but Will sensed his eyes following him.

Just then a cab pulled up and a round man in a fur hat started to step out. A woman who had been trying to flag a cab waited patiently for him to wrestle his briefcase out of the back seat. Will quickly stepped in front of her, scrambled into the cab and slammed the door. After a moment of stunned disbelief, the woman began to squawk loudly. The driver too was about to protest on her behalf, but the tone of Will's voice as he gave the order "Move out fast!" changed the driver's mind. He hit the gas pedal. Will turned back in time to see the man with the newspaper trying frantically to flag down a cab, too.

Smiling broadly, Will relaxed and gave the driver the address Marcie Manning had given him.

Fifteen minutes later, he was climbing the steep, narrow stairs to the second-floor landing of a loft building in SoHo. A decade after artists and artisans, desperate for large, cheap work areas, had seized these ancient, deserted factory buildings, the area south of Houston Street was a distinctive neighborhood, a hive of art galleries, shops and restaurants and, above them, artists' studios and apartments.

Will halted before a door with a lime-colored "Belinda" painted lavishly across it. "Manning" had been inked carefully in small letters on a strip of white adhesive tape below. Will was about to knock, but the door swung open at the first touch, revealing a wide, deep room full of modern furniture, inventive architectural constructions and subtle lighting. Pieces of sculpture rested on tables and in odd nooks. A blond man with a mustache sat at the huge Victorian desk engrossed in a phone conversation. Receiver tucked under his chin, he was busily writing notes as he talked. Noticing Will, he gestured upward with his head and eyes, pointing with his pen in the general direction of the stairway.

Will climbed to the third floor. A hum of voices grew louder. The door was open here too, and the loft was full of people. Although it was the same size as the one below, this space was starkly simple: two low bookcases dividing it, bare brick walls, century-old wooden beams supporting the ceiling.

Bolts of material were everywhere: stacked in orderly rows on a deep set of shelves along the far wall; leaning against the front wall; and on a table where several had partially unrolled, cascading and eddying colorfully down to the polished wood floor. Belts, ribbons and trimmings were tossed like a gay salad on one table near the door, jewelry on another. Beneath them were rows of shoes.

The front of the loft was illuminated by stark winter sunlight that fell across a low carpeted platform, a drafting table and the cork wall on which were pinned fashion sketches. A model on the platform was just stepping out of a full skirt. She handed it to a woman whose back was to Will. The woman began to examine the skirt's fabric, while the model, now wearing only a blouse and sheer panties, absent-mindedly watched a pigeon strut along an outside cornice.

The woman bent to an intercom and filled the design studio with her voice.

"Estrella, Max, to the front, please."

She turned around. It was Belinda. Seeing Will, she reacted with pleased surprise and held up a finger to indicate she would be with him in a moment. An older man and a woman were already scurrying toward her from the rear of the loft.

"This is the third time we've tried this skirt on Laura and the third time it has hung like a carcass." She spoke firmly, but with humor and patience. "Look at Laura. Are her hips curved?"

All heads turned. Laura, roused from her torpor, lifted her blouse to expose, not only her hips, but a dark triangle. She seemed unconcerned. The man and the woman nodded.

"Good, we're agreed on that. So the skirt should curve, too—can we also agree on that?"

They nodded again. Belinda took a pair of scissors from an end table beside the platform and began opening a seam at the waist. She explained what she wanted done to enhance the dirndl effect. Max would correct the pattern. Estrella would resew it.

Now a thin, willowy young man in tight pants and shirt came up to Belinda. He stood with his elbows and a hip jutting out at extravagant angles to the rest of him and held up a hanger on which a dark gown was draped. Belinda nodded. The young man beckoned to the model. She stepped down from the platform and followed him.

Belinda turned to Will, but before she could speak Marcie appeared, trailing the long extension cord of a white telephone she carried. "It's the hotel people. They say you can't install lighting!"

Belinda took the phone and began to speak. A moment later she clapped the two halves of the phone together like cymbals and dumped the instrument on a table. Her face was now a driving storm.

"What is it?" Marcie asked.

"Schactman! He told the hotel and suppliers that lights and scenery weren't necessary when we show the collection. Bring the contract and the budget. We're going up to his place." Belinda scooped her coat from an old-fashioned wooden coat rack.

"I . . . but we have a lunch date with Will. You promised to go with me."

"Good. He can come, too. We might need a lawyer."

"But it was *business*."

"That's exactly what we're going to see Schactman about—that low-down bastard!"

She launched herself down the stairs, the fury in her eyes fixed ahead of her in time and space to the clash she headed toward. At the second-floor landing she called out, "Ron! We're going to have it out with Schactman!" It sounded like a battle cry. She charged down the next set of stairs.

Will lumbered stiff-legged behind her. Books and files in her arms, Marcie passed him on the stairs. Then Ron burst out of the apartment ahead of him, too.

The three had hailed a cab and were waiting in it when Will finally stepped onto the sidewalk.

Ten minutes later they walked under the sign "Schactman Sophisticates" and into the pale-blue showroom.

Belinda swept through the showroom and into the office at the rear, Ron and Marcie a winged formation at her sides. A moment later they were back. Right behind Belinda was the balding middle-aged man Will remembered from the art gallery party. The long cigar was still lodged between the first and second fingers of his left hand like a surgical implant.

"The line is what sells. I'm not going to throw good money out the window on lights and scenery. What is this, a high-school play or a business?"

"You backed me because I have a sense of style that can sell,"

Belinda countered. "They don't know if I can design dresses, but they know I have flair and snap and style. That's what we've got to knock them on their asses with. Morris, this argument has been going on for a month. I tell you, when the effect's right they'll appreciate the dresses. Am I within my budget?"

Schactman shrugged noncommittally. Belinda glanced at Marcie, who nodded yes.

"Is every penny accounted for?" Belinda asked.

Marcie nodded again. After a moment Schactman nodded reluctantly.

"Then you give me no choice," Belinda said, and spun around to face Will. "Will, start preparing the court papers."

"You her lawyer?" Schactman asked in an unfazed tone.

He interpreted Will's neutral stare as confirmation. "What happened to the long thin one with the fag voice?"

"Gary's away for the holidays."

The dress manufacturer shook his head slowly. "Sure, fag lawyers can afford vacations! Do they have to meet a payroll?"

Ron Bailey stepped forward. Will could hear the fringe of anxiety in his voice. "Look, Belinda, maybe Mory would be willing to settle this by increasing our cash advance and then—"

Belinda was incredulous. "Can't you get it through your head that what I'm concerned about is the success of the whole line, of my career as a clothing designer?"

"But Belinda, honey, surely you—"

"Don't honey me! You're the businessman. You're supposed to be protecting me. Will, tell Schactman the grounds for our suit."

Will pronounced the words clearly to emphasize the harshness of the charges. "Misprision of a tortious redundancy. Open and shut."

Schactman seemed visibly to give way. "Okay, okay. I tried to save a few bucks. It's been a lousy season; the only thing good about it is that it's better than the fall. But it would be foolish to cripple new business before it even has a chance to get off the ground just to save a few dollars." He put his arm around Belinda. "Go, sweetheart. Spend. The worst that can happen is it turns out to be a lousy line and I go into Chapter Eleven." He eyed Will. "If you do bankruptcy work, stick around a few weeks. She may give you a client."

Belinda was all smiles as she kissed Schactman's cheek and bounded out the door. There her dark eyebrows pinched into an angry V and her mouth tightened.

"My budget's down in black and white, and he still tries to screw me out of it!" Her gaze lit on Ron and Marcie in turn. "That's why this show has to be a smash success. Unless I can write my own ticket and really be in control of everything, guys like Schactman will always be trying to tear out an extra piece of flesh."

Ron left them off at a restaurant, where they celebrated their success with red wine and good French cooking. When the waitress left to get the coffee, Belinda leaned across the table and confronted Will.

"All right, what is it you're trying to get out of Marcie?" Her eyes were wary, protective of her friend.

Taken aback by the abruptness of the inquiry, Will responded with candor. "Ben Buck wants to extend his right to vote Marcie's stock for two years. He'll pay well."

"She could get thirteen dollars a share for her stock. Why should she continue to deal with you?"

"She can't sell her stock till well into next year, when the contract expires. Nobody knows what it will sell for then. Buck'll pay cash right now for her to hold off selling for another two years. Add her dividends to that, and it should be quite a lot of cash for her to live on."

"What does he get out of it?"

"The certainty that he can vote the stock his way."

Belinda nodded in understanding. Her eyes narrowed once more on Will. "What do *you* get out of it?"

"Why, nothing, of course. I work for GUA."

"But you said Ben Buck was buying it personally. That isn't the same as GUA."

Will was stopped momentarily as much by the dark almond-shaped eyes as by the intuitive shrewdness of the perception. "Yes, that's true. If GUA held the voting rights or owned the stock itself, the stock couldn't be voted at all. Let's just say I think it's important that Buck continue to hold those voting rights and control GUA." Will was floundering in the face of Belinda's logic. He was very conscious of how attractive she was. "Does that answer the question?"

"No."

"Then I . . ."

"It just seems odd to me that the only person Marcie and I know connected with the company should want to meet with her to do a favor for someone else."

Will turned to Marcie, who had been sitting quietly, relying on her friend to guard her interests. "I told Buck I had met you, so he asked me to speak to you. There really is no grand plot here."

She smiled trustingly. "Belinda's very suspicious about people."

"And you should be, too," Belinda advised. "You're a very rich woman. People will try to take advantage of you." Her eyes shifted to Will, and he felt his breath catch.

A few minutes later, he couldn't help but feel pleased when Marcie announced she had an appointment to keep uptown and left him alone with Belinda, who had just ordered a second cup of coffee.

"I instinctively like you, Will," Belinda said honestly. "You were the only one at Carla's that night who wasn't a bore and a half. As a matter of fact, when I heard you had broken up with her, I tried to call you. But you must have already moved out of the city."

"That would have been a considerable inducement to come back," he said, intending to convey sincerity as well as gallantry.

"Even more so, when I tell you how horny I was at the time. I had just sent my Russian sculptor back to his wife. On the one hand, he kept wanting to be told how great an artist he was—and he was lousy. And, on the other hand, he kept wanting to be told how great a lover he was . . . and he was even lousier at that." She laughed. "My parents are Russian. I think Dimitri was my 'roots' period."

"I was into the Sierra Club type around then. Just out to Colorado. The scenery got to me. They had to be natural, earthy.

They didn't wear bras, but I seem to remember a lot of fumbling with backpack straps."

He recalled how Donna had early intrigued him because she was so different from the parade of such young women. Now, refusing to be satisfied with the Will Nye he offered on the surface, she sought from him a dedication stronger than he accorded to himself and the ambitions that drove him. Being with Belinda seemed a relief after all that. Quick, sharp, aggressive, she frankly appreciated those qualities in others. While Donna might intrigue him, Belinda was beginning to overwhelm him.

"Oh, God! Get me more than one mile away from Bloomingdale's and I get vertigo," she admitted. "Whenever I was really broke and couldn't even afford a tube of cadmium red and was ready to substitute my own blood for it, I used to go uptown and walk through Bloomie's just to get a sniff of luxury and chic. Like an ex-smoker who keeps maneuvering to get into smoky rooms."

The waitress appeared with the check. Will needed a moment to focus on it; he was experiencing the quickness of pulse, the rush of blood, that intense physical attraction produces.

"I wish I didn't have to leave New York this evening."

"Must you?" Belinda answered. Will could detect real regret—and invitation.

"I should be back and forth all the time now."

"How about New Year's Eve?"

"I really don't know yet. Let's leave it loose."

Belinda's answer was only a slow nod. But for an instant Will felt he was falling into the black infinity of her eyes.

Half an hour later, Will walked along the hall to his hotel room. The door was slightly ajar. On guard, he stepped sideways to shield his body behind the wall, then reached past the door buck to whip the door fully open. A man in a baggy brown suit was sitting in the armchair, fingertips touching, and gazing at him.

"Mr. Nye, I'm Charlie Benke."

"You with Faranco?"

"No, I'm with you. But the boys from Faranco were here."

Benke tossed a small object to Will.

"What is it?"
"Until I discovered it, it was a listening device that would have picked up every phone conversation and anything else that went on in this room."
He tossed Will a second one.
"And that bug was just in case you found the first one."
Will stepped into the room and closed the door behind him.
"Is it all right to speak now?"
Benke nodded. "I've been over every inch of the room, swept it twice with an electronics detector and traced the phone wires practically out to the street."
"I take it you're my detective?"
Will waited for the proof. Benke reached into his back pocket for his wallet. The identification listed him as "Charles Benke, Benke Detective Agency." Will called Masefield, Bevin & Parkhurst to verify that Benke was indeed who he claimed to be. Finally Will sat down on the bed to talk.
"Bill McCormick just said he'd trust you with his life."
Big and broad, pushing fifty, tending to jowls, Benke was a former FBI man with contacts all around the country. He was moved by Will's compliment. "I'm the one who owes *him*. I was up against it once . . . and, well, I owe him. He a friend of yours?"
Will nodded. "I used to work for the Masefield firm. Were you behind my car this morning?"
"A guy who sometimes works for me was. This is one of the people you were tailing."
Benke held up a photo. Slightly fuzzy, it was a telephoto shot of the Faranco limousine driver. "Eddie Leeds. He was a good light-heavy till he couldn't make the weight. Two or three better-class heavyweights put him on unemployment. He's Girard's driver during the day. Do you recognize any of these guys?"
Will leafed through the other photos Benke had brought.
"No, who are they?"
"Faranco's security people. It's set up something like the CIA—intelligence, counterintelligence, field operatives."
Will couldn't believe it. "We're talking about a public business corporation."

"Mr. Nye, businesses run on ideas and information. You stop the other guy from getting yours and you try to get his. Take another look at their faces—for future reference."

Will went through the stack once more, this time slowly. "Not a particularly eminent-looking crowd."

Benke's face twisted in distaste. "They're the bottom of the barrel. Firkling, who runs that operation at Faranco, was a bad cop with a lot of political friends who saved his ass when a brutality scandal was about to break. They let him take early retirement and introduced him to Faranco. He hired guys just like himself for his operation, but they're all employed by a phony corporation with no visible connection to Faranco."

Benke held up a picture of a sallow, furtive man trying to blend into the crowd on the plaza outside the Faranco Building. "The front-desk clerk identified him as the one who looked at your messages. His name's Meredith. An electronics expert who does a lot of work for Faranco. He is not on their company payroll, either. If he gets picked up, there's no link to implicate Faranco."

"I guess they really do take this stuff seriously. Do you know anything about the character who told us he was Desmond with *Newsweek,* but turned out to be Coburn?"

Benke shook his head. "If he's with Faranco, then he's one of the field operatives I told you about, undercover industrial spies."

"And maybe bombers."

"I've seen competitors go after each other's factories, after warehouses stocked with inventory."

"Land of opportunity," Will observed lightly. "All it takes is hard work and explosives, and a man can become a millionaire."

Benke drew a notebook from his jacket. "Besides Craig Merrill they've hired a scheduler who was at GUA till last month and another one of your accounting people who was laid off a few months ago—it's not Coburn. According to my source at Faranco, they've practically turned one room into a mini-operations center. Reports come in from all over the world. They've got a line on your flights and the passenger load as soon as they leave a gate. They seem to want your company real bad."

"The attraction's not mutual. The reason we hired you was to uncover something that might put a block in their way or give them second thoughts."

Benke nodded. "The investigation is divided into two sections: the company and Girard. I've told you what we've come up with for the company so far. And there's also some illegal payments they made overseas, but I understand you know as much about those as I do, which isn't much. The stuff is so secret I don't even think they keep the books in this country."

"Anything on Girard personally?"

"We're having a hard time with that." He raised apologetic eyes to Will's. "A man like that, rich as he is, shouldn't be so tough to do a background on. A man who gets that rich usually wants everyone to know it and be in the limelight. But he's very—'withdrawn' isn't the right word . . . 'private' maybe. Most people are easy to check out because they fill out long forms to get credit cards, insurance and bank loans. Girard doesn't do any of that."

"There are certain known items in his past to start from, aren't there?"

"He graduated Harvard. B.A. with all kinds of honors. All the time he was there the only home address Harvard had for him was a P.O. box in Houston, Texas. His prep school, Carleton, lists a P.O. box also, that one in Norfolk, Virginia. I've had investigators in both cities try to come up with family or more information, but so far no luck."

"What about since college?"

"He just seemed to have a knack for making money. Started a small company and built it up, then started buying up other companies. When the whole conglomerate thing heated up, with takeovers and selling securities to the public, he took off like a rocket. Brilliant, tricky stuff. Nothing wrong with that. But Girard was always ruthless, always just inside the law. It disappointed me."

"What did?"

"No arrests."

Will was startled. "I didn't think there would be."

"That's sure the sort of scandal threat that can give a guy like Girard second thoughts about taking you over. I had a hunch we might come up with an arrest, Girard being so quiet about himself, and so ruthless in business. A mob connection maybe, a fraud indictment. Do you want me to check into his wife?"

Will was suddenly uneasy. He had been offended by an invasion of his own privacy a few minutes before; this seemed more distressing because the woman was a bystander in this fight.

Benke sensed his conflict. His voice softened. "She has to be checked out."

Will thought it over for several more seconds before he finally acquiesced. "Information about the company itself can go right to the lawyers or Pope as well as me. Anything you dig up on the Girards personally goes only to me. I still haven't made up my mind about it."

"I understand."

"What do we do about the guy whose picture you showed me?"

Benke shrugged. "We can only prove that he asked to see your messages. The same with Coburn—impersonating a reporter isn't the same as impersonating a police officer. They didn't break laws. That's the problem, Mr. Nye. There's a thin line. And often it's only scruples that keep you from going over it."

"You make integrity sound like a handicap."

"We just have to work harder. Guys like that tend to take the easy way out. They miss things. We can't afford to. If there's anything out there to find, I give you my word I'll find it."

As Global Universal's phalanx of lawyers and witnesses walked out of the State Division of Securities, they were solemn indeed. Although they were bringing actions in other states, they had been high on their chances of halting the tender offer here, where GUA was incorporated, by relying on the state takeover statute. But the Commissioner would not intervene in their behalf. No one knew why, except J. Stephen Girard, who had bought the man off so far in advance that the hearing had been just a formality.

Then the next day the pendulum swung the other way. In New York City, federal judge Metucci issued a preliminary injunction against permitting Faranco Inc. to commence the tender offer. He agreed to hear arguments in the early part of January for and against making that injunction permanent.

The CAB too indicated it would meet in early January to hear testimony on Faranco's application to acquire control.

Until then, GUA had breathing space.

11

Will Nye spent the days ending the year in marathon phone calls and trips to plan the takeover defense, and a lot of time aiding the local FBI's dogged but fruitless search for possible sabotage suspects within the company. Christmas Eve he flew to Ohio to visit with his folks. The next night he was back in Denver and at his desk. By the time Donna finally returned to Denver, he was wrung out from too much work and too little sleep. He hoped they could put their differences behind them. He needed warmth, simplicity, gentle talk.

He shopped for really good steaks, fresh vegetables flown up from the South and the ingredients for an elegant dessert. There was newly sweet pleasure in examining the properties of a stringbean after hours spent groping through a forest of tricky forays; the selection of a burgundy made the dark specter of figures flitting past guards with fuses and mounds of plastic fade to insignificance. When he finally picked up Donna and drove to the cabin, he had regained some sense of himself as more than a decision machine.

Donna too was tired. She had ferried planes stuffed to the last seat with vacationers. Snacks and drinks overlapped with meals that nearly overlapped with landings; then a quick turnaround and the process started all over again. She sat contentedly by the wide stone fireplace and refused to lift the smallest segment of her little finger to help.

"I'm going skiing New Year's weekend with some friends. We're leaving this Friday. Want to come?"

"No," he answered. He added a dash of mustard to the salad dressing. "With only one leg left, I'll do my best to keep it in one piece, thank you."

"You used to ski, you said. There are a lot of one-legged skiers. They use outrigger skis on their poles."

"There are nuts everywhere. Have a nice weekend." He began tossing the salad.

Her voice softened. "Can't change your mind?"

"About every six months or so I get this terrible nightmare that I'm sliding out of control on an icy slope. That's skiing enough for me."

For a brief moment Will considered asking her to stay with him that weekend, and something—pride, he thought—held him back. Then he remembered meetings set in New York for the thirty-first. After that he remembered Belinda.

Donna spoke up. "Dee called me today."

"How is she?"

"Not too well. She can't seem to get started yet. She says she doesn't cry too much anymore."

"Merry Christmas," Will said softly. Tal had been much in his thoughts over the holiday; pursuit of Tal's murderer had fixed itself in his mind as an obligation of honor.

"Thank you for the gift," Donna said. "I know how busy you are."

He had sent her designer sunglasses; hers had gotten lost on the island. She had sent him a cashmere muffler.

"You've made me feel guilty about forgetting things like that," Will admitted. "And guilty about feeling guilty."

"Hey, I just realized this is a record for me."

Will gave the salad a last toss. "What kind of record?"

"As short a time as we've known each other, it's longer than I've let myself hang in there with anyone in three years."

He placed the salad on the table and stopped to gaze at her as he asked, "How much of that is due to me? How much to a schedule that keeps us apart a lot?"

"I don't know yet. Sometimes you get on my nerves. I suppose I get on yours just as often. But it never seems as bad as separating would be."

"After we argued when I saw you last, I wondered later on why we do it to each other when we have such a short time together."

"We get scared. Not just you. Me too."

"Of what?"

"Did I ever tell you about Amos Taylor?" She was feeling unusually nostalgic.

"No."

"Amos Taylor was my high-school boyfriend."

"Halfback?"

"Quarterback."

Will tipped his head respectfully. "And you were a cheerleader."

"Women's basketball and track."

"Nothing in the fall?"

"Harvest." She sipped her drink. "Amos's father owned one of the best farms in the county. Two months before graduation Amos said we should go all the way, get engaged and get married. He said his father had three hundred and twenty-three choice acres, fifty-seven dairy cows, three tractors, all in working order, and a lot of other things that I can't remember anymore, and that I would fit right in. I said I'd think about it. Graduation day I grabbed my diploma, took the money I'd saved and skedaddled out of town. Funny thing is I really loved Amos. But too many relatives had rights over me all my life. So I always figured someday I would cut out and start to live on my own. I was scared to death of making the arrangement with Amos permanent, of being owned by anyone."

"What happened to Amos?"

"Mary Ellen Sloat."

Will dumped the drained stringbeans into a bowl and added butter. He looked up in inquiry.

"Mary Ellen really *was* a cheerleader. The bouncy kind," she added. "He had her a month pregnant graduation day and married her the week after I left. She's already had five kids, good old Mary Ellen."

"The steaks are ready."

He set the platter on the table and poured the wine. As they both took seats, Will remembered. "You never said what I'm scared of."

"Oh, you're scared of me."

"What's that supposed to mean?" His tone was more belligerent than he intended.

"See what I mean? And that time I didn't even half try."

During dinner Donna entertained Will with anecdotes about the trials and tribulations of being slotted into flights as a replacement for attendants out sick. In January she would be back flying the schedule she had bid on.

"How's the reading coming?" Will asked.

"I've been wrestling with *Moby Dick*." She paused. "I don't understand it."

"Look, you don't have to read it just because I handed it to you."

"No, the book is terrific. What I don't understand is why you said you felt like Ishmael. You remind me a lot more of someone else in the book."

"The White Whale?"

"No." She laughed. "That's Ben Buck. You remind me of Captain Ahab."

Will's face grew dark. "Right down to the peg leg. Thanks."

"That never occurred to me. I meant you're both driven to go after things that seem impossible to other people, and you're willing to give up things that usually satisfy other people. The White Whale got Ahab in the end. That's what usually happens."

"You finished the book?"

"No, I just read the ending to see how it comes out."

"Doesn't that ruin the story?"

"Only if you haven't thought once or twice what it might be like to be Mrs. Ahab."

"If you're trying to convince me I'm lousy husband material, you're not the first." Will had looked forward to an evening of easy companionship. Now it was being transformed into an opportunity for Donna to appraise his character—and his failures. And she was herding him once again between narrowing fences.

"Will, I'm only telling you about myself. You asked a question and then got defensive when I gave you my honest answer. You're afraid of being made obligated by my words, Mr. Lawyer. As a matter of fact, you should feel flattered that I open up to you. I wish you were as open with me about your thoughts and feelings."

"I am. If you've got something specific in mind . . ."

"Just as an example, mind you, we don't have to make love every time we're together. You've been working very hard. You look knocked out. You probably would be just as happy to pass up sex and get a good night's sleep. There's nothing wrong with that. And there's nothing wrong with telling me."

Will's answer was an aggressive, insistent embrace. Later, as she fell asleep, Donna realized that, while the lovemaking had satisfied the physical self Will had no reluctance to share, it had also effectively cut off their discussion.

Early afternoon on the day before New Year's Eve, Owen Clayton called Will with news. Craig Merrill had returned from Africa that morning. New York FBI agents had just questioned him at length about his movements on the days of the crashes, but he had refused to answer.

"Damn it," Clayton exploded, "we can't arrest him without more evidence, and he knows it. He's the only barely warm lead we've got, him and the watches. Part of an identical pocket watch was found in the wreckage of the Zion crash."

"I'm flying to New York tomorrow for meetings. It'll give me the chance to put it to Merrill myself. He isn't likely to disappear again, is he?"

"Our people are going to question him again in the morning. He said he'd be there for a couple of days at least."

"If you need me, Owen, our New York City office will know where to reach me."

Clayton was silent for a moment. Then he said, "Will, don't do anything rash."

"I won't."

Another beat of silence and then, "And, Will, I hope the New Year's a good one for you."

"Thanks, Owen. Happy New Year."

"Colonel Merrill will see you now, Mr. Nye."

Merrill could be the saboteur, Will had concluded during the long, dark hours when the fatigue of work had not weighed heavily enough to seal his mind with sleep. Merrill was a man who saw only the structural purity of a concept—like the polished metal apparatus in the white sterile rooms astronauts are trained in. He could have devised the most savage means for vindication, weighing only its efficacy as engineering and never the appalling "incidental" consequences to the passengers and crew. There had been so many in Vietnam like him. They plotted the war on maps and attacked with pointers and colored pins, and then sent their younger duplicates to locate the coordinates high over cities and jungles, press a button, and return home like commuters. Merrill could have done it, Will thought with certainty as the secretary led him down the hall.

Not personalized in any way, Merrill's small spare office had the atmosphere of a way station. Will wondered whether he was putting off bringing in family photos and small knickknacks until he was permanently ensconced in Ben Buck's office. Was that to be the ultimate vindication?

Merrill stared expressionlessly at Will and said, "You and the FBI seem very interested in my travel plans."

Will took a seat across the desk from Merrill.

Straight-backed and military in the desk chair, the former astronaut continued. "I agreed to see you in order to tell you that I resent your going to my home and distressing my wife."

"And I resent the death of four hundred and eighty-one persons."

"Are you implying I had something to do with it?" Merrill asked tightly.

"Why did you get off 211 in Chicago just before it went down?"

Merrill paused. "I'll tell you the same thing I told the FBI. I took 211 because Bill Benson was piloting. He headed the pilots' local. I went aboard early. If I could convince him the airline needed stronger security measures, then the pilots would get behind me."

"But you had already resigned."

"If company policy could have been changed, I would have gladly stayed." His tone became sarcastic. "You might be surprised to learn that those safety measures would have been important to me whether I left or not."

"What was Benson's reaction?"

"It's damned ironic now. He said the pilots were concerned about skyjacking, but that meant slipping weapons on board. The magnetometers at security checkpoints had put a stop to the problem. Their main concern now was getting the same sort of surveillance at airports outside the U.S."

"So you just got off at the next stop because you wanted to fly on a different-colored plane?" Will couldn't keep the sarcasm out of his own voice.

"My meeting with J. Stephen Girard the next morning was obviously not for the whole world to know about. He asked me to come to New York, to discuss some sort of position. I didn't know what, but all of us on senior staff knew he was interested in Global Universal. It just made sense that fewer people would become aware I was in New York if I didn't arrive on a Global Universal plane."

"And where were you before 519 left L.A. the day it crashed?"

Merrill hesitated. "There might be . . . It has a suspicious appearance—I admit that. The FBI just learned about it and asked me, so there's no point in not telling you. I went fishing for a few hours very early and afterward I stopped off for a minute or two at Los Angeles Airport."

"You what!" Will caught his breath.

"It's not like it sounds. Somebody's car had broken down at the side of the road. He'd have missed the plane, so I gave him a lift to the airport."

"And of course you never got his name or license number."

"Bob something," Merrill said nervously.

"Very fortunate coincidences!" Will spat. "Two crashes, and you're at the airport before takeoff both times. Because of your job, you had keys to every door at our terminals and were the supervisor of a lot of the people working there. A military man too, who's no doubt had a lot of experience handling explosives. Probably still have plenty of friends in the service with access to them. On the first flight you were even 'lucky' enough to switch planes before the one you were on exploded. The most fortuitous coincidences on God's green earth!"

"Not even the FBI suggested I was involved in those crashes!" Merrill was hot with indignation. "The coincidences are just my—my karma."

Will looked at him. "That's your explanation?"

Merrill nodded abruptly.

"Do you remember what you said to me when you learned I had been able to get my friend Tal's name moved up the seniority list?" That angry dialogue had been replayed dozens of times in Will's mind as he sought in it a motive for Merrill sabotaging Flight 519.

"Exactly what I would tell you right now. That tampering with the qualifications required to make the flight deck was flirting with death."

"As you know only too well, Tal wasn't killed by inexperience—he had plenty of experience. He was killed by a bomb." Something clicked in Will's memory. "Do you know Darlene Valentine?"

"We met a few times at—at seances in L.A. . . . attended by a good many prominent people," Merrill added defensively, noting Will's expression.

"I should have known."

Will probed for several more minutes but could elicit no additional information. The telephone rang, and Merrill answered it. He listened and made notes. Will gazed at the few objects on the desk: some papers Merrill had flipped over when Will entered, a clock, a pen, an open calendar-appointment book. The only entry was near the bottom. Will strained to read it upside down, finally making out the words "Securities Gala."

Merrill hung up the phone. "Will, I think you have the mistaken idea that I'd jeopardize my reputation and my family's security, not to mention liquidating hundreds of people, just to satisfy some terrible desire for . . . for . . . I don't know, retribution, let's say. I would have everything to lose and nothing to gain. If you weren't so blindly loyal, you might see that the man with the biggest motive here is Ben Buck."

"What?"

"I admit to being as taken in by him as everyone else for a long time. But think about it for a second. Who's in a better position to plant bombs than the man who's virtually a dictator at the airline? Who profits most from the destruction of superfluous hardware? Every lost plane wipes out millions each year in lease payments to the loan certificate holders and brings in millions more in insurance payments. I only ask you to consider it, Will. You were willing to condemn me because, on the surface, so many facts appeared to fit. At least be open-minded enough to consider *another* suspect with a possible motive."

Will searched the features of the man across from him for the lie that had to be trembling behind them. Will felt his leg muscles bunching and his shoulders hunching forward. His body was poised at the very edge of tolerance, wanting to dive at Merrill's throat.

Instead he flung himself into a standing position and strode in fury from the room.

Will's black rage carried him blindly to Central Park South. He walked past the St. Moritz (where he was registered under the name Abner Boone, to avoid any surveillance) to the garage where he had left his rented car. Fifteen minutes later, he was parked across the street from the delivery entrance of Basehart Abrasives. Fury had aimed him there for want of an alternative. Only now, as the heat ebbed, did he wonder how he could get inside and what the value would be if he did. He had almost convinced himself to return to Manhattan, when he noticed a familiar figure stepping out of a taxi, valise in one hand, attaché case in the other. Coburn, the erstwhile *Newsweek* impostor. The man glanced quickly to either side, then hurried into the alley that led to the rear of the building.

Quickly, Will stripped off his suit jacket and tie, got out of his car, and crossed the street. A Basehart truck had been left near the alley. A nondescript blue parka was on the seat. Will took it. With the parka's collar pulled high, his face was well concealed. He strode toward the building's rear entrance.

Despite the cold, some workmen were eating lunch on the rear loading dock. None paid him any attention as he walked past them, awkwardly climbed the three steps and entered the building.

He found himself in a dingy corridor leading to stairs on the right and a door on the left. Indistinct voices floated down the stairway. He chose the stairs and began to climb, one strained step at a time.

Near the second-floor landing, he began to be able to distinguish words.

". . . Not this time." A high voice, the way he remembered Coburn's.

". . . orders." Heavy voice.

". . . risk my neck . . ." The high voice again. ". . . take credit."

Will came to the landing. He peered through the narrow crack between the door and the jamb. Coburn's back was to him, but Will could see clearly the heavyset man behind the desk with whom Coburn was arguing.

"I run this department," he was telling Coburn. "I'm the only one who deals with Firkling. Don't you think I tell him what a great job you're doing for us?"

"I sure don't. If it's my neck, Firkling should know I'm the one who pulled off the operation."

The bull-faced man at the desk thought about that for a moment. He seemed to decide that Coburn was not to be easily placated this time. "How about if I call him? We can meet him at a diner or something. You can turn the papers over there."

"Fine." Coburn's voice had turned amicable. "All I want is some of the recognition. It was pretty hairy a couple of times back there."

The other man had decided to be cooperative now. "Sure," he said. "You're entitled to that, Ralph." Then he rose and left the room.

Will was in a quandary about what to do next. Noises in the corridor below decided for him. Fearing someone might be coming up the stairs behind him, Will ducked his chin low in the upright collar, swung the door open and stepped inside. Coburn was standing near the window, looking out on the street.

Finding a pack of cigarettes in the parka pocket, Will stuffed one into his mouth and walked into the room.

"Got a light?"

Barely noticing the newcomer, still peering out the window,

Coburn reached into his coat pocket. As he extended the lighter toward Will, the chop caught him at the base of the neck, and he crumpled. Will pulled the limp body over his shoulder and straightened up. Through the window he could see the bull-faced man crossing the street in the direction of a pay phone—Firkling was obviously a cautious man. Almost as an afterthought, Will scooped up Coburn's attaché case.

He leaned heavily to his right as he walked, fearing the extra weight across his shoulder might cause the knee spring in the artificial leg to buckle. At the stairway he let the man drop and, gripping under his arms, began pulling him down the steps. The man's heels made a heavy bumping sound as they clomped down step after step.

Suddenly, Will stopped, nearly at the bottom. Voices. He could hear footsteps getting nearer. There was no door at the first level to shield him. The footsteps stopped. One man seemed to be giving orders to others. Coburn was beginning to groan softly. Will knew now that he could not make it out with Coburn. Half a loaf, he decided, was the better part of valor. He dropped the body onto the step, pulled up his collar and strode toward the rear exit.

"Hey, you!"

Will continued to walk, as if the speaker could not be calling him.

"Hey, you with the briefcase!"

Will stopped and turned slightly. A group of men stood at the other end of the hallway. The man who had called to him appeared to be the foreman.

"Where are you going with that briefcase?" he said.

"Firkling," Will answered. "He wants it right away."

The foreman nodded. Will walked briskly toward the rear door.

He had almost made it to the street when he heard the door slam open behind him and heavy footsteps coming toward him—they must have found Coburn. He ran, skipping on the good leg so that it landed twice for every time the wooden one did.

The key! He could not locate it among all the change in his pocket as he neared the car door. A glance behind him. Two brawny men were pounding out of the alleyway. The key! Shit, now he remembered—he had slipped it into his shirt pocket. He opened the door, got in and yanked it closed behind him. He fished for the ignition. He turned the key, his foot pumping the accelerator. The car started with a roar.

Ten minutes later he was parked in front of the Benke Detective Agency on lower Broadway.

"He'll be gone by the time the FBI gets there," Benke declared knowledgeably. "And no one there will have heard of him. I can't understand why they continued to use him after his cover was blown."

Will had expected an office out of *The Maltese Falcon,* with a secretary who had seen too many nights with too many men, beat-up old furniture and file cabinets, linoleum floors, and a wide window one story above the street with the firm's name stenciled across it. Surprisingly, that was exactly what he had found, except that the secretary was only a few months out of high school and still fighting acne, and Benke looked nothing like Bogart.

Benke opened a jackknife and forced the lock on Coburn's attaché case. Inside was an envelope. In the envelope was an original birth certificate for a female infant named Ivers. No first name. Parents listed as Warren and Consuela Ivers. The date was May 10, 1925. The city issuing it was Birmingham, Alabama.

"Look at the dried glue on the back. Someone stole it out of the Birmingham city records."

"What could be so important about it? Coburn sounded like he'd just found buried treasure."

"Blackmail? Ben Buck? Your directors?"

Will thought a bit. "Or maybe Faranco is trying to prevent blackmail."

"Maybe something they want to hide about Marie Girard?"

"It *could* be her. The age is about right."

"Well, it's a start." Benke rubbed a knuckle across the end of his large nose. "I could send one of the guys who works for me, but if you don't mind spending a little more for my time, I'd like to follow up myself. This investigation is getting to me. I never worked on a case where so little was known about somebody so well known."

"Whatever you find," Will said, "I want it reported directly to me. No one else."

As he departed Will found himself depressed by the prospect of discovering some long-buried secret about Marie Girard he could turn to advantage. Will had little doubt that once Benke's pit-dog jaws locked onto something, nothing would pry them loose. For a moment Will thought about returning to call off the hunt.

Will had two appointments that last afternoon of the year. First he, Eli Teicher and Teicher's associates reviewed arguments they could muster against the new counterclaim Faranco had just raised in Judge Metucci's federal district court. GUA management, like most targets, had been seeking relief in every possible state court based on the dizzying profusion of state takeover laws—one success anywhere could end Faranco's takeover effort. Faranco was maintaining that the state laws were a burden on interstate commerce and that the federal statute—the Williams Act—took precedence; in effect, tenders were a federal, not a state, matter.

The second appointment had been arranged by Serge Bergheim. After obtaining Buck's enthusiastic approval of a scheme to raise seventy million dollars by refinancing GUA's fleet of 707s, Bergheim had telephoned Will the day before.

"The 707s are all paid off now free and clear," Will had agreed, "with a lot longer life left than anyone could have expected after we bought them. How would the arrangement work?"

"You'd sell seventy million dollars' worth of guaranteed loan certificates backed by your old 707s. With that money you'd redeem the airline's eleven-and-a-half-percent bonds. Interest rates now are a lot lower than you're paying on the bonds—three percent less—so the airline would save over two million dollars a year that would go directly to increase the company's projected earnings. Our firm has never underwritten an airplane lease financing, but we do business with James Kean, who's a real expert in the field. If his firm takes the lead, we'll form part of the syndicate. He had an appointment with his allergist, but he shifted around his schedule to see you tomorrow afternoon."

Like many men who deal in high numbers on the basis of their own intuition, James Kean (which he pronounced "cane") projected a cool, aloof, but not ungracious manner. He was a tall thin man in his fifties, with a florid complexion and gray appraising eyes.

"I'm sorry I interfered with your doctor's appointment," Will said.

Kean shook his head in resignation. "There are so many things in the city air I'm allergic to, one appointment more or less hardly matters."

Out of habit, Will had been scanning the objects in the room. Nearly all the books were securities texts, except for one on the end with Kean's name on the cover as author—*The Troubled Post Office: A Study in the Failure of Authoritarian Economics and Administration.*

"Serge Bergheim told me you used to teach college economics, Mr. Kean. What made you decide to leave?" Will inquired politely.

"I realized I had an unquenchable gambling streak and a desire to be rich. I figured the only place I could indulge both was on Wall Street." A bemused smile flickered briefly across Kean's lips. "The truth is that all of us down here are gamblers, Mr. Nye. Oh, we may conjugate three-syllable verbs correctly once in a while, but we're gamblers underneath. And on a much bigger scale than the workingman with a race track habit."

Despite Kean's flippant small talk, he was, Will suspected, a man whose work was a calling and whose success resulted from careful attention to the most minute particulars. On the low wooden cabinets and the coffee and end tables, Will had noticed exquisite scale models of sea vessels, railroad cars and air transports. When pressed, Kean revealed he had built each one.

"We don't participate in many underwritings at a small firm like this one, Mr. Nye. But we have been privileged to be involved in some exceptional ones." He gestured around the room at the models. "These help me commemorate them."

"From your tone I gather that financing for GUA doesn't fall into that category."

Kean nodded. "This firm would earn a fee, of course, and that's a consideration. Serge Bergheim is a very powerful man in the financial community, and that's another consideration." The tip of Kean's index finger was on his lower lip. "But to be honest with you, Mr. Nye, I find your proposal a messy business. This sort of jerry-built refinancing of odds and ends is aesthetically displeasing. It smacks of desperation and suggests that present management is wasting time better spent elsewhere during this critical period."

"You mean because it will take months to conclude?"

"Yes."

"We're optimistic."

"Overly optimistic, from where I sit. If you'll forgive my saying so, I don't give present management past the end of February."

"Have you seen our projected year-end financials?"

"Bergheim's office sent them over this morning. They're much better than I had supposed. Your securities have been trading so low for so long, but these new figures ought to give them a real shot in the arm."

"So will a refinancing that reduces our debt service by over two million dollars a year. If your clients are holding any of our Series B guaranteed loan certificates, you know how solidly we backed them and how quickly we acted to redeem the proportionate share of them after the planes crashed. We put a lot of pressure on the insurance companies to expedite payment, simply to protect our image in the financial community."

"It was impressive, I'll grant you that."

"Mr. Kean, something is bothering me. When I was in Max Creighton's office the end of last month, he mentioned you and said your two firms often work together."

Kean's expression darkened. "We *did.*"

"Max Creighton's no friend of GUA."

"Nor of mine, anymore."

"Do you mind my asking why?"

"He reneged on giving us the right to sell twenty million dollars of a large debt issue after we worked exhaustively to convince our clients that it was a worthwhile investment. As a matter of fact, it was part of Faranco's recent hundred-million-dollar financing."

"I take it that's not what one old boy does to another old boy down here."

"If I *were* an old boy," Kean said, suddenly bitter, "Max Creighton would never have acted so dishonorably. But he knows very well that my folks are immigrants. I had to work my way through Catholic colleges and ended up here—at a small firm that needs Creighton more than he needs us. But I'm also a patient man, Mr. Nye, with an excellent memory. My time will come, and when it does, Max Creighton will be repaid."

Will found Kean's openness disarming. "A small start could be made by helping GUA beat Faranco. Creighton would lose a one-and-three-quarter-million-dollar fee."

Kean cleared his throat. "Then let's get down to business," he said with enthusiasm.

For a long while the two men hammered out terms and conditions of the proposed issue. It was nearly four o'clock when Kean terminated the meeting. He had some trading to finish off before the market closed for the weekend.

The two men stood up.

"Do you have big plans to ring in the New Year?" Will asked.

Thumbs hooked into his vest pockets, Kean replied, "I have to go to a big charity dinner tonight—I'm on the Board. I spend a good deal of time raising money for worthy causes. But, tonight, I'd be much happier in my study with a good book." Sighing, he gestured toward some liquids in medicine bottles on the cabinet behind him—labeled aspirin and pyrobenzamine. "I'll either get a headache from drinking too much or else sneeze my fool head off from the smoke."

Will and Kean agreed to meet again when their law firms had finished the next phase of the negotiations.

"If management is still around," Kean said, the corners of his mouth curled into a wry grin at Will's obviously misplaced confidence.

Will stood on the sidewalk, hands thrust deep into his coat pockets. All his business was concluded, and he would not meet

Belinda until nine. He tried to decide what to do with his next hours. He felt aimless, as if these few free hours were his margin of error left over at the end of the hectic year. He began walking.

The end of the year. When he was a boy his mother had made him sit down at the kitchen table and think about the year just past and how he could improve in the coming one. He remembered he had had to write down each resolution carefully. This year, he had made his vow early: to unmask Tal's murderer. How easy that had seemed when his thoughts were blood-red with anger! He felt sure that it had to be either Merrill or Girard. But which one? Could they have conspired? How satisfying if, at the bottom of it all, was J. Stephen Girard, the man who was also trying to steal away Will's dream of controlling GUA.

Will imagined him barricaded tonight behind his guards, corporate structures, factories and enormous wealth, contentedly raising a crystal glass of exquisite champagne and toasting his success—unaware that somewhere an avenger, burning with hatred, was forging a righteous resolution to strike him down.

Will found himself approaching the East River. At the lower end of Manhattan the FDR Drive was on stilts, allowing passage beneath to the river. A city blessed by water on all sides, New York had chosen to yield up its banks to the automobile, walling in the people. But at South Street a gap in both time and space had miraculously survived, a place where those who cared about such things had lavished love on old buildings and shops and piers and sailing ships.

On a gray winter day, the very last of the year, Will Nye, who had nothing else to do, sat on a bench at the end of the old wooden pier and observed the scene before him: the river that rushed too quickly for a waterway so close to the ocean; the solid security of the Brooklyn Bridge, the miracle hewn out of a man's mind that had taken away the very idea of the water; the ships gliding past self-importantly, as if no man were wise or strong enough to control them; and the edge of Brooklyn on the other side, sweeping around to the ocean—its docks, like fingers, interlaced with the fingers of the river to which it was wed. During these last, leftover hours, Will finally had time to think about such things.

12

"When are you going to pose nude for me?" the bearded painter was saying to Belinda with a grand leer. It was one of those New Year's Eve parties—noisy and so crowded that conversation was nearly impossible. "You may have sold out for the almighty dollar, but nobody looks better doing it than you."

"Simon," Belinda replied lightly, "I'll pose for you when you move your easel and your mind out of the bedroom."

"Ah, but that's where my talent lies," he said, laughing. "You should take advantage of it."

"If only it weren't such a *small* talent—and always still lifes." Simon pouted into his beard. "Besides, I've already promised Will here that I'll pose nude for him."

"What do you do?" Simon asked Will, resentfully.

"Whoever I can," replied Will over his shoulder.

So many people stopped to make conversation that it was a while before Belinda and Will could escape. Allison Hargrove was drunkenly trying to organize a group to go skinny-dipping in the fountain outside the Plaza Hotel. That it was too cold and there was no water in the fountain didn't seem to matter; she was determined to prove that the income tax had not killed off the effete aristocracy. Bob Weingarten invited Belinda and Will to fly to the Jersey shore with him for dinner at either Evelyn's Seafood Restaurant or the Old Mill Inn. Two stoned artists tried to enlist Belinda into giving up dress designing and devoting the rest of her life to a really important project they had just hit upon—putting bodies to the faces on Mount Rushmore.

Will and Belinda pushed through the crowd until, finally, they were near the front door. In a corner, Marcie and Ron were giggling about something. Marcie's face was flushed.

"Do you think they might want to join us?" Belinda asked.

"From the looks of it, I'd say they want to get laid."

She hesitated for a moment and then shrugged her shoulders. "I guess you're right. Why don't we just go off by ourselves for dinner?"

"That sounds wonderful."

Belinda made a quick phone call, then she and Will walked out behind a couple Will had been chatting with: Larry Goldman, a real estate developer, and a blond actress now making a name for herself, Laurie Chock.

Outside, Belinda was subdued. Will had noticed her staring at Laurie's dress as the actress was helped on with her coat. "What did you think of that dress?" he asked.

"It was beautiful," she burst out. "A Bill Blass. God, will anyone look at my things and be impressed like that?"

"Are you wearing one of your dresses?"

"No. They're locked up at night like gold. There's only one of each. Just for the showing. Schactman will make them up when the orders come in."

They had reached the car. Will unlocked the door for Belinda, and just before she stepped inside he asked, "Now that you're finally successful at it, why give up painting for designing?" But she didn't seem to hear him.

Will circled to the driver's side. "Any choice of restaurant?" he asked, and started the engine.

"I just confirmed our reservations at Windows on the World, but if you'd rather go somewhere else, that's fine with me."

"No, that's all right." But Will was put off. She had maneuvered him into taking her to a wildly expensive restaurant, just the sort of behavior that annoyed him about the pack she ran with. Well, so what? She was beautiful and witty and openly sexual. That was enough.

"I asked you a question before. You were a successful painter. What's the reason for the switch?"

She thought a moment. "There was no one reason, but boredom was part of it. My energy was flagging. I needed something totally new. Someone asked me to try my hand at textiles. I loved the fact that a single design would be in thousands of homes. A painting is the only one of its kind. And I could never keep a canvas. If I didn't sell, I didn't eat."

"And I gather you love to eat well."

She failed to notice the sarcasm.

"No matter how well I did, I could never live well enough . . . as well as I wanted to."

"That's rather materialistic for an artist."

"If artists could afford it, they'd live better than anybody. Money is freedom. I want to be able to walk barefoot along the beach at Coney Island and know that I can afford to do it the next day at Cannes. Or spend a year on a painting and then hang it in my own living room."

"That's not much of an aspiration."

She laughed. "When I die—very old and very rich—have them put just one word on my gravestone: 'Rosebud.'" She thought a moment. "Oh, and another thing. Have them take five years off my real age. By that time I'll have had ten facelifts and be lying outrageously about it."

He returned to the point. "An artist is supposed to have more integrity."

They were at a stop light and could look at each other.

"Artists are just more self-centered, not necessarily more honest. Half the time our integrity is simply stubbornness and ego. For me integrity means not being satisfied with less than everything."

"Does that mean one of these days Marcie will be asked to fork up for all your generosity?"

"Marcie is my friend!" she retorted angrily. "Loyalty to my friends means a lot to me."

"I don't doubt that. I just wonder *why* Marcie became your friend."

They pulled into the garage, and the conversation broke off.

For several minutes after being seated, they were silent, looking at the menu, wrapped in their own thoughts. The lights of New York spread everywhere around them like baubles at an Eastern bazaar. Occasionally, without her noticing, Will would gaze for long moments at Belinda's remarkable face. She was magnetic, born for the spotlight on center stage. She seemed to feel highs and lows passionately, and she swept one up in them. Although he took pride in being self-contained, independent, never wanting what was in the power of others to give, Will was very much aware that he wanted her.

A little while after they had ordered, Belinda resumed the conversation as if it had never been interrupted.

"If you want to know why I've chosen Marcie for a friend, I'll tell you. The reason is she's never tried to hurt me. She's grateful for anything one does for her. And she doesn't have any ulterior motives. Nor do I."

"You say that as if you suppose I do."

"Will, for all your open, boyish, faultless style, I always get the feeling you're holding something back. Your mind seems always to be working out the best path to the next objective. You're so smart you usually get away without people sensing it."

"What about you? Aren't you like that?"

"I don't think so. I live on my passions."

The waiter set down the appetizers. Will waited for him to leave before responding.

"Doesn't that just mean we're alike at the core, but our means of getting there differ?"

Belinda put down her fork. "When we met at Carla's dinner party, you were filled with a wonderful fervor. Some little guy with a grocery store had been abused by the Internal Revenue Service. They attached all his money in the bank. His little business was practically ruined. You had taken the case for free—even though you were with a high-priced law firm—and had gotten the government to back down."

"I'm flattered you remember."

"There seemed to be an intense positive power in you. I found it incredibly attractive."

"You shouldn't have. Like a lot of *your* passions, I suspect, the commitment was only skin deep. My enthusiasm probably stemmed from boredom with everything else I was working on."

"And now you're concerned with something more compelling?"

"Much. The thrill of winning. You and I are both hooked by it—in our careers and in our relationships. Earlier, I mentioned integrity. My own definition is simply that it's the line we draw, the place we won't go beyond to get what we want. If the stakes are high enough, and we eventually reach that place, we have to make a choice."

"That's very easy for me. I told you, values like friendship, artistic freedom—they mean a lot. Will, there must be one special friend who means a lot to you. Or are you too ambitious even for that?"

An image of Tal the last time he had seen him flashed into Will's mind. He continued to cut the same piece of meat until the knife edge grated loudly against the plate. Finally he grinned and said, "Now I know why dumb blonds are always so popular."

Belinda's wine goblet halted in midair. "Oh, shit, I said something wrong. I'm sorry, I really am. I've looked forward to this date with you and I didn't want our conversation to be just small talk . . ."

"It's not your fault. Just the wrong time of the year. An odd thing just occurred to me. One of the qualities that drew me to my friend is very much the same as one that draws you to Marcie. He idolized me without reserve."

The atmosphere had grown somber, introspective. Belinda smiled with an entertainer's coyness, trying to restore, repair, the earlier mood. "I may not be many laughs tonight, but how am I doing on depth of character? They don't pay much for it around the massage parlors, but I figured at a posh restaurant like this it might have some appeal."

Will laughed. "You're doing fine," he said honestly. "A little overpowering maybe."

"I have all the charm of radiation therapy. It can be beneficial, but you have to build up a tolerance for it."

"What time is it? We don't want to miss the New Year. I left my watch on the dresser in Abner Boone's hotel room."

Her eyebrows lifted with suspicion. "I knew the New Year was starting off too nicely."

"I'm registered under another name at the hotel," he explained.

"I usually carry a watch in my purse, but I didn't have time to transfer everything to this one."

The waiter was near the table. She asked the time—it was eleven—and, handing him a credit card, requested the check.

Will was dumbfounded. "You can't do that."

The waiter was already on his way to the other end of the room.

"Why not?"

"But that's ridiculous."

"They take credit cards."

"No, paying for me."

"I owe you at least that for standing in as my lawyer with Schactman last week. Call it a fee. You don't think I'd invite you to a restaurant like this and expect you to pay?"

"But it makes me feel like a gigolo!"

She allowed a sensual smile to sneak across her face.

"Be serious," he insisted.

"I have a good income. I can pay my own way, and in this case my guest's way too. Why *should* you pay?"

"It's traditional, you know that as well as I do."

"So's the missionary position, the outhouse and beriberi."

Will laughed. "At least let me take *you* somewhere now. My treat."

Paolo popped the cork at an angle so that it flew high over the stern rail into the moonlit lagoon, shattering the mirror surface into slivers. The huge white yacht was anchored, the Girards the only passengers. A few hundred yards away the lights of the Caribbean island's little port city winked a welcome, and occasional laughing voices skipped across the water to them.

The ship had anchored around noon. A car had been rented, and the Girards had been driven to a charming hotel. They had swum at the beach and sipped cocktails on the patio—potent drinks their hostess had called Merriwether Hurricanes. Marie had been so happy, and that had made him happy. Jamie had thought of buying the little hotel for her, but she became so gloomy at the mention of it that he had changed the subject. Perhaps if it were a surprise, for a special occasion . . . But he was buying her the airline. She would love that. He had never forgotten the joy that had shone from her face so many years earlier, after she had just spent part of their hard-earned money—hers more than his—to buy a seat on the flying boat for the day. That day had been enough for her, she had said. Every penny from then on would be for him. And it had been.

He raised the glass Paolo had poured.

"I can never repay you," he said.

She put a finger to his lips an instant too late to silence him. "To us and the New Year."

It was still early in Denver. Buck had already tried to carouse the New Year in, but cheeriness had avoided him. He had drunk too much, then dropped by Rose's Place and joked with the hookers. Even the young ones, flirting in short nighties, had failed to lift the heaviness.

Now home alone, alternately pacing and brooding darkly in an armchair, he had put in a call to Gunther Velheim in Switzerland. As he waited he sank lower into depression. No new flashes of intuition had struck him, no brilliant thrusts with which to set upon the adversary.

The phone finally rang. Velheim. They were old friends. Many years before, Buck had bought Gunther Velheim's airline to gain entry to and ground facilities in parts of South America. Velheim's Brazilian company owned five percent of Global Universal as a result. The Swiss businessman warmly agreed to withhold his stock from Faranco and the market; he would of course side with his old friend.

One conversation and Buck's spirits had leaped high enough to dance across the mountains outside the wide window. A call to Rose's. He would send a car for some of the girls. Maybe old

Pres and a few others were still looking for some excitement. This was a night for celebrating. Hell, it was a *great* night for celebrating!

At an intimate club high above Central Park South, Belinda and Will danced while candlelight flickered around them. The music was slow and soft, an invitation to hold each other, swaying. The heady smell of her perfume brought back to Will the New Year's Eves of his teen years, when the night carried a license to stay out late and kiss and grope and breathlessly excuse indiscretion. Tonight the cries of "Happy New Year," the multichromatic explosions bursting over Central Park with surprised beauty, the faces pressing flushed around them, once more granted permission, and they kissed. The inner concussion startled them both, and the fire that swept across them, and the sudden weakness—they were too old for such reactions.

"Oh, shit!" moaned Belinda. "Let's go somewhere we can take our clothes off!"

A short time later, in the quietness of Belinda's loft, Will sat at the butcher-block table while Belinda prepared coffee. There had been little conversation in the car: a momentary reticence had set in, a desire to step back for an instant and regain control. She reached up to the rack hung above the island counter in the center of the room and took down the coffee pot.

The conversation that began now was much simpler and more leisurely. They talked about their pasts. He was from Ohio. She was from New York. He had been dependable and learned to be audacious. She had been audacious and learned to be dependable.

The coffee stopped percolating. Belinda rose to fetch the pot. And Will excused himself to use the hall bathroom.

The bathroom door was locked. He tapped against it—no sound answered from within. Will looked down. A dark liquid was leaking onto the carpet.

"Belinda! Come here quickly!"

He slammed his shoulder into the thin central panel. It gave. He reached in and twisted the lock open.

"What are you *doing*?" Belinda was hurrying down the hall. "Oh, my God!"

Marcie Manning lay in a pool of blood. Her wrists were slashed.

"She's still breathing," Will said. He spotted a pair of pantyhose hanging from a towel bar. He ripped them apart and swiftly improvised tourniquets.

He spoke as he worked. "Call the police. Nine-one-one. Have them call the nearest hospital to stand by with blood."

Less than a minute later Marcie, wrapped in Will's jacket, was slung over his shoulder head down to facilitate blood flow to the brain. Two steps at a time he descended the stairs to the street. His car was at the curb. A quarter of an hour later doctors were working over Marcie.

After the rush to the hospital, the long hours of waiting that followed seemed doubly difficult to endure. Finally, the young doctor emerged.

"The only reason she's alive is she was in such a rush to kill herself that the razor cuts were too shallow. The bleeding was slow. If you hadn't found her when you did, though, she wouldn't have made it."

"Any permanent damage?" Belinda asked.

"Scars, sure, but that's all. I'm not a psychiatrist, so I can't tell you what the inner damage is. But I do recognize a bad case of shame for having tried it."

He started to move off. "She's awake if you want to see her."

"Thank you, Doctor."

Belinda pushed open the heavy door. A lamp on the bureau provided the only illumination in the small room.

Marcie lay on the bed, two pillows under her head. Her hair was wet—a nurse had sponged it free of blood. Glucose dripped through an intravenous unit into the bend of her right arm. She looked up and saw Belinda's face peering through the crack in the door. Fumbling, she sought to shove her bandaged wrists below the sheet.

"You okay?" Belinda asked softly.

Marcie's nod was barely perceptible. Belinda turned to Will and motioned for him to follow her. His bloodstained jacket was folded back over his arm. Dried blood patches spotted his clothing. When Marcie saw him, she turned her face toward the window. Belinda moved to the bed.

"I thought you'd want to thank Will. He probably saved your life."

Marcie turned back. Eyes averted, she nodded her thanks.

"The bathroom must be a mess. God, I'm sorry," she muttered.

"That you tried it?"

"Yes."

"But *why*? Was it something you'd been thinking of doing?"

Marcie shook her head. "I just wanted to die."

"Where was Ron during all of this?"

Marcie was silent, biting the inside of her upper lip.

"Did he say something insulting? Was that it?"

Again Marcie's gaze went toward the window. Belinda patiently waited out the silence. In a small voice Marcie finally said, "We were at the Lynes' party. I was having such a good time. I thought he was, too." Her voice trailed off. Then, almost in a whisper, she went on. "There was a very good-looking actress there . . ."

"And Ron left with her," Belinda finished up.

Marcie nodded.

"Oh, honey, you can't let your life be someone else's yo-yo." Belinda's fingertips touched her friend's still-pale cheek.

"All I could think of at that moment was what a misfit I was. So many wonderfully clever, successful people there. Useful people I really admired. If any of them died, the *Times* would have written their obituary, but I knew if I died no one would probably notice till they swept up in the morning."

Belinda's heart was breaking for her friend. "Marcie, you've been through a lot. Better get some rest."

Marcie shook her head adamantly. Now she wanted to talk. "My funeral could have been held in a closet. You're my heir, did I ever tell you that?"

Belinda nodded. "After your mother's funeral. But you're wrong. There *are* people who care for you. I love you very much."

"I get in the way. You spend more time correcting my work than if you did it yourself."

"It's still new to you. You're learning fast." Belinda paused. "You're a good person, Marcie. That counts."

Marcie's eyes reflected her gratitude. "Thank you."

Neither of them could think of anything more to say. After a few minutes, Marcie's gaze fell on her bandages.

"The doctor said I could probably leave in a few days. What can I do about these?"

"Bracelets," Belinda said quickly. "Ricardo can make them up. Wide bangle bracelets."

Marcie nodded, and her eyes dropped. "Don't say anything to Ron, please."

"Not if you don't want me to."

"You could say I took a vacation for a day or two."

"If you want."

"It really was dumb, wasn't it?"

"It really was."

They smiled at each other. Belinda bent and kissed Marcie's cheek.

"Now get some sleep. I'll come by in the morning."

"Thanks," Marcie said once more to Will. He followed Belinda out and then closed the door gently behind them.

At the elevator, Belinda's arm shot out at the button like a punch.

"Damn it! Why does she always fall for the bastards like Ron? He's a good businessman, but a shitty human being."

"I guess if you don't think you're worthwhile, you fall for people who like to keep reminding you."

Belinda was about to answer when, like a car emerging from the House of Horrors at an amusement park, a stretcher table nosed between the far corridor doors. A form was strapped to it. As it cleared the doors, the orderly pushing it noticed that the sheet had pulled away from the chalk-white face. He reached lackadaisically forward and tugged the sheet back over the head. Belinda shuddered and fixed her eyes on the elevator door until it opened and she could escape inside.

All the lights had been left on in Belinda's loft, as if only a breath or an eyeblink had occurred between entrances. Will stared down the long hallway at the splintered bathroom door.

"She was so sad and felt so useless."

"I really thought she seemed happier since coming to live here. I guess everything fell apart for her on the wrong night of the year."

They walked into the kitchen. She fixed eggs and reheated the coffee while Will set the table.

As she put the omelette on the table and took a seat, she spoke earnestly. "You were amazing. I would have fallen apart seeing Marcie bleeding on the bathroom floor."

He shrugged. "You would have managed, if you'd been alone."

"What, heave her over my shoulder and bound down the stairs on one leg, then drive to the hospital like A. J. Foyt? I doubt it."

"How do you know about my leg?" Then he remembered. "Ah, trust Carla to kiss and tell."

"The gang at the beauty parlor could hardly wait for her weekly appointment. It was better than instant replay. You couldn't want better advertising. I'm sold. And I can't wait to see the leg."

"You bring it up enough."

"You mean you ignore it, so I should? Sorry, but it sounds provocative, like a beauty mark in an intimate place. It brings out the poet in me." Her eyes gazed off toward an unseen horizon. "'He limps in beauty like the night . . .'"

Will laughed in spite of himself. The coffee in his cup sloshed dangerously from side to side. He put the cup down and stood up.

"I know my place, lady." He stood up. "Where's the mop and bucket?"

She pointed to a closet. "I'll change into jeans and be there in a minute."

Barefoot, he swabbed the bathroom floor, and she wiped down the walls, the sink and the tub. When they had finished, Belinda turned on the water in the large stall shower and pulled Will under the spray before he could object. Soap in hand, she immediately started to work up a lather on the bloodstains across the front of his shirt.

"What are you doing?" he sputtered.

"Us traditional women love to do our menfolk's laundry."

The water cascaded over them. Her face glistened with the sheen of wetness. He pulled her to him and kissed her. Her lips were warm and slippery.

"Mmmm." She sighed and opened her eyes. "Now I know why we love it."

"But us modern men do our share."

He took the bar of soap and began to move it over the front of her T-shirt. She pulled the shirt over her head. Slick hands slid across slick skin. Her arms circled his neck. Lips again found lips. Clothes fell away. Hands slipped lower. She pulled him down on top of her, pressed him into her. The water beat upon his back and ran down his buttocks and thighs. Their bodies slapped together in urgent rhythm. He heard a strangled gargle deep in her throat, felt her body arch to engulf him and allowed the explosion to shudder in his loins.

Later, in bed, they made love again. This time more slowly, with greater curiosity. She touched the stump, now that the prosthetic leg was off. Then she kissed it. Her hands and tongue moved upward. His senses felt hypnotized by her, drugged. His hands were drawn to every crevice. His mouth hungered to taste the hidden parts of her.

Afterward, propped up on her elbows, eyelids heavy, she spoke.

"Will, I can't afford commitments now, the distraction of loving someone. The truth is I'm probably not very good at it either. Make a pact with me, and it can be terrific for us. Nothing held back when we're together, but no obligations, promises or restraints when we're apart."

He kissed her to seal the pact.

When she fell asleep, he lay with one arm around her and the other behind his head.

Uncharacteristically, Will had spent most of his free time for the past month with only one woman—Donna. He felt reassured, elated, by tonight's confirmation of his freedom and of the pleasure he took in diversity. Earlier he had defined for Belinda the essence of the only commitment he was willing to make—to his career. He wasn't ready—or maybe wasn't cut out anymore—for a commitment to a person. He sought whatever prize society held up before him.

His eyes went to the clock. Five-forty-six. Nearly dawn. Some sleep, and then he would be back on the trail of the bomber. All the facts pointed straight at Craig Merrill. The astronaut's face hung in the darkness above the bed, burning the air like St. Elmo's fire. He would pay.

Will closed his eyes, unaware that the year just past still held two major surprises. When he awoke he would learn that, on a tip, Pennsylvania police and the FBI had raided a farmhouse near Pittsburgh and arrested two men and a woman long sought in a series of bombings of public and corporate buildings across the country. The woman, identified as Susan Harper, was carrying a Social Security card issued in the name of Barbara LaVigne, which matched the name given by a passenger wanted for questioning in the Indiana crash of Global Universal's Flight 211. Also found in the farmhouse were arms and explosives. The suspects denied any knowledge of the aircraft bombings.

In the morning Will would also learn that, shortly before midnight, Craig Merrill had been shot and killed.

13

The metal screen in the window slid up.
"Is this the body of Craig Merrill?"
Will stared at the head exposed through a hole in the black rubber sheet.
"Yes, that's Merrill."
The screen descended. Will was escorted out of the morgue's identification room. The police detective and the FBI agent who had brought Will here were waiting in the office of the Chief Medical Examiner.
"That was Merrill, no mistake?" the police detective, Rovere, queried.
"That was Merrill."
The two investigators shifted in their chairs toward the desk as the medical examiner resumed his seat. Rovere spoke.
"Thanks for doing the autopsy so fast, Doc. What's the story?"
The forensic pathologist opened an envelope and allowed the contents to spill onto the desk top.
"He was killed by these."
The FBI man, Ted Klaver, leaned forward to examine one of the bullets. He turned to the detective.
"It's from a forty-five. Military."

"High-velocity," the Medical Examiner confirmed. He put on his glasses and scanned the report. "Two bullets were found lodged against the interior of his ribs on his left side. A third exited the left side. They entered at various heights on the right. Tore through his organs."

"What time did he die?" the police detective asked.

"Judging by the state of the body and the extent of digestion of the stomach's contents—you did say dinner was served at nine or so and was over by ten-thirty?"

"Yes."

"Around eleven-thirty last night. Half an hour either way."

"That jibes with the time on his watch," the policeman said. "It probably came out of his pocket and smashed when he fell. It reads eleven-thirty-three. The neighbors say they heard shots about then."

The FBI agent interrupted. "Could you let Mr. Nye see the watch?"

A silver pocket watch was extracted from an envelope. Rovere held it by a paper clip through the ring around the winding stem.

"Do you recognize it?"

"Yes."

"Like the one that detonated the bombs on your aircraft?"

He examined the face. Beneath the crushed crystal were the silver hands.

"Yes."

The FBI man stood up and extended a hand across the desk. "Thanks, Doc." Then he turned to the others. "We'd better go back to the apartment. We can drop the watch and gun off at the lab."

"Do you mind if I tag along?" Will asked.

"Clayton asked me to bring you. He's going to meet us there when he arrives from Pittsburgh. We captured a group there that might be involved in the bombings."

Will was still dazed by unalterable facts to which his mind could not quite adjust. The Merrill he knew was a flaming quarry hovering at the border between his conscious and his subconscious, not a bleached white fish of a face bobbing atop a rubber sea.

Will had called the local GUA switchboard after breakfast.

The lone message was from Owen Clayton: "Merrill was shot and killed last night. Contact Ted Klaver, FBI New York office." On the phone Klaver had asked whether Will knew Merrill personally and then requested that he come down to identify the corpse.

Before meeting the others at the morgue, Will had returned to his hotel to change his clothes. As he had approached the St. Moritz's entrance, seeking a parking space, he spotted a car parked nearby. The driver was the man with the newspaper who had not been quick enough in finding a taxi the last time around. His photo had been among those Benke had presented. Realizing that Faranco's troops must be covering all the major hotels in midtown Manhattan and that the car he was driving would be a dead giveaway, Will had sought a parking garage, left the car there and found a rear entrance to the hotel.

He had gone upstairs and changed into a green blazer, gray slacks and turtleneck. He had telephoned Charlie Benke, then had slipped out the same rear entrance.

Now, an hour later, Will and the officers were leaving the morgue. They drove down to Police Headquarters and then back uptown to Merrill's apartment building. Rovere pointed out the place where the body had been found, around the corner from the entrance. No one had witnessed the killing itself. The body sprawl was still outlined in chalk on the sidewalk. Splotches of blood were visible within the white perimeter. A policeman lounged nearby, posted to guard the site. He advised Rovere that a .45 bullet had been found and sent down to the lab.

"The girl's upstairs," the detective said. "She should have calmed down by now."

"What girl?" Will was surprised.

"Merrill's girl friend." Rovere's eyes narrowed. "I thought you knew him. I mean not just from newspaper photos."

"I . . . I didn't know he had a girlfriend. The only woman I ever saw him with was his wife."

"Well, he had one all right. Lived with her here. Strange kind of girl, too, especially when you figure he was a celebrity."

Just before they walked away, Will cast a surreptitious glance about him. A man was leaning against a building across the street. Will pretended not to have seen him and continued around the corner and into the apartment house with the detective.

There was no name in the slot below the peephole on the door, only the gold decal reading "3B." A heavyset woman answered the door.

"How is she?" Klaver asked.

"Better. You can try speaking to her now."

Will was the last one into the apartment. Simple, unadorned, utilitarian. Furniture rented or sublet with the place.

A pale frightened face jerked up from the brown velvet sofa as they entered the living room. The dull-blond hair was plaited into a single braid that fell forward across one shoulder. She wore a gray wool hand-knit sweater and darker wool slacks. On her lap was a blue Himalayan cat.

"Miss . . . er . . . Miss . . . Dandelion, we have questions and we want answers."

Klaver was, by nature, a blunt man. He had wanted to be polite, but attaching "Miss" to such an odd name had thrown him. Now he signaled Will and Rovere to be seated. The interrogation was about to begin.

"What'd you want to know?" she responded. The voice was gentle and ingenuous.

"All about Craig Merrill's killing, of course."

She flinched at the statement. Her mouth opened as if to speak, but no sound came from it. The cat gazed up at her. She stroked it. Language seemed difficult for her; several seconds passed before she began to speak.

She was twenty-two, she told them finally. Her real name, Alice Barton, had been abandoned after she quit college two years before. Now she was Dandelion. She and Merrill had met a few months earlier at a lecture he had given in Chicago. A friend had asked her to help with refreshments served after the lecture, and she had nothing else to do that night, so she agreed. She rarely looked at a newspaper or watched a television set. She had heard rumors in high school that, among other vagaries of the factual world other people inhabited, men had walked on the moon. Suddenly, one of them was actually before her. Dandelion had been seized with an irresistible compulsion to meet this moonman, to talk to him. That very night the affair had begun.

"He was like a child," she told them, suddenly displaying an adult woman's awareness of the invisible sinews binding man to woman. "He was so straight. He had never, you know, made it with anyone but his wife."

As an airline executive he could arrange frequently to be in Chicago. When he flew East after Thanksgiving weekend, she had joined him at O'Hare. They had flown to New York together. He had paid for her ticket with cash, so that the charge would not show up on his credit card. He had even switched planes because he was so well known at Global Universal, and so that they could be seated together.

Will was dumbstruck. Merrill had maintained all along he had a good reason for switching planes. Here she was. Will asked about her whereabouts the date of the second airline crash.

"When Merrill went back to California," Will suggested.

"Oh, I was there, too, at a motel. Most of the time he was out doing his family number."

"When did you leave?"

"We were supposed to stay, you know, all weekend, but Cat was here alone and . . . I had had it with the L. A. scene. Besides, we were really into each other's heads, and I flashed having me and his wife in the same city was too heavy a trip for Craig."

Klaver appeared baffled.

Dandelion's wondering eyes fixed on his. "Craig was about to go on a bummer of an anxiety trip."

"Where to?" Klaver's pencil was poised above the pad.

"I decided to split to New York. Craig put me on a plane. We didn't expect to see each other like for a few days, but there was a plane crash or something, and he had to get back to New York that night for business."

"Did you use your own name at the motel and on the plane ticket?" Will asked.

She nodded. "We got to the airport just before my plane took off."

"What airline?"

"A lot of red in the colors, I think."

Many airlines used red in their color schemes, Will recalled. All of them could be checked. She was the person Merrill had claimed to have taken to the Los Angeles Airport that morning, but could not name. She could also be checked out on American's manifest for the Chicago–New York flight Thanksgiving weekend. Her story was the confirmation of innocence Merrill had refused to use, for fear of damaging either her reputation or his own. Will's logic sought the flaw: Merrill could still have set the bomb on the first plane and used her presence as an alibi to switch airlines. But if that were his purpose, would he have gone to such lengths to conceal her presence?

"That plane you took from Los Angeles, was it red only or red, white and blue?"

"Only red, I think."

"TWA?"

Her mouth turned up in the slightest recollection of a smile. "That was it. I remember grooving on how my airplane had its own initials. I like dug the flight. The stewardesses were really into good space."

Rovere spoke up. "You two can reminisce later."

Will picked up the phone and called a friend at TWA.

Klaver twisted back to Dandelion. "Do you mind telling us how you happened to be the one who found the body?"

She took a deep breath and began. "Craig was supposed to come home early from some dinner. We were going to go to Times Square. You know on New Year's Eve at midnight how the ball climbs the pole and . . . like maybe a million people freak out when it lights up Happy New Year? He promised to pick me up by quarter past eleven. I was supposed to meet him downstairs. But I got like really uptight when it got way past that, because he forgot his watch in the morning."

She reached deep into the pocket of her slacks and pulled out a wristwatch. Will recognized the aviator's chronograph Merrill always wore.

"That looks like his watch," Will confirmed.

"So you were downstairs," Rovere prompted.

She nodded.

"Why didn't you wait in the lobby?"

"The hotel was only a few blocks down the street. He'd be walking."

"Why did you shoot him?" Klaver said harshly, hoping to catch her off guard.

Shock and fear flew into her eyes. "I . . . I didn't."

"You were the only one who could have. You must have hidden between parked cars, and knowing he'd have to walk in that direction, you shot him as he passed you."

"No!" The sorrow enfolding her earlier like a soft blanket had been ripped away by animal terror. "I heard the . . . the shots just as I came around the corner. He was on the ground . . . when I saw him."

"Did you see anyone else?"

"No."

"You and Merrill were alone when the policeman who heard the shots ran up."

"That's not what happened."

Her arms were around the cat, and she had begun to rock unconsciously forward and back.

"Was he about to leave you? Is that it? About to leave you and go back to his wife?"

"Oh, no, no. We were really up front with each other and still getting it on like . . . wow. If we hadn't been, I'd have split. That's the time to move on."

The doorbell rang. It was Owen Clayton. He looked more tired and the brown suit even more rumpled than the last time Will had seen him. Clayton had been up all night: a flight to Pittsburgh, interrogation, a flight to New York. He collapsed with relief into an armchair. The other men quickly summarized what had been brought out so far.

Still on the phone, Will began to scribble a note on a scrap of paper. "Thanks," he said, and hung up. He relayed the report. "Alice Barton was on the TWA flight that left Los Angeles only five minutes before GUA 519 left for Denver."

Klaver corrected him. "Someone using that name was on the plane. But even if this girl— Dandelion—really was, we only have her word that Merrill drove her to the airport or that they both weren't at the airport hours before takeoff."

Will asked the young woman if she remembered the name of her motel in Los Angeles. The vague expression lifted a bit and her forehead wrinkled as she strained to comply.

"It was a dynamite violet color . . . I remember that. Oh, and the dude that owned it had these really kind eyes. You could tell he really dug where being in love was at."

When Will tried to pinpoint the address, she promptly replied, "There was a great big football next door, and they served Mexican food inside it, but only with . . . with animal flesh. On the other side was a McDonald's, with a sign saying they'd served billions of hamburgers. It really brought me down to think of all the poor cows they'd killed."

Clayton gestured to gain Rovere's attention. "Can we go in the other room to talk alone?"

Rovere nodded.

Clayton smiled politely at the young woman. "Will you excuse us for a few minutes?"

He led the men into the bedroom. He sat on the edge of the unmade bed and filled them in on the conclusions he had arrived at in Pittsburgh. The weaponry in the farmhouse was definitely from the Alabama army base. But no plastic explosive was found—dynamite, but no plastic.

"None of them would talk, but when I asked Susan Harper, the LaVigne on 211—" he cast a sidelong glance at Will—"and the boobs really are great—when I asked her about there not being any plastic explosive, I hit a raw nerve. She was angry with the sellers, who told her that her budget couldn't cover the price. The plastic was already promised to another group."

Clayton paused, awaiting a reaction. No one spoke, so he continued. "All right, I'll tell you what I think she meant. Exactly what she said—that someone who had possession of the stolen material had it up for sale."

Klaver spoke up. "That means their organization didn't plant the aircraft bombs, because they were outbid for the stuff we know blew it up."

"Not necessarily. One more fact. The leader of the cell, a man named Arthur Prager, was graduated from the same high-school class as our friend in there, Alice Barton. Her file's on record for a small marijuana arrest."

The two FBI men exchanged weighty glances.

"How do you see it?" Rovere asked.

"I can construct a scenario which might be way off base but ties everything into one neat package."

"And puts Little Bo-Peep in there in the middle of it?"

Clayton nodded. "But it's all supposition."

"Try us."

Clayton leaned forward. "X stole a lot of weapons and explosives. X contacted different terrorist groups and offered to sell. Susan Harper's cell was outbid for the plastic by their buddies in another cell of the organization. Barton, alias Dandelion, had recruited Craig Merrill. He was using the organization to retaliate against Ben Buck and all the top brass at Global Universal Airlines."

"But why kill him?" Rovere interjected.

"Two reasons. We were closing in on him, and he was never really one of them. When we had him in custody, they were afraid he would break, like Patty Hearst."

Klaver slapped his thigh. "It fits."

"Let's try it," Rovere offered.

The three law officers filed back into the living room. Will stood silently in the doorway, leaning against the frame. For half an hour the men tried to obtain verification of the ties between Dandelion and Arthur Prager's group. She was shown a picture of him and thought they might have been in high school together. She wasn't sure, she said, because her graduating class comprised over six hundred students.

When Clayton stood up to stretch his legs, Will called him into the bedroom.

"What are you going to do?"

Clayton shrugged. "I'm willing to bet my next paycheck that Merrill was shot with the gun found near him, the forty-five, and that it came from the Alabama arsenal."

"So, like Klaver, you think everything fits."

"Doesn't it? Come up with a better theory. How's this? Merrill was accosted by a thief and was shot when he refused to turn over his money. Some big holes in that one. If I'm right, and the gun that killed him did come from the Alabama supply—sold to radical organizations for their own use—how did a common thief get hold of it? And isn't it a hell of a coincidence that the explosives we're seeking and the murder weapon both came from the same place? Finally, even if I'm wrong about the pistol, no one except the girl was on the street, right?"

The lawyer nodded. A policeman had arrived in seconds. He had scanned doorways and the spaces between parked cars as he ran to aid the victim.

"That pocket watch bothers me. Merrill always wore a wristwatch. His girl friend still has it."

"So he had two watches. Maybe it got to be a fetish after he started using them for the bombs."

"What about Darlene Valentine, did you check her out?"

"She was on *The Johnny Carson Show* last night, and it wasn't a rerun. After that she was at a premiere."

The FBI man let his body slump back against the dresser. "What about my theory that Dandelion killed him?"

"All of that's possible. I just don't know if it's probable. You're drawing a picture of a ruthless political activist. Is that what she is? I don't think she could earn half credit on naming our two major political parties. She's the last of the flower children."

"Want to bet I could dig for a day or two and come up with two or three activist organizations she's connected with?"

"Sure, if you mean they bought a mailing list with her name on it and sent her literature. Or she signed a petition against tuna fishermen killing porpoises or farmers who, I don't know, are unkind to soybean plants." Will sought Clayton's eyes. "Why are you in such a hurry to say she's the one?"

Clayton's gaze did not waver. They had spent a good many hours with each other in the last month. They could be frank.

"My superiors are screaming. The public is worried. And I'm just plain tired. So if it wasn't her and Merrill acting alone to sabotage those planes, it was them working with the Pittsburgh gang."

"Because this Dandelion and Prager happened to have been in the same high school. But you yourself had the feeling Susan Harper couldn't buy plastic explosive."

Clayton's hands flew up from his sides in exasperation. "So I was wrong. She fooled me. She's a better actress than I give her credit for. So's Little Bo-Peep in the living room. The odds are damned good that if it isn't Dandelion and Merrill who did the bombings, it's Harper and her friends—ninety percent sure at least. With over four hundred killed already, would you take chances?"

"What if neither one did it and another plane goes down?"

"Then I guess we'll know for sure."

"You're not the callous type, Owen. It's out of character."

The heavyset man straightened up. "Sometimes you get to the

point where you have no choice." He jerked his thumb toward the living room behind him. "There's too much evidence against her. If she's innocent it will surface as we check everything out. Do you happen to know where Merrill was walking from last night?"

"A dinner at a hotel a few blocks away." Will supplied the name.

"We'll question the agents and the help and check for people who might have been looking out a window or walking on the street. We'll make sure he left alone and no one followed him. Don't worry, we don't go eeny-meeny-miney-mo."

"And you keep backing off from taking a hard look at Girard and company."

"Damn it!" Clayton reacted with annoyance. "Why would Faranco kill off their own guy? That doesn't make sense."

"A falling out? Maybe he knew too much." Will's tone was sharp. "I saw our friend Coburn yesterday, Owen." He related the entire incident in detail, holding back only one point—the attaché case. Will's conviction was strong that its contents did not pertain to the bombings, but mentioning it would have been admission of a larceny.

"Will, industrial spying is about as common as the cold. So far that's all you've got on Coburn—or Faranco. The Pittsburgh group, on the other hand, had weapons from the same cache and a terrorist history. Any reasonable person would believe we had caught the people who killed his friend and hundreds more."

"Are you convinced?"

"So far."

Will shrugged. "I'm not. Or maybe knowing they're caught isn't satisfaction enough. I'll be honest with you, Owen. Maybe it only would have been enough if I could have tied it all to Faranco or if I had been the one to do the catching."

Clayton stared at him with sympathy. "Funny about human nature. A few seconds ago you were wondering whether she might be telling the truth. If she was, then maybe Merrill was innocent, too. But that's a lot tougher for you to accept." He sighed and walked to the phone. "I told you ninety percent was worth going with. Covering that last ten percent of doubt is what gets to you. After I make this call I'll check out Faranco and Coburn."

Clayton made a collect call to Conklin at the FBI's Los Angeles office. He wanted to know if anyone at a violet-colored motel, between a Taco Football stand and a McDonald's, remembered one Alice "Dandelion" Barton. And—oh, yes—it was run by a man with kind eyes who really dug where being in love was at.

Four hours after the news of Craig Merrill's death reached Girard, he was landing at La Guardia. First he would tape an interview he hoped would be used on the news segment of *Good Morning America.* Later he would have a full press conference. By dinnertime, he would be back on the yacht. With him in the limousine driving into Manhattan were Carl Raymond and Jackson Lubeck, Faranco's head of public relations. In the three hours since being prematurely awakened by his boss's phone call, Lubeck had arranged the press conference and revised the press release announcing Grant Eckman as Merrill's replacement. Instead of a line declaring Merrill's respect for Eckman, there was now a short eulogy of "our beloved astronaut and aviation leader, the late Craig Merrill."

Of course, Merrill had been as totally unaware of Eckman's hiring as he had been of the killer lying in wait for him. Bringing in an eminent aviation man like Eckman had been a secret well kept, particularly from Merrill. Eckman's name would be a big boost for Faranco at the CAB hearings.

After Lubeck completed the briefing, Girard sat silently, thinking. Craig Merrill's death had been advantageously timed. The astronaut had undoubtedly served a vital function for the takeover scheme, but his efficacy was rapidly reaching its end. For the next phase Grant Eckman was much more valuable. Girard knew that he could not control Eckman as he could the astronaut, but Eckman was hungry to get his hands on Ben Buck's airline. He was willing to leave the means to Girard.

"You understand how I want the press conference handled, Jack."

"Yes. Several reporters who've tried to interview you over the years were stunned that you'd have one."

"It will be a long time before I do it again. In this case the benefits were too great to be ignored." Girard turned to Raymond. "Now, then, how are we doing on recruiting an insider helpful to our cause high up in GUA management?"

"Very well, I think," Carl Raymond said.

Girard nodded, closed his eyes and silently began to review the points he wanted to make at the press conference. Everything was going so well.

Klaver and Rovere were on their way back to their respective offices when Will picked up his rented car at the nearby garage and drove Clayton to the Faranco Building. He drove slowly so as not to inadvertently shake the green Cougar once again on his tail. After receiving Will's phone call, Benke had placed something in Will's car.

Barred by Clayton from accompanying him up to Faranco, Will spent a few minutes at the lobby newsstand. Coburn's attaché case was gone from the back seat of the rented car when he returned and drove off again. If he was lucky that would call off the hunt.

The party, given by a fashion magazine, was in full swing when Will arrived at the rambling penthouse. Cup of eggnog in hand, he let the people and the conversation swirl about him. Belinda introduced him to two men who he gathered were among Belinda's former—or maybe even present—lovers. Joe appeared to Will to be about six and a half feet of solid muscle. He said very little, smiled and flexed a lot. That seemed quite enough. Darrell looked like a department-store mannequin and (in contrast to Joe) was very articulate, spouting inside jokes that convulsed Belinda, about people who seemed to have only first names and to live in Europe. Will began to feel that all the others there were members of a club about to blackball him. But even more unpleasant was the feeling that he seemed to have become part of a process, the latest model chosen for Belinda's inventory—presentable to others and entertaining in bed.

Why should he be angry? he asked himself. He was happily obtaining exactly the same benefits as she. And perhaps he had chosen Belinda based on his own version of the same criteria.

With that perception he finished off his third eggnog and immediately ordered another. A model whose face seemed reminiscent of dozens of magazine covers remarked lightly, "You must have a hollow leg."

"Yes, I do, knock on wood." Will tapped his lower leg.

"How do you do that?" she inquired, startled.

Will asked the bartender to make his drink a double.

Toward evening Will wandered into the study and watched part of a football bowl game, then caught a news program. The lead story was the death of "famed astronaut Craig Merrill, shot and killed late last night on a Manhattan street." The camera moved in for a closeup of Dandelion as she was being taken in for what was termed "intensive questioning." She appeared frightened and bewildered. The reporter's voice described her as "the married victim's alleged love interest" and declared that the authorities were attempting to link her to suspected terrorists.

Belinda entered the study during the news report. She perched on the wide arm of Will's upholstered chair.

The last part of the story was a filmed news conference with J. Stephen Girard. Admitting he had always shunned the spotlight, Girard declared he was speaking out now because of "grief and rage over the shocking death" of his "dear friend, Craig Merrill." He touched on Merrill's crusade for safety and his concern about uncovering "lapses that caused two airline crashes in ten days at Global Universal." While GUA management was never blamed directly for Merrill's death, an impressionable viewer might well have had his suspicions aroused.

"We are determined to win our battle to wrest control of Global Universal Airlines from a management which declares dividends while its planes are exploding like a string of firecrackers. I am proud to announce that Grant Eckman has agreed to join Faranco. Mr. Eckman was formerly head of the Federal Aviation Administration—the agency charged with monitoring air safety—and of one of the largest airlines in the world. We intend to name Grant president of GUA when our tender offer is successful and we obtain control of the airline."

Will let out a low whistle. Grant Eckman was an impressive name in the industry. Any claim that Faranco lacked administrative experience was now going to be much more difficult to sustain.

"In Craig's name," Girard concluded, "the trustees of the Girard Foundation have voted to establish a one-million-dollar fund, to be known as the Craig Merrill Memorial Fund. Its purpose will be to carry on research in and promote the furtherance of air safety."

A reporter tried to ask a question, but Girard asserted he was too grief-stricken to continue and, head down, left the microphones. The press conference was over.

"That girl with the braid, did she kill him?" Belinda asked.

Will turned off the TV. "What throws me is the girl's personality. I don't think she's capable of the planning and split-second execution the murder required. Unless I'm a total fool about people, take that girl out of a bedroom and she develops a bad case of incompetence. Assuming she's innocent and telling the truth, then she corroborates Merrill's innocence as well."

"You mean it could have been the Pittsburgh group, or anybody."

"It's just as likely to be Girard and his little army who engineered the whole thing, to cover their own tracks."

"Because you don't like him?" she chided. "Do you have any proof that Girard is anything worse than a tough successful businessman?"

"No," he admitted, then remembered something. "Is his wife like him?"

"Marie?" Belinda chuckled. "Hardly. She's warm, very simple and unassuming. I don't think she understands business or really takes any interest in it. She seems soft, but when something is important to her, she becomes quite determined."

"In what way?"

"She wanted to buy a painting I didn't want to sell. She wouldn't be diverted—I tried my best. The painting had personal meaning for me, but I guess it touched something personal in her too. She said it looked like water spurting up a window and then said something like that was once the key to dinner when she was young."

"I don't understand."

"Neither did I. I tried to get her to explain what she meant, but she wouldn't." Belinda turned wary as a thought struck her. "What does Marie have to do with anything? She doesn't participate in her husband's work. I'm very fond of her, Will. If I thought you were doing anything to embarrass her . . . If you want to investigate somebody, stick to those terrorists. Or investigate me—I ran with a pretty radical crowd when I was studying in Europe. But leave her alone."

Will stood up. "I thought I might drop around to see whether the cops have learned anything more about Merrill's murder. After that it's my turn to take you out to dinner."

"If you want, but I thought I'd go home and make dinner with my own two little hands. It should be ready by the time you get back to the apartment."

Will called Clayton at the FBI office and learned he was out. He called Rovere at Police Headquarters, who said they were all there together and Will could join them. The detective dejectedly added, "But if you're looking for assurance that the bombing is over or that we know who killed Craig Merrill, you won't find it here."

"What's happened?"

"No fingerprints on either the forty-five or the pocket watch. The watch didn't even have Merrill's own fingerprints on it."

At Police Headquarters Will joined Clayton in the lounge. That night the FBI man would be flying back to Chicago.

"She's already been released," Clayton said as he allowed the second spoon of sugar to drop into his paper coffee cup. "A woman claimed she had looked out her window just as the shots rang out. She saw Merrill falling and Dandelion come around the corner of the building an instant later."

"Did she appear reliable?"

"Even without the eyewitness, they would have had to let the girl go," Clayton observed. "The cop on the beat showed up only a few seconds after the shot. The forty-five was free of fingerprints, and so was the watch. She would have had to fire the three shots from the curb side of the pavement, wipe the gun clean, then throw the gun and watch away from her without getting fingerprints on them—all before the cop arrived."

"It doesn't sound that hard."

"It is when you aren't wearing gloves and the only clothing you have on is made of wool. You met her. She's a nut for natural stuff: coat, sweater, pants. Wool would leave greasy streaks. The cop searched her carefully—not even a handkerchief on her."

Will thought for a while. Finally he said, "In her case I guess natural products really were better for her health. Have you heard from Conklin?"

Clayton smiled joylessly. "There really is a Taco Football. Out there there's at least one crazy everything."

"And a violet motel?"

"A kind-eyed man too. He recognized Craig Merrill, even without Conklin showing him the photo. Says Merrill and the girl were in the motel room together all morning. Merrill paid him quickly because they were late for the airport. They would have had just time enough to make it. The owner found the receipt. It had the checkout time stamped on it."

"So Merrill might be dead, but he's in the clear as the bomber."

"Yeah, and the New York City cops have a hell of a tough murder to solve. Merrill left the dinner right after his own speech, but just before the head of the New York Stock Exchange spoke. Merrill stopped to buy a newspaper on a corner halfway between the hotel and the apartment building. The newsman says he was alone. And he was alone on the street when he was shot by the weapon found lying beside him." Clayton pulled a sheaf of pages from his jacket pocket. "Here are lists of everyone the police or our people spoke to."

Will scanned the list. Half the participants in the takeover fight had been at the Securities Gala: Serge Bergheim (dais), Bill Tait (Table 23), M. J. Winn of Creighton's firm (Table 11), Samuel Friedman with his wife, Mary, as guests of Carl Raymond (Table 3).

Raymond and the investment banker Murray Eskenazi had gone out separately through the left doorway (two witnesses). The woman in the hat-check room remembered that Raymond bought a pack of cigarettes on the way back in but was unsure of the time. People at his Table 3 contended his absence was only a few minutes. The people at Eskenazi's Table 1 claimed he was gone for less than five minutes as well. James Kean was watching the organization's accountant tally the receipts in an adjoining office. Eli Teicher was just coming in from the men's room as Merrill was leaving through the right doorway (three witnesses). Clarisse Hook, a waitress, saw the astronaut leave and hurriedly asked for his autograph. The Secretary of the Treasury was late coming from the airport to the Gala. He passed Merrill in the lobby and exchanged greetings (11:21 P.M., according to a police escort). The front doorman (Philip Crane) offered to flag a cab for Merrill, who refused and headed north on the avenue all alone (approximate time 11:25 P.M.). John Mortimer, the blind newsdealer from whom Merrill customarily bought his newspaper, said Merrill stopped there at about 11:30 P.M. Merrill mentioned that he would be going down to Times Square in a few minutes to welcome in the new year. He was shot two blocks north. Mortimer was the last person known to have spoken to Merrill.

There was another list of names, apartment dwellers on the block. The only one who knew anything was a Ms. Judith Morgan, the woman who saw Dandelion round the corner just after the shots rang out.

"What about the pistol?" Will asked.

Clayton took a resigned breath. "I get to keep my next paycheck. The serial number matches the missing Alabama stuff."

"Did you arrest Raymond?"

Clayton flashed a scornful look at Will. "On what grounds?"

"Do I have to draw you a picture? The man followed Merrill out of the ballroom."

"People at his table say he was back only a few minutes later with a fresh pack of cigarettes."

"Did you read the list of who they were? All on the Faranco team."

"You mean for the tender offer?"

"You say it as if the tender-offer fight wasn't the motive, or at least tied into everything else. What about Coburn? I'll bet Raymond wouldn't admit ever having heard of the guy, just like when your people interviewed him after we almost caught Coburn at the demonstration in our parking lot."

"Today he not only admitted having heard of Coburn, he brought it up first. He said Coburn had gone to a security officer at one of their subsidiaries yesterday and tried to sell information stolen from GUA, but their man threw him out."

"Threw him out?"

"Raymond says they get a lot of similar offers when they're in a takeover fight, and their people know they won't stoop to that level."

Will was disgusted. "Owen, they followed our car this morning."

"Why didn't you let me know?"

Will's impulsive concealment that morning of the attaché case and the memo in it now appeared foolish and shortsighted. Disclosure would only convince Clayton that Will's purpose all along had been to build a case against Faranco. "So Raymond and Faranco are off the hook."

"Until I have proof against them."

"In the beginning you had a lot of suspects and no firm clues. Now there's a bushel of clues and no firm suspects. What's the next step?"

"Have our people keep following up on Faranco and Raymond. Work on the Pittsburgh group and try to track the route their weapons traveled from Alabama—my gut feeling is that the underground is up to its ass in this. And we'll just keep slogging through investigations on crash victims and suspects." His face brightened. "An interesting lead just came up. We got word that an S. Wojuski was arrested for arson in Chicago. That's pretty close to the 'S. Wojelski' we've been looking for. The rumor is this guy was in California until recently."

Will was depressed. "That's it? Everybody back to the starting line?"

"One less suspect—Merrill."

"That's a rough way to narrow the field." Will rolled forward onto his feet and stood up, his shoulders slumped. "This is a job for professionals. I haven't got the endurance for it. I'm going to step back for a while. With athletes the legs go first. With me it's the emotions."

In her kitchen, Belinda was trying to fathom why, when two of the best-looking women at the party had asked her for Will's phone number, she had been so annoyed that she gave them the number for Dial-A-Prayer. Distracted, she let the Hollandaise sauce curdle and then became furious with herself for not being able to cook as well as she did everything else.

Only later, in bed with Will, was she able to relax and allow the physical sensations to crowd out thought.

Near midnight she rose to go to the bathroom, not bothering to close the bathroom door. Returning, still naked, she stopped at the bureau to run a brush through her black hair. Will stared at her as she stared at herself in the mirror. Her face was compelling, enigmatic in its beauty, as if in some earlier life she had been high priestess of a pagan tribe.

Will recalled that his wife had always worn a nightgown in bed and had been uncomfortable making love with the lights on. When he had once tried to joke about it, she had censured him for his coarseness and pulled away. She had always dressed almost secretively, at a feverish pace, her back to him in the tiny bedroom, until the forbidden areas were covered. He had felt like a voyeur trying to catch a glimpse of her, restricted in intimacy to moments when she was either clothed or invisible.

Belinda turned and glided back toward the bed, her nipples puckered and hard in the cold loft. His senses felt suddenly assaulted by swiftly closing proximity. They made love again. When it was over, he reflected with surprise that the intensity and hunger had been as great as the first time. Although Donna had certainly not lost the power to arouse, with Belinda the sole focus was unrestrainedly sexual; nothing more was asked of him. Talk seemed either foreplay or courtesy. He and Belinda were like Siamese twins joined at the groin.

14

Not normally a magnet for reporters, the Civil Aeronautics Board's hearing room in Washington, D.C., attracted journalists in droves throughout the several days of testimony on Faranco's application for permission to acquire control of Global Universal Airlines. In general the press was favorable to GUA. Bill Tait encouraged sympathetic stories about the widely admired aviation old-timer Ben Buck. And he suggested reporters consider whether size was an economic virtue to be fostered at the expense of all else.

With the CAB members, however, Faranco seemed to be making much better headway. Eckman and the former Secretary of Commerce, Atwater, who were slated to be president and chairman of the Board, respectively, after the takeover, were warmly received at the hearing. Although no firm opinion was expressed by the CAB members, the quickness with which delaying motions were dispatched and the tone of the questioning left little doubt that the members were leaning strongly toward Faranco. Their only hesitation occurred when Al Goetz attacked Faranco's secrecy about the illegal foreign payments. He pressed home that failure to disclose them violated both CAB and SEC rules.

The GUA lawyers agreed that if the reaction of the Faranco team was any test, Goetz had struck a vital organ.

Two days later the issue blew up in GUA's face.

Jack Anderson broke a story claiming that Global Universal Airlines had indirectly made illegal payments to foreign officials in Asia. The purpose had been to remove wildly high fees for landing and for use of the airspace in certain Eastern countries that had made air service there virtually impossible. He accused GUA of duplicity in having done exactly what it now decried Faranco doing.

The article's initial repercussions were predictable. The CAB immediately ordered the hearings reopened to explore the matter of foreign payments. Faranco filed a flurry of court motions. And Ben Buck broke almost every glass unlucky enough to be in his office at the moment he first learned of Anderson's revelations.

Will Nye stormed into the corner office just as one of the last highball glasses was hurtling toward the door. It crashed against the doorframe inches above his head. Will never even paused.

"You lied to me, you son of a bitch! I took you at your word, and you were lying all the time!"

The Old Man spied a Steuben ashtray on the coffee table and dove for it. He flung it toward the illuminated map. It struck just above the map, gouged a hole in the wall and cracked apart.

"Stop acting like a two-year-old and give me some answers fast," Will shouted. "And straight, for a change!"

Buck finally seemed to hear and stopped careering about in search of more glass. Gulping large breaths, he eyed the intruder with hostility.

"I'll give you my fist if you don't get your ass out of here in two seconds flat!"

"Some answers, General! When you offered me a job here, I asked you some hard questions. One of them was 'Have you knowledge of any illegal act or payment made by your company?' Another one was 'Have you failed to report any illegal act or payment?'" Will flung the Anderson story at the chief executive. "It says here you're up to your ears in it, that you approved the overcharges."

"One more word and you're fired!" But a lot of the steam was gone from Buck's threat.

"If I don't get answers, I may have already quit."

His chest heaving, the white-haired man sought a chair and collapsed into it. Will waited for him to catch his breath, but he was having trouble. He struggled to pull a key case from his pocket.

"Pills. In the middle desk drawer." He thrust the keys toward Will.

For an instant, intent on his angry inquisition, Will failed to register what Buck was saying. Then he moved quickly to the front of the desk and inserted the roundheaded desk key into the lock. A small bottle lay on its side near the front of the drawer. Buck motioned heavily for Will to remove a pill for him. He placed it under his tongue. Several minutes passed in silence.

"How long have you been on nitroglycerin?" Will asked finally.

"You're a great one for questions. If it's not one thing, it's another." Ben Buck breathed in again, more deeply than before. "About three or four months. It started way before that, but it only got really bad enough to scare me a few weeks ago."

"I never thought I'd hear you use a word like 'scare.'"

"I shouldn't let myself get carried away like I just did. That's when I feel the strain on the ticker." Buck peered up at Will nervously. "Swear to me you won't tell a soul about this!"

"The stockholders might have a right to know about your health if they're choosing between you and Eckman."

Buck snorted. "This is one issue that prick won't raise. He's had more heart trouble than the cardiac ward at the Medical Center. That's why he retired from the airline industry at fifty-four."

Buck stared at the pile of shattered glass at the base of the far wall. Then he said quietly, "Why do you think I decided to pick a successor? I made it pretty clear that's partly what the Future Planning Committee's about. I would have stepped down this year, but I couldn't shake the feeling that without my reputation up against him, Girard rolls over us like the German Army rolled over France." He fell silent for a moment, a bitter knowledge on his face. "As soon as this Faranco battle is over, I step down, Will. I don't have any choice. Oh, I'll stay on as a director or in some advisory role, but, win or lose, my days of running Global Universal are numbered."

"I don't know whether to believe you," Will said, weighing aloud the large man's credibility. "Somebody once asked me whether I liked you. I said yes, but that I didn't trust you."

"Shows good sense on your part."

Will glanced up. "How sick are you?"

"Not bad. I can do just about everything . . . in moderation. I can't let myself get angry like that, though. I watch what I eat now and cut down on the drinking and try to get enough rest. Thank God I never took up smoking. That would be too much to give up all at once." He tossed a hand upward. "Shit, I'm nearly seventy-five years old, Will. No way around that. I'm lucky to have held out this long. But I want to leave one thing behind me when I resign—a healthy airline that will thrive when I'm gone. Girard will destroy it, because he doesn't understand it. He's a numbers man. He reduces everything to income and sales, routes and dollars. That's important. But keep your eye only on that and passengers will stop buying tickets." Buck's hand made a small circle in the air as he cast about for the precise expression. "Girard has no . . . no *humility.* Sometimes things don't happen just because you choose the right tactics. Eckman is like that, too, trying to bully the world into line with what he wants. A passenger's a fickle lover, Will. People like Girard and Eckman lack sensitivity. They don't know how to put themselves in the other fellow's place. We don't manufacture anything. This business is just people, our people serving all the others out there. Planes are only what we carry them in. How far do *you* think this airline can go under deregulation without that sensitivity?"

Will suddenly seized the last glass on the bar, spun away from the Old Man and heaved it against the far wall.

"Feels good, doesn't it?" Buck grunted.

"You're trying to sucker me in again. 'Just hang in there and keep quiet to give a sick old man his last wish on earth. The future of forty thousand employees and a lot of stockholders is on your shoulders, Will, so just forget I lied to you and to our government.'"

Buck studied the tense young man's face. "I didn't lie about the foreign payments. The trading company asked a certain contract price for clearing our licenses. We paid it. All very normal. All very ordinary. That's all we knew."

"And the day after that their government just happened to yield on a lot of issues you'd been pushing for."

"We didn't get anything more than we were entitled to, and we had no control over how the trading company cleared things. But we knew if they did, it would be worth a lot more than we were paying."

Will's eyes were anthracite black and hard. "There'll be a hue and cry over this, General. Faranco will see to that. And so will opposition parties in three quarters of the countries we fly to. The fact you kept your blindfold on during every dirty transaction won't seem like much of an excuse."

"Shit," Buck exploded, "that's the only way you can do business in a lot of countries. They've done it that way for thousands of years until we decided everybody had to live by our holier-than-thou moral code. Look at how many upright U.S. companies admitted having to give bribes abroad. Damn it, you don't think our top government people didn't know about it! Over there your hand better wash theirs or it'll come up empty."

"Any other deals like this?"

"A few. Just as clean."

"And we have employees all over the world who will have to testify under oath here that they knew exactly what they were buying with those contracts."

Anger surged through Buck again. "Somebody on our side had to be the leak to Anderson! He names names and countries, so it had to be someone high up here, like Jessup or Conway. Whoever the traitor is, I'll find him and hang his balls from the control tower out there. Leaking all that stuff has got to be some kind of crime, Will!"

"What, exercising the right of free speech and refusing to keep quiet about an illegal act?" Will answered with heavy sarcasm. "No wonder it had to be leaked to a journalist."

Buck was assessing him shrewdly. "What do you suggest?"

"List all the payments. Say that they're questionable and may have gone for illegal uses. Say that you always hired local parties to handle local arrangements but that you're listing everything in the interests of honest disclosure. Next, our auditors figure out how much we owe the IRS for deductions we shouldn't have taken—bribes aren't deductible."

"How long can we delay having to reduce earnings?"

"Long enough. In most cases the tax statute of limitations has expired and we owe nothing."

"Okay." Buck sighed. "If you think it's the smart thing to do, draw up a statement or a list, whatever you want."

"First I want to see the files—*all* of them," declared Will sharply. "I'll probably want to speak to people who were involved. And everything goes in the statement, regardless of whether Anderson knows about it yet or not."

"The files are locked up. Eloise will show you where."

Will had the disclosure he had come for. Buck was the type who normally fought interminably to assert actual or professed innocence. But now that word of one payment was out, it was futile to conceal the others.

With a start Will realized that Buck's eyes were fixed on him, pleading for the charity of silence—not about the company's wounds, but about his own, seeking hope in the last refuge of the helpless, pity.

"You can really hold it together for, say, half a year?" Will asked unemotionally. "Not just survive, but do what has to be done?"

Buck nodded.

"And by then you'll announce who your successor will be?" He pressed further. "No games or tricks?"

"I promise you, Will, before God Almighty, that if we beat Girard, not more than a month later I will name the man to follow me. Not more than six months after that he takes my place completely. So help me God."

Will held the little pill bottle up to the light. He turned it slowly, first one way and then the other, peering in deep concentration at the tiny saviors within. Finally he let it fall back into his fist, walked to the desk and dropped it into the still-open drawer. Slowly he pushed the drawer closed and turned the key.

"I am shocked and dismayed by these disclosures."

Judge Metucci waved GUA's affidavits at the plaintiff's lawyers. They had been given ten days to investigate Jack Anderson's charges and submit affidavits. Will had done little else since then but track down questionable transactions.

"The accuser's hands are as dirty as the accused's. I was prepared to give great weight to Global Universal's contentions that their shareholders are entitled to judge between the relative integrity of the two sides in this controversy. Now I say there is little to choose between you. A plague on both your houses."

His attention shifted to Faranco's lawyers. "The court grants Faranco's motion for dismissal. As of this moment the preliminary injunction earlier placed on the tender offer is lifted. Furthermore, Faranco's motion to enjoin any state from interfering with the tendering process is also granted. We find the state takeover statutes an undue burden on interstate commerce. Global Universal's shareholders cannot be prevented by local concerns from selling their property to a bidder who conforms to the dictates of the Willams Act; the federal act has preempted legislation in the field."

The gavel descended.

The CAB quickly followed suit. The Board held that the acquisition would "not be adverse to the public interest" and "not result in a monopoly." Faranco's application for the tender offer was granted, subject only to approval by the White House, because of the airline's foreign routes. The CAB flatly rejected the voting trust proposal, indicating it might revoke its approval completely if Faranco tried to go forward before the President signed. Faranco was a step closer, but it had to sit and wait.

The public's fears about the Global Universal crashes had been set to rest with the capture of the radical terrorists in Pittsburgh. But GUA employees were not so easily lulled. If terrorists *had* been sabotaging GUA aircraft, then others might still be at large. If they had not been, then the real bomber was still at large. GUA flight employees came to work on edge. When they finally left their planes at the end of a work day, they breathed a common sigh of relief at their survival. And the next shift then had to wait out the hours.

A figure with merciless eyes stared at the passengers gathering into a line before the security barrier, placing hand luggage on the X-ray conveyor, then waiting their turn to step through the magnetometer lintel themselves. A German shepherd stood near them, watching, nose testing the air. These airport dogs were bad business; they could sniff a bomb or even the makings of a bomb.

The opportunity had presented itself to strike, to carry out the last part of the plan ahead of schedule. But now it was clear that it would be a mistake. Security was much too tight here in the U.S. Boarding would be safer outside the country. So many airports in Africa and South America, and some in Europe, were lax about security. Out of the country it would have to be, then. But of course that depended on Global Universal—and the plane.

One more plane must go down, one more jumbo 747. But not yet. Once the plan had been set and Global Universal chosen as the target, there was no turning back. But the timing had to be right, the preparations for escape and a new identity all made before the risk was taken. A person with one name would be lost with that last plane. A few hours later and thousands of miles away another would be born.

The figure spun around and strode back toward the airport's concourse.

Ears pricked, alert, the German shepherd stepped through the open frame with her blind master. On the other side of the magnetometer, the GUA Customer Service representative stepped up to escort the man and his Seeing Eye dog down the corridor to the gate their plane was scheduled to leave from.

Although dozens of lawyers were engaged in pursuing existing legal actions or thinking up new ones, an unmistakable lull had descended on the takeover contest, as if two sleek sailing ships racing for the China prize had cut too close to the Doldrums and found themselves becalmed at opposite horizons. The investigations of the crashes and of Craig Merrill's murder also wallowed, making little headway. Will considered himself wise for having stepped back for the time being; they could go on for months, or even years, without a breakthrough.

The first morning back in Denver, Will reviewed Legal Department developments with his deputy, Mel Farber; they were fairly routine. Then, finding himself between the tempest behind and the tempest surely ahead, he decided to use his much freer schedule to turn his attention away from the crashes and the takeover and confront the issues before the Future Planning Committee. In that connection, Lee Conway had requested a meeting. Will was to meet him at the GUA hangar.

The wide entrance doors to the first hangar were closed to lock out the winter wind. Several transports were undergoing maintenance there. Conway was in the adjoining hangar, which contained the painting dock. Standing nearby was a 747 surrounded by a multistory scaffold. Men in spattered coveralls worked along the rails beside the big transport. Will made his way to Conway's side. Every time he saw Conway, Will couldn't help but wonder if this was the moment when Conway would finally confront Will about the short affair with his wife.

"What do you see, Will?"

"The paint's being taken off one of our planes."

"And do you know why the paint's coming off?"

Will shook his head. He was beginning to relax.

"Have you met Boyle, in Keller's division?"

"Yes."

"Boyle took his deadly little calculator out one day and figured that we could save an average of seven dollars in jet fuel on each flight if we removed all but a fuselage stripe, an insignia on the tail and some lettering—that's it. Keller ran to Bannister. He told him how not only did it weigh less, but it was cheaper to maintain—no down time for repainting and easier to detect corrosion. Seven whole dollars! I don't need to tell you Arnold started doing cartwheels. You know the power trip he's on with all the emphasis right now on cost-cutting to goose up profits and make our P and L look better for stockholders. I was sandbagged. Here, look at the sketch."

A silver-skinned aircraft with a minimum of markings was depicted in profile.

"See for yourself, Will. You'll need a magnifying glass to tell it from anyone else's. Painting our planes purple and gold ten years ago was the best publicity this airline ever had. Passenger traffic jumped. Everybody knows we're the purple-and-gold airline. If that's not worth a lousy seven dollars a flight . . ."

Resigned, Conway turned his back on the paint dock. As always, Will found himself put off by the contrast between Conway's boyish enthusiasm and the age lines deepening at eye, forehead and jowl. Yet, for the first time, Will could understand what Helen must have seen in him when they married. His buoyancy was contagious.

He and Conway had never been close and never would be, Will realized, but the relationship would always sustain itself because they were part of something that continued, the corporation, the business. Men learned as boys it was the game itself that was important—the right to keep playing.

Conway led Will to one side of the hangar, where a mock-up section of a 727 had been redesigned to contain three rows of new high-density seating and a galley. The Marketing V.P. explained that he wanted to gain more seating capacity by adding thinner seats and narrowing the aisles, and he wanted Will's support when he presented thc plan. But Conway saw this as only a stopgap measure. Lower fares were inevitable, he felt. The President was pushing for them and for freer competition. It was part of Conway's Future Plan to have GUA take the industry lead in sharply discounting fares—carefully tailoring the discount to attract new pleasure passengers without reducing revenue from business travelers. In addition, Conway wanted more planes.

"I want to be able to fling more frequent flights and more seating capacity against the competition on a route than they can fling against me," he explained. "Flight frequency, that's what dominates routes."

Conway suddenly glanced down at his wristwatch. "I just remembered something. Got a minute?"

Will nodded. They walked across the concrete hangar floor toward a door opening onto the tarmac.

"It's a strange thing, Will. That first day, when we were all so worried, it never occurred to me the Faranco offer could have a good side to it."

Will cocked his head as Conway continued.

"Lately I've gotten to thinking about it in another way. At thirteen dollars a share, I'm worth nearly two hundred thousand dollars. That's a lot of money. And Grant Eckman's not a bad guy. We've always gotten along well. It doesn't seem like he's got a team all picked out to bring in. He's been away from the industry for five years. The only one he's out to get is the Old Man."

They had reached the hangar door when Will finally responded. "You're a director, Lee. What will you do when it comes to a vote?"

Conway's mouth tightened. "Would you believe it, Will, with all the anger and the strategies, it's only just now coming to me that the directors have a real decision to make. I'm really on the line."

Both men understood there would be repercussions no matter how Conway voted. If he voted with Faranco and Buck won, or voted with Buck and Faranco won, he would have voted himself out of his job. Employee-directors rarely voted contrary to their chief executive, but in this case a personal decision was unavoidable. Will thought he read fear on Conway's face.

Conway opened the door. The cold air hit them. They were facing the runways.

"What are we looking for?" Will inquired.

"My wife." Conway glanced squarely at Will. Was it only Will's imagination that Conway was observing his reaction before squinting into sunny skies? After a minute or two Conway spoke with annoyance. "I promised her I'd be here to watch her land. With all the other problems on my shoulders, she seems determined to . . . She's soloing today for the first time."

The white-and-red single-engine Cessna completed a semicircle and then swung into a line leading straight to the runway. The plane glided downward with wings perfectly level, then flared and touched down on target without a bounce.

"That was a hell of a nice landing for a solo flight," Will declared.

"Hey, it sure was." A big smile creased the middle-aged executive's face. "She said she'd taxi over here."

A few minutes later the four-place Cessna rolled up to the hangar doorway. The engine cut out, and the plane's door swung back. Helen Conway sat at the yoke.

"You were great!" her husband shouted as he trotted toward her. "Terrific!"

Her face broke into an enormous smile. When he was beside the fuselage, staring up at her, she said to him, "Now, *that's* what I wanted to hear."

Taking care not to arouse the wariness of the named participants in the race, Will began to develop his own plan for GUA's future growth and for promoting his own candidacy to replace Ben Buck at the company's helm. He would have to find a posture that capitalized on his own attributes the way Conway had. He spent days studying route maps—all the feeder or spoke routes to hub cities where GUA's longer, dense routes emanated from. He pored over the financials. He consulted experts in technical areas. But he was at a loss so far. Realistically, he had to conclude that a lawyer in his thirties, less than a year with the company, did not seem much competition for the others.

These weeks were quiet for Will. One day flowed seamlessly into the next. When Donna was in town, they automatically assumed they would be spending their free time together. Invariably, the first night or two were marvelous fun for them both. Dinners out. Tickets to the Center for the Performing Arts or to see the Nuggets play basketball. Hours of lovemaking. Followed by hours of contentment just to be together—having breakfast, visiting shops, wandering through the art museum. After that Will would begin to grow edgy, suspecting that some commitment was now expected.

Away from her, he would propel himself into a whirlwind succession of comfortable, predictable old lovers and new dates whose personalities rarely matched the looks that had attracted him. Soon, Will would find Donna's image crowding into his thoughts and he would realize how eager he was to see her. Often he would be at the airport to greet her plane.

In early February rumors began to fly that the White House was about to sign the CAB's order. GUA had been quite careful about its contact with public officials, keeping in mind the antipathy aroused by American Airlines' campaign to raise support for its proposed merger with Western in the early seventies. The general feeling then was that private meetings set up with influential officials at the Department of Justice and Transportation and even with members of the CAB had done more harm than good. But a friend of Will's, Peter Kory, was about to be appointed Undersecretary of Commerce by the President. He had not yet been formally named (although the appointment was imminent), and so would not be compromising himself by agreeing to a meeting. Will decided to fly to Cincinnati.

He had given Donna his word he would be in Denver that night when she returned and regretted having to call from the airport servicing Cincinnati to tell her not to expect him. He could hear annoyance in her voice—an unfortunate feminine inability to put priorities in their proper perspective, he thought. And that triggered his own resentment at having his potential freedom limited.

"One night more or less can't be that important," he pointed out. "I'll be back in the morning."

Usually now each sensed the other's sore points early and drew back before getting too close, but this time she refused to.

"Will, you swore to me you'd be here tonight."

"Sorry, but I just can't. Look, I know you like to see me the first night you're back, but I have responsibilities to my job. Besides, I've made it plain there are no commitments."

She took a deep breath. "I was giving you a surprise party. Your friends were invited. Today's February third. Happy birthday, Will."

She hung up.

Will stood with the phone in his hand until he realized he looked as foolish as he felt. Then he took a cab to Peter Kory's address.

In an office overlooking the city, as lights began to twinkle through the gathering dusk, the two men had the last frank exchange they could have until after Kory stepped down as Undersecretary.

When the meeting was nearly over, Will understood that the President was not merely backing deregulation to lower fares to the public. He wanted to make an unequivocal declaration that government was out to end both its intrusion into private business and the power of the unions to extract wage increases that the CAB automatically passed along to the consumer. Within a few days the President intended to sign the CAB order approving Faranco's application. There was no way to change that fact.

"Pete, please understand I don't wish to influence the President in any way . . ."

Out of habit Kory ran his fingers through his dark hair as he suppressed a smile.

"But if he really wants the regulatory process to operate evenhandedly and get the CAB off its fanny at the same time," Will went on, "he might insist the CAB make a decision on the West African routes."

"West African routes?"

"The Administrative Law Judge decided in our favor nearly a year ago. The full Board held its hearing months ago."

"It means a good deal to the airline?" Kory chose between the cigarettes and the pipe on his desk, lighting the latter.

Will had time to select his words carefully. "If the route award comes through *after* the tender offer expires, Faranco gets a fat windfall and a lot of shareholders get a fat shafting."

Kory said nothing. But Will had not expected that he would. Will stood up, wished his friend good luck, and headed back to the airport.

While waiting for the last plane out, Will telephoned Eli Teicher. The last card had to be played. Papers had been ready for weeks. Early in the morning they would be served.

Will thought about phoning Donna, but decided against it. He would call in the morning. In the minutes remaining, he wandered through the airport shops, searching for a gift and trying to frame an apology.

For several weeks now, Donna had refused to let herself think beyond the pleasure she felt being with Will. Perhaps she had tried to rush him the night they had argued in the cabin, she decided. But in the days after Will missed the birthday party she had planned for him—with the relationship never deepening, replaying itself over and over like a stuck record—she began to feel used.

One morning after Will had left the cabin for work, while packing her valise before driving to the airport for a duty flight, she opened one of the bedroom bureau drawers. Inside she found another woman's red bikini panties.

That night Will arrived home to find them affixed to the headboard of the bed with the point of a carving knife.

During this time Will heard from Belinda only once. She telephoned late at night after a long, trying work day. Schactman was harassing her. The new designs seemed uninspired. Her best seamstress had just left her, and none of the replacements she had interviewed seemed to know which end of the needle was for threading and which for sewing. She needed to unburden herself to someone who wouldn't feel let down by her momentary weakness or take advantage of it. At the end of the conversation, Will thanked her for trusting him enough to call. He meant it.

After he hung up, his mind kept returning to their unrestrained sexual bouts and her exorbitant beauty. The seeming finality of Donna's abrupt leave-taking had left him unhappy. But any doubt that it might have caused about the joys of being free and single, the joys of diversity, were quickly erased by these recollections of Belinda.

Samuel Friedman's professional gaze skipped most of the complaint's opening incantations: naming parties, reciting corporate citizenry, asserting the court's jurisdiction, and so on. This new lawsuit had to be GUA's last, futile attempt to avoid the inevitable, he reasoned; he was certain Eli Teicher had no more arrows left in his quiver. Pausing to sip his morning mug of coffee, Friedman reviewed the course of the takeover fight with satisfaction. Although quite complicated, it had run the gauntlet almost exactly as planned and almost exactly on time. The Circuit Court of Appeals had refused to hear an appeal from Judge Metucci's decision. Only the President's signature was needed to permit the final countdown to begin, and that was expected any day. Everything was breaking Faranco's way, including the fact that arbitrageurs had bid up GUA stock to 12 5/8.

As he flipped the pages upward, Friedman's eye fell upon the allegations. An instant later the shock wave hit. He hurriedly turned back to the very top of the complaint. Faranco was not the only defendant in this action. Teicher was also bringing suit against Creighton, Cromwell & Co. Friedman jumped back to the allegations, forcing himself to slow his reading pace and absorb every word. When he was finished, he pressed the intercom button twice. His secretary, a sunny-faced blond woman in her middle years, entered his office.

"Edith, photocopy this for every lawyer working on Faranco. Have them read it at once. I don't care what they're doing. They're all to be in the conference room to discuss it in twenty minutes."

The woman rushed from the room. Friedman picked up the phone receiver and dialed Max Creighton. When the conversation ended a few minutes later, Samuel Friedman had his answer—and his work cut out for him. Creighton, Cromwell & Co. was holding warrants to purchase two hundred thousand shares of GUA stock at twelve dollars a share as a result of an equity financing done many years earlier. No one at the investment banking firm had remembered they were still in existence. The brokerage house might be held to be part of an investing "group" joined with Farnaco to acquire control, and no mention had been made in the tender documents of its stock interest. The stench of apparent fraud might well fill the nostrils of shareholders, of arbitrageurs and, most dangerously, of the SEC. By exercising its option at twelve dollars and tendering at thirteen, the investment banking firm stood to gain two hundred thousand dollars and shift a large block of shares to Faranco—all while acting as the offerer's dealer-manager for a fee that could reach $1,175,000.

The takeover assault launched so confidently two months before was suddenly in real danger of falling apart.

Will in Denver, Teicher in New York and Goetz in Washington were on a three-party conference call.

Eli Teicher spoke. "We brought suit in Washington to avoid Metucci. My bet is the Washington judge will wait for the SEC to decide. He'll try to stay out of it."

Will Nye thought about Teicher's opinion for an instant before replying. "That makes sense. If the SEC rules Creighton, Cromwell's infraction was inadvertent, Faranco will put Humpty Dumpty back together again with an amended filing, whitewash the whole thing and put us back in the hole again. The Judge can just follow the SEC's lead."

Will had a question. "Jenabelle Draper was just confirmed by the Senate as head of the SEC. Which way do you think she'll jump, Al?"

"No one's sure yet," replied Goetz. "She's still too new. She'll probably stay out of it and leave it to staff."

"If only we had something on Girard. Any luck on that front yet?" Teicher asked Will.

Benke had called Will the day before. Frustrated, he had been trying in vain to find leads in Birmingham, Alabama, that could shed light on the birth certificate found in the attaché case.

"Not a thing." Will's voice became rueful. "The last time we had something on Faranco it was foreign bribes, and the ricochet almost took our heads off."

"Now everything's riding on the SEC," said Teicher, "and none of us knows what the hell they're thinking."

Jenabelle Draper treasured Wednesday nights. As she changed into a sheer nightgown she had happily paid too much for at lunchtime, she thought of him reclining on the bed, watching the closed bathroom door as he waited for her to emerge. It was all so new to her, but every time she was with him, the magic was there. She wished they did not have to sneak around like this, but with her chairmanship of the SEC barely begun—the one job she had coveted all her years in government—the risk of scandal in gossip-ridden Washington dictated that she take the most extreme precautions to preserve discretion.

Every Wednesday night, they rented a room at a motel, driving up in separate cars. By 10:30 P.M., she was on her way back to Washington alone, with a lovely glow that would last through the weekend she spent with her husband in the small town where he practiced medicine. There she would play at her third role—dutiful and devoted wife. The role was not new. Fearing spinsterhood, she had married a professional man who would allow her to pursue her own profession. In the beginning there had been some affection, but nothing like what she felt now, with *him*—so handsome and admired, such a principled man.

In the few weeks since this fever had engulfed them, they had never talked about marriage. Just being together, having each other this way, seemed enough. But he had said he loved her. Perhaps someday, if it could be handled without scandal, without anyone knowing what had prompted it, she could ask her husband for a divorce. Once that was granted, maybe then she could even think of starting a new life, so that the magic could be hers always.

She opened the bathroom door and turned off the bathroom light. One small lamp was lit in the bedroom. As always, he was lying on his side waiting for her—smiling and waiting.

"That's a beautiful negligee, but I love you better just the way God made you."

She smiled, seeing the love in his eyes, and let the garment slip to the floor. She lay down on the bed and turned toward him. He put his arms about her naked body.

As his lips moved close to hers, the door was suddenly smashed open. Flashbulbs popped. She screamed. The flashbulbs, brilliant, blinding, seemed to go on for minutes. Finally, when her vision began to clear and the hands allowed her to clutch the sheet around her, the person with the camera was gone. The man remaining in the doorway was her husband.

"We were so careful," she whispered. "I don't see how you could have found out."

"It doesn't particularly matter to me one way or another what you do," he said. The indifference in his voice seemed even crueler than the break-in. "But someone wants a favor. I had to be sure you would deliver."

He reached for the door handle.

"Good night, Jenabelle. Good night, Mr. Goetz."

SEC CLEARS CREIGHTON, CROMWELL OF WRONGDOING

WASHINGTON (AP)—In a decision issued today, the Securities and Exchange Commission cleared the well-known investment banking firm of Creighton, Cromwell & Co. of charges raised in the tender offer fight for control of Global Universal Airlines.

The air carrier had claimed the firm was violating securities law by failing to disclose it held warrants to purchase 200,000 shares of the airline's stock at the same time that it represented Faranco Inc. in the latter's attempt to gain control of GUA. Securities experts agreed that an adverse decision could have placed Faranco's takeover effort in jeopardy. However, the Commission's Enforcement Division ruled today that a simple amendment of Faranco's original filings was sufficient to clarify the matter in light of Creighton, Cromwell's intention to return the unexercised warrants, worth $2.6 million, to the airline.

With the President any day expected to sign the Civil Aeronautics Board's suggested order approving the giant conglomerate's right to tender for a majority of GUA shares, the stage now seems set for the tender offer to take effect after more than two months of legal wrangling. Faranco is expected to announce in the next day or so the new date for the offering period to commence.

GUA BOARD TO MEET

The directors of Global Universal are scheduled to meet shortly to consider whether to recommend acceptance of the tender offer to their shareholders.

The exceptionally bitter battle began in mid-December when Faranco offered to pay shareholders a quarter of a billion dollars for control of the huge airline. The offer was met with angry charges . . .

Al Goetz considered himself a very practical man. He did not fight for lost causes. He salvaged his position as best he could and survived. When, weeks before, it was clear that the CAB would give its blessings to Faranco's efforts, he had decided the war was as good as lost. Not wanting to be part of any mopping-up action, he had discreetly allowed Grant Eckman to win him over ("My conscience will not permit me to undermine the best interests of GUA shareholders by opposing your generous tender offer"). A very handsome deal was set by Faranco for Goetz's role in the GUA of the future. He would be executive vice-president, Eckman's chief of staff. The only thing left for him to do was make certain that by some perverse miracle, Ben Buck did not reverse the tide and win.

One maneuver toward that end had been to shift the use Goetz had originally intended to make of Jenabelle Draper. But the more involved their relationship had become, the less certain he was about how to insure her cooperation. Affection alone would not sway her from a decision she felt it her duty to render. When he explained the problem to Carl Raymond during their strategy meeting, Raymond had smiled and said he thought they could supply the necessary insurance. Goetz had simply to provide Jenabelle Draper's schedule. Only after the incident at the motel did Goetz realize that he too had been trapped by the photos. If Buck were to see those photos of him being intimate with the woman who headed the agency that had ruled against GUA, Buck would draw a connection to a prior betrayal—the leaking to Jack Anderson of GUA's illegal payments scandal. For Al Goetz there was no turning back.

The greatest service he could now render to cement his position with Faranco and demonstrate the extent of his new loyalty was to guarantee that GUA's Board of Directors did not needlessly delay the inevitable defeat by rejecting Faranco's offer. Buck had induced two of the less dependable directors to resign. Of the remaining eleven, seven were business or professional men from outside the company. Of those seven Goetz felt certain that three could now be counted on to vote against Buck. Hodges and Eaton were hardheaded businessmen who would analyze the figures and conclude that thirteen dollars a share was too high a price to decline. Clarkson, the timid old college professor who had feared that the responsibility for the foreign payments might be laid at the Board's doorstep, was now in a sweat over Goetz's insinuation that stockholders might sue directors who voted down a tender which might be in their best financial interest.

With six votes constituting a majority, Goetz needed two more votes in addition to his own. The Washington lawyer decided he required an ally in counteracting Buck's overwhelming influence with other members of the Board. He went to the one person in the company who he was positive would know secrets about some of the directors incriminating enough to force a few votes Faranco's way. In return, Goetz believed he could offer the single reward that person would demand, assurance he would not be fired when Faranco took over.

Pres Frey, it turned out, was as anxious about his own future as Al Goetz was about his and was most relieved when the latter had cautiously approached him. Ben Buck had been very good to him, but the handwriting was on the wall; it was every man for himself. After thinking for a while, Frey told Goetz he could deliver two director votes. One belonged to Edward W. Chaikowski, president of Mid-National Standard Gas Transmission, past chairman of several key committees of the American Chamber of Commerce, pillar of the Catholic Church, Knight of Malta, father of seven, and currently payer of the rent on a Denver high-rise apartment leased to a woman in whose bed he spent most of his spare time while in town. He invariably arrived two days early for a Board meeting and left one day late. Frey had introduced the happy couple after a broad hint from Chaikowski about how ill his wife was and how difficult that was for a man with normal, healthy desires.

The other director Frey thought he could deliver was Lee Conway.

15

Several days before the GUA Board of Directors meeting, Al Goetz's assistant was undecided whether to mention to his boss the CAB's rush request for more information related to GUA's application for an African route. Instead, he went into Madeline Naybaugh's office to talk over his qualms.

Goetz had been acting strangely, and it concerned the diligent assistant, John Rosenthal.

"He's, well, secretive now . . . all the time. And lately he's been stalling on things, sitting on them."

Naybaugh too had noticed that Goetz was preoccupied, but she had chalked it up to anxieties over the takeover—they were all on edge. Yet Goetz had been through a hundred crises without losing his poise. Maybe there was something else.

"Why don't you just handle this one yourself, John? I mean it's no big deal if you just put the material together and send it out."

Rosenthal tugged uncomfortably at his red beard. Certainly he could put it together; he had done it many times. But not on something this important without informing Goetz. Madeline Naybaugh assured him that this time an "oversight" made sense.

"Have you heard anything?" the young lawyer asked.

"Nothing definite. A few rumors that don't add up." And that was all she was willing to say.

Early in the morning of the day the GUA Board of Directors was scheduled to meet, Pres Frey stood at the apartment door, ringing the bell.

The woman who answered it still had sleep in her eyes, and tousled hair. She was about thirty and good-looking, just a touch overweight, as if that were a problem for her and she had to work at dieting. She clutched an apricot-colored robe in front to hold it closed. The chain was pulled tight across the door opening.

"Fran, I've got to speak to Ed. It's something really important. I swear to God wild horses couldn't have dragged me here if it wasn't really important."

There were some shuffling noises inside the apartment, and then the woman released the chain.

A moment later Ed Chaikowski appeared in the bedroom doorway, barefoot, wearing a sleeveless undershirt, and still in the process of pulling up the fly of his black suit pants.

"Jesus, you know what time it is, Pres? The Board meeting's not till ten o'clock."

"It's later in New York. That's where this telephone call came from."

They sat down in the living room. Chaikowski reached forward and extracted a cigarette from the open pack on the coffee table. He was in his fifties and looked older, but in the strong way some successful men get older; the lines in his face lent him authority, as if they had been earned by hard-won experience. He lit the cigarette and sat back.

"You got a call?"

Pres Frey nodded. "I swear to you, Ed, if the call wasn't important I wouldn't come within ten blocks of this building. I mean a man's home is sacred, and this is practically a second home, you and Fran being so . . . so close and all. She worships the ground you walk on, Ed. Did you know that? I ran into her at the shopping center last weekend and she said she'll be grateful to me till the day she dies for introducing her to as fine a man as Ed Chaikowski. I know he's got a wife and family he can't ever leave, she says, him being such a devout Catholic and all, but when we're together it's like we're a family, too, and he's been away on a long business trip, she says. That's why this call really shook me up."

"Who was it from?"

"Once in a while I get a call from the secretary of Faranco. We belong to this association of corporate secretaries and know each other pretty well. Faranco keeps trying to get hold of our stockholder list so they can send their offer and other letters direct to the stockholders and their soliciting firm can telephone. I thought that was why he was calling me. But instead it was someone else from Faranco. Wouldn't give me his name, but he said he had a message for you."

Chaikowski was leaning forward anxiously, puffing on the cigarette and depositing the ash as soon as any appeared. Frey bent toward him. His voice lowered.

"He told me to tell you it would be 'unfortunate,' that was the word, 'unfortunate,' if people found out about you pumping Fran on the side, you being a married man and Martha being so sick and—"

"Shit! Just like that? On the phone?"

"He knew Fran's name, this address, everything. They're ruthless people, Ed."

The hand holding the cigarette was shaking. Some of the ashes fell on the lip of the ashtray.

The bathroom door opened. Fran had washed up and brushed her hair. She had not put on any makeup. As she crossed toward the kitchen, Frey smiled at her.

"You're a picture, Fran, you know that? A Rembrandt picture. How many women in this world look like that in the morning? Right, Ed? Maybe one in a thousand. She's one in a thousand, no, a million. Just looking at you two here together I can see how much she means to you."

Fran smiled happily and disappeared into the kitchen.

"Hey, Pres," Chaikowski cautioned. "She's got enough ideas already. That's all I need, with so much stock in Martha's name." He crushed the cigarette into the ashtray. "Of all the shitty things to happen! Did they say what it was they wanted?"

Frey hesitated, as if torn between loyalties. "They didn't have to spell it out, Ed. They just want to be sure you're voting for the offer. The truth is they probably have it won already without your vote, but they're taking no chances." Frey fell silent and waited for Chaikowski to look up. "No way the Old Man can win, Ed. It tears my heart out—we were so close all these years—but it's over for him. I just wanted to be sure your ass isn't caught in the wringer for no reason."

"Thanks, Pres." Chaikowski was smiling now. "Thanks a lot. I appreciate your coming here."

They stood up and headed toward the door. The woman poked her head out of the kitchen.

"Aren't you going to stay for some breakfast, Pres?"

"No thanks, Fran. I have to get back to the office, get things ready for the meeting of all those important types, like your man here. He's a really important man, Fran, really respected."

Pres Frey found himself dancing little jig steps all the way to the elevator.

The directors meeting was as tightly closed as any that GUA had ever held. The eleven directors were in the Board Room, along with Will, Teicher, Parkhurst, Frey and Frey's deputy, and Natalie Harmon, a capable woman lawyer Will had insisted on putting in the corporate secretary's office as a check against Frey's muddling. Both Harmon and Pres Frey took notes for the minutes. A guard had been posted outside the door. The reporters were allowed no further than the reception area.

The discussion had been going on for nearly four hours, with all the arguments hashed and rehashed, when Ben Buck finally said, "Well, I guess it's about time we put this thing to a vote. Do I hear a motion?"

Crane spoke. "I move for a roll-call vote on whether to accept Faranco's offer."

Bannister seconded.

Buck felt little concern about the actual vote. He was confident about the four inside votes and at least an equal number of outside directors. Eaton and Hodges would vote for the offer, but he had been expecting that. Clarkson was nervously rubbing his hands, so that probably meant he was lost as well. No matter. Buck had almost asked him to resign when he put it to the other two, but that would have left an even number on the Board.

Eight to three. He needed only six votes—five others besides himself. He began to call the roll in the order they were seated around the table.

"Fuller."

"No."

"Crane."

"No."

"Eaton."

"Yes."

"Hodges."

"Yes."

"Dillingham."

"No."

"Clarkson."

A hesitation. "Yes."

The three yes votes right where he expected them.

"Chaikowski."

An even longer hesitation. Buck sought his gaze, but he was looking down.

"Yes."

Three to four. "I didn't hear you, Ed."

Louder. "Yes."

"Bannister."

"No."

"Goetz."

"Yes."

Buck's silence was like a thunderclap. He stood up.

"I've suddenly got a wicked urge to piss."

He moved toward the side of the room, but he kept talking. "You know, it's a strange thing what the need to survive will do to a man. He gets cornered, he suddenly changes his priorities."

Buck pushed open an almost hidden door cut into the paneling. It led to a small bathroom. Then he did an extraordinary thing. He pulled down his fly, stepped into the bathroom just behind the still-open door, and began to urinate. Stunned eyes around the table met and instantly turned aside as the liquid sound rang loudly through the conference room. Buck's voice continued to boom out as well.

"Now, I can understand all the pressures on a man, all the

fears, the temptations. A man tends to mislay little things like honor and virtue and loyalty. He also tends to forget that old friends can be as deadly as new friends. Take me, for instance. If I thought someone I trusted had double-crossed me, well, I'd probably spend every cent I had, use every weapon, just to . . . destroy him." The urine seemed inexhaustible. "Now, some people might think that kind of savagery went out a long time ago, that people today could never be so barbaric."

The liquid chime was diminishing in volume. Gradually it died away. A flush. Then Buck emerged from the bathroom zipping up his fly. All eyes were on his immense bulk filling the doorway.

"I guess you all understand now I'm one of those people who isn't that refined. I would stomp their balls into a meat grinder and serve the hamburgers to their kids."

He sauntered slowly back to the head of the table. "Now, where were we? Oh, yes, Al was about to vote."

Goetz seemed incapable of breathing.

The outside door opened a crack. The guard entered and handed Will a note.

"She said it was urgent," the guard whispered apologetically.

Will peered through the opening to the outside corridor. Lorna, his secretary, was pointing at the note, a wide smile on her face. Will unfolded the paper and read it. He smiled back at her and handed it on to Buck, who glowered at the interruption. But then, reading it, he too smiled.

"This is from our Washington counsel. You'll all be pleased to know that the CAB just recommended this airline be given the West African route. The scuttlebut is the President will sign the recommendation at the same time he signs the Faranco approval." Buck stared at Goetz. "How much did we estimate the route was worth in added net income each year, Al?"

Goetz was all smiles now. "Well, that certainly turns things around, General. That's great news. If memory serves, it's worth seven to ten million in two years. And fifteen to twenty in four years. The higher numbers if the world economy is good."

"So you would say this airline is now worth a lot more than thirteen dollars a share?"

"Well, that depends on whether the President approves the

route award and the U.S. can negotiate favorable treaties with the countries involved and landing rights and—"

Buck's fist smashed against the table. "Yes or no, Al. Are we worth more than thirteen dollars a share?"

"Yes."

"Thank you, Al." Buck turned to Bannister. "How much is the route worth at, say, seven times its annual earnings?"

"By 1981 at least a hundred to a hundred and forty million dollars. Two and a half to three and a half dollars a share."

Buck resumed his seat and allowed his gaze to circle the table slowly. Finally he spoke again.

"There's a motion on the floor. I've lost track of the vote. Why don't we start all over again?"

This time no one voted against the offer.

Lee Conway was the last to cast his ballot, but, hesitantly, he spoke instead, as if honesty about his private acts and feelings were very new to him. "I worked for an office machine company before coming here. My boss was on the take. I was just out of college and didn't have two nickels to rub together. When the roof caved in, he threw the blame on me. That was easy, because the suppliers gave me the envelopes to deliver to him. I knew what was in them but needed the job too much to say anything. Even afterward I kept my mouth shut, because he promised to find me another job. He knew someone here, and I got the job. But that other company has a file on me and in it there's a piece of paper that says I was fired for taking kickbacks."

"And somebody knew about the file?" inquired Buck.

"Until a few days ago I was sure the whole thing was dead and buried." He reached into his inside jacket pocket. "Then I got this in the mail."

He tossed a piece of paper onto the table. "It's a copy of my file at that other company. A note is typed on top telling me to vote for Faranco's offer."

No one reached for the paper.

"Which way do you vote?" Buck asked quietly.

"No," Conway said.

"It's unanimous," Buck announced.

Teicher spoke up. "I'd take one more vote, General, just among us for the time being. Faranco will probably raise its offer. If they come in two and a half dollars higher, do you also turn it down?"

The new vote was also unanimous. Bill Tait drew from his briefcase the version of the press release that fit the just-completed vote and went out to the reporters. No one else left the room.

Buck and Chaikowski spoke privately in a corner for a few minutes. The gas pipeline executive shamefacedly admitted he was seriously involved with a woman—the first time he had strayed in twenty-six years of marriage. Buck asked the name of this rare woman who had proved so captivating. When told she was Fran Mitchell, he clapped a hand on the Midwesterner's back.

"Damn, no wonder you're so starry-eyed. Old Fran's one of the top lays in Denver."

Bewildered, Chaikowski began relating the morning's surprise conversation with Pres Frey. The Old Man's face turned grim as death. Faced with this accusation, Frey admitted he had lied to Chaikowski about the phone call and had been the one who put in a word for Conway at GUA twenty years before—he had kept secret until a few days ago the damning file from Conway's employer. Goetz, however, simply said he did not believe incumbent management could beat Faranco. He resigned from the Board. For them the war had ended, and they left.

Will was given both men's departments; they would be combined with his own to form the new Corporate Affairs Division. He insisted on making some promotions to department head: Farber (Legal), Naybaugh (Governmental Affairs), Rosenthal (Regulatory Relations), and Harmon (Corporate Secretary). The directors approved the reorganization.

And the tumultuous meeting was over.

A few minutes later, as Will passed by an empty office, he glimpsed a large figure at the window. It was Ben Buck, and he was looking down at the building's entrance. Curious, Will walked to Buck's side and gazed in the same direction. Pres Frey, accompanied by a guard, was carrying an armful of personal belongings to his car.

Buck glanced at Will and then down to the pavement.

"Pres and Al were both with me since the war. Poor old Pres

must have been getting awfully worried wondering if my backside was going to be around much longer to kiss." His tone was very gentle and very sad. He turned away from the window, suddenly weary. "How about a drink, Will? It's been a hell of a day."

As they reviewed the day's events, Buck expressed second thoughts about naming a woman to as presently hot a spot as corporate secretary.

"If Natalie can take your pissing performance, she can handle anything," Will said.

Buck smiled mischievously. "Did she mention it to you?"

Will nodded.

"What did she say?" Buck asked.

"She said she wouldn't have missed it for the world." Will tipped his head respectfully. "The opposition was bowled over."

Buck's face became drawn. "It got me out of the room long enough to take a pill."

For weeks, Charles Benke had slogged through Birmingham neighborhoods until they became as familiar as his own Maspeth section of Queens. Each approach had led nowhere: birth, marriage and death records; old phone books; interviews with older residents. Finally, at a loss for any other way to continue the investigation, he began to walk the rows of headstones at every cemetery in the city.

Bushes had grown wild in a corner of a small cemetery on the city's outskirts. If Benke had not been so persistent, if he had not bent the brambles aside to peer at the name carved on the headstone, he might not have discovered the burial place of Consuela Ivers, listed as the mother on the birth certificate discovered in Coburn's attaché case. Consuela Ivers had died on July 7, 1936. Perplexed, Benke had stared at the inscription. He had carefully searched Birmingham death certificates and found nothing. Yet hers was such an unusual name that there was little chance that this was not the woman he sought.

Few plots remained for the cemetery's manager to sell, and he welcomed the twenty-dollar bill Benke offered in exchange for a photocopy of the woman's forty-year-old burial papers. The woman had not died in Birmingham, Alabama, but in Mobile, and her body had been shipped for burial back to Birmingham, where her husband owned a two-grave family plot. The woman's death certificate had been issued in Mobile. All the documents gave the same Mobile address for the husband, Warren Ivers, the man listed as the father on the birth certificate Coburn had stolen from the Birmingham records. The second grave was still empty; the last communication in the cemetery's files was the wife's burial papers.

The next day Benke drove south to Mobile and sought the address. A shopping center stood on the site. He drove on to the repository of the city's records.

Checking the death date listed on Consuela Ivers's death certificate had yielded nothing. The page had been torn out of the book. Somebody—Coburn, probably—was working hard to cover things up, but might have left enough small clues to lead somewhere. For a start the burial papers at the Birmingham cemetery had been overlooked. But if Faranco was behind Coburn, they might have others blocking the trail as well. In any case, Benke thought, he had to be careful; the closer he drew to whatever lay at the end of this investigation, the more people would gather there to stop him.

For the next several days, Benke pursued the tedious routine he had earlier followed in Birmingham. Old records revealed no trace of either Warren or Consuela Ivers. He decided, at that point, to concentrate on the address given in the cemetery papers. For another week Benke searched for anyone who had lived near the Ivers house about the time of Consuela's death. At an old-age home he finally found someone who had lived next door.

Frail and ill, the woman was allowed visitors for only two hours a day. Benke was the lonely woman's only visitor. He would arrive promptly at two o'clock in the afternoon and sit beside her bed in the tiny room. She would pretend lapses of memory or purposely let her reminiscences stray from her topic. Only as four o'clock approached would she yield at last the tiny tidbit of information that would lure Benke back the next day, spinning out her story like a withered Scheherazade.

On the sixth afternoon, after Benke claimed that his employer, an insurance company, was about to recall him because so little information had been gleaned, she disclosed that the name of the Iverses' oldest child was Marie. Her age roughly coincided with the dates on the birth certificate in the attaché case.

The next day she told him the family used to disappear in the winter months and return in the spring.

On the ninth afternoon, Benke showed her a plane ticket north for later that afternoon. Only then did she finally release the one nugget carefully kept from him until all the lesser ones were gone: Consuela Ivers was a working prostitute, and Warren Ivers was her purveyor as well as her husband. The old woman, who had been so loquacious for so long, fell silent. Her fluttering hands lay still and heavy as white marble on the blanket. She had nothing left with which to entice her visitor back, and she knew he would come no more. Benke sat beside the old woman until she fell asleep, and only then did he leave.

Benke used the nursing home's pay phone to call Will Nye. One news story in his file gave Marie Girard's maiden name as Marie Logan. Benke had to prove the connection, but he had little doubt that Marie Girard, Marie Logan and Marie Ivers were the same person. The cover-up was evidently being undertaken to expunge her family taint. But it was not very much of a scandal, Benke and Will agreed. Continuing the investigation did not seem to warrant the cost. Will called it off.

Flying back to New York that night, Benke felt cheated by the inconsequence of what he had spent so much time to discover.

Nine when her mother died, Marie Girard remembered her very well. She was warm and earthy and used to wake Marie up with surprises when she came home very late at night. But most of all Marie remembered that after her death there had been nobody to protect her from her father. For the first year or two, all he did was beat the daylights out of her. After that it got worse. The only place to which she could escape from the pain and the shame of being used by him was inside herself. In her imagination life was always lovely and genteel. Only there could she make believe she was away from people—far out to sea or high above houses and trees, among the clouds.

She pulled herself back to the present. She had been lying on her stomach on the topmost deck of the yacht, watching the sunset. As she sat up and began gathering the few articles spread around her, she remembered that sunset had been a special time when she was a child—the time when she and her little brother could run home and wake her mother and tell her about their day.

Now it was dinnertime that was important to Marie. She would dress carefully, formally, and sit at her husband's side. She would do most of the talking, prattling about her activities, her thoughts. His own concerns were so monumental, she was sure his laughter came because hers were minor and silly. But she would feel so isolated without those moments.

Recently, they were becoming fewer and fewer. Jamie maintained it was because he had been so unusually busy. But she felt different. Despite their love, which she never doubted, they had been alone together too long. As much as they had always denied the need for it, she was convinced the stimulation of other people was now essential if they were not to begin to wear on each other. That was why she had begun to coax Jamie to include others in their once-private dinners and to take her to an occasional restaurant. Twice they had even attended parties for short periods. Despite her trepidation, Jamie had enjoyed himself and been ebullient afterward. So many years had passed that she no longer feared anything would come out. The time had arrived when other considerations were paramount.

As she stepped out of the marble shower and enveloped herself in the billowing towel, she began to consider the Palm Beach charity party. She and Jamie had agreed to the use of their ship. What easier way to break the seclusion of the past than on their own yacht? She would invite one or two of their few friends that night to ease the way even more. She would speak to Jamie about it at dinner.

She cast a quick eye at the clock. He was in the study, already dressed and doing some business things, no doubt—only occasionally would he carry concerns in to dinner with him. But she was late. Naked, she sat before her mirror and began to apply makeup. Her body was still remarkably slim and firm, almost girlish considering her age. Yet when she was a girl, how womanly it had looked, and, she remembered, what a terrible curse that had been.

* * *

West Africa. His hole card. Why had the route suddenly been awarded today? In only two weeks he would have owned Global Universal. No wonder the Board rejected the offer, with a gem like that suddenly dropping into their laps. He could put a damper of sorts on the value of the new route by having Odalu and the others announce their displeasure at the choice. But that would be self-defeating. He would own the airline soon. How then to win back the route? Perhaps they could point out that GUA's control of the route was not a sure thing because exclusive landing rights had been granted to Aéronautique Eur-Afrique et Mondiale, a Swiss air charter service. Faranco's connection to the little company was too well hidden ever to come out.

But all those moves were merely to salvage a disadvantageous turn of events. Thirteen dollars a share, which had looked so grand only a few weeks before, was now clearly inadequate. Girard had to raise the offer. If he failed to act quickly, the market itself might well bid the stock higher in the morning and that could be a real psychological boost for Buck. But how high to raise it? He had hoped to get a feel for the inside numbers and the GUA Board's choking point from that fellow Goetz, but something had obviously gone wrong. Goetz had resigned from the Board and was taking no calls. Well, that meant only that he would have to calculate it himself.

Early in the game Girard had decided that fifteen dollars was the highest he would go. That was close to three hundred million dollars for only fifty-one percent. Yet jumping an even two dollars, from a round number to a round number, gave the impression he might go higher, as if it were an auction. But with no bidder on the other side, he was bidding only against the feeling of the shareholder that it would prove more profitable to sell than to hold out. Maybe he should come down a bit, not offer a round number, make it appear the new offering price had been arrived at after careful analysis of myriad variables. Fourteen dollars and seventy-five cents. That had a good, responsible ring to it. Close enough to fifteen dollars for the shareholder to tell himself it just wasn't worth holding on for the last quarter of a point. Yet that quarter of a point would save Faranco four million dollars. Fourteen seventy-five it would be, then. The announcement would be made before the market opened in the morning.

One way management could be pressured was if its banking contacts started making things harder. Girard had been pleased when Creighton suggested inviting Winstead of Metrobank to the charity party to be held aboard the yacht. Metro was GUA's lead bank, and one Faranco had done little financing with. The expectation of new business from Faranco—or the loss of business when Faranco gained control of Global Universal—might move the man.

Girard liked the idea of the party. Lately he had been getting a bit bored, just the two of them without company on the yacht. At dinner he might raise with Marie the idea of their attending. She would be reluctant because of her fears about what increased exposure might eventually lead others to discover. But now he could assure her that that could never happen. His people had made certain that the past was dead and buried—and would stay that way.

16

Owen Clayton had hardly reached his office after his New Year's Day trips to Pittsburgh and New York when the Teletype had begun clattering additional disappointment at him. Stanislaus Wojuski had been serving a six-month sentence for vagrancy in a San Bernardino jail during both air crashes. This had turned into a bastard of a case, with little easy glory. Clayton had the distinct impression that a lot of his superiors were very pleased to retire from the forefront of publicity. But Clayton was not interested in advancing up the desk-job ladder. He loved the hunt, and the complexity of tracking down this particular killer fascinated him.

Unfortunately, the investigation was not his sole concern. The doctor was increasingly pessimistic. Edna had not been getting any stronger. Mrs. Evans had taken a full-time job elsewhere, and finding a replacement had taken him nearly a month. He had had to drag his body out of bed when the alarm clanged each morning.

But tedious, day-to-day detective work had begun to pay off. Three watchmakers manufactured the silver pocket watch, an exact copy of a famous antique timepiece. The watch found with Craig Merrill was, surprisingly, not a reproduction, as those found in the crashes had been, but one of the few originals, made by a famous London watchmaker of an earlier century. At first Clayton had tried to locate the owner of the watch through collectors, museums, dealers and auction houses. But this particular watch had never surfaced before. The sales records of the three companies that manufactured replicas had had to be laboriously checked by hand by FBI employees, and then the retailers ordering the model checked as well. No leads panned out.

Keeping pressure on Susan Harper had proved more productive. In return for immunity for herself and with an assurance that she would not have to divulge anything about her collaborators in the underground, she had agreed to testify off the record about the weapons purchase.

Two days later a group of FBI and county lawmen had made a surprise raid on a farmhouse off the beaten track in Southern California. No weapons or explosives were found, but the farm's owner had admitted that someone claiming to be an old army buddy had used the place for storage. The farmer had not remembered the man or his confederate, but was willing to rent them, from mid-October to mid-December, the back of the old barn he did not use anymore. "Who wouldn't," he had told the authorities, "when someone's willing to pay five thousand dollars?"

The men who rented were both muscular tough-talking types about average height. The one who had called himself "Skipper" was white and had a Southern accent. The other, who had called himself "Bud," was black. The farmer had never learned their real names. He might never have found out what they were storing if their truck had not broken down while their buyers were waiting at four different motels for the "auction" to begin. This was at the end of November. The farmer would not loan them his pickup truck, but had agreed to drive them from motel to motel with some of the samples they had pulled out of the barn. He gathered from their talk that a middleman had located potential buyers and that none of the buyers and sellers had known each other or their real names. The largest buyers were a woman in her twenties and a man with a big black mustache. Everybody had paid cash, half down and the rest when they picked up their purchases. Over the next few days the two weapons merchants would periodically load up their repaired truck, rendezvous with the buyers and exchange weapons for money. When all the crates were gone, the two men left.

Conklin had arrested the farmer for possession of stolen property and aiding and abetting its sale. After days of questioning, his story had still not changed. He identified Susan Harper from a photograph as one of the buyers. The FBI had already spent hundreds of hours to no avail among the waterfront, construction and transportation trades, checking out Pearse, the tall, dark, mustachioed passenger on 211.

This day Owen Clayton sat in his O'Hare office and decided that his only recourse now was rechecking matters already examined. He flipped a mental coin. Pocket watches won. Clayton placed his files in the locked area, went home, packed a suitcase, kissed Edna goodbye and returned to the airport to slog his painfully weary body onto an airplane for Boston. One of the watch companies was located there. If rechecking its records failed to pan out, he would try the other two, on Long Island and about thirty miles farther on, in New Jersey. Maybe the book on him was right, that he disliked delegating responsibility. On the other hand, the nagging belief that the answer lay in the pocket watch could be tested only if he checked for himself.

Toward the end of a telephone conversation with Bill Tait a few days later, the public-relations consultant told Will an interesting piece of news he had just gleaned from a well-known syndicated gossip columnist. Palm Beach was buzzing about a party to be given on the Girards' yacht. Marie Girard had confided to a few friends, whom she had invited to the party, that she and her husband would attend. Belinda was one of those invited.

Belinda had asked Will to the showing of her collection that night. He was supposed to telephone and confirm earlier in the week but had forgotten. He felt embarrassed making the call the day of the showing, embarrassed and jealous. What if she had made new plans with some other guy? Like that Joe or that Darrell—what a name for a forty-year-old man; it sounded like something chosen to match a shearling coat, Gucci loafers and body jewelry. But Belinda sounded delighted to hear Will could be at the showing. A few hours later Will hopped a TWA flight to New York.

Only when he was in the cab about to drive from the airport to Manhattan and reading the address on the invitation Belinda had sent him did Will realize the hotel was the same one Merrill had been at the night he was killed.

Will arrived too early for the showing, it turned out. A dress rehearsal was on. He waved to Belinda, to let her know he was there, and wandered into the lobby. The door was open to the small office beside the ballroom. Ron Bailey was deep in conversation with Morris Schactman.

Will ambled back out to the lobby and examined the entrance. The Secretary of the Treasury had entered through these glass doors. Somewhere between them and the ballroom, Craig Merrill had spoken to him. Then Merrill had proceeded to the doors and said a word or two to the doorman before walking up the avenue. The doorman was busy now. He had just flagged a taxi for a couple and taken the keys of a black Chrysler from a guest about to register, who had tipped him heavily. Will watched the doorman for several minutes. He double-parked the Chrysler next to a Cadillac. A minute or so later a couple emerged from the hotel's cocktail lounge and got into the Cadillac. As they drove off, the doorman zipped the Chrysler into the space.

Will went out on the sidewalk to have a few words with the doorman, explaining who he was and what he wanted to know about the night of Merrill's murder: Could there have been a car?

"Funny you should bring that up," the burgundy-uniformed doorman replied. "A guy rushed out of the hotel and got into his car right after I was speaking to the astronaut—I didn't remember Merrill's name then, just that he was one of the guys who had been to the moon."

"The man who rushed out, would you remember what he looked like?"

"After all this time? Not a chance. I think maybe the car was one of the little foreign jobbies. Usually I can remember the cars better than the people. You know, a Mercedes, a Cadillac, a red Fairlane. But it's been too long."

"Did the police question you about it at the time? Maybe you gave them a description."

"Nah, they only asked if I saw somebody following Merrill, and what Merrill had talked to me about, and was he frightened when he talked to me."

"Then why can you remember that someone jumped into his car right after Merrill left?"

"Because it was strange. He was back here not fifteen minutes later, giving me the keys to park it again."

Excited now, Will began walking north along the avenue. It was well lit by gas vapor street lamps arching high overhead.

He found the blind newsman's stand. Initially, the old man was suspicious. For months someone had been coming along at night and grabbing a newspaper without paying.

"Damned cops don't do anything. Twenty cents every night. It adds up, but they don't want to know about it."

Will asked whether he had heard a car right after Merrill left him that night.

"I thought the car was going to stop and whoever was in it get out for a paper, he was going so slow. Sometimes they do that, double-park and buy a paper. When it passed I figured he must be looking for a parking place."

A few blocks farther on Will reached the quiet block where Merrill had been murdered. Two apartment buildings shared the block. The entrance to the near one was on the avenue, but even now the doorman was inside. On a cold night like New Year's Eve was, he had doubtless stayed in the lobby as well. The far half of the block displayed no other entrance, because the doorway of Merrill's apartment house was on the side street. Then Will saw what he had suspected. The policeman hearing the shots and hurrying onto this sidewalk would have viewed a solid wall of cars parked along the curb. A car moving along the avenue halfway down the block, a small foreign one perhaps, would have been well hidden from his view. Dandelion would probably not have seen it either, although it was moving in her direction. Moreover, her eyes were on Merrill as she ran to him. The policeman had looked for the killer between parked cars as he raced up the block, but it was already too late. The murder had indeed been accomplished from between parked cars, but not by a person on foot, rather by a man in a car. The murderer had slowed or even stopped for an instant between parked cars, fired, thrown out the gun and the watch, and continued on his way. The killer had been inconspicuous because he had blended into the cityscape.

Will strode across the street to the apartment house where Judith Morgan, the only witness, lived. The doorman rang her on the house phone. She came down to the lobby. In her thirties, intelligent and objective, Will observed. She explained that at the time of the murder she had been having a small party with a few friends to celebrate the incoming year. She heard shots and looked out the window. A moment later a woman rounded the corner and ran up to a man who was lying on the sidewalk. Yes, she remembered an automobile on the avenue, now that Will mentioned it—the only one, as a matter of fact. But it had seemed to be part of normal traffic. She had not really thought of it until now.

Will thanked the woman and walked back to the hotel, deep in thought. He found a pay phone and called the local FBI office. Klaver was out of town. Will refused help from anyone else. He telephoned the local police precinct and left a message for Rovere that he would call again in the morning.

The ballroom was filling up, and Will took a seat. He scanned the room's entrance. The room was a sieve built for ease of access. Two double doors opening onto the corridor. Two single doors on the side wall into the kitchen. A fire exit on the far wall. Anyone could have watched Merrill during that evening and then left when he did. The outer corridor led directly into the lobby. Someone could have been waiting, his car at the ready. Or maybe someone suddenly spotted the astronaut and seized the unexpected opportunity to strike down a moon walker or a corporate executive or a cheating husband. Or what?

There had to be a motive, even if it was one as insane as disliking Merrill's face. But when he limited speculation to rational motives, only one name kept leaping into Will's thoughts: *J. Stephen Girard.* His lieutenant, Carl Raymond, had attended the Gala and left for a few minutes when Merrill did. But why kill Merrill? To clear the way for Eckman? Perhaps Merrill had learned something he was not supposed to.

Girard certainly had the thugs to handle a little detail like murder—half the faces and bios Benke had showed him would not have been out of place on Death Row. Knowing that Merrill's travel schedule coincided with the bombings, the killer had thrown the objects out of the car. If the police and the FBI bought Merrill's complicity in the bombings, then the heat was off Faranco. And who else but Girard could so easily buy and dispose of stolen weapons and explosives? In crates labeled "Machine Tools" or "Specialty Steel Parts," they could be shipped anywhere. The world market for arms was booming, in the legitimate as well as the black market. Once the arms were smuggled out of the country, the buyers and the profits were nearly limitless. That was big business, on a scale to entice even someone like J. Stephen Girard.

The lights dimmed. A lone flute began to play a simple, seductive melody. The curtains opened. The stage was filled with large slate-black shapes that evoked the primitive monumentality of Stonehenge. From behind one of the great vertical blocks stepped a young woman in a white flowing gown, looking like a priestess at dawn. Belinda. Applause began like rolling thunder. She moved to the side of the stage, where a microphone had been placed, and waited nearly a minute for the applause to end before she began to speak.

The first model stepped out from behind another of the dark shapes. The loose, flowing, colorful fashions were set off dramatically against the elemental stage set. The audience reacted with unrestrained admiration for Belinda's designs. The show was an instant, dazzling success.

One hour later, after the final presentation, screens were removed along the side walls to reveal tables laden with food and drink. As the guests rose and moved toward them, workmen moved most of the chairs out of the way so that people could mingle. Belinda was everywhere at once, soliciting orders and drumming up publicity. Bailey, Schactman and Marcie were doing the same, but Will's eyes were only on Belinda, who seemed to be ignoring him, alighting beside man after man, greeting many with a fond kiss. Will felt pangs of jealousy he had thought were an aberration of his youth.

Perhaps he misunderstood, and had been invited only as a

guest for the showing. Once Marcie offered him a smile in passing. Concluding that pity had been in her eyes and that Belinda was playing him for a fool, he considered leaving. For an instant he recalled waiting awkwardly, ostentatiously, in front of other doors while she viewed his mutilation. And then he realized that the *déjà vu* was at another place, with another woman—his wife. Old wounds hurt more than new ones, he decided.

He hesitated a moment before leaving, and Belinda glanced his way, a query in her eyes. Will shook his head: no, he wasn't leaving. She smiled warmly at him, excused herself from a group, and came to him.

"I'm so glad you could be here, Will. How was it?"

"A four-star smash."

"The orders are pouring in. A couple of the fashion reporters swear they're going to give me raves. I think it might be okay."

She slipped her arm through his. "Let's have champagne to celebrate," she said.

She led him back into the room and began introducing him to people whose names he instantly forgot. He was sure they were doing the same with his.

After the party ended, the insiders, elated, animated, gathered at the hotel's coffee shop. The first orders had nearly deluged them. Tomorrow, in the showroom, many more people would place orders. There was no doubt about the trend. Schactman had a surefire line for the fall, and Ron's horse had come home a winner. Marcie's eyes never left Ron as he talked excitedly about his plans and ideas. Will hoped the self-centered young man would be moved by either lust or compassion enough tonight to sleep with this lonely young woman who wore a thick gold band around one wrist and a half a dozen heavy chains around the other.

The quietest of all was Belinda. The triumph was hers. The greatest rewards would also be hers. She was savoring the joy. Once, without her even looking at him, her hand had sought Will's, squeezed it, then slid across his thigh to his crotch, cupping his genitals as if they were a trophy.

When the other couples went off in other directions, Will and Belinda took a cab back to her loft.

Will was barely undressed when Belinda mounted him and

was quickly possessed by a succession of keening orgasms that might have continued forever if he had not finally ejaculated. She collapsed on him, her fingers massaging his shoulders convulsively. He felt raped.

In the morning, while he was dressing, he found her note—loving, thoughtful—taped to the bathroom mirror. She would be at the showroom all day to meet with buyers and to run through several smaller versions of last night's fashion show. She wouldn't have time to make dinner, although she wanted to. Could they go out tonight or maybe bring something home? Since she didn't know where he'd be today, could he call her later at the showroom? She left the phone number.

Will ripped the note from the mirror and shoved it into his pocket. He didn't know what his plans would be after he called Rovere.

When he did, Rovere agreed that Will's deductions the night before made sense, and he wanted to question the accountant who had been in the office adjacent to the ballroom when Merrill left the Gala—the man might have seen something. They arranged to meet for breakfast and then drop in on the accountant.

Patches of faded flesh-colored paint curled back like skin seared by the single exposed light bulb. Most of the offices along the dingy corridor were unrented. Below Sidney Spielvogel's name on the frosted-glass door panel were the names of several organizations, among them the Securities Gala. Below those were the words "Public Accountant" and "Notary Public."

Rovere knocked. An indistinct voice called out from within. A few moments later the door opened a crack. An eye peered at them above the security chain.

"Rovere, New York police."

He held his credentials up to the eye. The door closed. They heard the chain being snapped out of the slot. The door swung open. A small, balding man in his sixties stood beside it, fearful sagging eyes flicking from Rovere to Will and back again. Then Will comprehended the reason for the anxiety. Numbers tattooed on his left forearm were visible below the rolled-up threadbare shirt cuff. Once a knock on the door from different police had brought years of terror.

"We're just here for some information," Will said gently.

The man's face seemed to relax. He gestured toward two old wooden chairs which faced a desk piled high with ledgers and files. Rovere and Will went in and sat down. Spielvogel circled the desk, buttoning his shirt cuffs. He slipped on a suit jacket that did not match the pants.

"Mr. Spielvogel," Rovere began, "you were in the small office at the Gala when Craig Merrill left. Did you notice anything unusual in the hallway?"

The little man hesitated.

Rovere recognized from experience the man's reluctance to become involved. "It's very important, Mr. Spielvogel, I assure you."

Spielvogel nodded. "First I saw the man who got killed and then I saw somebody else." He spoke with a light German accent.

"Did you tell this to the policeman who questioned you?"

The little man shook his head. "All he wanted to know was did anyone leave the room I was in. Nobody asked me about seeing somebody in the hall."

"You were in that little office next to the ballroom?"

Spielvogel nodded. "I was sitting at the desk in the hotel office, counting the receipts. A lot of my business is I do the books for the small charities. They use my address to save overhead. One rule I got. When I count the receipts, someone from the charity is there to watch. I get their signature on a voucher, so I have some protection."

"James Kean was with you," Rovere said, scanning his notebook.

"Just the two of us."

Spielvogel rose and went to a file in a metal cabinet, its green paint chipped, its side dented. He returned with a voucher. Kean had approved the total.

"Anyway, I was counting the receipts. Mr. Kean asked me a question. I looked up. The fellow who was killed went by the door. I haven't got a very good head for faces. But next day when I saw his picture in the paper, I recognized him. I looked back down at my papers after he passed to find the answer to the question. When I looked up again, the other man was just moving across the doorway. Average size, I remember. On the fat side. In a dark suit, maybe a tux."

"Anything else? Hair color? Age?"

Spielvogel shrugged.

Rovere had a thought. "If we put you together with our artists, could you describe his profile?"

The sorrow-worn face turned apologetic. "You got to keep in mind it wasn't a big thing then. I saw a guy walk by, like a thousand times a day, maybe on the subway, you see a guy walk by."

"Could Kean have seen him?" Will asked.

The man shrugged. "His back was to the door. I was facing it. I don't even know this guy I saw wasn't just going to the toilet."

"It's not much to go on," Rovere explained. "We know someone left the hotel shortly after Merrill."

Will had been reluctant to prompt the little man, to put descriptions into his memory that might not really be there. But Carl Raymond had left the ballroom just as Merrill was leaving. He was the logical one to have either killed Merrill or pointed him out to the actual hit man. Uncontrollably, the rage for vengeance flared up once more.

"The man you saw," Will burst out, "was he very tall, stooped shoulders, blond hair? That *had* to be the man!"

"No," demurred Spielvogel, taken aback by Will's sudden vehemence. "No. I told you. Average size. A little fat, I think."

"Thanks for your help, Mr. Spielvogel," Rovere interjected, and stood up.

"I only wish I could help you a little more," the man said plaintively, "but it happened so fast. It didn't seem important enough even to take a good look."

In the elevator, Will told Rovere he was going to see James Kean in a few minutes to discuss aircraft financing and invited the detective to come along. Rovere declined. He had already questioned Kean; they would learn nothing new there. Instead he was going to speak again with Murray Eskenazi, the investment banker, who had been leaving the ballroom when Merrill left. Perhaps he too had seen a man in the corridor behind Merrill, but had not been asked about it.

They drove the short distance from lower Broadway to Wall Street. Will got out of the police car and entered the skyscraper housing Willoughby Securities.

Kean was at the bank of elevators as Will approached. Will was about to shake hands when a chattering couple with a barking St. Bernard dog rushed between them into the elevator, nearly knocking Kean down. Kean eyed the group with distaste and held Will back until the elevator doors closed.

"I've never particularly liked dogs, perhaps because I'm allergic to them. But these days their owners don't seem to exercise any control over them. Maybe that's why the world is coming apart at the seams—no control. No self-discipline, no rules, anywhere." He led Will into the next elevator.

Upon arriving at his office, Kean found a news service Teletype printout on his desk. The White House had just announced that the President was planning to sign both CAB orders within a few days. Faranco had instantly raised its bid to $14.75. GUA had yet to reply.

Will immediately telephoned Serge Bergheim. Bergheim had been able to obtain a suspension of trading in GUA stock just before the opening, on the ground that the airline's management needed time to prepare and announce projected earnings that included the new West African route. If Will could induce Kean to agree on the terms of the refinancing, the savings in interest payments would further increase GUA's net income and enhance the stock's value. Fourteen dollars and seventy-five cents was not the sort of killer bid that could crush GUA's morale or bowl over its shareholders. By nickel-and-diming it, Girard had left himself open to a counterattack.

"I'm not happy the SEC gave Creighton, Cromwell a clean bill of health on those warrants." Kean's eyes had turned cold as ice. "You know my opinion of Max Creighton. If Faranco fails, that will be some satisfaction to me."

"Will the sale of these 707 loan certificates be hampered without Creighton, Cromwell to market a large share of them to the public? They'll badmouth the issue all over the Street."

Kean's mouth was set tightly. "I'll try to form a syndicate of investment banking firms that will buy the certificates for their own accounts. The planes backing the certificates are insured. The company has a strong income now."

"You sound like you have doubts about pulling it off."

"I won't fail." And the eyes once again were bitter cold. Will was grateful for the motivating animosity Creighton had provoked in Kean.

For a couple of hours, the two men negotiated points their lawyers had been unable to settle, with Will stressing how important the refinancing had become for Global Universal.

As Will was preparing to leave, he reminded Kean they had first met on New Year's Eve, the night Craig Merrill had been murdered. Sadly, Kean remembered speaking casually to the astronaut during the cocktail party preceding the actual dinner. The aviation executive had seemed apprehensive about something, but Kean had no idea what. They had not spoken the rest of the evening. Kean reconfirmed what Will already knew, that he had not been facing the door to the corridor and so had failed to glimpse the two men who had hurried by.

But someone at the hotel that night just might have; that second man, Will was now convinced, was the key to solving everything.

Buyers and the press had inundated the showroom. It was after two o'clock before Marcie and Belinda could take refuge in a back office at Schactman Sophisticates to eat a hurried lunch. But they were both too excited by their success to get down more than a bite or two. Several times during the morning Mory Schactman had tried to draw Belinda aside to discuss extending their one-season arrangement into a permanent one. He obviously had already discussed it with Ron, because the latter remarked at one point, too offhandedly to be innocent, "Wouldn't it be great if we could get a long-term deal out of Schactman?"

"You don't really want a long-term contract with Schactman, do you?" Marcie asked Belinda.

"Maybe if he was willing to put up enough capital and keep his hands off the creative end."

"Oh, I had thought . . . the way you argued with him all the time, you would be dead set against it no matter what."

Belinda did not want to think about it. In a few days, when the wildly fulfilled feeling began to ebb, her judgment would be better. "How was your evening with Ron?" she asked, changing the subject.

"All right, I guess. We went to a discotheque, met a lot of people we knew, danced a lot."

"Does 'met a lot of people we knew' mean Ron took *you* home or took someone else?"

Marcie shrugged. "This time I didn't give him a chance to leave me hanging. I left before he did." She smiled. "I must be learning at last. How was your evening?"

"Super."

"God, he's attractive."

"Will?"

Marcie nodded. "Uh-huh. You always get the feeling that he's in total control of everything." She chuckled. "Like Ron would like to think of himself, but Will really is. You two getting to be more than friends and lovers?"

"You know me better than that."

When they had finished eating their lunch and were leaving the little room, Marcie suddenly flung an arm around her friend and exclaimed impulsively, "Wouldn't it be wonderful if we didn't need people like Schactman, if it could be just the two of us?"

Later that afternoon Will called Belinda from GUA's New York offices. The next minute their relationship nearly ended. In the same ecstatic tones with which she told him how great the crush of buyers had been all day, she mentioned that an important Wall Street friend she had just spoken to was convinced Faranco couldn't lose.

"I wish you'd keep your other lovers out of our life," Will said testily. "That was the deal, wasn't it?"

"What's that supposed to mean?"

"I get the distinct feeling that you really miss me because I'm wearing your dildo."

For several seconds there was silence on Belinda's end of the line. When her rage became controlled enough for her to speak, she only said tersely, "We'll talk about it at my place tonight. Seven o'clock."

Click.

At exactly two minutes past seven she was standing, arms akimbo, on the second level as Will made the turn midway up the stairs.

"All right, you son of a bitch, let's have it out. Do you always get your jollies pouring water on someone else's parade?"

Will looked up, said nothing and commenced the second half of the slow climb. At the top he hobbled by her into the apartment.

She stormed in after him. "You haven't limped in all the time I've known you!"

Inside the living room he tossed his overcoat on an armchair and turned to face her.

"Don't bother," she warned. "You might not be staying that long."

He ignored her. "You delude yourself that you have this warm, intimate, special relationship with a bunch of men I'm beginning to think is equal in size to the Sixth Fleet. You're fooling yourself. The men don't matter as long as they're pleasant and bathe on a fairly regular schedule. The only differences in them you care about are the ones that stir your lust. I think that's why you were so fascinated by my missing leg. You set up the rules right at the beginning so you never really have to give anything of yourself to a guy. You don't love anyone, but you want the euphoric illusion of loving—it's a drug that heightens the sex."

"Oh, no, you don't. I had the most fantastic night and day of my life, and you're not going to ruin the glow with your personal hangups. You're jealous of the other men in my life. You're intimidated by them and the fact that I'm not just the usual adoring moron who can be circumscribed by your traditional morality."

She was working herself into a towering rage, but a lot of the steam escaped when she noticed that Will was hardly listening. Perhaps half a minute passed before he spoke again.

"Maybe you're too self-centered to love. Your goals are so all-consuming and so personal—like painting, and now becoming a fashion tycoon—that there's little of you left to share with your lovers. So you simply use them. You give generously only to those who are incapable of demanding real commitment from you. It's another kind of using."

"You mean people like Marcie?"

Will nodded, rejecting the sudden perception that he might be criticizing Belinda for failing to demonstrate some of the same commitment he had denied Donna. "Instead of understanding how depressed I would feel if Faranco all but wrapped things up, you sounded on the phone like it was my birthday." He paused. "Okay, I've had my say."

She exhaled the last of her rage. "I'll have to think about what you said for a while. The easy thing to do is point out that you're just angry at seeing yourself in someone else's shoes. But that's too easy—and maybe it's also not quite true. What you said was too uncomfortable to ignore." Her voice became more tentative than Will had ever heard it. "Are you trying to tell me you want to break things off between us?"

"No. A small part of you is more exciting than all of most women. Just don't try to use me."

She cocked her head. Slowly, the smile that stirred Will so began to insinuate itself on her lips. "Does that mean I have to be really polite and wait until after dinner to fuck?"

A couple of hours later they began to dress to go out to dinner. As she watched Will slip on the prosthetic leg and buckle its belt around his body, she felt a swell of tenderness. Will happened to glance at her at that instant, and his expression turned quizzical. She shook her head: nothing was on her mind.

Perhaps the unanticipated denunciation had been the cause. Perhaps Will's strength alone would have been enough eventually. But as Belinda reached for Will's shirt to hand it to him, she could no longer doubt she was breaking her own rule. She was falling in love.

Will began carefully. "I've been thinking of going somewhere warm this weekend. You've earned a little bit of vacation yourself after your great success."

"As a matter of fact, I *was* planning to go away this weekend."

"Where to?"

"Palm Beach."

"Sounds perfect . . . unless of course you already had company."

"No, but I'm not sure you'd be comfortable at the party I was invited to—or welcome."

"Being given by one of your lovers?"

She smiled. "Certainly not one of yours. The Girards."

Will appeared properly surprised. "Might be interesting."

Belinda probed Will's tone for intent. "If you went, could you behave yourself and act civilized even though you're in this takeover battle? You'd have to promise me that, Will."

"I don't like the man, but it's not personal. It's business."

"You don't sound very convincing."

"Of course I'll be a perfect gentleman. What I'm really looking forward to is some sun and sand."

"I have a reservation at a beach hotel."

"If you'd rather I not invite myself along, just tell me."

Belinda smiled. "You're not inviting yourself," she decided. "I'm inviting you."

He leaned over and kissed her. "We probably won't get out of bed long enough to go to any parties."

Her reply was lighthearted. "Where else could I find a man who can travel for free and has a clean tux?" The real reason she wanted his company was still too startling for her to face—and could very well conflict with plans that only in the past few hours had begun to form in her head.

17

The next morning, while Will was in the air between New York and Denver, the President signed both of the CAB orders and opposing lawyers appeared in state court to wrangle over the last barrier to commencing the tendering period—release of the stockholders list, which GUA's lawyers had managed to retain as a "confidential communication."

J. Stephen Girard had flown up to New York City the day before. His mood had turned foul over his lawyers' repeated failure to gain access to the list of shareholders. While waiting for the result of his appeal, he refused to see anyone.

All the while a small, determined visitor named Herbert Kimble was being passed from one secretary at Faranco to the next without being able to gain a hearing. Returning by chance to his office in Corporate Communications just as Kimble arrived, Jackson Lubeck stopped to ask the man his business. Amazement growing, Lubeck drew Kimble into his office and made him repeat his story before dragging him down the hall to Girard's suite.

Girard's secretary would not admit him, but Lubeck said he would assume the responsibility and stepped by her, pulling Kimble behind him. The elderly businessman had hardly begun to tell his story when Girard exclaimed, "You want to sell what?"

"No big deal, Mr. Girard. The newspapers say you want the GUA stockholders list. I'll sell you my copy for whatever it cost me. It's not very old."

"How much did it cost you?"

"Three thousand dollars."

"Mr. Kimble, you have a deal!"

By late afternoon, when new offering ads were being transported to the *Wall Street Journal* and the *Times* and amended filings were going to the SEC, the state judge peremptorily ordered GUA to turn over its list of stockholders to Faranco. The decision was no surprise. Not after Friedman's startling revelation that GUA's so-called confidentiality had extended to selling the list to a mail-order luggage firm for three thousand dollars.

By evening Faranco's offering material would be on its way to all GUA stockholders. During the next ten days, they would have to decide whether to submit their shares to Faranco's dealer-manager for sale at $14.75 per share or continue to hold them for investment.

"Pres Frey sold some luggage dealer our stockholder list?" Buck roared like a wounded bull elephant.

"Nothing evil about it," explained Will. "Just shortsighted. He was in charge of marketing our intangible resources."

"Don't you give me that gobbledygook, Will. He was in charge of that little gift catalogue we put on the planes."

"He decided GUA could also make money by selling the stockholders list to magazine publishers, charities and mail-order houses."

"Oh, shit! We just keep stabbing ourselves in the back. We ought to change our name to Kamikaze Airlines."

But that very afternoon one of the most heavily strained bolts holding Global Universal together, the loyalty of GUA's stockholder-employees, was tested, and held.

Vail, the spokesman for the pilots' local, had decided to use the present crisis as leverage to gain advantages for his union. The two sides met in a small conference room in Industrial Relations. Vail quickly outlined his demands.

"That's it in a nutshell, General. If we ask our pilots and the other employees not to tender the stock they own, we want your assurance that labor contracts coming up this year will contain at least a fifteen-percent wage hike and a no-layoff clause. There are a few other things we want, but those are the important ones. Faranco people tell us they'll buy our deal on wage hikes and no layoffs."

Will glanced at Buck, Keller, and Glover, head of Industrial Relations. If they chose not to answer, the task would fall to him. But the Old Man's ferocious gaze was fixed on Vail; he was going to answer for management himself. Years later, Will would look back on this moment as one of Buck's finest. Everyone was expecting Buck to respond with fury. Instead his voice was as gentle as a child's.

"The easiest thing for me to do right now, Mitch, is give in to you. I don't have to tell you that the employees' shares are crucial. But if I bargained away this airline's future by accepting your terms, I would be betraying you as both stockholders and employees as surely as if I scuttled all our aircraft. There's a whole new air transport industry out there waiting to be born. No one is quite sure what it will look like. But I'm sure that any airline with its hands tied will lose out. And I'm also sure that only the best managed airlines will survive."

His gaze moved slowly along the line of employee representatives. "I've always said Global Universal was a family. I could try to win your support by playing on your heartstrings, bringing up all the triumphs and trials we've shared. That would be unfair and might even take your minds off the larger question: which management team can best assure all of you that a strong and successful Global Universal Airlines will still be here in five or ten years, the one who gave away the store now or the one who refused to?"

He stood up, allowed his gaze to catch each pair of eyes across the table for an instant and left the room. The others on his side of the table followed.

Two hours later the union representatives announced they would recommend that employees *not* sell their shares to Faranco.

* * *

Several people were filing out of Will's office as Donna entered. Her plane had landed a few minutes earlier, and she still wore her violet uniform and carried her saffron valise. She hadn't seen or communicated with Will since the morning she found another woman's panties in his cabin. Yanking the door closed behind her, she stepped up to Will, drew his face down to hers, and kissed him.

"Mmmm. How I've missed that!" She separated from him, then looked about her with distaste. "I still get itchy in this building." Finally her gaze returned to Will. "When I left your place, I made up my mind I was through with you. But all the time I was away I couldn't stop thinking about you. You've gotten under my skin. This relationship ranks high among the stupid things I've done in my life."

Will bristled, but waited for Donna to go on.

"I'll swallow my pride just this once," she said. Then she cocked her head. "Want to move in with me?"

"No."

"Want me to move in with you?"

"No."

"Do you have plans for the weekend?"

"Yes."

"See what I mean? Stupid. This weekend of yours—is it business or pleasure?"

"Both."

"Who's the pleasure part?"

"I don't ask you who you've been with."

"That's only because lately you know you don't have to."

"What happened to the young woman who told me in a Washington, D.C., airport that she wasn't the kind to get tied down?"

She searched Will's face for quite a long while before she answered. "You tell me."

"It depends on what you're looking for."

Donna spun around abruptly. "I guess I just got my answer, straight from the lawyer's mouth. See you around, Will."

She strode from the room before Will could come up with words calculated to stop her.

The softly lit yacht looked like an ornate Japanese lantern

hung from the dark sky. Will and Belinda stood beside several other couples in the launch as it closed the distance between the pier and the yacht.

"Pity the rich," Will whispered, "with all those responsibilities."

"You don't come across as a very convincing Bolshevik in that suntan and tuxedo."

"I'm really a well trained guerrilla team in disguise. Once on board, the revolution starts, building on the unrest of downtrodden millionaires who can't afford more than a fifty-footer. To paraphrase a certain radical dress designer, it's not social oppression that moves us wild-eyed revolutionaries, it's envy pure and simple."

Belinda laughed unrestrainedly. "I'll bet it all started when you were a little boy and your sailboat sank in the bathtub."

"Today the bathtub, tomorrow Palm Beach! Southampton, Greenwich and Newport will fall like dominoes!"

Belinda was wearing her most spectacular gown. Soon after they reached the yacht's main deck, she spiraled away to promote her budding dress line and Will began meandering among the guests. He spied Bob Winstead, but, sensing the banker's chilliness, decided not to inquire about the stock escrow plan. Instead, he began chatting with a succession of striking women, with whom he traded promising innuendoes and phone numbers. But his interest soon began to wane, and he realized his motivation was rooted more in habit than in desire.

An hour later he was leaning against a rail, drink in hand, when J. Stephen Girard's path finally crossed his. Until the moment Girard spoke, Will had no idea whether he had been recognized.

"Mr. Nye, if memory serves. Welcome aboard."

"I'm flattered that you remember." Flattered, and flushed by a victory of sorts.

"You've made your name quite prominent in my affairs. You would be difficult to ignore."

"The feeling is decidedly mutual. You have a certain knack for acquisition also difficult to ignore."

"Have you been around the ship yet? Some excellent pieces from my art collection are on board. The Tintoretto is particularly fine. I had to outbid the Metropolitan for it." Girard paused a beat to underline what he was about to say. "Nye, I never lose."

"Your life is about to become more complicated," Will countered. "I have that same nagging habit."

"From all reports, quite true. You are a force I hadn't reckoned with. I had counted on management flailing pointlessly about, at the whim of Ben Buck's impulsiveness. But you've kept them well on target. Management didn't have a chance, but you've played a poor hand as if it were a straight flush."

Will waited without expression for the predator's strike sure to come.

"We can both come out on top, Nye. We can both get what we want. With your help I can quickly end the useless delay and take control of Global Universal. Buck listens to you more than to most."

"And what can you possibly give me that I want?"

"Why, the same thing I want, of course—Global Universal. You're much too ambitious to want anything less."

Will felt suddenly naked.

"Eckman will stay on as president for no more than two years. I'll give you an ironclad contract that you get the presidency and the chief-executive-officer title too, when he steps down."

"What about Al Goetz? I figured that was *his* payoff."

"He's taken himself out of the ball game."

"I'll bet he had an ironclad contract, too." Will took a deep breath. Girard had smelled desire like an open wound and had torn at it. "You're about four hundred and fifty deaths too late. You and your goons are ruthless about stomping all over people. You seem to get away with everything. I want you paid back for every shortcut, every dirty little trick, every life."

"Which means you want to stick with Buck."

"Buck's victory is part of it. And so is your losing—and the knowledge that I had something to do with it."

"You'll regret not taking my offer, Nye."

"I'd regret taking it a whole lot more."

Girard barely nodded before walking off in the direction from which he had come. Throughout the conversation Will had tried to peer into Girard's eyes, seeking guilt or shame or evil, but all Will had seen was himself mirrored in Girard's dark glasses.

Belinda was speaking to a small well-tanned woman with delicate features when Will found her in a sitting room. Belinda introduced him to Marie Girard. She was not what Will had imagined Girard's wife would be. She seemed totally without pretensions or guile. Her shoes were off and her feet drawn up under her.

When Belinda mentioned that Will was with Global Universal Airlines, Marie's mild interest seemed only courtesy. She knew the name, to be sure, and probably that her husband had some vague business with it, but the reference merely prodded an old recollection of her first airplane ride. She had flown in a Clipper down here, she told them, the old flying boat that was once queen of the skies. Landing and taking off on water seemed so much safer, so much friendlier than on land. She had always been in love with the sea. That was why she loved the yacht so.

After a while, Will noticed that Marie Girard was asking him questions for the most basic and homely of reasons: to determine whether he would be suitable husband material for her friend.

When she inquired whether they would enjoy touring the below-deck area of the yacht which had been closed off for the party, Belinda bounded to her feet. Marie walked them to the stairway and then left them to wander below.

At each new stateroom and sitting room, Belinda's hunger to own similar possessions grew. Luxury surrounded her so far beyond the fantasy goals for which she had been striving that she was dumbstruck. Furniture chosen with exquisite taste and cost no consideration. Walls covered with rich silks and adorned with extraordinary paintings spanning half a millennium, enclosed in airtight frames for protection from salt and moisture. The decorators had chosen woods that glowed like honey, material and carpeting that blended colors like magic. Belinda's fingertips ran along the edge of a writing table so lightly one might have thought she feared that all before her was illusion.

In the Girards' white bedroom, wide windows instead of portholes looked out across the water, and a Renoir nude hung over the bed. Belinda locked the door, reached behind her and pulled down her dress zipper. The dress fell to her feet. Bra and pantyhose followed an instant later. She stretched out on the thick carpet.

"I've never been so hot in my life," she breathed, reaching for Will's fly.

As the hour grew later, guests clustered in small groups. On deck, Senator Dale Mickelson, a member of the Senate Banking Committee, was vigorously lecturing Bob Winstead. Not one to nurse a drink, he had started imbibing at noon, and his tact was now rather ragged. After haranguing Winstead about Metrobank's choice of real-estate loans, he veered in another direction.

"And now you guys have all that money out to a shaky operation like Global Universal!"

Winstead had been extending courtesy to a man who had been merely boring up until that moment. Now he perceived that the invitation and this encounter had been carefully prearranged. Both the manipulation and Mickelson himself were insulting.

"Scnator, wc makc it a practice *not* to lend to shaky operations."

"Well, you fellows sure blew this one."

Mickelson took another sip of his bourbon and water. He failed to note the fury leaping to Winstead's eyes.

"I've been monitoring that loan myself, Senator. Perhaps you didn't see GUA's latest figures."

"What the hell difference do they make, Bob? Sure as God's in his heaven that company's going to have a new boss in a couple of weeks." He leaned close to the banker's face. "You don't want to end up sucking hind tit, Bobby, you better stop backing the losers and get with the winners."

Winstead's teeth were clenched. "As long as I'm head of Metrobank, that's exactly how we *don't* do business."

Mickelson shook his head. "No wonder you end up loaning money to has-beens like Ben Buck. Shit, we ought to investigate that kind of irresponsible banking. Talking to you is like spitting into the wind."

Winstead whipped the contents of his drink over the rail, set down the glass and spun away from Mickelson.

Will Nye was just coming out on deck again when Winstead located him.

"Will, are your people still interested in Metrobank holding that extra GUA stock as security for the fifty million?"

"I'm sure we are, Bob."

"Understand, I have no concern at all about GUA's ability to repay the loan. Headly Parkhurst thought our voting that stock might help in the takeover fight."

"It will help a good deal," said Will quietly. "It will put maybe five million shares more into the total pool, five million shares that will be voted for management and that Faranco has no chance of buying. It could be the difference."

"I hope so, Will. I sincerely do."

Will considered whether it would be discreet to inquire why, after two months, Winstead's mind had suddenly changed. He decided against it. The act itself was too momentous to jeopardize with an imprudent word. A most unexpected pinion had held.

"Thank you, Bob."

"I'm happy to do it. Good night, Will."

"Good night."

As Will watched, Bob Winstead collected his wife, and they made their way to the gangladder and down to the launch tied up at its base.

A short time later Will and Belinda followed.

"What did you think of Marie?" Belinda inquired as the launch edged away from the side of the ship and into open water.

"Good-hearted. Simple. Untouched by her husband's wealth or his dealings." Will considered a moment before giving words to his next thought. "But if you're thinking about them for partners, you ought to drop the idea. Business is jungle combat to Girard. He makes Schactman look like Saint Francis of Assisi."

"I guess you're right," replied Belinda regretfully. "It's not a very wise idea."

"Was my behavior at the party acceptable, ma'am?"

She was deep in thought and took several seconds to respond. "Behavior? Oh, yes." A wide smile broke across her face. "Will Nye, you were, as always, a perfect gentleman."

They lay in the sun most of the next day until it was time to leave for the airport. Will's plane to Denver departed only a short time after Belinda's flight to New York, but something Marie

Girard had said the previous night had jogged his memory. It seemed so unimportant, but curiosity prevailed. He canceled his reservation, got back in the rented car and drove to Miami.

It was early evening when Will found the turnoff from 95 and headed out to the key. He had an image in his memory of a photo he had once seen: an old terminal, an abandoned hangar, and a few antique flying boats tied to the piers—all that was left of the base Pan Am had built for its famed Flying Clippers, the fabled four-engine sea transports that carved routes out of the Caribbean and South American skies.

Will halted the car on a wide, well-lit boulevard. A sign read "Dinner Key," and Will turned left. Landfill had long ago joined the tiny island to the adjacent mainland. Will was prepared for that. But he was unprepared for the modern civic auditorium on the right, the boat marina's long fingers jutting out from the shore, and the low white building at the end of the drive, with the words "Miami City Hall" above the entrance.

The doors were locked. A cleaning man outside knew nothing of any seaplanes. Will was about to leave when he noticed the insignia on either side of the building's title: bas-reliefs of the Western Hemisphere—with wings. Driving out, he noticed that the road was named Pan American Drive. Will decided to cross the boulevard to the Dinner Key Lodge, a neatly kept motel. In the office his questions were answered. The woman behind the counter pointed to a photograph, among other nostalgia on the wall. It was of a plaque which used to be on the key, but had been taken down when the auditorium replaced the hangar. Will wrote out the relevant phrases.

DINNER KEY

Picknickers in sailboat days gave the key its name. . . . In 1930, Pan American World Airways here inaugurated flying boat service to Latin America, erecting huge hangars and a terminal. . . . Over 100,000 visitors a month came to see the giant Flying Clippers.

. . . In World War II, Navy and Pan American operated flying boats here until Latin American airports built for hemisphere defense enabled use of more economical landplanes. The City of Miami purchased the key in 1946.

"City Hall used to be the passenger terminal," the woman explained.

Statements that hadn't made sense to Will originally were suddenly clear. On New Year's Day, when talking to him about Marie Girard, Belinda had quoted her both correctly and incorrectly. The painting Marie Girard had purchased from Belinda reminded her of "water spurting up the window" because that would happen during a flying boat's takeoff or landing. But Marie had probably not told Belinda it was "the key to dinner." The reference had undoubtedly been to the site where the flight commenced, to this place, Dinner Key.

Marie Girard's trail might have been lost in Mobile, but she had definitely been here between 1932 and 1942, when the base was converted to war use and private passengers could no longer go up. Soon after that, flying boats, like the great blue whales they resembled, began to become extinct.

Will walked outside and gazed out to the key. He realized that this side trip had been as much a pilgrimage into his own past, the romance with aviation that had drawn him aloft as a boy, as a search into Marie Girard's. Now that he had met her, he was glad that he had called Benke off. Belinda was right: this was not Marie's fight. And he was not a voracious beast like Girard, feeding without limit or conscience. Whatever might be buried in the history of Marie Girard's family would stay buried.

Will drove to Miami International Airport and caught the next flight to Denver.

The ten days that followed were a marathon. Both sides used print ads, telephone solicitations and the mails to influence stockholders. Charges and countercharges of payoffs and private deals flew. But none of the charges could be proved. Ben Buck held a press conference in New York City for financial reporters and estimated that the coming year's earnings would top three dollars a share by a good margin. Speedy startup of the new West African route could push the figure even higher. Anticipating a raised bid from Faranco, arbitrageurs bid GUA's stock to fifteen and a quarter. When none was forthcoming, the price sank to fourteen and a quarter.

As the 5 P.M. deadline of the tenth day of the tender offer approached, Faranco's team was gathered at Creighton, Cromwell, with two open telephone lines: one to Lorillard Bank, which was serving as a depositary for tendered shares, and the other to J. Stephen Girard. The GUA team was at Bergheim, Mack, with an open line to GUA's management in Buck's office.

But 5 P.M. came and went, and the tender offer expired, with no announcement.

Champagne bottles in hand, Ben Buck raced down the executive corridors roaring his jubilation. A growing, laughing crowd followed him like the Pied Piper. He had won! They had won!

Max Creighton was shocked that as the shares were counted and the disappointing totals communicated, Girard refused to top $14.75. Creighton, Cromwell's fee arrangement depended on the offer succeeding in full. When the deadline passed with only some thirty percent of GUA's outstanding shares owned by Faranco, $1,750,000 slipped through the brokerage firm's fingers.

J. Stephen Girard knew exactly what he was doing. He had hoped to draw more shares. But thirty percent was most satisfactory. A clear victory would have required an eighteen- to twenty-dollar bid—sixty to a hundred million dollars more, not counting Max Creighton's one and three-quarters million—an expense that brought no additional stock. Now that the tender offer had expired, the law permitted Faranco to begin purchasing stock again other than through the offer. A higher price for certain specific large blocks made sense. But offering a higher price for *all* the shares tendered—and pushing up the market price with each purchase—would have been profligate. Let other conglomerators get carried away by ego and overspend in the heat of battle. Such victories could literally cost their careers. He would gain control of Global Universal on his terms—by judicious stock purchases and a proxy fight for control of GUA's Board.

The next day Faranco declared its opposition to present GUA management and its intention to vote for an opposition directors slate at the annual stockholders meeting. Under the airline's corporate charter, the meeting had to be held on the first Thursday in May. The ultimate confrontation had now been shifted to May 5, some nine weeks away.

18

A proxy fight is an election campaign. A shareholder can cast a vote in two ways: by voting in person at the stockholders meeting or by granting a proxy to representatives of a particular side to cast the vote for him. The number of votes a shareholder possesses corresponds to the number of shares of stock he owns that are entitled to vote. And he can switch sides as often as he wishes, merely by filling out and signing a new proxy form.

Although Global Universal's charter called for as few as three directors, its Board traditionally comprised thirteen. GUA management would propose a slate of thirteen candidates. Faranco and every other stockholder also had the right to propose a slate. During the next few weeks, each side would wage an all-out campaign for the support of uncommitted shareholders. After the votes cast at the May 5 meeting were tallied, one or the other slate would control the company's destiny for the upcoming year.

For the first time in a charmed life, Ben Buck was acutely aware of his mortality. That knowledge stripped away whatever few illusions still remained to him. As he reclined in his desk chair and gazed out the far windows at his beloved Rockies, he realized he was even more superfluous to the present conflict than to the one just ended. He was a figurehead, a symbol, a name to be waved by canny professionals to rally troops to his cause.

But Ben Buck intended to put these nine weeks to very good use. He spun back to his desk, rang for Eloise Cooper and dictated a rush memo to the Future Planning Committee. They were to have their proposals ready for presentation the next day. Even if these nine weeks were his last weeks at the helm of Global Universal—or on earth—the airline would be set on a path which no one, not even J. Stephen Girard, could change.

The memo caught Will off guard; he had almost forgotten about the Future Planning Committee in the acceleration of activity during the tender offer. Now he reached into the bottom desk drawer for the thick manila folder in which he had collected background material and his own thoughts. But just as he opened the file, the phone rang: Teicher was calling from New York. The call ended an hour later only because Glidden, the proxy solicitor, was on the phone with an urgent matter. That conversation gave way to a three-city conference call among lawyers.

It was late in the evening when Will finally hung up the receiver and looked back at his desk. With a start he caught sight of the open file.

He took a deep breath and began to read the top page. Two paragraphs later he slammed the file together and stood up. He would take the material home and deal with it there.

But five minutes after he had set the open file, a sandwich and a beer on the coffee table in the cabin, he fell asleep.

He woke when the sun was already rising into the sky. The sandwich still sat uneaten on the plate. For a moment Will could not remember what the papers before him were, only that they seemed a lot less important after a night's sleep.

His eyes lifted to the empty clearing. Bright motley was being cast on the snow as the sun shone through the spaces between the pine boughs. As Will watched the camouflage shrink back away from itself toward the woods, he was overcome by a torpor alien to him since his purgatory days in the V.A. hospital. He sat immobile and totally without thought, as if some motor deep within him had suddenly seized and he possessed no inner purpose to force critical parts into moving once more.

Eventually, a doe, brave with winter hunger, ventured into the clearing and began to dig away the snow, searching for food. Until, without warning, she lifted her head and stared straight at Will for what seemed a very long time. Then, with a sudden flash of white tail, she bounded away.

The automatic coffee maker began gurgling a moment later. Rousing himself and shuffling off to a cold shower seemed to require the utmost effort Will could muster.

An hour later, shaven and freshly dressed, the file once again inside the briefcase, driving back to an office he seemed to have just left, Will Nye could not shake the disconcerting feeling that he was trapped in a body going through the motions of someone else's life, living up to someone else's aspirations. If he was ever to find peace of mind, he decided, he must sever himself from the ambition that blocked nearly all else from his mind, and seek the essence of his own nature and needs. The serenity that reclined just beyond his reach seemed to beckon more seductively than a thousand scepters of absolute power. It seemed to beckon to his soul.

Conway's and Keller's presentations to Future Planning, complete with slides, graphs, statistics and a question period, lasted until lunch. Bannister's took up the early afternoon. For Will, who had observed the evolution of each, there were no surprises. Each man had emphasized a different aspect of the airline business in his scheme for the future. Not surprisingly, the views coincided with each man's field of experience. Conway advocated heavy aircraft purchases in all sizes in order to expand the route network rapidly when deregulation came and to wipe out route competition with a massing of flights and seating capacity. Keller emphasized buying new, more efficient aircraft better matched to a similarly expanded route system, a plan he felt required an early commitment to Boeing, so as to maximize GUA's influence on the design of a new 180- to 210-passenger jetliner. Bannister urged caution on purchases so that a strong cash reserve would build and permit the airline to reduce its debt and attract bank financing; cash was his key to surviving the intense route competition sure to come.

The late afternoon was set aside for debating the various proposals. Will listened calmly. Ambition had made him presumptuous, he felt, and the overreaching had induced dissatisfaction. Now, reconciled to the certainty that this was someone else's competition, he was at peace with himself.

Will's eyes occasionally strayed to Ben Buck, the man faced with this most difficult and least clear-cut of decisions. Buck's frustration rose perceptibly through the afternoon as he twisted this way and that, vainly seeking firm ground on which to rest a ladder to the future. Then, without warning, he revolved a full quarter turn in his chair and faced Will.

"What's your opinion, Nye?"

Until that moment Will was not certain that he had an opinion, but the knowledge that he no longer clung desperately to the outcome seemed to free his words and thoughts. He spoke in a relaxed, almost offhand manner.

"In one way or another, all the proposals assume we ought to go for a lot of new routes after deregulation becomes final. I ask myself why someone would want to fly GUA. The answer I come up with is very basic: we do a good job. As long as we match a competitor's lower fare, we'll succeed by concentrating our strength in the markets we already dominate. That means the routes originating at and connecting our major hubs. We have the ground facilities and strong public identification there. We can defend those routes when other carriers challenge them. For one thing, major airports are so cramped for space that new airlines will have a tough time getting in." Will leaned forward, about to make his principal point. "Nobody in a free market could defend the hodgepodge of routes the CAB awarded us. Maybe it's airline heresy, but I think we ought to *shrink* our domestic route system to its strongest, most sensible size. When we add new routes and go into new markets, they should follow logically and enhance what we already have."

After weeks of groping, the path into the next decade had suddenly become apparent to Will.

"There's a second point—equipment. With the coming free-for-all in the domestic market, everyone agrees some smaller carriers may go under when the stronger lines attack their routes with lower prices and more flights. We'll be in big trouble ourselves on the medium and long hauls if we can offer only a few jumbo jets while our competitors are able to offer many more flight times, because they have many more two-hundred-passenger planes. Let's face it, we're already underutilizing our jumbos in the off-seasons and on medium-haul routes. They're not efficient unless we're flying fairly full over a long distance. Without a midsized, cost-efficient, modern airplane—one that burns the least amount of fuel and has quiet engines that meet federal noise regulations—we'll get killed in the domestic market when deregulation comes."

"That's what I've been saying all along," Keller interjected.

"With all due respect," Will responded, "a way has to be found to start buying that aircraft *now*. Otherwise, if deregulation doesn't kill us, inflation in the cost of buying the plane will."

Bannister was about to speak when Ben Buck stood up.

"Nine o'clock tomorrow morning."

He left the conference room. The meeting was at an end.

Will had a stunning dinner date that night, but his mind kept wandering. He felt foolish; these other men were longtime professionals who had studied the industry long and hard. Why hadn't he simply declared that he had no opinion? At least the Old Man had been gracious enough to cut off the broadsides about to be fired by the others.

His resolve to abdicate ambition's heights, so easily formulated, had not been so easily achieved. When Buck called on him, he had charged forward to answer, relaxed perhaps, but nonetheless eager to shine. The restraint that the knowledge of his own inexperience should have engendered was trampled underfoot. The detachment and serenity he had sought were quickly forgotten.

Will had a sudden insight: he saw himself, with absolute clarity, as a sullen child instinctively reaching for and simultaneously rejecting every bonbon on the plate. He had left New York in part to gain tranquility; now he knew that the disquiet was within, that it could not be tricked by sudden relocations or easy vows.

Later that night, as he walked fitfully around the cabin, the feeling assaulted Will that there was no place in all the world that could ever really be his, where he would finally and forever be content.

The meeting the next morning began with Buck declaring, "I agree with Will's evaluation. And his conclusion. We need a new aircraft *now* that will meet our needs for the next fifteen years. If we wait four or five years for a new design, the game may already be lost." His eyes circled the table. "I've decided to send a team to Europe right away to see the Airbus. The A-300 is far and away the most economical wide-body. It's got only two engines, so it uses twenty-five percent less fuel than any other wide-body. It carries two hundred and thirty or so passengers, which is as close as we're likely to get to the two hundred that would be ideal, and they're working on a smaller model for the future. We don't have to wait five years to see what a prototype looks like; they're flying right now in Europe and have a good safety record. Most importantly, European governments own the company that makes them and they'll fall all over themselves to arrange financing for us so they can break into the American market."

Ben Buck leaned back and waited for the reaction. He had stunned them. Bannister hemmed and hawed and finally admitted that the idea made financial sense. Conway declared that passengers no longer had strong aircraft preferences and that he could sell the Airbus.

"Jim, how do you feel about it?" the Old Man finally asked.

Keller raised his head. "When I came here, it was made clear that I'd have a free hand to standardize the fleet. We decided on Boeing. We've been able to cut maintenance costs and down time. The new plane Boeing's working on will fit our needs and fit in with the commonality of spare parts, servicing and support equipment we're aiming for. Now that we finally have a handle on costs and a way out of the chaos, you're throwing us right back into it."

Buck replied with simple logic. "We can't afford to wait for a plane that might never come and that we might not be able to pay for if it does."

Keller restated his objections.

At last Buck said, "If the plane checks out and the financing is there, I insist on it, Jim."

After a long pause, Keller said quietly, "I'll stay on until after the stockholders meeting, so as not to make problems for you. But as of this moment, I've resigned from Global Universal."

In the early-morning hours, when Ben Buck had finally, unalterably, decided on this course, he had feared that Keller's resignation would be inevitable. That sole consideration had almost made him turn back. He respected Jim Keller as much as he did any man who had ever been with GUA, and he secretly felt Keller was the right person to replace him. But he worried that the man's viewpoint had been so narrowed by the concerns of his current job that his judgments on larger issues had been sacrificed. This moment had been a test. Keller had failed it. He was as fine an operations man as there was. But he could never be a chief executive officer.

Buck began to discuss the impact of the European Airbus on the company's fortunes, but in his eyes Will thought he could detect another message—that the wagons in the circle around him, once all manned by friends, were drastically diminishing in number, tightening like a noose.

In the eyes of Bannister and Conway, Will believed he read something else, that he was no longer considered merely a bright young courtier. Despite his own burgeoning indifference, he was now to be treated as a very dangerous rival for Ben Buck's crown.

Bannister had been driving the auditors for weeks to complete the annual financial statements. When their job was done and he was satisfied that net income was as high as he could possibly peg it, the statements were incorporated into the annual report and sent to the printer. Then the statements would be added to the long proxy statement and to the proxy card that stockholders would be asked to sign. The package would be sent out at least thirty days before the shareholders met. "Fight" letters attacking the other side would have preceded it.

While others contacted the larger shareholders, Ben Buck spent his time redesigning the company's route system. He insisted that the plan to retrench gradually to the airline's strongest markets be in process before the shareholders met, at least to the extent that present CAB regulations allowed.

Buck's main concession to the coming proxy fight had been to induce prominent people who might attract votes to run as part of management's director slate, among them a former Cabinet officer and an ex-astronaut; the last had been added as a way of confusing stockholders who might have been swayed by Craig Merrill's public pronouncements. Bob Winstead of Metrobank had volunteered. Several incumbents had not been renominated. Will had replaced Al Goetz.

There was no way Will could diplomatically refuse the invitation, though he very much wanted to. As general counsel he could retain some degree of distance from decisions and warn Buck and others of potential pitfalls. As a director he would be resented if he opposed management's proposals, compromised if he did not. As a man he knew it would be more difficult to pull up stakes and move on to a new horizon.

Just after dinner on their flight to France, Will tried to broach the topic with Buck. The annual reports had not yet been run off; another's name could be stripped in. But the Old Man cut him off. Unless Will wanted to talk about the Airbus they were going to view, Buck wasn't interested, nor did he want to be told that their time could be spent more valuably back home working on the proxy fight. GUA's team of experts had been in Toulouse evaluating the Airbus. Buck shoved the report from GUA's V.P. of Flight Operations over to Will.

"Paul Engel said it flew like a dream, Will. He said it was everything a pilot could want. It will fit our gates. The fuel consumption and noise level are as low as they claim. If they'll make the right deal for it, I'll take thirty now and an option for twenty-five more with a right to switch to any other model they make in the future."

"General, if they're as anxious as you say to lease or sell us this Airbus, maybe we can try a few for six months or a year free of charge, with an option to order if it works out."

"We buy *now*!"

Will finally understood. Ben Buck was not merely picking a plane to fit his vision of the company's future needs, he was picking it to dictate for the next fifteen or twenty years the kind of airline GUA would have to be. Success on this trip meant that even if he were to lose on May 5, Buck would still have won.

"Duhamel called me this morning from Gomala," Buck said,

seemingly starting on a new topic. Jean-Pierre Duhamel, GUA's V.P. for European Operations, had been dispatched to Gomala to facilitate the opening of GUA air service to West Africa. "He says the American ambassador presented a very fair air treaty to the Gomalan President, but was told that exclusive landing rights had already been granted to a Swiss air charter outfit that runs a rinky-dink airline there." Buck pulled a slip of paper from the breast pocket of his sport shirt. "Aéronautique Eur-Afrique et Mondiale. They fly a few old planes to some countries in the area. An exclusive there too."

Buck paused, and when he spoke again he sounded very tired. Will realized that all the remarks had been part of the same concern: the time he had left. "My father and grandfather both died when they were seventy-five, did you know that?"

Buck was not expecting an answer. He closed his eyes. A few minutes later, when Will looked over at his battered features, he could not tell whether Buck was sleeping or lost in thought.

Will soon came to the opinion that Ben Buck was happier during the days in Toulouse than at any time since Will had joined the company. Often the lawyer would corner his chief executive to get some answers, only to have the Old Man suddenly mutter something like "I wonder if there's tail strike on rotation during an engine-out takeoff." And then he would run outside to fly the A-300 again.

The Global Universal people with them in France agreed with Buck that the Airbus was right for their needs. Buck quickly overrode the few reservations that were voiced. A deal was struck on very favorable terms to GUA because, as Buck had foreseen, the manufacturing consortium had run out of European customers and was anxious to crack the American market.

Will and Buck had just begun a discussion of the contract terms when a secretary brought word that Gunther Velheim was telephoning from Geneva. Buck's animated face quickly grew somber as he spoke to Velheim. He said very little. When he hung up, he told the younger man, "After we sign the Airbus agreements, we have to fly to Geneva. Velheim's banks have called some of his loans—thirty million dollars' worth. He's strapped for cash right now. By a strange coincidence, they also seem to have come up with a buyer willing to pay sixteen dollars a share for his GUA stock. A buck above the market. A little over thirty million dollars."

"By another strange coincidence that buyer wouldn't happen to be Faranco Inc., would it?"

"No, it's that Swiss company, Aéronautique Eur-Afrique."

Attired in a black velvet smoking jacket, Gunther Velheim graciously showed his two American guests through the large mansion overlooking Lake Geneva, ending up in a sunny room with a view of the snow-covered peaks. Velheim peered at his guests from wise, apologetic eyes which refused to rush the amenities that made life pleasant. Only after dessert and cigars were passed around did he broach the subject that had brought the Americans here.

Brazindustrial had weathered three recession-tossed years only because the banks had ridden with Velheim. The day before, without warning, the head of one of the largest Swiss banks had telephoned to demand repayment of thirty million dollars in outstanding loans. Later, at a private dinner, he had revealed the precipitating cause: Kalex Metallurgy, a giant Swiss company, had insisted that the banks force Brazindustrial to pay the notes or, alternatively, to sell its GUA stock to Eur-Afrique.

"It's strange that Faranco's name appears nowhere in this," Will observed.

"Not directly, no," Velheim said slowly. "My belief is that Kalex is merely doing a small favor for a friend. Faranco is its joint-venture partner in West Africa. Unfortunately, Ben, I am the small fly they are brushing off their friend's back."

"If Global Universal were to buy your shares, would that satisfy the bank?" Buck suddenly asked.

"I do not know."

"Will, when can you close on the 707 refinancing with Kean?"

"A month to six weeks."

"Can we use some of the money to buy Gunther's stock?"

"Sure. When we took down the Metrobank loan, we covered ourselves with a catchall statement that the funds might be part of a larger stock repurchase plan."

"Good. Very good." Buck swung back to his old friend. "Gunther, is Helmut Braschkopf still in the government?"

"Yes."

"May I call him on the phone?"

Fifteen minutes later, after Buck spoke to the man he had first befriended when Braschkopf was a minor Air Ministry official, Braschkopf called back with the information Buck sought. It could never be proven and the banking laws would protect the transaction's confidentiality, but the head of the private bank owning the stock of Aéronautique Eur-Afrique et Mondiale had admitted that the bank was merely custodian for a European subsidiary of Faranco Inc.

"It's a shame we can't prove it publicly," Will said. "Faranco contended in their CAB papers they owned no aviation interests."

Buck pulled at the corners of his mouth. "But Girard can't be sure that we *won't* be able to prove it. The trick is to make it cheaper for him to back down a little now. Gunther, if I could phone one more time. I want to call Girard."

Buck wasted no time on hypocritical preliminaries when Girard came on the line. "I'm offering you one dollar to buy that Swiss air charter company, Eur-Afrique. You and the banks give Velheim sixty days either to come up with the cash or sell his GUA shares to you—in writing. And I want real cooperation from you people in sewing up the West African arrangements. If you win the proxy fight, they're yours anyway."

Girard's voice through the phone was unruffled. "Assuming I have some influence with those parties, what do I get in return?"

"You have my word that I don't blow the whistle about your owning Eur-Afrique."

There was only the slightest pause from Girard's end.

"He has forty-five days, and in writing; Faranco automatically gets to buy his stock if the loans aren't paid by then. Anything else?"

"No, that's it."

There was a click. Buck turned to Velheim.

"He gave us until just before the stockholders meeting to buy you out, Gunther. His buyout will automatically take effect if we strike out. He'll put it in writing. You'll be safe either way."

"Thank you, my friend. Sometimes it is good to be only a fly when giants are fighting for the heavens."

Buck was ecstatic in the cab to the airport. He related the details of the short telephone conversation again and again to Will, roaring with laughter each time. Only once did his mood break. "It's a shame about Gunther. He's gotten old."

For Buck the European trip had been an unalloyed success. When the takeover attempt first commenced, he had been imprisoned by Girard's initiatives and the maze of legal dictates, where his experience was negligible and his own initiatives restricted. Perplexed, uncertain, like a man newly blinded, he had been forced to rely on others for the most part. His powerlessness had enraged and humiliated him.

Now, watching the white-haired giant move gregariously through the aircraft's cabin to chat with passengers and flirt with stewardesses, Will knew that during the past week he had finally observed the essence of the Ben Buck of legend. He was an aviation man, at last in his own arena. And if this was his final appearance, the last defense of his crown before retirement or defeat, he was making it a grand one.

19

In the hectic weeks that followed the Airbus purchase, time was measured by the inexorable diminution of days remaining until the stockholders meeting. With a new plane and a new domestic route system laid out, Buck now turned his attention to reorganizing the company's management structure, holing up with Conway and Bannister for long hours, emerging occasionally only on the page of a terse, upheaving memo.

Ignored, Will was left alone to direct the fight against Girard. He had no time for any social life beyond a quick drink now and then after work. Once he flew to New York to meet with James Kean and their lawyers to push forward the 707 financing. He phoned Belinda, but she was out of town with Schactman. Lunch with Marcie proved tedious. The contract with Buck would terminate a few days before the shareholders meeting. But without Belinda to rely on, Marcie refused to come to any decision about voting her stock.

Will saw nothing of Donna. That was her loss, he assured himself. Once, very late at night, he called Crew Scheduling to locate her and was told she was out of the country, assigned to a London flight.

* * *

In fact, at that moment, Donna was enjoying the luxury of a free day in London before the turnaround. It was a raw morning, and she was pleased to be in the warm, quaint antique shops filled to the rafters with old and interesting objects. A carved wooden carrousel horse. Hundred-year-old bureaus and desks. An early typewriter. A ship's bell. An old peg leg.

Donna halted. She suddenly remembered Will's moment of indecision their first morning on the island as she stood before him in her bikini, waiting for him to change. She missed his company most, she realized, when she wanted someone to show this pompous John Bull coin bank to, or to make silly jokes with about those old stereoscope photos of Egypt, or just to glance at from time to time. Maybe that was the greatest loss; she never grew tired of looking at him.

Well, tonight she had a date with that good-looking English actor in first class on the way over—he had been both put off and intrigued by her not knowing who he was. She guessed that would be fun. And tomorrow, back home, she had plans for the evening as well. Keeping busy was important, she told herself, and concentrating on other things.

But, in the very next shop, she saw a pre-Raphaelite painting of a young knight on a quest that brought Will to mind yet again. "St. George," the title plate read. Although the horse was rearing, the knight's dark, implacable eyes were fixed unwaveringly on the huge dragon in front of him.

To scold herself about this romanticized glossing-over of her and Will's very different outlooks, she added another thought: No doubt, at the very next castle, he'll find a maiden in distress—or, at the very least, a lady in waiting.

Their tour of department stores around the country had taken Belinda and Marcie west. Belinda had arranged to stop off in Denver to see Will for the evening. Marcie had traveled ahead to set up the collection in San Francisco. Belinda would catch an early plane and join her.

At dinner Belinda was full of humorous stories about her trip and was obviously happy to be with Will again. As they were leaving the restaurant, the two stood aside to let another couple enter. Will did not know the man. The woman was Donna.

"Hi," she said breezily. "Crew Scheduling said you were looking for me, but I guess it couldn't have been anything too important."

Will, uncharacteristically at a loss, forced out an awkward introduction of the two women.

"And this is Chuck Balis, my gynecologist," Donna replied.

Will stared at the man's blond, wholesome good looks. Not "Doctor Balis" or even "Charles," he thought, but "Chuck." They probably had cocktails in her bedroom before coming here. He probably knows every little technique to drive her out of her mind.

Balis extended a friendly hand to Will.

Donna smiled brightly at Belinda. "So you're the city mouse."

Belinda laughed. "You don't look much like a country mouse."

"I try my best. So long, Will."

As Donna and her escort edged by, Belinda remarked, "We must do this again sometime."

Outside, Belinda was silent for a moment. Then she exclaimed, "Shit, she's a knockout! I was hoping the home-town product needed emergency orthodontistry and dermatology."

"No, just gynecology. He makes house calls."

"I have my doubts."

"It's over between us."

"You might try telling *her* that."

"How are my pals Joe and Darrell doing?"

"*Touché.*"

At the cabin Belinda was charmed by the rustic setting and spent quite a while looking at Will's possessions. She stared at the roughhewn wooden bed and the thick patchwork comforter. Of all the men she had known, she decided, Will was among the very few who never stepped out of character, even for an instant, to play a role he mistakenly thought might appeal to her; Will merely revealed another aspect of himself.

"You *must* be special," she said, curling up on the comforter. "The amount of mileage I have to roll up to get laid!"

In the morning, while driving her to the airport, Will exacted a promise from Belinda. The contract with Buck would end before the stockholders meeting, and Marcie had not decided on the course of action to take with her stock. If Marcie wanted to retain her stock for investment, management wanted her proxy. If she wanted to sell, Buck would arrange somehow to buy. Will sought Belinda's word that she would try to convince Marcie to side with Buck in either case. In a few days, Will would be in New York for the closing with James Kean and could buy Marcie's stock then, if that was what Marcie decided on.

Belinda squeezed his hand and nodded her agreement. If one friend could help another, that was wonderful. And she would only have to go a few more days before seeing Will again. One thing, of course, could be firmly established right now.

"There is no doubt that Marcie will be *selling.*"

After so long with so few results, Owen Clayton felt the accident that brought the first real lead in many weeks was deserved and long overdue. A crate labeled "KITCHEN WARE" slipped out of the sling as it was being hoisted aboard a freighter. It smashed open on the pier. The harbor police found rifles thrusting through the excelsior. The next case they opened revealed rows of gleaming black hand grenades marching in lethal procession. There were thirty-one cases in all.

Clayton, who had been checking through watch company records for weeks, was on the pier within two hours. There was no doubt. The weaponry was from the army arsenal. He and the other FBI agents moved quickly to trace the shipping documents to the sender, a small New Jersey freight forwarder, before word of the accident could get back to him.

After a day of questioning, the man caved in. He revealed that the armament was destined for a splinter group fighting in Northern Ireland. Pro-Catholic but anti-IRA, it called itself the XE Brigade. He was not a member but had agreed to handle their illegal shipping out of the U.S. for a fee. The head of the rebel group in Ireland, One-Eye Johnny Doheeny, had contacted him through channels and made the deal on one of his secret trips to the States. An Irishman named Dan Ward had brought him the packed crates. The last consignment was expected the next day and would have been put aboard a different ship—if one shipment was discovered, the other might still get through. Each would follow circuitous routes and be transferred to other ships before finding their way into the hands of the XE Brigade in Ireland.

When Dan Ward showed up at the forwarder the next day, he found himself surrounded by a dozen law enforcement officers —all with guns drawn.

Tall and blond, with eyes opaque as blue granite, he refused during days of questioning to speak about himself, his group or the card found in his pocket that identified him as a representative of an Irish relief agency. Nor was he likely to. The records sent by British authorities suggested that Ward had survived much worse treatment during several incarcerations by the British. The relief agency had never heard of him.

The sullen rebel's only topic was the injustice of the British and the Protestants. As a last resort Clayton read Ward the list of weapons and amounts of materiel recovered by the FBI. Ward erupted.

"There was more *plastique* and more pistols," he shouted. "You bastards have taken the stuff yourselves, to resell it."

"Looks like somebody did."

Ward glowered with rage, but held his tongue. The outburst was not repeated.

Wearing a stevedore's cap, a false black mustache and a hand tattoo, he might have been the weapons buyer and 211 passenger who seemed a logical suspect. But Clayton doubted it. This young man was one who relied on muscle and courage. Someone else much more wily had negotiated the weapons purchase. Ward had only trucked it cross-country, probably already packed in sealed cases. The British described Doheeny as a small, wiry man, so he couldn't have been the weapons buyer either.

Things were beginning to fall into place in Clayton's mind. He had a hunch that the relief-agency angle would lead somewhere. And another hunch, finally, about where in the watch companies' records he should be looking.

The sense of excitement was beginning to grow in him at last. Clayton knew that meant he was getting close.

Snow had been unusually sparse in the early winter. But once begun, it had come with a vengeance and, as it often did in the

Rockies, was falling heavily at the end of April. GUA's public-relations staff feared that the storm would not cease by May 1, the day of the celebration planned for Global Universal's fiftieth anniversary. But the first May morning, a Sunday, while still cold, was clear and sunny.

The high point of the festivities was when the Old Man took up a duplicate of the original plane on which he had flown the airline's first mail delivery from South America. He circled the field a few times, gently put the little high-winged monoplane down and rolled up to the Airbus parked in front of GUA's hangars. Ben Buck's eyes were glistening with what had to be tears as he stepped from the cockpit dressed in the same kind of outfit he had worn fifty years before—even to the .45 automatic strapped to his hip, which was once required equipment for all U.S. airmail pilots.

Then there were speeches, by Buck and others, followed by a buffet that had been set up in a large hangar for the several thousand guests and GUA employees.

Will hung at the periphery of the crowd and stared at the mammoth 747 transport under which the party was taking place. Graceful, beautiful, overwhelming in its awesome size, the airliner could have tucked an entire DC-3, once the miracle of air transportation, under each wing. How quickly our perception of the miraculous changes, Will thought.

"He's still out there somewhere. That's what you're thinking, isn't it?"

Will's head turned toward the woman's voice. Helen Conway, a drink in her hand, had come up beside him. Lee was a step behind her.

"*Who's* out there?" Will asked.

"The bomber. They've never caught him, have they?"

"No."

"I was sure it wasn't the Pittsburgh Three."

"That what they've taken to calling them now? No, it probably wasn't the Pittsburgh group. The FBI thinks the man who did it slipped out of the country."

"An American?"

"No, a foreign terrorist."

"But they're not sure. And they can't be sure he isn't coming back."

"That's true."

Helen Conway's eyes swung to her husband.

"Out of the question," he muttered.

"Lee, I swear to you we will," she retorted, a steel edge in her voice.

"Let's not discuss it here." He cast an angry sidelong glance at Will.

"Then where? You avoid the issue. You keep thinking if you don't discuss it with me it'll go away."

"I think I'll get a drink," Will said politely, and started toward the bar.

"Please don't, Will." Helen's hand on his arm halted him. "Lee said you were more involved in the investigation than anyone else in the company. If you tell me the bomber won't be back, that the kids and I will be a hundred percent safe from him flying GUA to Hawaii next week, then we will."

"Look, you folks can settle this without me."

"But you can't give me that guarantee?"

"No."

Will was unable to move off quickly enough through the crowd to avoid hearing Lee Conway's threat.

"I warn you, Helen, if you humiliate me by flying on another airline, that will be the end between us! And it will be your fault."

Helen's voice was louder and, thus, also unavoidable.

"If you put your job ahead of your family's safety, then I'll be glad to call it quits. Your job *better* be important to you then, because I'll want a lot of alimony."

The glance Conway had directed at Will stuck like a splinter in the lawyer's thoughts. The intimate hand Helen had placed on his arm and the warm, reliant tone she had instinctively assumed with him were as obvious an indication of their former relationship as if Lee had discovered Will naked in their bedroom closet. Perhaps she had already listed him among the infidelities with which she may have taunted her husband.

But Conway had another reason for anger lately. The Old Man had procrastinated on the deep fare discounts Conway had advocated; and now other lines had already announced drastically lowered fares, stealing Global Universal's thunder. Lower fares, Conway had been maintaining, were the wave of the future, and he had insinuated that, despite the Airbus purchase, time seemed to have finally passed Buck by.

Will wandered off in the general direction of Ben Buck, to whom he wanted to offer his own fiftieth-anniversary congratulations.

A familiar figure, tall with dark-red hair, appeared in his path. Donna.

"Well, look who's here," she declared with an easy smile, "the Playboy of the Western World."

"You've become a bit literary, haven't you?"

"Your effect, I admit it. I read constantly now. A friend gave me some of the reading lists and lecture notes for courses at the university. I'm already through the basic literature courses and working on some of the electives."

"I'm impressed."

Honesty seemed to ambush her face with the surprised smile he remembered so well. "You were supposed to be. I'm impressed myself."

"How have you been?"

"Pretty good, for a person who found herself feeling like a damned fool for a while."

"I've missed you."

"Thanks, but I doubt it. That's the reason I broke it off when I did. To this day you probably don't understand why. It had very little to do with wanting to live together for its own sake and a lot to do with the fact that one sometimes gets to the point where people aren't interchangeable in one's life. Another date on Saturday night just wasn't the same thing as being with you."

"I felt the same way."

"But you weren't grown up enough to limit your life as a result of it. You were still like a kid in a candy store."

"Maybe." Will reflected for a moment. "That's probably true. But I've still missed you."

"That's nice to know, but you haven't given up the candy store."

"Can we have dinner one night?"

Her laugh sounded very wise. "Oh, no you don't! Let's leave well enough alone and just wish it could have been different."

She kissed him delicately on the cheek, then moved off toward the buffet.

Will stared after her until the chestnut hair was swallowed by the sea of people.

Several old men were gathered around Ben Buck, faces smiling, hands occasionally imitating a plane's swoop or a roll. He was "Buckie" now. And despite their protruding belt lines and receding hairlines, they were "Slim" or "Curly" or "Red." Captivated, Will stood at the edge of the little circle and listened until Buck had to break away to speak with other guests.

"Hey, Will," Buck exclaimed, catching sight of him, "why don't you take the old plane up? God, you forget with all these hydraulics and instruments and computers what it was like to really *fly* the plane."

"I'll leave that to the real pilots, like you and those fellows. Congratulations, General," Will said sincerely. "Fifty years is a magnificent accomplishment."

"Hell, the way I feel, I'm good for another fifty!"

He turned abruptly to other people.

As Will headed toward the exit, Lee Conway stepped into his path. A faint smile failed to conceal the anger and humiliation he felt.

"Say, Will, I've been meaning to tell you—you know that reorganization the Old Man is working on? It's set now that all your departments will be part of Administration—reporting directly to Bannister! Sorry about that."

Out of the corner of his eye, Will sensed that a figure nearby had suddenly stopped moving. Will glanced to the side. Arnold Bannister was staring at him, his mouth bent into a malicious smile.

Will stepped around Conway with a look of utter contempt.

Outside, pickets marched in front of the gate in the high chain-link fence surrounding the airfield. There were about a hundred or so, chanting loudly, "GUA grounds women! GUA grounds women!" They were a diverse assemblage, Will observed as he went toward the parking lot, well-dressed matrons to ski-parka-clad college kids. Sally Emerson was at the head of the circling parade. In her hands was a large sign proclaiming "GUA DISCRIMINATES AGAINST WOMEN EMPLOYEES."

She charged up and tried to engage Will in a debate over GUA's female hiring and promotion practices. As Will moved past her toward his car, Sally loudly accused him of callousness toward the plight of women.

As Will drove away he noticed that Helen Conway had joined the pickets and was being lustily cheered.

That night Will sat by the picture window in his living room and contemplated all the issues he had stored in his mind's attic, some for months, some for years. Conway's disclosure of the coming reorganization had shaken him. Undoubtedly, the Old Man had made up his mind to squash the only employee who knew the secret of his ill-health and to whom he had vowed he would resign. Will had often thought he might be happiest in a little law office in some small Colorado town, eking out an honorable living and occasionally, like Sally Emerson and Ralph Nader and Jimmy Stewart, courageously backing his beliefs by taking on the big guys. What a pretty self-delusion that was, he suddenly perceived, for the defender of an ill and lying Ben Buck—briber of foreign officials and suppressor of evidence that Faranco had lied to the CAB.

Perhaps his bristly independence was only a pose to cover the fear of failure, so good that even Will himself was fooled—a tough Dead End Kid bluff that, if called, would leave him cowering, his tail between his legs. There might be nothing within the walls of his inner sanctuary, neither the courage nor the beliefs. Open up the little vault in his heart where he had always told himself had been deposited for safekeeping all the emotions which might be set upon if left exposed, all the vulnerable needs, and he might find only a few grains of dust, the final residue of self-delusion.

And Buck knew that. He owned Will Nye, had raised Will's hopes long enough to get the most out of him, and planned to discard him when his usefulness was at an end. Buck knew Will would accept whatever was imposed on him. Donna had called him a hired gun. Was it true? Was he committed only and always to playing out mindlessly the game society had set up and expected of him, on whatever team he happened to find himself?

He started to reflect on the past weeks and stopped at a Friday night in Florida, the first night there. He and Belinda had gone to the dog track. Yapping packs of unfed greyhounds raced after a rabbit skin on a rail. Someone had explained that the few dogs who ever managed to catch the spurious quarry went through an extended depression and had to be retrained for months to race once more after the artificial prey. Was that the canine equivalent of the state in which he now found himself, eager to be retrained to ignore the shabbiness of the bait leading him around the endless track on which he foolishly thought he freely ran? Was he—for all his pretensions of integrity—just like the others yapping in the pack?

His thoughts were interrupted by the phone. Will had half a mind to let it keep ringing, but it could be the Old Man. He lifted the receiver.

"Hello."

"Hello, Will. Your mother gave me your phone number. . . . She says you're doing fine."

Eight years had passed since their last exchange, but his ex-wife's voice was as vivid in his memory as if it had been yesterday.

"As soon as you left the hospital, my leg grew back."

There was a pause. Then she replied, "That anger is what chased me away then."

"I guess speaking to you again opened old wounds—as they say. I'm sorry. Why are you calling?"

"Some men have been around asking questions about you. They say it's for a government appointment, but they sounded too menacing. When I wouldn't tell them anything, they offered me money. After that they threatened me."

"Thanks, Karen. I know who sent them. I just didn't know I was important enough game. I appreciate your calling to let me know. There's only a few days left. They probably won't bother you anymore."

He waited for her goodbye and was about to cut it short himself when she said, "I'm happy, Will, I really am. My husband

and I teach at the same college, and he's a good man. We're expecting a second child soon."

There was a long silence before he responded. "I'm very glad for you, Karen. And I'm glad you called."

"Goodbye, Will."

"Goodbye."

The pain was gone, pain of such long standing that only when it was no longer there did he realize that it had ever been.

Nearly a minute passed before he became aware of an emotion that had burst forth during the phone conversation: blowtorch anger at Girard. Will had canceled the investigation of Girard's and Marie's private lives. Such scruples, Will decided, were an admission of weakness to the likes of Girard, an opening for the sneak dirty blow. To beat him, one played with a single rule: Winning is the only morality. Will wanted to beat this murderer of his friend, this violator of his privacy, with all the fury of which his soul was capable.

He lifted the phone and dialed Benke's office. He did not expect to find the detective there so late, but, to Will's surprise, the phone was answered by a voice as angry as his own. The office had been ransacked, file locks smashed and files stolen. All the Faranco files.

"It's a damned good thing I know these bastards, Will. I had photocopies of everything on Faranco and Girard in my bank vault."

"That couldn't have been too much, Charlie."

"More than before. I couldn't just let the investigation drop altogether, so I wrote a letter asking friends who are also in the association of former FBI agents to do some checking on my behalf, particularly in Houston—Girard listed that as a college home address—and in Virginia, his high-school home address. A few things popped up: the Girards' marriage license in Houston and an old Virginia newspaper clipping that mentioned a car crash in which Girard's parents had been killed. I asked my friend to pursue that one a little farther, see if he could track down the exact place they had died. As a matter of fact, I came back here tonight because I'm waiting for another friend who finally was able to spring Girard's records from the Carleton School. He should be here soon."

"Nothing came in about the Miami, Florida, area?"
"That's never been mentioned before."
"I know Marie Girard was there sometime before the Second World War. She took a trip from Dinner Key on a Pan Am flying boat between 1932 and 1941."
There was a silence before Benke spoke again.
"You sure you want me to look into Girard's wife as well as him?"
"We have only four days before the stockholders meeting. Whatever will stop that maniac is fair game. His rules."
"Miami, then. I'll catch a late plane tonight. A scandal about himself he might ignore. If it's about his wife, you've got him by the balls."
"That's where I want him, Charlie. And then I want to squeeze."

20

Tuesday, the third of May. The phonc and the alarm clock rang at almost the same time. Will started to answer the clock, then his mind cleared. He turned off the alarm and lifted the receiver.

"Will, Owen Clayton here. I'm calling from New York."

"Oh, good morning, Owen. What's up?"

"Do you know a woman named Rifkin?"

"Rifkin?"

"Belinda Rifkin. She's a dress designer, with a studio on . . . " He seemed to be referring to notes. "On West Broadway. She claims to have been with you New Year's Eve."

"What time New Year's Eve?"

"When Craig Merrill was killed—eleven-thirty."

"I can verify that."

"Do you know anything about her background?"

"What do you mean, her background? Come on, Owen, level with me. What's this about?"

Clayton was coughing. Will waited for the fit to pass and repeated what he had said.

"Let me start from the beginning," Clayton said. "We found the bulk of the weapons we were looking for and an Irish national in this country illegally by the name of Dan Ward. In his pocket was a piece of paper with the name on it of one of the relief agencies distributing to the needy in Ireland."

"What does that have to do with Belinda?"

"The relief agency over there had never heard of Dan Ward. We began checking in this country. Some very prominent people are involved in fund raising for the agency here."

"And Belinda's one of them?"

"She was at a party for them in the spring and gave a party at her studio last summer. One of her paintings was donated and auctioned off. Other artists did the same thing." Clayton's speech had slowed. He seemed to be scanning his notes again. "Oh, she spent one year at the University of Dublin and got in with some pretty radical types."

"And the year before she studied in Paris, so you can blame the '68 student riots on her, too."

"We're just checking, Will, that's all."

"I still don't understand what."

"Our best guess is that part of the money raised in this country for the relief agency never got there but went to buy weapons for the terrorist group Ward was with, the XE Brigade. The relief agency probably knew nothing about it. They were happy with whatever they got."

"Did they tell you who sent them their money?"

"Yeah, Carl Raymond."

There was a long silence.

"You still there, Will?"

"Yes, I'm here." Will struggled to control his elation. "Carl Raymond doesn't sound very Irish."

"He shortened Carroll to Carl as a kid so it wouldn't sound like he had a girl's name. Raymond was a French merchant who settled in Ireland a couple of hundred years ago."

"That's the clincher, then, Owen."

"I'm not completely sure yet. He showed us the books he kept. Every penny that came in was accounted for. A lot of people took on the job of doing the actual fund raising and then turned over the money to him."

"Like Belinda?"

"And Riordan, the Senator. O'Dea, the film producer. O'Brien of O'Brien Crude Oil. Dolan of Transatlantic Lumber and Trading. The Mulvaney family raised a quarter of a million dollars in one afternoon in East Hampton. Any one of them could have held back something."

"They're all too rich for that. Is J. Stephen Girard involved at all?"

"The Girard Foundation donated ten thousand dollars. Raymond says they did it as a favor to him."

"You sound as if you've got to catch him wrapping the wire around the detonator before you can arrest him."

"We're watching Raymond like a hawk. But we still have some things to check out to be a hundred percent sure. All I've got to do is smear him and Faranco by mistake—how many days before the vote?"

"Three."

"Three days before the vote—and my ass would be swinging higher than the Sears Tower."

"Did you find out anything that would connect them to the pocket watches?"

"No, and I spent a solid two months checking out every receipt and ledger entry at those watch companies." Clayton chuckled. "One owner tried to hire me as his new controller."

"I'll be in New York City tonight. Can we meet so you can fill me in?"

"Will, this is an investigation. Until we make an actual arrest in the case . . ."

"Don't do that to me, Owen. I didn't take any action on my own or leak anything where Craig Merrill was concerned."

"And keep in mind how guilty *he* turned out to be."

Will tried to block a pleading tone from slipping into his voice, but he could almost taste the kill. "I want to be there at the finish, Owen. I'm owed that much by the . . . the Fates, at least."

"Nobody ever ends up with what they deserve." Clayton's voice was bitter. "Okay, Will. We should know by tomorrow morning if Raymond is guilty and how deeply Girard and the company are implicated. Meet me at eight-thirty tomorrow morning in the lobby of the Waldorf, near the front entrance. It's near the Faranco Building. I want our people to move in on it in force, make the arrests, seize records, the whole shebang."

"Thanks. That's one I owe you."

"If something comes up and I can't be there, I'll leave a message at the front desk."

"The Waldorf. Tomorrow. Eight-thirty in the morning."

" 'Bye."

As he hung up, Clayton wondered how much more adamant Will would have been if he had revealed that Carl Raymond's silver pocket watch was identical to those used as timers on the bombs.

Another coughing fit overcame him. Less than four hours had passed since the last pill, but he had to take one more to dull the pain.

Snow was threatening again, and the roads into Denver were glass. Will, driving slowly, was late for the meeting in the Board Room, but he realized he had missed little. The others, who were not at the center of the maelstrom as Will was, were being brought up to date on the latest developments in the proxy contest. Confidence that victory was within reach was apparent in the relaxed atmosphere.

"You can be very proud, General. You too, Arnold," Bergheim was saying. "The financial institutions that own your stock are voting overwhelmingly for management. They know things weren't easy for the aviation industry and respect the way you attacked the problems, kept all your creditors and stockholders informed, and have come out of it. Bergheim, Mack got to them early, but it would have meant nothing if they didn't respect the job you've done."

"What about the banks and insurance companies associated with Faranco?" asked Buck.

"Most of them sold out at the tender. In our estimates we're figuring that the stock owned by Creighton, Cromwell, Lorillard Bank, First Federal and one or two other institutions will go to Faranco. But we kept on their tails to make sure that they sent on our proxy material to beneficial shareholders whose stock they don't have a right to vote—where they're just the nominee or there's a co-trustee. Eli and I personally took the envelopes with the material to the president of each, with GUA's check for postage."

"Max Creighton must have shit purple," Buck guffawed.

"We're getting a very heavy response, even from Faranco's institutions. Most shareholders vote for management's slate of directors automatically. Our follow-through with the institutions and using local airline employees to call local shareholders has been very effective. When we give you the totals we project, you'll see just how effective."

"And we were up against a very difficult problem here," Bill Tait explained to the others. "Faranco was careful not to nominate any of their own officers or directors to their slate, so they wouldn't have to reveal their wheeling and dealing in our stock after the tender period expired."

"To the casual observer Faranco isn't involved in this proxy fight at all," Glidden added. "Faranco will vote its share just as any other stockholder has a right to do . . . for the Eckman slate."

Glidden gestured toward Natalie Harmon and stepped to a blackboard resting on an easel. She joined him.

"We've analyzed GUA's past proxy returns," Glidden stated, "and the flow we're receiving now. We've done extensive telephone surveys and got advance information from the institutions that haven't submitted their proxies yet. Here's the way we're pretty sure the vote will break down."

Harmon had a sheet of paper in her hand. Referring to it, she began to write columns of numbers on the blackboard, while explaining their significance. As of the completion of the tender offer, Faranco owned 30.3 percent of GUA's outstanding common stock. The Girard Foundation owned 3 percent. A recent private purchase from a mutual fund amounted to 2.3 percent of outstanding stock and brought the total under Girard's putative control to 35.6 percent. After a lot of inquiries and deduction, the GUA experts were convinced that Faranco had managed to obtain voting commitments of only about 4.6 percent from institutions—for a 40.2 percent total.

Buck owned just under 10 percent and the Buck Foundation just under 5 percent. However, institutional blocks pledged to management, including the Metrobank block, and proxies already in hand totaled about 29 percent, for a known vote in GUA's favor of about 44 percent.

The rest of the proxies looked as if they would break down

with a quarter not voting and the rest running three to one in favor of management.

"What about the Velheim and Manning stock?" Bannister asked when he realized that those blocks were missing from Harmon's figures.

"I was just getting to that, Arnold," the young woman said. "They're the balance of power here. We're scheduled to buy the Velheim stock tomorrow with the proceeds of the 707 refinancing and receive his proxy at the same time. Without the Velheim stock we have forty-eight and a half percent. With it we have fifty-three percent."

"Then there's no doubt we've won," Conway burst out. He turned toward Will. "Is there any chance that we won't close on the 707s?"

"None that I can foresee," Will answered. "The closing is scheduled for tomorrow morning at Willoughby Securities, the lead underwriter. The SEC's last comments are being incorporated into the papers right now. They'll be at the printer by afternoon for sure. James Kean of Willoughby has approved everything and put together a syndicate of institutions to take the debt issue. Bergheim, Mack is taking a good part of it. Serge, do you see any reason why it might not go through?"

Bergheim shook his head. "After the closing, money will be released in Zurich to pay Velheim."

Will went on. "Just in time to meet tomorrow night's midnight time limit, when our option to buy the Velheim block expires. Girard calculated it carefully and obviously knew that our charter didn't permit an earlier stockholders meeting."

Conway spoke up again. "It was my understanding a company couldn't vote stock it owned."

"*We're* not actually buying Velheim's stock, Lee. As you know, we're borrowed up to our eyelashes. Bob Winstead got his Board to agree that Metrobank would buy the Velheim and Manning stock if we reduced our debt to the bank by an equivalent amount. We'll use the first thirty million of the seventy we get from tomorrow's 707 financing to pay back thirty of the one-fifty we owe Metrobank. They'll then buy Velheim's stock with their own funds."

"And of course there's not the shadow of a doubt you'll be able to pay Velheim on time." Sarcasm was edging into Conway's voice.

"If we can't make the payment on time, the stock and the proxy go to Faranco automatically. They'll be able to vote the stock a few hours later at the shareholders meeting. We're really cutting it close."

Teicher shifted in his seat. "In these things, you almost always end up cutting it close—one way or the other."

"Which," Harmon resumed, "brings us right to the matter at hand. The Velheim stock gives our side a very small but still a clear win. If something prevents us—that is, Metrobank—from buying Velheim's stock, the Manning stock can tip it either way, about one point eight percent of the company."

All eyes turned toward Will.

"I'm meeting Marcie Manning in New York tonight," Will told them. "She's held off selling out to Girard pending our coming up with cash. We'll set a price tonight."

Buck was full of good cheer. "If she wants your body instead of the cash, you're fired if you turn her down."

"The timing is awfully tight," Greer, the treasurer, remarked.

"This one is a piece of cake," said Bill Tait airily. "I remember a Board meeting where a director stopped a takeover by pulling a phone out of the wall to prevent another director from telephoning in the deciding vote."

"I remember a takeover," Harmon reminded them, "that was stopped when the chairman pulled out something a lot more shocking that that!"

The room exploded. Buck loved it. Harmon was one of the boys.

As Teicher and Glidden began to review the procedures to be followed at the shareholders meeting, Lorna broke into the room and hurried up to Will's side. A moment later Will excused himself to return to his office for an urgent phone call from a hospital in Miami regarding Charlie Benke.

He closed the door and picked up the phone. "Will Nye here."

"Hello, Mr. Nye." A woman's voice. In her twenties probably. "Charles Benke asked me to call you. He said you would know I was really calling for him if I told you the name Abner Boone."

"Okay, you're from Charlie. Has something happened?"

The woman's voice seemed to falter a bit as she began to answer. "Mr. Nye, I'm a nurse here. I'm calling for him because he was found badly beaten up and unconscious early this morning. When he came to a little while ago, he insisted that I tell you. He's very weak and has several fractures, but he wouldn't take any medication until I promised to deliver a message to you."

"What's the message?"

She spoke slowly as she repeated what he had told her. "'Get here fast. They didn't get it from me.'"

"Did he say what it was someone was trying to get?"

"No. He repeated the same message twice." She paused a moment, weighing whether to say what was on her mind. "He's critical, Mr. Nye. His skull was fractured. The doctors will decide later today whether to operate to relieve pressure on the brain. He insisted nothing be done until you arrive."

"I should be there this afternoon. What's your name, Nurse?"

"Elizabeth Steihl." She spelled it.

"Tell him I'm on my way, Ms. Steihl."

"Yes, sir."

While Lorna checked the *Airline Guide* and confirmed Will's suspicion that commercial flights would take too long, Will called Flight Operations. A Westwind was available, but they would have to dig up a second pilot. Could he allow them an hour? Time was something Will had little of, with Benke critically injured and onto something important. He had to get there as quickly as possible. Will told them he would be the second pilot himself.

Twenty minutes later he was in the air, headed southeast.

"Nurse Steihl, please."

A short Hispanic cleaning woman pointed farther down the hospital corridor. Will thanked her and hurried toward the rectangle cut out of the wall at the junction with another corridor.

Will leaned into the room behind the opening. A black nurse was writing on a chart. She looked up.

"Can I help you?"

"Nurse Steihl?"

"Are you the gentleman from Denver to see Mr. Benke?"

"Yes. My name's Nye."

She quickly tucked the chart under her arm and moved to the

door. "Please follow me. Miss Steihl is with him. He keeps losing consciousness."

She moved with surprising quickness. Will strained to keep up with her.

"Did she tell you much when she called, Mr. Nye?"

"Only that he was found badly beaten up, several fractures."

"All his clothes had been ripped off him. The police thought he had been hit by a truck, but then they saw his wallet had been taken . . . everything he was wearing."

She led him into a small ward with four beds. Only one was occupied. At first Will thought he was looking at a cartoon: the man in the bed was enveloped in plaster casts and bandages; a leg and an arm were suspended. A dark-haired nurse who had been sitting in a chair beside the bed rose and came to the door. She was in her twenties, as he had gathered from her voice. But her thin, plain face looked older.

"This is Mr. Nye, Betty."

She offered him her hand to shake. The black nurse withdrew.

"He went back under soon after I called you," the woman said in a whisper. "But his pulse and respiration are strong."

She led Will to the side of the bed. Only Benke's eyes and mouth were free of gauze and tape. At least two teeth had been broken.

"Oh, Lord!" Will gasped. "Do they know who did it?"

"No. The police had to identify him through his fingerprints. He had once been with the FBI, they say."

"You said his skull may be operated on."

"That's why I was so pleased when his eyes opened and he spoke. It was just after I came back on this morning. I immediately called in a doctor to see him. Mr. Benke kept insisting I call you before they operated."

"What was his exact message again, Nurse?"

"'Get here fast. They didn't get it from me.'"

"The other nurse said he wasn't wearing anything when he was found. Where could he have hidden whatever it is he wants me to have?" Will thought about the problem for a while and examined every inch of the near-mummy before him. The skin of one hand and one leg were exposed. "Could he have swallowed something?"

"I don't think so. A body scan was done when he was admitted, to check for internal injuries—a kidney was badly injured. Any foreign object would have shown up."

Will had trouble concentrating on the problem. The savagery inflicted on Benke must have been meant to kill him. Will noticed a precise row of welts near the right eye—brass knuckles. What secret could have been so terrible that one human being would order such violence inflicted on another?

"He has a strong body, Mr. Nye. He'll pull through. He has deep religious faith too. That will be a source of great strength as well." Will nodded at her words without hearing. "At first we thought it was a cross he was clutching around his neck and we were about to call a priest for the—you know—the last rites. But then we saw it was the ornament with prayers that Jews wear. They have them on their doors. The rabbi came by, I understand, but Mr. Benke was still unconscious."

Will looked down at Benke's free hand. He could just make out the top of the gold mezuzah in the clenched fist. The gold chain on which the prayer tube hung circled Benke's neck. Odd that Benke is Jewish, Will thought. The FBI didn't take many Jews back then. And then Will suddenly understood. Many people wear some kind of religious ornament. But a mezuzah is hollow. Prayers are written out on parchment and rolled up inside. The attackers must have thought it just another solid religious medal and ignored it, perhaps even superstitiously avoided tearing it from his body.

Will reached down to remove the small article from Benke's hand. Reflexively the fingers tightened even more strongly. Will bent to the injured man's ear and whispered.

"It's me, Charlie, Will Nye. I'm here. You can give it to me. Will Nye—*Abner Boone.*"

The hand relaxed. The eyes fluttered, then opened. The dry lips moved. "Watching here," Benke said. "Watching the building."

A minute motion of Benke's hand indicated he wanted to whisper. Will put his ear close to Benke's mouth.

"It's all . . . in there. I was afraid . . . something like this. One more . . ." He raised his head slightly. The pain cut off his speech for an instant. "One more place . . . understand?"

"Yes, to check out."

Benke forced clarity into the words. "But about husband. Not . . . wife. Crippville . . . Virginia . Say it back."

Will repeated the whisper into Benke's ear, then positioned himself to listen once more.

"Louis J. Girard. Isabel Girard. Parents."

Benke's voice trailed off. Speaking was becoming too much of an effort. The eyeballs started to roll up.

"Is that where the newspapers say they crashed and were killed?" Will asked.

Benke's head moved slightly forward in assent. As much of a smile as the pain would allow creased his mouth.

Will straightened up. He wanted to put his gratitude into words but could not think of anything adequate to Benke's sacrifice and dedication. One thing he could do was put the hospital bills on Global Universal's tab and hire guards to protect Benke while he was recovering. Until then the clock on his services would continue to run. Will told Benke and thanked him as best he could before the eyelids relaxed and closed.

"He's asleep now," Steihl remarked softly. "Not unconscious."

Will drew her to the other side of the room. Speaking in whispers, he put through a collect telephone call to Eloise Cooper. She would handle all the arrangements confidentially. Will hung up and, still in subdued tones, addressed Elizabeth Steihl.

"I've asked her to order round-the-clock nurses, Ms. Steihl. I'd appreciate your staying on."

"I'd rather not."

Will was surprised. "But he's in no condition to do anything for himself."

"No, I didn't mean that. And I'm sure he'll pull through. The hospital will arrange for someone to replace me." Will realized the young woman's voice was cracking with strain.

"Might I ask why?"

"It would serve no purpose."

"Look, if I did something to offend you without realizing it, Ms. Steihl . . . I'd like to make it up somehow."

"Mr. Nye," she said harshly, "my brother and sister-in-law were killed on one of your planes last year. Two very young kids have no parents. I have to work half a day just to pay for the woman who cares for them so I can be out working the whole day. Creepy men keep coming around from your airline trying to get me to sign away the children's claims against you for next to nothing . . ."

"They're not from us, they're from the insurance company. We have very little control—"

The young woman interrupted sharply. "Harry and Molly were killed on a plane, not on an insurance company!"

"I apologize, Ms. Steihl. I'll try to see that it stops. Do you have a lawyer?"

"There's a lawyer with the union who said he would handle it."

"With all due respect to him, it's a field for specialists. If you don't think I'm interfering or trying to take advantage of you, I'd like to send you the names of several specialists who usually pin the airlines' ears back. To begin with, they can give you knowledgeable advice." Will had another thought. "When you choose one, have him call me. I'll then arrange for some money for the kids against any future settlement or award, as long as you agree it won't prejudice our case."

"Do airlines usually do that?"

"No."

"Thank you."

Will walked to the window. He pushed aside the edge of the curtain. A man stood across the street, his eyes fixed on the hospital's entrance.

"If I could ask for a couple more favors, Nurse. Some stationery, stamps and a way out of the building without being seen."

"The stationery and stamps are easy." She went for them. In her head she ticked off each entrance to the building, and when she reached Emergency she realized how it could be done.

Five minutes later Will had dropped a special-delivery letter to Ben Buck in the mail chute and was riding the elevator to the basement. The short, dark-complexioned cleaning woman watched him leave Benke's room, then slipped in. Seeing the nurse there, she smiled and began to mop. As the wide arcs of the mop brought her close to the bed, she began to take quick glances at the patient. If something had changed since the last time she was in the room, those men who had paid her so well would want to know.

* * *

The ambulance raced onto the street, lights flashing. As it swung around the corner, Will cautiously lifted his head high enough to peer out the side window. The man watching the hospital entrance had shot the ambulance only the most cursory of glances as it passed.

"Don't you give it another thought, old buddy," the driver called to him with a heavy Southern accent. "We'll have you at the airport in a jiffy."

"She's a good woman, Betsy is," the other man, a tall blond in his thirties, was saying. "The missus and I went over to visit after she lost her brother and his wife. They were on that 747 that crashed Thanksgiving weekend."

"I heard," said Will softly.

"She said you came to see that fellow we picked up just off the MacArthur Causeway. The kind of pain he had to be in it was a lucky thing he was unconscious. To tell you the truth, there was a minute or two there Bubba and me thought he was dead."

"I'd like to get my hands on those sons of bitches!" the driver spat.

"Just get me to the airport fast. The faster I'm out of here, the quicker they'll be paid back."

"You got it. Hang on."

Fifteen minutes later they were approaching the airport. The Westwind was parked near the service gate. The white ambulance swung through the chain-link fence and onto the tarmac.

"This is fine, guys. I appreciate it." Will slipped out of the back of the ambulance.

As he approached the executive jet, the door opened and a man jumped down. The face was one Will recognized from Benke's stack of Faranco glossies. A blank face. Gray, expressionless eyes. In his hand was a pistol. Will had an instant of surprise that it wasn't a .45 automatic.

"The gold thing Benke had around his neck. Give it to me, Nye."

"Where's the pilot?"

"He'll live. But you might not make it if you keep me waiting." The voice was as devoid of feeling as the eyes.

Will slowly pulled the mezuzah and chain from his pocket and tossed them off to the side. The gunman's stare never left Will's face as he crossed to where they lay. Just as he bent down, his eyes still on Will, the gun level, the ambulance roared forward and caught him broadside. He flipped upward and crumpled as he hit the ground.

The attendants stepped lazily from the ambulance. They pulled a stretcher from the rear and ambled over to where the man lay. The Southerner was shaking his head. He squatted down to check for injuries.

"It's a shame about these hit-and-run drivers. Why, would you believe this very morning we found a man in the same condition off the MacArthur Causeway?"

Will picked up the mezuzah and chain and dropped them into his pocket. "If the police want me as a witness, Ms. Steihl knows where I can be reached. Would you mind taking a look at the pilot for me?"

"Sure," the tall blond replied. "My other patient doesn't seem in any hurry."

The attendants left the Faranco man beside the stretcher and joined Will inside the Westwind. The pilot was trussed up in the lavatory, a welt on his forehead. He was still groggy, but he refused to wait around for a doctor to see him. This was one town he wanted to get out of fast. He staggered into the right-hand seat and belted himself in.

The ambulance headed toward the highway, the Westwind toward Virginia.

"Yep, you name it, son, it's all here. Births. Deaths. Deeds. Mortgages. Over there's weddings. You can come near tracing a person's whole life in this room if they've been born and lived in these parts."

The old man's honey-sweet Virginia accent rolled like the hills Will had driven across to find this county recording office. Everything was here, all right, as the talkative old man said, but he had been here over forty years—and he was the index.

"It's been a long time, but I seem to remember that name. They weren't from around here. We don't have any Girards around here. Some Jenners around Newland, but I'd know if there were any Girards. No, they were visitors, I remember." He stood before the shelves, surveying the gilt imprinted on the large book spines. One hand cupped an elbow, the other his chin. His ample girth filled a plaid flannel shirt and dungaree pants. The mud from morning chores was still on his work shoes. "Around Crippville, you say."

"Yes, it would probably have been fifteen or twenty years ago. In a car crash."

The old man snapped his fingers. "Now I remember. Bad storm. Skidded off the road, wasn't it?"

"I guess so."

"Just driving through, they were."

He pulled down one volume and scanned the names on the opening pages, put it back and did the same with the next, and then the next.

"Here it is. 'Girard, Isabel.' 'Girard, Louis J.' "

The old man strolled toward the counter as he flipped the large pages over. He set the book down before Will.

"Would it be possible to get copies of the death certificates?" inquired Will.

"Two dollars each."

Will handed the old man eight dollars and asked for two copies of each.

A few minutes later the old man emerged from a back room and handed Will four photocopies. Louis J. and Isabel Girard had been killed on September 19, 1956, on County Line Road.

"This Dr. Cyrus Johnson who signed the death certificates, is he still alive?"

"Sure is. Lives about a quarter of a mile north on Main Street after you go through Crippville."

Will thanked him and went out to the rented car.

The old man watched him depart and then shuffled toward the back room to retrieve the book and replace it on the shelf. Something didn't sit right with a stranger traveling all this way and going back that far in the records, the old man told himself. He stopped at his desk and picked up the phone. With all the trouble last week in Meridian, it didn't hurt to be too careful. He called Doc Johnson and let him know a stranger might be stopping by who had been asking about death certificates Doc had signed for a couple of people named Girard.

Will debated whether to drive the additional fifteen miles that the map showed to Crippville. He noted the time and decided he could still make his evening appointment with Marcie Manning. As a precaution, he slipped a copy of each death certificate between the bottom of the rear seat and the floor.

The bell rang off and on for several minutes before a crack appeared between the door and the frame and a man's face peered through it.

"I'd like to see the doctor."

"About what?"

"Twenty years ago or so he signed death certificates for a couple named Girard."

The man slammed the door, but it would not close. A leg had been slipped through the door opening. He slammed harder, using all his strength. His eyes slowly widened. Not the slightest hint of pain appeared on the stranger's face. Finally, in frustration, the man allowed the door to swing back, revealing himself. Will moved his good leg inside the doctor's office as well.

"You the doctor?" The man nodded. "You're liable to give people the idea you're not friendly."

"Who are you?" The doctor's accent was soft Virginian.

"My name's William Nye. I work for Global Universal Airlines. We're in the middle of a little altercation with J. Stephen Girard. You signed his parents' death certificates."

The doctor moved warily behind his desk. "Do you have any identification?"

Will dropped a business card and his employee ID on the desk and took a seat. The man's eyes went from the photo to Will's face several times before the tightened lines around them relaxed. He was in his fifties. His office might have been as old—oak furniture and heavy curtains. The examining room behind it was outfitted with modern equipment.

"Please excuse my rudeness, Mr. Nye," the doctor said, "but we're all a little jumpy around here. A family in a nearby town was murdered last week. A stranger was seen in their neighborhood just a few hours before the murder."

"All I want is some information about Mr. and Mrs. Girard's deaths."

"I remember it well, a terrible accident. A storm was hitting us that night. Lightning, thunder, heavy rain. One of the County Police called, said there'd been a car accident near my property on County Line Road and asked me to meet him there. As a matter of fact, the car had skidded off the road through my fence and hit a tree. They were dead when I got there. As near as I could reckon it, they'd been killed instantly."

"Were they buried around here?"

"No, their son intended to cremate them. He picked up their bodies the next day."

"Did you meet him?"

"Yes, I did. He thanked me for going out. We spoke for a few minutes. Of course, he wasn't as rich and famous as he's since become."

"No, I suppose not. Do you have any idea where the Girards were traveling when they were killed?"

The doctor's voice seemed to soften with the remembered sorrow. "Their son was about to be married and they were driving to the wedding. That made it even more tragic. To Texas, I believe. I don't recall where they were coming from."

"Is the officer who called you that night still alive?"

"Frank Tolliver? No, coronary. Died about five years ago."

"Well, I guess that's it, Doctor. Thanks for your time."

Will stood up and shook the doctor's hand.

"I'm sorry for being so cautious before, but you understand," the doctor said.

As Will turned to leave, a photograph caught his eye. It was of a mature woman, professionally posed. Will thought her face looked familiar.

"Isn't that Jenabelle Draper, the head of the SEC?"

"Yes. She's also my wife. Draper was her maiden name. She chose to keep it when she began practicing law—rather daring in those days."

"Thank you again, Doctor."

Will left and started the long drive back to the airport. On a hunch he stopped on the main street in Crippville and asked directions to the local newspaper's office.

Will spent twenty minutes going through old issues of the *Crippville Chronicle.* There was no doubt. The edition printed the day after the accident was missing. Will checked all the dates for a month before and after—only that copy was missing. Now why, he wondered, would someone remove that particular edition? He pondered it all the way to the airport.

"That Mr. Trobard from Faranco increased the offer for my stock, Will. He said he would pay fourteen million five hundred thousand dollars."

About eighteen dollars a share for Marcie Manning's stock, Will calculated. "What did you tell him?"

"That I had promised to sell to you. But when?" She poured Will and herself more coffee. Belinda would be home soon. She was having dinner at a restaurant while being interviewed for a magazine.

"Is tomorrow too soon?"

"Tomorrow!"

"You look like a kid on Christmas morning."

"That's just what it feels like. I'm really going to be rich."

"Aren't you going to ask how much I'll pay?"

"You wouldn't try to cheat me. You saved my life."

Will shook his head. "This is business, Marcie."

"But it's not your money, it's Global Universal's."

"Actually, it's not even Global Universal's. A bank will be buying it. They said I could meet any other offer to buy the stock, so they'll pay fourteen and a half million."

"Mr. Trobard said when I sold I'd have to give him my vote at the same time."

"Because you'd still be listed as the owner on our records. Marcie, this election is important. Somebody doing work for us was almost killed, another man was hurt. Today, I was threatened with a gun—"

Marcie gasped.

"And I'm pretty sure the other side is also responsible for putting bombs on our planes."

"I'll be glad to be out of it tomorrow." She stood up and began clearing the table. "The wine bottle's empty. Why don't you go into the living room and make us some drinks? Cognac for me."

Will finished pouring two cognacs as Marcie came into the living room. She clicked her glass against his. "Here's to my future." She led Will to the brown velvet sofa.

"How's it going with Ron?" asked Will.

"It isn't. I don't even think he knows when I'm in the room."

The front door slammed. Belinda swept in.

"*People* magazine, kiddies. Interview was a smash. The interviewer they sent was gorgeous. One look at him and I was squirming in my chair. But I think he was gay. He took more of an interest in the waiter. Is that cognac you're drinking?"

They nodded. She poured herself one.

"Next week *Us* may do a story on how I'm the latest fashion star. Some star! All day long Schactman tells me his costs are so high there are no profits for me to share in." She dropped into a chair. "At least I haven't let him see the new sketches."

Marcie leaned forward. "Will is buying my stock tomorrow, Belinda. I'll have fourteen and a half million dollars in cash."

Belinda emitted an involuntary whistle as Marcie rushed on.

"I can pay you back now. But I'll do more than that. I'll put up the money for a new company. We can be partners."

Belinda jumped up and hugged her friend. "Oh, Marcie, that's incredible, that's just incredible."

For five minutes the two women plunged into a flurry of plans. Will got the impression that the arrangement had been worked out in Belinda's mind long before Marcie "surprised" her, but her joy seemed genuine.

"Wine! We've got to have some wine!"

Belinda raced into the kitchen and returned with three bottles of white wine poking out of a plastic bucket filled with ice.

By the third round of toasts, the wine was cold. By the third bottle they were all drunk. Belinda decided this was not enough of a celebration of the new partnership.

"Let's all three of us go to bed together. You could screw us both, Will, kind of to seal the pact." She threw an arm around a beaming Marcie. "He's really very good, really good." Belinda flung her other arm around Will and pulled the three of them close together. "Once he fucks you, you'll know why I love him so." She smiled with simple ingenuousness at Will. "I really do love you, you know."

Marcie kissed Will sweetly on the cheek. "I wouldn't be imposing on you, would I, Will?"

He stretched his arms around the women. All his lascivious

fantasies should have danced behind his eyes. He should have felt weak, his breath short. Instead he felt as if he were about to step into the ring for a few quick rounds of sparring. That wasn't enough.

"Ladies, I have bad news for you. With all this wine I couldn't even raise a flag. The spirit's willing, but, as they say, the flesh is weak."

"Oooh, poor Will," Belinda cooed, and kissed him tenderly. "Maybe if Marcie and I . . . "

"No, I don't think so." He backed away. "Besides, I'm awfully tired. I'd better be heading back to the hotel."

Belinda lifted her arms up to his neck and kissed him. "Mmmmm. Are you very sure?"

"Good night, ladies."

Will moved to the door and down the stairs. In the street, he stopped to look up at the lighted window. What a strange time to grow up, Will thought. You give up toys and games, but you don't give up what they mean to you.

He shoved his hands into his pockets, began strolling toward the corner and wondered where, in all the wide world, Donna was.

21

The fourth of May was warm and sunny in New York. Will chose to wait for Owen Clayton on the sidewalk just outside the Waldorf-Astoria's front entrance. He watched the pedestrians moving by on their way to work, and thought about his telephone conversation with Belinda that morning. The subject of Belinda's fund raising for the Irish charitable organization had seemed inappropriate the night before.

Belinda had a hangover, remembered very little of the previous night, but was willing to talk. Will asked whether Clayton had questioned her about her involvement with the group. He had not, nor had anyone else. She said she had nothing to hide; she had never denied her activist youth, but those days were long since gone. Deirdre Mulvaney knew that she had spent a year in Ireland back then and that she would be willing to help the widows and orphans in the North. Deirdre had invited her to a fund-raising party in the spring, and each had given one in the summer. Few, if any, at the affairs had had a connection with the charity itself. There was really no formal structure to the organization. People who wished to raise funds for it would do so and send the money on to the organization. She and Deirdre had both sent theirs to Carl Raymond.

And Raymond meant Girard, Will told himself. Everything had come together. Every piece had fallen into place. Even as he stood thinking about it in the agreeable morning air, Will could feel his muscles tense and his heartbeat race at the prospect of retribution, of going in after the prey at last.

Clayton was overdue by nearly twenty minutes when Will finally recalled his saying he would leave a message at the front desk of the hotel if the plans changed. There was an envelope with Will's name on it, left the night before. The message read, "Important new facts coming to light. Had to return to Chicago."

Will smashed the note into a ball, fury for revenge transformed into fury at being thwarted in gaining it. He stomped away, the wooden leg thumping against the floor like a club against a war drum.

Darlene Valentine had closed up her Beverly Hills home abruptly and driven nonstop, without telling anyone, to the small house in the desert. One of the scandal rag weeklies had learned that she and Rolf had entered into a separation agreement just before he died and that they were not the blissful couple she had pretended they were during the publicity tour for *Greater Good.* Another had unearthed the affair she had had with Woody Walker when the split with Rolf had become irreparable. Well, Darlene thought, that was why she paid her public-relations people so well. They would just have to handle the brouhaha without her.

Darlene arrived at the house at 2 A.M., thinking she would sleep like a log after such a long drive. But sleep was fitful. Finally, at around six, she had a dream. She was back in the Los Angeles Airport waiting area, nearly hysterical with fear over the crash she knew would soon occur. In the dream her husband was naked and the plane was full of women much younger than she. She begged him not to go aboard, but he said his cock was like a magnet and the girls inside were too pretty to resist the pull. Just as he disappeared into the plane, she had a sudden sensation that her face and body were covered with wrinkles like an eighty-year-old woman's. Then an old man emerged from the tunnel leading from the airplane, but, despite his age, he did not have a wrinkle on his face. Even he did not desire her.

That was when Darlene awoke. Sweat covered her body. She remembered the old man. He had emerged from the plane first, though, not last. The vision of the plane in flames had come at the instant she had first noticed him. The vision had been so overwhelming that she had forgotten the strange details associated with the old man until now. His clothes were baggy, as though meant for someone fatter. His skin had been smooth and young-looking. And his gray mustache had seemed to sit at a strange angle—before his hand flicked up to his face and the mustache was back in place.

That face! She had seen that face only a day or two before the crash, she was sure. Without a mustache or glasses or a hearing aid. Without gray in the hair. And wearing a well-tailored suit. Now she remembered: it was at Jane Kelly's fund-raising party at the Beverly Wilshire. Jane was an agent famous for her celebrity friends and clients. She had invited a good many to the party in order to raise money for a group providing food and clothing to people made needy by the strife in Northern Ireland. The man who had solicited their contributions was the same man who had rushed out of the Global Universal plane.

Darlene was nearly an hour from the nearest telephone. But even if she did drive to a phone and call the authorities, they would probably snicker as they had done when questioning her about the vision that had kept her off the plane in the first place. Or else think she was seeking publicity for her film. . . . Then she recalled the hundreds who had died in the bombed planes and that hundreds more might die in the future.

A few minutes later, just a little past six, Darlene Valentine threw on jeans and a T-shirt, slipped into the red Ferrari and began driving back the way she had come.

Several people were already waiting in the reception area when Will arrived: lawyers, including three from Masefield, Bevin & Parkhurst; investment bankers; and two people from Metrobank. Kean and a few others were still to come. Despite the importance of the imminent closing on the 707 note issue, Will had not yet been able to rein in his frustrated rage. He was grateful for the additional few minutes.

By ten o'clock all the participants except Kean had arrived. When the outer doors opened, they thought this must surely be he, but, instead, a middle-aged woman entered and asked if she could see him. She had no appointment and, although she was told he would be busy all day, decided to wait in the hope he could meet with her for a minute or two.

None could guess how much anguish she had suffered before finally summoning the strength to come here. Her friend Lotte had recommended Mr. Kean to her as someone who might help her invest her husband's estate. Except for a trip every week or two to the supermarket, she had not left her house since her husband had been killed months before when the airliner went down. This morning she had dressed carefully, driven to the station and taken the train into the city.

Will noted the tension in her face. It seemed to take as much energy for her to stay as to leave. She chose a seat near Will.

"He should be able to take a few minutes to speak with you," Will said to her.

She jumped at the first words, then relaxed enough to smile as she realized the young man beside her was trying to be kind. "I hope so. I don't know any . . . investment people. My friend Lotte's husband is partners with him in the factory. Perhaps I should have made an appointment first, but he was out of the office when I called yesterday, so I just took a chance on coming in."

Will nodded politely and turned toward the others. He was about to suggest that they might start to lay out the documents in the conference room, when the woman spoke again.

"You know, I really wanted to make a good impression on Mr. Kean." Her hands were kneading each other. "I'm so glad it's warm today. It would have been awful if I'd had to wear my fur."

Will looked at her blankly.

"Lotte told me not to wear it," she said, suddenly uncertain.

Will stared. "Why?"

"Because Mr. Kean is allergic to fur, Lotte says. He got furious when Lotte tried to shake hands with him once while she was wearing her mink. They were all at a jewelry convention, and she was terribly embarrassed. They do business with all those people."

Of course, an allergy to fur! That would also explain why the stevedore wouldn't hold the coat. And the drinking. Suddenly,

Will's mind was exploding in a chain reaction of realizations. All that fund raising! And the open door! What about the watches?

Will seized the woman's hands. Frightened, she tried to pull away. Will was nearly shouting. Now he understood everything.

"The factory your friend's husband and Kean are partners in, does it make pocket watches?"

"They make all kinds of watches," she answered fearfully. "I'm wearing one."

Will looked at her wrist. The name on the watch face was "Superba Timepieces."

"But do they make reproductions of old pocket watches?"

"I think so."

Will leaped to his feet and rushed past the receptionist toward Kean's office. Kean's secretary was at her desk, a tall young woman in a high-necked blouse. Her brown hair was pulled back neatly.

"Miss . . ."

"Marley."

"Miss Marley, do you have Mr. Kean's appointment book for last year?"

"Yes."

"Where was he on Thanksgiving weekend?"

"Mr. Nye, if Mr. Kean wishes me to . . ."

"Have you heard from him today?"

"No, he left rather hurriedly yesterday around noon, but I imagine he should be in very soon."

"The closing was supposed to start at nine-forty-five."

"What closing was that?"

"GUA. Seventy million dollars."

She checked her appointment book. "I remember Mr. Kean dictating some letters on it a while ago, but he didn't ask me to schedule a closing. I didn't even put a hold on the conference room for this morning."

The signs were ominous. "Did Mr. Kean arrive at work with a suitcase yesterday morning?"

"Yes. I assumed he was away for the weekend. But how did you know?"

"Perhaps there was an unusual call or visitor here just before he left?"

She was about to say that such prying was not a practice in which she indulged, when Will's urgency overcame her discretion. She opened the appointment book again.

"A Mr. Clayton. They left together. Mr. Kean returned about half an hour later, just as I was about to leave for lunch. I offered to stay if he needed me, but he said I could go. When I left he was making calls in his office with the door closed."

"And when you returned, he and his suitcase were gone."

"Yes. Is something wrong? I don't understand."

"One more question first. Is Kean one of those people who has trouble swallowing pills?"

"Yes, he is, but how did you know? Oh, the liquid aspirin and pyrobenzamine on his cabinet."

"It's not just dogs he's allergic to. He's violently allergic to all animal fur, isn't he?"

The young woman nodded. "Once one of the girls here was moving away and all the other girls chipped in to buy her a kitten. It happened to wander into Mr. Kean's office. I honestly thought he was angry enough to have killed the kitten if I hadn't carried it away. But I'm sure that was only my imagination."

"He always seemed to me to be an unusually cold and solitary man, Miss Marley."

She looked down at her lap for an instant. "I rather appreciate that . . . reserve, Mr. Nye. I'm not a very demonstrative person myself."

What she had considered a reserve that put her own anxieties at ease, Will sensed, might be instead an impenetrable indifference to human relationships. Kean had chosen a profession that removed him from direct contact with people. He dealt in amounts, ratios, concepts, the business operations of others, from which he was separated by telephones and floor traders and order clerks. His hobby was making miniature models, perfect in every detail but lifeless, and he was their deity, the god who created them. Those were only characteristics, but if Will was right, they were manifestations of a truth so monstrous that he almost dared not believe it.

"Does Kean's watch company make reproductions of old pocket watches?"

"Yes. As I understand it, Mr. Kean suggested that they get into that line. The first few were based on Mr. Kean's own collection. Several other companies copied them. He gave me one of the pocket watches for Christmas."

The watch she pulled from her purse was identical to those extracted from the bombed planes and found on the sidewalk beside the body of Craig Merrill.

"He was rather proud of how close to the original it was," the young woman said. "Often he would have me send one to a person who had helped with raising funds for his Irish charity."

"Like Carl Raymond."

"Yes. I sent one of the first to him, perhaps a year ago, when Mr. Kean first became interested in that charity."

"He wasn't interested in the relief agency before then?"

"No, he had several other charity events and groups he was associated with."

"Like the Securities Gala?" She was about to answer when Will interrupted. "Do you have Spielvogel's telephone number, the accountant?"

"Oh, I'm sorry, but Mr. Spielvogel retired and moved to Israel several months ago."

"I'll bet he did," Will said aloud.

And I know why and how, he thought with anguish. That open door! I should have known right from the start. But we all missed it. Kean and Spielvogel had to have been lying. No one would count that many thousands of dollars with the door open, particularly a cautious accountant whose own office door was always kept locked. Spielvogel lied about seeing someone pass by the open door at the Gala in order to throw suspicion elsewhere. Kean must have spoken to Merrill sometime that evening, as he had claimed. But Merrill must have kept trying to place Kean's face. Fearing that sooner or later the astronaut would remember seeing him in stevedore garb and mustache in the first-class section of Flight 211, Kean decided to kill him. He probably watched Merrill all evening, waiting for an opportunity. When Merrill slipped from the room, Kean followed him. His car was parked at the front entrance, and he used it to accomplish the murder. The .45 must have been locked in the glove compartment. He threw that and his own watch—the original antique—out the car window. Kean then drove back and went to the little office where Spielvogel was counting the receipts. Maybe he tried to lie about what the time was or maybe he made the deal with Spielvogel then and there. By the time the police spoke to Spielvogel, Kean had bought the threadbare little man's testimony at a price high enough for Spielvogel to retire and move to a place of sanctuary.

Will suddenly slammed his fist to his palm and rushed to the bookcase in Kean's office. Kean's book, written in his youth, was no arid study of postal systems. *The Troubled Post Office* was an analysis of the abortive 1916 Easter Rebellion in "troubled" Ireland. A group of rebels were eventually hanged by the British, who beseiged the Dublin post office the insurgents had holed up in. Will turned to the dedication page, knowing beforehand what he would find: "Dedicated to the memory of two martyrs for liberty, Padraic Pearse and James Connally, who led those that stood their ground." Using their names on the plane tickets had been a scholar's conceit.

Voices outside the office neared the doorway. Will looked up.

"I tell you," an authoritative man's voice was saying, "he hasn't arrived yet." Two men entered.

"And he won't either, Ted," Will said. One of the men was Ted Klaver, of the FBI's New York office. The other, in his sixties, introduced himself as Hugh Willoughby, head of the securities firm.

"What are you doing here, Nye?" Klaver asked curtly by way of greeting.

"I thought I was coming here for a closing. What about you?"

Klaver explained that the Los Angeles office had passed on an "oddball message" from Darlene Valentine about the second plane that crashed. She claimed to have recalled seeing James Kean disembarking from GUA 519 in Los Angeles just before it took off on the fatal flight to Denver. She said he had been disguised as an old man, wearing baggy clothes, spectacles, hearing aid, whitened hair and false mustache.

Will told Klaver his own suspicions about Kean. He figured that when buying the weapons Kean had been dressed as a stevedore, with a dark Mongol mustache and maybe dark glasses. He was still dressed the same way when checking in on 211 to Chicago. A woman had asked him to hold her fur coat. Fearing an allergy attack, he had caused an argument with her that gave him a pretext not to touch the coat. At the gate he had made certain he would not be seated beside her. As a precaution he had swallowed liquid allergy medicine, probably pyrobenzamine—he gagged on pills. The woman thought he was drinking whiskey. He planted the bomb and disembarked in Chicago, changing planes to New York. On 519 ten days later he dressed as an old man.

"How did Kean smuggle the plastic explosive onto the planes?" Klaver asked.

"He was a lot fatter getting on the planes than getting off. Darlene Valentine described him as having worn baggy clothes. The hearing aid had wires and batteries. Add one small detonator and a pocket watch, and you have a time bomb. Dressed as a stevedore, he could have brought, say, a pocket radio on board, with the parts he needed hidden inside it."

"But why? Why bomb a 747? The one thing that little terrorist group didn't need was enemies in America. This was the XE Brigade's breadbasket."

Hugh Willoughby had listened first in amazement, then with growing self-righteous anger. The eyebrows that overshadowed his eyes like gray valances moved up and down as each new revelation came forth. At this point he could restrain his acrimony no longer. "I warned him no good could come from wasting time with that Irish nonsense. He had always raised money for prominent charities. One makes very good contacts that way. But the Irish business was too controversial to be helpful. Besides, when he started with it, his own finances had deteriorated drastically. Large losses in commodities and the stock market. I tried to warn him that his own finances needed looking after a lot more than some people across the ocean."

"He was a wealthy man, wasn't he? This firm is doing well," Will said.

"For a small firm we do quite well, but as of last fall James Kean was no longer a partner. He withdrew his capital and receives only a percentage of his department's business. The odd thing was that all his debts had been repaid by then."

Will's voice grew excited again. "But the investment with the Irish charity started well before that?"

"Yes, in the spring or summer. I knew he was of Irish extraction, of course, and took an interest in the history and literature. But that charity became an obsession with him. He traveled everywhere to raise money."

"For a very good reason," Will declared.

"For those terrorists," Klaver offered. "He was skimming from the charity to buy guns and arms for that XE Brigade group he had thrown in with."

Will's own deduction went further. "I think he was playing the terrorist group along, too. He paid off his debts before withdrawing his capital from this firm, but after spending a lot of time fund raising for the relief-agency charity. That could very well mean he was shortchanging both the charity and the terrorists by keeping a lot of what he raised. When the XE Brigade got word that a really big supply of arms was for sale, he had his chance. He was a businessman, so he stepped in to handle the negotiations. He used part of the money he had collected for the Irish group to buy the armament, probably keeping most of the money and some of the plastic explosive and guns for himself."

Klaver thrust his square face forward. "But, Nye, that still doesn't explain why he'd want to blow up planes!"

"Until now I thought it was only a coincidence that the two 747s that went down were both financed by the same guaranteed loan certificates. And this whole idea would seem crazy if James Kean wasn't one of the financial industry's foremost experts in loan certificates. But what I think Kean did was beg, borrow and steal every dollar he could lay his hands on to buy GUA's Series B loan certificates when they fell way down in price last year. That issue was fully secured by three 747s built consecutively by Boeing. Each time he blew one up, by the terms of those loan certificates, the insurance on the plane first went to buy back one third of the certificates—at full face value. Then Kean could use the additional funds to buy more of the remaining certificates. If he bought a million dollars' worth of certificates *in toto,* let's say when they were at sixty-six cents on the dollar, and if he then blew up all three planes, he would get back half again more than he invested—a profit of half a million dollars—because the insurance company paid off a hundred cents on the dollar. Nice profit."

Willoughby had a thought. "If he borrowed another million from a bank using the certificates as collateral security, his profit would be twice as high. His original million dollars would produce a million in profit, less the interest paid to the bank for borrowing."

"And no risk," Will added, "because he knew that the insurance company stood one hundred percent behind the planes he would bomb."

Klaver threw up his hands. "It seems impossible that someone could just go out and pick the exact airplanes he wants to invest in."

"That sort of investment was James's specialty," Willoughby said bitterly.

"Something else just occurred to me," Will added. "He could borrow only half the money to buy securities at a bank in this country. But in some countries he could borrow a lot more. I'll bet if you checked your records you'd find that one or maybe several foreign banks bought our Series B certificates very heavily with Kean as the broker—and then bought more each time another third of the certificates was called."

Willoughby broke in. "For months I've been disappointed in Kean's performance. He seemed to have lost interest in his work. I was about to have it out with him when he told me he was putting together a large underwriting for you people. Occasionally I would ask how it was going, whether the syndicate had been formed yet, and he would either give me glowing reports or put me off with vague answers. My guess is he either couldn't put the syndicate together or just didn't try."

The remark fell upon Will's shoulders heavily. In a quiet voice, he asked, "Would you go out and check whether we have a financing or not, Mr. Willoughby?"

Gravely, Willoughby left the room.

Will punched the top of a chair in exasperation. "Shit! We looked for passengers who might have been killed for money or revenge, employees who might have had a grudge against the airline, terrorists with a political motive. But none of that mattered at all! That vermin didn't care who was on the plane. Or even which airline it was. He chose Global Universal simply because the price of its certificates was lower than other airlines'. If the price had been higher when he concocted his scheme, some other's planes might have gone down. And Kean was in the perfect position to keep buying up certificates."

Klaver suddenly blanched. "That means two things. One is that someone at your airline had to be feeding him flight schedules for those 747s."

"Probably someone in Aircraft Scheduling who sympathized with the Irish cause. Kean's phone records should track the person down. What's the other thing?"

"There's one more 747 left to complete the parlay."

Will was moving to the desk telephone. "If that scares you, try this on for size. Kean arrived at the office yesterday with a suitcase. He and the suitcase left at noon. No one's heard from Kean since. A dozen or so people showed up here today to close on a seventy-million-dollar debt issue, an appointment that Kean clearly had no intention of keeping."

Willoughby hurried back into Kean's office with the anticipated bad tidings. Kean had lied about the successful syndication. A quick head count revealed that less than twenty-five of the seventy million had been raised among the institutions supposedly subscribing, and a good part of that had been taken by Bergheim, Mack. There would be no signing today. And finding a willing lead underwriter and hammering out new terms would take days, if not weeks.

Will dialed GUA Operations Control in Denver. Within seconds the reply came back: the third 747 was in the air; it had boarded in Italy after an overnight stop and would be landing at JFK in less than an hour.

"Which means," Klaver said, voicing the obvious conclusion, "either that Kean is aboard now and will get off when it lands, leaving behind a pretty little surprise package for the next flight . . . or else he's about to try to get on board with it for the next leg. What's the next stop?"

"Back to Paris, then Rome. There's another plane flying the route in the opposite direction."

"Maybe the guy is just happy to make a getaway."

"Maybe. But he showed up yesterday with a suitcase—he had thought it through ahead of time and planned to leave. He wanted to be away before the closing."

Already on the phone with his office, Klaver quickly gave them Kean's description. Within minutes the GUA terminal at JFK would be completely staked out. In addition, Klaver would try to find a photo and drop it off at the New York office on his way to the airport. It would be Telefaxed to JFK and other airports, transportation points and FBI offices around the country.

Will asked Willoughby to telephone Ben Buck and fill him in on all that had just occurred. He wrote out an additional message: Velheim's stock could not be purchased by that night because the 707 refinancing had fallen apart; and without the funding, Will would have to try to negotiate a new deal for Marcie Manning's stock. Her stock would be enough for victory at tomorrow's stockholders meeting.

Will raced out of the Willoughby offices in time to get into the elevator with Klaver. He would be there at the finish. But something of the triumph would be lost. Kean was a man whose evil stemmed not from passionate vice but from cold, isolated indifference. It should have been Girard! God Almighty, if there had been any justice, it *would* have been Girard!

22

The aircraft had been repeating the pattern for quite a long time. Donna was tired and restless. Bad weather in Paris had forced delays, so the crew's Rome stopover had been shortened. By the time Donna was able to fall asleep, it seemed she was dragging her body out of bed again to get to Leonardo Da Vinci Airport and make the return trip. She had ten days off coming up now. A lot of them would be for sleeping.

She also planned to get back to jogging again and read some of the books that had been piling up on her night table. But Donna did not feel the heightened anticipation she used to, when she knew Will would be waiting to greet her. She had loved only two men: her high-school boyfriend, Amos, and Will Nye. But with Amos, cutting off had not hurt this way . . . for so long. Just when she was finally certain she had gotten over Will, last weekend—seeing him again—all the old feelings had revived, and so had the doubts about what she had chosen to do. She had been breezy and self-confident and strong enough to cut each of the strings that had started tangling together with his. But she had not been able to rid her mind of him.

This leg of the trip had been the easiest for the flight attendants. Most Atlantic traffic went east in the early summer and west in the late. There were many more empty seats than passengers—some off-season tourists, some businesspeople. She directed her thoughts to the passengers. A few were unusual, Donna noted, mostly negatively so. Mrs. Reade, a little old lady with a nasty disposition and a ready hand on the call button, had demanded every item for passenger convenience on board. They kept disappearing into her large shoulder bag. First she was napping with a blanket, then the blanket was gone. Magazines and a deck of cards had dropped out of sight as soon as Donna turned her back. The dinner tray had come back without flatware. The woman was a petty thief, and Donna planned to request a surprise inspection just before disembarkation. Across from Mrs. Reade was a Greek who bragged of being a wealthy businessman and had offered to let Donna shop wholesale in his coat factory in Athens. Donna did not trust him—his manners were too good. She had decided he was really a headwaiter. On the left side of the cabin was a middle-aged woman she felt sorry for, a nun, wearing old-fashioned wire-frame glasses, floor-length black habit and starched white wimple. Obviously very timid, perhaps even under a vow of silence, the woman was probably returning home to visit her family after many years in an Italian convent. The woman would find many changes. The one she was probably least prepared for was that the average lay person no longer deferred to the clergy, increasingly viewing them as no more or less worthy of respect than the rest of the population.

That much was clear in the attitude of the man across the aisle from the nun. What cruel eyes he had! If the word hadn't sounded so outdated, Donna might have called them "evil." He seemed to take perverse pleasure in staring at the sister and, alternatively, attempting to engage her in conversation. Earlier in the flight, when the woman returned from the lavatory and tried to sit two rows farther back, he insisted on moving two rows back as well, upon *his* return from the lavatory. Donna could not help being impressed by the tall plain woman's serene dignity.

"This is Captain Drew again." Donna checked her watch. The airline liked the captain on the P.A. system every half hour or so. Nervous passengers seemed to feel things were well in hand if he had time to chat with them. "Air traffic control has still got us circling around up here. I wish I could be a little more definite about when we'll finally get you all to the gate. There's quite a line waiting ahead of us. Once we land there'll be a wait for our gate as well, so your best bet is to sit back and just relax and enjoy the view. We'll let you know just as soon as we're cleared."

In the cockpit the others nodded at Drew. The announcement had sounded matter-of-fact, ordinary. Yet the three men were only awaiting word that hurried ground preparations had been completed before they would be cleared and streak in for a landing. They had been moved up to number-one priority in the pattern.

At the very last minute, only when that word was received, would the flight engineer go out into the cabin to alert selected flight attendants about the situation and the roles they would have to play in the suddenly accelerated drama.

James Kean had grown concerned. He had set the bomb to detonate three hours after the next leg's scheduled departure for Paris. He didn't want this aircraft going down in an area where it might be recoverable. The longer the delay, the greater the risk that this just might happen.

Planning for this final operation had been meticulous. He had been able to put off the FBI agent yesterday. The man's suspicions had almost ruined everything. The final crash would have occurred a month or two earlier if this particular plane had not been routed out of the country so late this year. And although all the insurance money was quickly pumped back into additional series B certificates, he still had set himself the task of convincing Max Creighton to fly with him to France. For that, he fabricated a secret meeting to be held with France's Minister of Finance. Creighton's eyes had bulged with greed as Kean described the massive, but spurious, American offering of French government bonds. Creighton had been planning to attend GUA's stockholders meeting tomorrow, but this took precedence. Just before boarding, Creighton would get a message that Kean had had to change his travel connections and would meet him at the George V in Paris this evening. But of course "James Kean" *would* be aboard. All the world would believe that he had died in the plane crash and his body was lost at sea along with Max Creighton's and the others'.

Kean reached for his pocket watch, then remembered it had

been affixed to the bomb. Out of the corner of his eye he glimpsed the wristwatch of a man moving down the aisle. The time was very much later than he had judged. And more delays to come. It took all his restraint to rise casually and slow his steps down the aisle to the lavatory. Middle one on the left. A small white-haired woman with a cumbersome shoulder bag scurried to the rear of the plane a step ahead of Kean. She opened the door to the lavatory toward which he had been heading. He tried to thrust himself between her and the door. She was too quick and slipped in under his arm.

"Take another one. They're all empty," the old woman cackled, and yanked the door toward her. He grabbed for the outer handle, halting its progress.

"I'll call the stewardess!" she warned with a mean, pleased smile.

He let the door handle slip from his hand. She slammed it closed and shot the bolt across. *Occupied.*

A few minutes later he knocked. There was no answer from within. He knocked again.

"Beat it!" the old woman's voice snarled in reply.

Donna noted the seat belt sign. "I'm sorry, but we're about to land. Please take your seat."

He had no alternative.

Klaver raised his voice above the engine sound of the police helicopter in which they were flying. "Ordinarily with a bomb threat our first priority is to get the passengers off fast. But we're afraid if Kean is on board he'll get suspicious if we undertake emergency procedures for disembarking. He might have a weapon or the bomb on him and hold the passengers and crew hostage before we can get to him."

"So we all rush right in as soon as it pulls up," Will confirmed.

"Right."

The helicopter was beginning to descend to the airport. Klaver pointed the pilot toward the GUA cargo area.

"Over there. Keep it out of the way behind the building." He shifted back to Will. "They say no one named Kean's aboard, but a few fit the description. The pilot will aim for the ramps. The flight crew will open the doors right away and armed agents will rush into the cabin dressed as GUA employees. Try to point out Kean to us fast."

"What about the next leg, to Paris?"

"We have agents and plainclothes police mingling with the passengers in the boarding area. Anybody looks like him, they'll take him aside."

Will gestured toward the horizon. A tiny silver silhouette was angled toward the end of a runway. "That's ours. A 747."

The helicopter pilot flipped the radio dial to the ATC landing frequency to catch the talk between GUA's Flight 12 and the tower.

"Global One Two at the outer marker inbound," a voice in the loudspeaker said.

"Global One Two, you're cleared to land Runway Three One left. Do not contact Ground. Remain this frequency. You understand the emergency procedures. Acknowledge."

"Roger."

Will and Klaver clambered out of the helicopter and ran to the corner of the building. Men with rifles and bulletproof vests had taken positions out of sight. Several men in coveralls seemed to be lounging by two mobile ramps in the open. Three minibuses designed to ferry passengers between gate and aircraft were parked nearby. Armed agents inside them would duck down when the plane rolled up. Out of sight around the corner, two policemen knelt beside a pair of German shepherds, stroking their coats. Behind them a platoon of ambulances and emergency trucks stood ready to roll.

A few moments later Klaver and Will, in purple coveralls, sauntered out toward one of the two white stairways on wheels. Will was wearing a cap to hide his face in case Kean happened to look directly at him.

"They gave me a list of the crew," Klaver was saying. "You might know some of them."

Will glanced at the pencil-scrawled list. He had to read the next-to-last name twice before he understood that Donna Harney was on board. Klaver pointed to her name.

"She's the one opening the door we're going through. I hope she's strong enough to do it fast."

She's strong as an ox, Will wanted to assure the FBI agent, but his mouth was too dry for speech.

Donna had moved to the jump seat in the coach section and now faced backward, all thought of inspecting the little old lady's bag abandoned. Dave Jacobs, the flight engineer, had caught her eye just as she was starting to herd people back to their seats. She had gone forward, where he told her a bomb might be aboard and described the man who might have placed it. The captain would announce that all gates were full; the passengers would be bussed to the terminal. As soon as the plane stopped moving, Donna was to open the door beside her as quickly as she could and step out of the way.

The captain was just now explaining to the passengers how much time the buses would save. Donna hoped she could be as calm.

The ground was rushing up at the plane. Donna allowed herself to glance at the tall man with the black mustache seated across from the nun. His eyes stared back at her. She tried to smile at him with a reassurance she did not feel and glanced toward the windows.

The plane touched down. Reverse thrust roared out of the engines. The plane decelerated abruptly and turned onto a taxiway. Donna reached for the microphone, trying to pretend that this was any ordinary flight.

"On behalf of Captain Drew and the entire flight crew I wish to thank you for flying Global Universal, America's premier air—" she stumbled over the word "—airline. We hope when you're planning your next trip you'll think of Global Universal."

The man must have known something was up, she was so nervous. She fought the impulse to glance back at him and lifted the microphone again.

"Please remain in your seats with your seat belts fastened until the aircraft has come to a complete standstill."

She slipped the microphone back on the cradle and released her seat belt.

The 747 was coming toward them from the right. No turn

would be needed for its doors to be accessible to the rolling stairways. For an instant Will thought the plane's speed might be too great, but then it slowed and, its doors adjacent to the ramps, stopped.

Will pretended to be pushing the rear ramp along with the others, but his gaze was directed up at the plane's windows.

The top of the ramp was against the fuselage. The door swung out. Klaver and several other men were up the steps immediately and inside the plane by the time Will reached the top.

Passengers were starting to take coats and packages down from the storage bins as Will entered the cabin. Donna had flattened herself against the bulkhead so that the FBI people could storm aboard. Will caught her eye for only the briefest instant as he passed, long enough to be certain she was safe and to notice her pleasure overcoming surprise as she caught sight of him. The men in purple coveralls had fanned out and were moving along both aisles. Most of the passengers were too busy gathering belongings to notice the newcomers. A few were startled by the roughness with which they were shoved aside.

Will scanned faces hurriedly. A male passenger toward the rear was bent over. Will moved toward him and was about five feet away when the man straightened up, still facing away from Will. The build was Kean's. Observing Will's actions, Klaver charged toward the rear, twisting and cutting by passengers, nearly knocking over the nun. Just as Will was about to dive at the man's back, the man turned around. It wasn't Kean. Will's shoulders sagged.

"Are you sure?" Klaver said tensely. His hand was inside the top of his coveralls.

"Yes. It's not him."

Will's head spun around. His eyes darted from one man's face to the next.

"He's not here."

The dogs were inside the aircraft now, and more law officers were pouring in behind them. Passengers were becoming panicky. They jumped out of the aisle to let the German shepherds pass. Suddenly, the dogs began to bark and leap against their leashes. The nun tried to step out of their path, but she fell over the arm of an aisle seat. Frightened, she tried futilely to scramble backward crablike.

"She'll get hurt," Klaver muttered, and ran to help her, Will just behind.

The woman was terrified by the dogs. One of them had the hem of her habit in its teeth and was ripping at it.

"Get them away!" she screamed with a man's voice.

"That's Kean!" Will shouted.

Men grabbed for the nun's hands. Klaver's gun was out, and an instant later he had it aimed at Kean's head.

"My God, those men are animals," a woman yelled out. "Somebody help her. They'll kill her!"

A moment later the wimple had been ripped away, and there was no doubt.

Will wanted to leap at Kean's eyes and tear them from their sockets. And then he was struck by the unrelieved ordinariness of the man, just as he had been struck by it in the televised face of another mass murderer, Adolf Eichmann. Kean in hand, like Eichmann, was an agonizing anticlimax.

Will stepped back. Kean was pulled to his feet and quickly frisked.

"There's nothing on him," an FBI man announced.

"Then he's still got enough smell of explosives on his hands for the dogs to pick it up," said a handler.

"That means he's already planted it," Klaver warned. "Get everybody off fast!"

"Where'd you put it?" an officer asked Kean threateningly.

Kean stared straight ahead silently.

As the plane crew began evacuating the passengers, Will raced toward the rear lavatories. Right side, he remembered from the Zion crash.

Will peered closely at the lavatory ceiling. The buttons covering screw holes were askew, as if replaced in a hurry. He yanked out the waste bin below the sink, dumping the contents into the corridor. Along with the wet towels, a penknife with a screwdriver attachment tumbled out.

"Don't touch it!" Klaver warned him. "We'll need the fingerprints."

The dogs were barking wildly into the lavatory.

Will took the screwdriver offered by a man in overalls, pried out the buttons and began to remove the ceiling panel. The dogs were led away. A second man in overalls moved into the lavatory beside him and started to remove screws at the same time.

"Do you know the bomb?" the man inquired quietly.

Will spoke as he worked. "If it's like the other two, the charge is plastic, an electric fuse, batteries and a pocket watch as the timer. Probably only one hand on the watch, the hour hand."

"No crystal? Comes around and makes contact with an exposed wire?"

"Right."

All the screws were out. Their hands held the panel in place. The demolitions expert glanced back over his shoulder.

"Anyone left on the plane, Gene?"

A second bomb squad man was just outside the lavatory door. Beside him was a thick steel box and netting made of heavy steel cable.

"You'd better go," the second bomb squad policeman said to Klaver. A few seconds later his head swiveled back toward the lavatory. "All clear. The buses are pulling out."

"Step back, Gene," the first man said. Then he spoke to Will. "Let it down very slowly. I'll try to look inside for a dead-man switch."

He positioned himself.

"Okay, start lowering," he said.

Slowly, Will allowed the panel to descend. A slight crack through to the space behind it appeared between the panel and the ceiling.

"Hold it!"

Will stopped. The other man, eye to the crack, was searching for the bomb.

"Gene, give me a hand. I want to go around to the other side for a look."

He shifted position but could see nothing. "Drop it a tiny bit more."

Will did.

"I see it!" the man declared.

He stared into the recess for what seemed like eternity.

"You can let it down. There's no switch."

Will handed the panel to the second bomb man.

"Just like you said," confirmed the first man. "Were there any booby traps on the other ones?"

"I don't know. They went off."

"Thank God my mother thinks I have a nice safe desk job," the man remarked, and stepped onto the toilet. He removed wire cutters from his pocket and lifted his head into the cavity.

"No wonder he wore a dress to hide it. There's enough plastic up here to blow out the tail of this plane like a champagne cork."

There was silence for many long seconds, interrupted only by the tick of the pocket watch resounding off the metal around it. Then the man standing on the toilet spoke again.

"I'm going for the wires."

He reached upward. Will could feel the sweat sliding down his body.

"Shine a flashlight up here. My head's blocking the light from the fixture."

Will aimed the beam of the flashlight he had been handed.

"Good," the man said.

Several eternities passed tick by tock.

Snip!

He handed the wire cutters to Will behind him, then extended both free hands upward. A moment later he reached back down with the batteries.

"There doesn't seem to be any other power source. Let me have the cutters again."

Within half a minute the fuse and the watch were handed backward.

The last item out was the large tan mass. It went into the steel box. The man who had defused the bomb wiped his sleeve across his dripping brow.

"How much time did we have left?" he asked.

"You don't want to know," Will said.

The GUA Customer Service representative conscientiously sought out Maxwell Creighton in the boarding lounge of the Paris flight. He handed Creighton an envelope containing a message that had been left the previous day, just before James Kean boarded the flight to Rome using the first of two false passports. Max Creighton walked down the ramp and into the first-class cabin, confident he would meet Kean for dinner that evening at their Paris hotel.

One-Eye Johnny Doheeny had left it up to the American to get him out of the country on this trip. The photo in Kean's passport that rested now in Doheeny's inside pocket had been changed to match Johnny's own austere, reproving face with the one glass eye. Although in jail, Dan Ward had secretly passed word that he was suspicious of Kean. But how could a man not trust someone who had put himself on the line so completely by giving Johnny his very own identity?

The Irishman waited until only a few minutes before flight time before striding down the corridor to the gate. At the counter he handed over the ticket bought in Kean's name. The gate agent's eyes flicked from the ticket to another man standing nearby. The latter immediately stepped forward to question Doheeny. Rough hands grabbed Doheeny's arms so he could not run. Was it only a moment before that Johnny had been counting it good fortune that he had such friends as James Kean?

The passengers from the Rome flight that had just landed were still clearing Customs as Will arrived at the GUA dome, but the crew had already passed through. With Klaver running interference, he and Will rushed through Customs and onto the concourse. At the Crew Lounge in the Crew Operations area, Will finally found Donna. An FBI agent was taking her statement. Will waited to one side. She caught his eye, and he smiled self-consciously.

The agent interviewing her was young and good-looking and seemed to be taking an inordinately long time. He's probably asking her out, Will fretted. She keeps smiling. What the hell could be so enjoyable about an FBI once-over?

Finally they both stood up, and Donna crossed the room to Will.

"I've been worried sick," she said. "I saw all the others get off the plane but not you."

"I love you," said Will simply. The words slipped out by themselves, before he could think. And they did not hurt when he uttered them.

Donna's eyes peered into his, searching for sincerity. For that moment self-assurance deserted her. Never had Will seen so deeply through the sapphire blueness into her vulnerability. All his memories of her, the newly discovered immensity of her significance to him, and all that blueness took his breath away. He was afraid that if he tried again to tell her he loved her, it would sound forced and contrived. He kissed her.

"I love you," she said.

23

The helicopter floated down onto the pad in Manhattan like a stork delivering a royal baby. During the first half of the short trip, Will had felt exhilarated. But the ordeal on the plane and his tension and fatigue finally caught up with him. During the second half of the ride, his muscles went weak and he began to shiver, as if his body were inflicting a flash fever to punish his mind for jeopardizing them both by such inane behavior

Will wanted very much to stay with Donna. They had been apart for so long that leaving each other even for the few hours until they met for dinner in Denver seemed painful. But Will first had to see Marcie Manning about her stock—all of the arrangements were in disarray, and she was the key to winning the proxy fight. No matter what the outcome, by tomorrow night the stockholders meeting would be over. His duty would be ended as well. Then he and Donna would have time to be alone together—maybe to go off somewhere. That thought would make the next twenty-four hours bearable.

When Marcie saw Will walk into the studio, she started to go for her coat. Will had to sit her down and explain the hurricane of events that had just whipped so many lives about.

Without the 707 refinancing, the money was not available today to buy Marcie's stock. Will suggested a new arrangement: signing a contract tomorrow morning in Denver with Ben Buck, who would guarantee to pay her fifteen million dollars in thirty days—with interest. And she would give him her proxy.

Marcie was bitterly disappointed. She had trusted Will to make good. Out of gratitude, she had refused Faranco's offer in favor of Will's, although they were identical. Just a few moments before, Belinda had run out for lunch with Ron and Morris Schactman. She was going to tell Schactman exactly what he could do with his offer to renew the present deal. Now Will had let Marcie and Belinda down. Reluctantly, Marcie agreed to accept the new proposal but wanted to be sure a signed contract was in hand before she relinquished the vote all sides seemed so intent on getting from her.

Will telephoned collect to Ben Buck, who already knew about Kean's capture. Will explained the deal he had renegotiated with Marcie Manning. Buck agreed. All of his stock was already tied up as collateral for loans he had earlier taken to buy more stock, but in thirty days Serge Bergheim would certainly have pushed the new 707 refinancing through and the resources would then be available for Metrobank to work out funding for the Manning stock purchase.

Will would arrange for Marcie to fly to Denver tonight. He could close with her at GUA's Denver bank tomorrow morning and bring her proxy to the stockholders meeting.

"Reserve a hotel room for her at the Brown Palace," Will said. Then he added, "I sent you a special-delivery letter."

"Nothing's come in. Somebody went through the mailroom like a buzz saw before the boys arrived this morning. That could have been what they were after."

"It will probably get there this afternoon. When it arrives, don't open it. Just put it in the vault."

"What's in it?"

Will chose not to answer directly. "And have Pope run another check for a tap on the phone line."

Reluctantly, Buck yielded. "I'll keep an eye out for the letter."

They hung up, and Will turned back to Marcie to confirm they had a deal. A limousine would pick her up and have her on tonight's GUA eight o'clock to Denver. Will would meet her at the

Denver airport tonight when she arrived and take her to the Brown Palace Hotel. At eight-thirty the next morning he would meet her again for breakfast in the coffee shop.

"Why don't you fly there with me tonight?" asked Marcie.

"I can't. Something's troubling me. I want to stop off somewhere on my way back."

"Where?"

"Chicago."

Will stopped in at the O'Hare FBI office right after the Westwind touched down. He was looking for Owen Clayton. Uncertain what to say, a woman finally stammered that he was out of the office today.

Will took a cab to Clayton's home. He wanted to know why Clayton had not arrested Kean the day before, although he had to have known by then of Kean's fund-raising activities for the relief agency and, after purported weeks of extensive investigation, of his partnership in Superba Timepieces. On the telephone Clayton could put him off. Will was seeking a face-to-face confrontation.

A doctor met Will at the front door of the old two-story brick house. His name was Howard Rappaport. A large man with black hair parted in the middle, black mustache and black-framed glasses, he was there to minister not to Clayton, but to his invalid wife, who was in shock. Owen Clayton had shot and killed himself that morning with his service revolver.

FBI agents and police had swarmed over the house for several hours, finally satisfying themselves that the act was a manly choice in the face of inevitability, and not an escape from imminent incrimination. Perhaps only his sense of duty had allowed Clayton to hang on as long as he did, they reasoned. His last act had been to file a report that charged James Kean with the GUA bombings on the basis of ties to Irish terrorists and Superba Timepieces, just discovered among the massive piles of papers turned up in the case. His work done, he could allow himself at last the ultimate surcease from his pain. The old friends who stayed to comfort the widow made much of his dedication.

Will was shaken.

"There was no mystery to his taking his life," the doctor quietly avowed. "I told them flat out how Owen knew he had only a little while left. The cancer was very far gone and he was in pain. I gave them a signed statement. He knew since Thanksgiving weekend that it was inoperable, terminal. Nothing could be done, so he didn't tell Edna a thing—she's my patient, too. Owen wanted to keep working and taking care of her as long as he could."

Will knew Clayton's wife was chronically ill. But Clayton had kept his own disease a secret. When someone commented on how drawn he looked, Clayton would blame it on long hours spent trying to crack the GUA case.

"Why now, Doctor?" Will asked as they sat on the porch steps. "Why not last week or next week?"

"A few years back I was in New York City for a medical convention, and I heard a rumor that Hemingway had terminal cancer. I wasn't surprised to hear a few months after that he'd taken his life. Who knows why he thought that moment was the right time for him, not the week before or after?"

Will rose and went inside to pay his respects to the widow.

Edna was upstairs in bed. She was propped up with pillows like a stringless marionette. She had been heavily sedated; normal conversation was impossible. A young woman whom Edna might long ago have resembled sat quietly in the other bedside chair. She followed him out of the room when he departed.

"I'm their daughter, Hannah. May I speak to you?" Her eyes scanned the hall cautiously.

"Of course."

"You said you're a lawyer. Are you with the Bureau . . . or the police or D.A. or—"

"No," Will broke in. "I'm with Global Universal Airlines. Your father and I met while he was investigating two crashes involving our planes."

"Is it true a lawyer has to keep something you tell him confidential?"

"Yes, if you hire him. Consider me hired."

She hesitated, then drew an envelope from her pocket and handed it to Will. Inside he found a U.S. Treasury bond worth a hundred fifty thousand dollars, payable to the bond's bearer, whoever that might be.

"Late last night my father came to my apartment and said he was worried about his health, that he had sold his stamp collection and bought this. It's funny. I didn't try to tell him that he was fine and would live a lot of years. My heart was breaking, Mr. Nye. I knew this was too important for him to be imagining things, so I just listened. He said to keep what was in the envelope private from everyone, not to tell the Bureau or Mom or anybody. He was worried about what would happen to Mom when he was gone. He said I was to use it to take care of her, and of the baby and me too till I got back on my feet. It would give us all income, and I could always sell the bond if we needed cash."

"A reputable bank will take care of all that for you."

"Mr. Nye, I don't know how my father's stamp collection could have been worth so much. There were times when he was juggling every penny to pay bills. I don't know where he could have gotten this kind of money in any . . . in any normal way. I promised him not to tell anyone, but it doesn't seem right."

Will gazed down at the federal security. One hundred fifty thousand dollars. Untraceable. The bearer bond could have been obtained years ago or yesterday. Or yesterday. If Clayton had taken it yesterday, what had Kean received in payment? Probably twenty-four hours' lead time before the ax fell. Clayton probably never understood what Kean's real motive for the bombings was, because he had not investigated the airline's financing. He could not know that Kean acted out of personal greed, not Irish patriotism, and that Kean, suitcase packed, had already set his sights on the third and final prey, still on the wing.

"Hannah . . ." He had no idea of what advice to give her. Will glanced into the bedroom. Edna Clayton had begun to slip down the slope of pillows, unable to halt her own movement. Then Will knew what to say; he chose his words with care.

"I can't advise you to break the law, but your father must have thought very long and hard about the instructions he gave you. And must have cared very deeply about what would happen to you and your mother and your baby when he was no longer here."

Will replaced the bond in the envelope, which he handed to her.

"I think I understand," she said, and put the envelope back in her pocket.

Until he had gotten the telephone call and met with Wilfred Trobard, Ron Bailey had been frantic. Instead of agreeing on the long-term deal he had busted his butt to work out with Schactman, Belinda had pulled out of the whole arrangement. All she would say was she was starting a new company with a new partner.

Ron had decided to meet with Trobard because the man had said three intriguing things on the phone: that, as a demonstration of his seriousness, he would pay Ron a thousand dollars simply to attend the meeting, and a lot more could follow; that they would meet at the offices of Faranco Inc., where Trobard claimed to be vice-president of Financial Affairs; and that the call and the meeting were to be kept highly secret. Ron was aware that Faranco was a massive conglomerate run by that mysterious Girard whom Belinda had invited to her art show. As a check, Ron looked up Faranco's telephone number and dialed it. He asked to be put through to Wilfred Trobard and reached the same man. Ron was on his way to Faranco as quickly as he could sprint from phone to cab.

An hour later the meeting had ended, and Ron sat on a stool at Chock Full O' Nuts stirring a cup of coffee and thinking. Trobard would pay him forty-nine thousand more just to sell Marcie Manning on the idea of letting Faranco buy her stock in Global Universal Airlines. That was a shocker. All along he had thought the mousy little blonde a charity case Belinda had dragged out of the rain like a stray cat. Who'd have thought she was worth fifteen million bucks? Trust Belinda to maneuver things her way. That was where the money for her new company must be coming from. You ran a hell of a risk underestimating *that* chick. Marcie had the hots for him. That would make things easier. But time was short. Trobard had said the stock sale had to be made by tomorrow morning.

Ron tossed some change onto the counter and moved toward the door. This was a selling challenge, that's what it was. And he considered himself just about the best salesman there was, particularly where chicks were concerned. The forty-nine thou wasn't going to slip away without a hell of a struggle. And that was only for openers.

Snow had been falling lightly on Denver all day. Viewed at dusk from the cockpit of the approaching Westwind, the city in front of the mountains looked like the scene in a souvenir glass ball.

As Will entered the GUA Building, the security guard lifted the telephone receiver. "Mr. Buck wanted me to let him know as soon as you arrived."

"Would you call Mr. Pope and ask him to join us?"

Will entered the elevator and ascended to the top floor.

"Damned foolishness!" Buck bellowed as soon as Will came into view. "The fate of this company up for grabs, and you send me this asinine letter." He raised a crumpled piece of paper to his eyes and began to read aloud.

"DEAR BUCKAROO,

Roses are red,
Violets are blue,
Ben Buck wears lace panties
Beneath his tutu.

Your friend,
WILLIE.

"Eloise tells me a tutu's a skirt ballerinas wear. What the hell kind of joke is that? You a fag, Will?"

"When I called I said not to open it until I got back. Where's the envelope?"

"How the hell do I know? I threw it out."

Eloise marched firmly into the room, a white envelope in her hand. She winked at Will as she extended the envelope. Will began to scrape the stamps away. Underneath was a small black square.

"What is it?" Buck demanded.

"Microfilm. The detective we hired was able to keep it from Faranco's thugs."

Dan Pope entered the room. Will carefully handed the square of film to the company's Security chief.

"Have this processed, Dan. Right away."

"It's going to take some time."

"How much time?"

"I couldn't guarantee it before noon tomorrow."

"That's not good enough. I've got to have it before the stockholders meeting in the morning."

"I'll do my best."

"And put it under the tightest security you've got. A single copy. Deliver it to me or the General personally. No one else is to see the contents. The microfilm goes back into the vault. Handle the whole thing yourself, Dan."

Agape now, Buck asked, "What the hell could be on it, Will?"

Will shrugged his shoulders. "What do *you* think is worth trying to kill a man for?"

Learning that Will was expected back, Lorna Redmond had stayed late and was waiting when he reached his office. Will was grateful; her presence would speed things up. He dictated a short agreement covering the Manning stock. After he checked the draft over, it would be Telefaxcd to the mailroom at Masefield, Bevin & Parkhurst and then taken by messenger to Marcie's lawyer's home for approval.

Natalie Harmon came in to discuss the stockholders meeting agenda and to show Will the latest tabulation and projections on the voting. The Velheim block gave Faranco an edge. Marcie Manning's stock would be the deciding factor. Will and Harmon proceeded to Buck's office to review the same matters with him. The incumbent Board of Directors would meet at eight in the morning. The stockholders meeting would start at ten. Teicher, Parkhurst and several other lawyers would be there for management's side. But Buck had run many annual meetings. Complications would arise only if the insurgents tried to throw a legal curve during the proceedings.

Will slipped away while Harmon was graciously talking her way out of a dinner date with Buck. Will had a dinner date of his own and, after more than two months apart, did not intend to jeopardize this new beginning with Donna by being late.

He threw coat and suitcase into the trunk of the Porsche and started to drive out of the parking lot. He braked as he saw that the barrier was lowered across the parking-lot exit. A new man was on—rather late, Will thought. Will pressed the button to lower his window. He came to a stop and reached inside his jacket for his wallet and ID card.

"Don't make any funny moves!" the man warned.

Will turned to find himself staring into the open end of a pistol. The man holding the gun had the same look Will had faced on the Miami tarmac.

"Start by handing over the necklace Benke gave you," the man said in a flat tone as cold as the night.

Very slowly Will pulled his hand out of the front of the jacket and reached for the right side pocket. "It's all yours," he said deferentially. But in the next moment he knew that obtaining the mezuzah would not satisfy the gunman.

The man leaned into the car, putting the gun barrel only inches from Will's temple. "The guy you busted up yesterday in Miami was my brother. And it was the dumbest thing you ever did."

Will slowly lifted the gold chain out of his pocket. He tipped his head, as if glancing at the mezuzah, but his eyes were on the gunman. The gunman's own gaze shifted for an instant as he reached with his free hand. Will chose that instant to duck his head and smash his left hand upward into the hood's gun hand, slamming and holding it against the roof. Will's right hand flashed across his body to the window button. The window rose into the man's throat and arms. Struggling, he tried to scratch at Will's eyes with his free hand. Then he began to gasp for air. A bullet exploded into the car roof. Will pressed the accelerator to the floor. The car hurtled forward, dragging the gunman with it as it crashed through the wooden barrier. Will spun the wheel with his right hand. The man's body whipped outward like a rag doll as the car revolved in a tight circle on the deserted access road. The man's eyes were bulging as he tried desperately to breathe, his entire weight concentrated on the window edge that cut into his windpipe. He released the pistol and tried to tear out the window.

Will pulled at the window button, and the man was flung into the snowbank deposited beside the road by snow plows. The gold chain and the empty mezuzah were still tangled in his fingers.

At a nearby gas station, Will called the police. By the time they arrived back at the parking lot, the man was gone. Will turned over the pistol to the police. They cautioned him against going home for the night and followed his car into town as a precaution.

Will arrived at the restaurant twenty minutes late and said that he had had trouble starting his car.

As if all the experiences, thoughts and feelings of her past two months had been saved up for this occasion, Donna talked nonstop through dinner, hardly touching her food. Her new submersion into books, and more time in Europe, had begun to deepen her innate intelligence.

"I was a little afraid when I was with you before. You knew so much, had so much education and I was always sure in the very next sentence you'd find out just how ignorant I was."

Will smiled. "Why are you telling me now?"

"To put you on notice. There's so much out there waiting for me—and I'm coming on like an SST."

Will had changed, too, since their breakup. He was groping toward some new direction, he thought, but wasn't yet sure just what. More important to Donna, he wanted to talk about matters that he had habitually concealed behind a facade of flawless competence and charm.

"That morning at the cabin, when I just sat there, unable to move, I felt as if the weight of all the things I had tried to hold in had finally brought me to a halt. I had to get them out or lose all hope for the future. I wanted to talk to someone I trusted, but with you out of my life, there wasn't anyone I trusted left in it."

"Oh, how much I love you, Will Nye," Donna whispered.

At nine-thirty, Will and Donna reluctantly took leave of each other outside the restaurant. He had to pick up Marcie at the airport and take her to her hotel before going back to his office to review strategy. No doubt he would end up, as he often did, sleeping on his office couch.

As difficult as being separated tonight might be, it was only for a few more hours. And if Will was able to finish up early enough, they might even be together tonight.

The snow had not let up. As Will made his way to the car, he found the sidewalk icy and the footing unsure. He stepped into the street, where plowing and occasional traffic had scraped down to the asphalt.

After half a block he started off across the deserted street at an angle that would bring him to his car. As he reached the center line, a dark sedan on the far side suddenly started up and swung into the street, lights off. The rear door opened as the vehicle drew near. For the third time in two days, Will found himself peering into the muzzle of a gun. Behind the gun, motioning for him to get in, was the man he had encountered in the GUA parking lot. A thick bandage was around the man's throat. His face was contorted with hatred.

Will pulled his legs into the car just as the gun barrel smashed into the side of his head. The world behind his eyelids went blazing white, but he fought to stay conscious. When the pain began to stab holes through the white, he knew he could hang on. The gunman started to reach across Will's body to close the door, thought better of it and jabbed his message hard into Will's ribs. Will groped for the door handle and yanked.

The driver swung into a wide U turn and sped out of the city.

Will found himself in the back seat of a car that had three other occupants; the man with the gun was beside him and two men were in the front seat. Neither front-seat occupant turned around. Will stared at the silhouettes of the backs of their heads.

The driver seemed unfamiliar with the area and wove up ice-slick mountain roads until the car was miles past populated suburbs, past even the occasional solitary house.

Nobody had spoken a single word until the front-seat passenger said in a voice faintly familiar to Will, "Here okay?"

The car came to a halt. The driver turned on the interior light. The man in the right front seat shifted around toward the rear. The face was pinched with loathing, but still recognizable. It belonged to Ralph Coburn. The last time Will had seen it the face had been moaning up out of unconsciousness at the bottom of a stairway at Basehart Abrasives.

Nosing over the seat top was a black gun barrel.

"You lousy sneak-punch prick, if you only knew how I've waited for this moment! Make a move, prick! Just try going for the door!"

"That's enough!" the man on the left commanded. The voice was a deep rasp. At last he too rotated to face the rear. Will started. The man wore a metallic ski mask. Only his eyes and mouth were exposed. Will assumed he was Firkling, the former police official who now ran Faranco's Security Division. The hidden face nodded at Coburn. The latter's eyes darted back to Will.

"Where's whatever was in the Jewish prayer thing Guido took off you?" Coburn's high, reedy voice, cracking with emotion, sounded more menacing than any shout Will had ever heard.

"I don't know," Will answered honestly. He decided to keep as close to the truth as possible and hoped the sincerity being lent to his voice would convince them to let him go.

"You know all right. You carried it from Miami."

"I know it was microfilm but not what was on it. I turned it over to our Security people for safekeeping. They put it in a bank, I think."

Ski Mask did not buy the story. "You landed too late. The banks were closed. Don't lie, Counselor. It only gives me an excuse to let Guido stomp you. You hurt him real bad. He can't speak. He wants a return match with you, Counselor."

Will's head ached in jackhammer throbs. "Look, the one thing Faranco doesn't need is lousy publicity about beating up an opponent."

Coburn smiled mirthlessly. "If they ever find you."

"I honestly don't know what was in it. Guido had me terrified in my car. If I had what you want, you'd have had it then. If I even knew what it was, I'd have told you."

The ski mask tilted in totemic sadness. "It's always the smart guys who are too dumb to listen to good advice." Then it nodded almost imperceptibly. "Okay, Guido."

Guido jabbed with the gun. Then he jabbed a second time, harder. Reluctantly Will released the car door handle and pushed the door outward. A foot sent him crashing to the road. He stood up and was shoved toward the front of the car into the glare of the headlights.

A blow to his stomach doubled him over. He was able to dodge most of the knee aimed to his face and tried to grab at Guido's legs and wrestle him down. All the men were out of the car and around him. A kick from the side caught him in the ribs. Guido immediately karate-chopped at his neck from the front.

Will struggled to his feet. He had to get the car behind him to protect his back. A fist shot toward his face. He tried to duck and the artificial leg slipped out from under him on the glazed snow. He landed on his back, helpless.

"One last chance to tell us where it is." The silver ski mask was peering down at him like a malevolent idol.

"I don't have it," Will gasped.

"What the fuck difference could it make to you?" the voice asked incredulously.

Then a shoe Will never saw crashed against his ribs. Blows and kicks were coming from all directions. One caught him in the head, and everything disappeared.

When he came to, Will was very cold, and his head ached in great waves. He tried to pull his jacket around him and realized he wore none, nor pants either. His attackers would go through his clothing at their leisure to be certain he had been telling the truth. Far below were their headlights, melted into a single bubble of light following the road's curves away, marooning him.

Will tried to raise himself to his knees and collapsed with the shock of the pain. The second time he fell on his face. They had taken his prosthetic leg as well.

Never before had he felt so desolate, so terrified. In Vietnam he always had had a means of escape, however short the odds—a jungle to hide in, a plane to carry him out if he could hang on long enough. Here he was miles from any shelter, without even two legs on which to attempt walking to safety before the cold brought numbing death.

There were lights several miles below. In desperation Will clawed at the snow under him and started to slide down the road. His progress was slow. Whenever he picked up too much speed, he had only his naked limbs to scrape against the snow as brakes. Sometimes he would career off balance and begin to revolve, as if fulfilling his most hellish personal nightmare—toppling from a single ski and sliding on his back, head down, faster and faster, toward an unseen precipice.

Suddenly, he hit an ice patch and slid out of control, accelerating. He slammed into a snowbank, flailed wildly at it and ricocheted back onto the road, shooting downward like a bobsled run amok. Will's shirt and underwear were shredding and tearing away. The ice was ripping at his skin.

All at once headlights appeared below him, charging upward like the eyes of a great night-hunting cat. Will tried to tumble sideways off the road, but he had no way to propel himself obliquely. The huge eyes were almost upon him. A scant instant before death the car stopped and he bumped painfully into one of the tires.

A moment later a face was peering down at him through the snowflake haze, a most pleasing face. Then he recognized Donna. She was on her knees beside him, trying to cradle and warm his scraped and freezing body.

"Thank God!" she kept repeating. "Thank God! Thank God!" It was an incantation which could assure his safety now.

She wrapped him in her coat. His teeth were chattering; speech was impossible.

"I was watching you walk down the street. All of a sudden those men dragged you into their car," she explained softly, rocking him. "I followed in my car. After a while I lost sight of their headlights. Then their car passed me, and you weren't in it. I was terrified."

He looked so helpless, but she had to get him into the car. She swung his arm around her neck and strained upward to lift him. There wasn't the strength left in his body even to feign effort.

She dragged Will to the car and pushed him onto the seat. His head fell limply against the backrest. After a moment his eyelids opened again. He looked up at her with absolute, defenseless gratitude.

Donna slipped into the driver's seat and began the trip back down to Denver and the hospital. All the while, one arm held him close to her, sustaining them both.

Workers on the night shift were used to the Old Man arriving at all sorts of hours to wander through the huge buildings in which the engines were overhauled or the aircraft bodies checked and repaired. But tonight was not like other nights. The men knew that even before he showed up.

Buck arrived at one o'clock in the morning and slowly, with obvious effort, climbed a catwalk so as to be able to view all of the capacious jet-engine "hospital." This might be the last time. He did not move for two hours. Below him dozens of engines, for every aircraft in the fleet, hung on chains from the ceiling. Every now and then a yellow cart would roll by on tracks overhead, carrying a part sent by Inventory to a particular station. The men labored quietly, seemingly oblivious to him.

It was nearly three when the Old Man descended and walked through to the maintenance hangars. He stood silently beside a 747 stripped down for its annual checkup. Crates full of supplies covered the floor around him. Four days earlier this same plane had been the centerpiece of the fiftieth-anniversary party.

Nearly an hour later Buck turned and began to retrace his steps. Every man he passed looked up from his work to say, "Good night, General." A few added, "Good luck."

24

Like a young house cat out too late, spring finally jumped the Rocky Mountain fence that May fifth morning. The skies were a bright, cloudless blue and the air was warm. At another time, tomorrow maybe, Will could sit in his yard and watch the whiteness begin trickling off and the sun's heat wake the sleeping world beneath. This morning he had obligations that would not wait.

Donna had spent the night tucked into a chair in the hospital room. She helped him into a borrowed prosthetic leg that didn't quite fit and clothes out of the suitcase retrieved from the trunk of his car. His every action was agony. Two ribs had been cracked and, under the bands of adhesive constricting him from armpit to waist, stabbed back their resentment at being moved.

Donna drove Will to the Brown Palace Hotel. Marcie was waiting for him as he suffered the ordeal of lowering himself into a chair. He started to apologize for not being able to meet her at the airport, but she was too full of her own good news to wait through the sentence or two.

"Oh, it was all right, Will, Ron and I took a taxi."

"Ron?"

"Ron Bailey. He was so sweet yesterday. He asked me out, and when I told him I couldn't, that I had to fly here on business, he was as disappointed as a little boy. He begged to come with me." She smiled. "All the time I thought he was ignoring me, he was just too shy to approach me."

"But not too shy to approach the woman he left the New Year's Eve party with."

"He explained all that. She was an old friend in a lot of trouble. They went to the corner pub to talk for a few minutes. Because of my stupid jealousy, I ran out before he came back. He was so hurt; he thought *I* had stood *him* up." She clutched her coffee cup blissfully. "It must have taken all his courage just to ask me out again. Last night was just wonderful. He says he usually has difficulty, you know, making love . . . because of his shyness, but I never noticed a problem. It was incredible for us both."

"That sometimes happens to those shy guys out here," said Will with exaggerated solicitousness. "Denver's the sexual Lourdes."

He reached into his briefcase. "Marcie, this is the contract I drew up for the sale of your stock. I called your lawyer this morning, and he has no changes. If it's all right with you, I'd like us to eat something quickly and be at the bank at nine."

Marcie's brow clouded. She was busily engaged in setting her utensils perfectly perpendicular to the edge of the table. Then she smiled and looked up again.

"He asked me to marry him, Will. It just sort of slipped out, and he began to blush and apologize, but I said yes." Tiny tears of happiness were forming in the corners of her eyes. "Isn't it the most wonderful . . ."

"It's wonderful to see you so happy," Will said sincerely.

Her eyes dropped again. "But I did something you aren't going to like. Early this morning I sold my stock in your company to Faranco." She rushed on. "Ron convinced me it was the wise thing to do. It was so important to him that we start out our marriage and our new partnership with Belinda on the right foot. I called her then and there to tell her the good news."

"What did she say?"

"She said she was happy for me if I was sure Ron was the right man."

"What did she say about selling to Faranco?"

"That Ron was right. Too much was at stake to wait thirty days." Marcie's face was aglow. "Ron was just terrific. He insisted that we wouldn't sell for less than sixteen million dollars cash, and Faranco didn't let out a peep."

Marcie showed Will the check and her copy of the sale contract and proxy she had granted.

The fight for control of Global Universal Airlines had been lost.

"Marcie, I wish you the best." Abruptly, Will stood up. "If you'll excuse me. It's going to be a busy day."

Will had already left change on the table and was moving toward the door when Marcie noticed the anguish on his face and the bruises. But it was too late to ask about them.

As Will walked into the GUA Building, the sculpture above the entrance, its talons poised like knives, seemed about to dive at the back of his neck to extract retribution for his failure.

While the directors breakfasted in the Board Room, Will sat with Ben Buck in the large corner office. Only a few words were required to inform Buck of Marcie's action. They sat silently, trying to adjust to the inevitable. Someone else would be at this desk within a few days, directing the men and women of GUA into a future Buck had helped build out of struts and propellers and fan jets and plain raw nerve. How could they ever care as this old man did, Will asked himself, or see the outlines of tomorrow with the same clarity?

Buck had been thinking many of the same thoughts. "You know, I was born about the same time the first airplane flew, and I was lucky enough to be part of it all. But the pioneers have just about died out—I'm one of the last of the breed. The technicians have taken over the industry now. It's their turn. They understand the complex machinery and the numbers and procedures and financial statements—Lord, do they know the financial statements! But something is missing. I don't mean the sentiment, all that Wild Blue Yonder crap, but a vision of what you can make happen. Old men giving way to young men isn't the sad part; it's always been that way. But the vision they all had . . . losing that is the sad part."

Buck glanced at the clock, dropped his feet from the edge of the desk, and rose. The two men left the office.

Dan Pope and one of his security guards were hurrying up the corridor toward the General's office as Will and Buck waited for the elevator that would take them to the auditorium. Pope handed Will the manila envelope he carried. The blowup of the microfilm in the envelope was a memo from Benke to Will, with attachments. As he read the memo in the descending elevator, and then while walking onto the auditorium stage, Will understood at last why Girard would have stopped at nothing to prevent its contents from becoming known.

TO: WILLIAM NYE
FROM: CHARLES BENKE
RE: J. STEPHEN AND MARIE GIRARD

I am preparing this memo, microfilming it and the attached documents and hiding the microfilm because I'm certain that Girard's people are right behind me.

1. Attached is a copy of a 1942 police record from a small town outside of Miami, Florida. Although the original had been stolen, the records had been microfilmed several months earlier by the municipality, as a precaution against fire. The attached record is of the arrest of one Marie Ivers, aged sixteen years, on charges of prostitution. Because of her age she was granted a suspended sentence and released in the custody of her father, Warren Ivers, arrested at the same time for procuring, but released himself for lack of evidence. A copy of her first driver's license is also attached.

2. Enclosed from the city records of Houston, Texas, is a copy of a certificate of marriage, between J. Stephen Girard and one Marie Logan, dated September 24, 1956. Inspection of the signatures of Marie Ivers and Marie Logan reveals them to have been written by the same person fifteen years apart.

3. Attached is a copy of the birth certificate of James Ivers, born in 1929 in Miami, Florida. This birth certificate, found in the Miami city records, is, with certain forged substitutions, identical to the birth certificate of James Stephen Girard submitted later to the Carleton School.

4. There is no doubt that James Ivers assumed the name "Girard" when entering Carleton and fabricated imaginary parents. I am fully con-

vinced that this will be borne out by a visit to Crippville, Virginia, the site of the alleged death of those "parents," where no death records will be found, or else falsified ones. If the latter, then the cooperation of key police officials and the physician were probably bought and paid for by Girard.

5. Note that the parents on the enclosed birth certificate of Marie Ivers "Girard" and James Ivers "Girard" are identical. Therefore, the inescapable conclusion is that J. Stephen Girard and Marie Girard are brother and sister, as well as man and wife.

Shocked disbelief seized Will Nye as he stared at the memo. Only after that had passed and he realized that his heart was pounding wildly did Will understand the memo's import. They had won! There was no way Girard could continue the fight when this was shown to him. It would be made clear to him that the memo would remain in GUA's vault only as long as he kept his hands off the company. Just when it had seemed defeat was inevitable, the means for victory had been placed in their grasp.

J. Stephen Girard stepped out of the first limousine carrying their party. He himself helped Marie from the vehicle. He could not hide the beginnings of a jubilant smile at the corners of his mouth. Only a few minutes more and Global Universal would be his—the culmination of his career. That was why he wanted Marie to be with him. Her only interest in life was he. She had sacrificed so much for him for so long. He would lay Global Universal at her feet.

As they were about to enter the GUA Building, an object streaking across the sky caught Girard's eye: a fugitive falcon that had chosen that moment to break the invisible thread between it and its master was now fleeing back to the wild, its leather jesses still trailing behind like streamers. Marie followed Jamie's gaze and saw it, too. They watched until it was out of sight high in the mountains.

Ben Buck looked up from the memo Will had given him to read. They stood in the wings of the stage, just beyond the drawn-back curtains. A bustle in the rear of the auditorium attracted everyone's attention. Girard and his entourage of wife, Carl Raymond, Grant Eckman, lawyers and vice-presidents were just entering. Buck watched them for a few minutes and then spoke very quietly to Will.

"I want this memo and the microfilm burned as soon as the shareholders meeting is over. No one else is to see it. For whatever little time remains to me at the head of this company, we will not lower ourselves to violating the sanctity of those people's privacy, no matter how repul—no matter what! We will not use it!"

Will was stunned. Never would he have thought Ben Buck unwilling to use that ammunition to save himself, never, particularly against as ruthless an opponent as Girard.

"Just *show* it to Girard," Will hissed. "We'll never have to release it. It'll go into the vault. Girard only has to know it's there, and we've won. He can't let this get out. The scandal of having married his own sister would destroy him and destroy her. We've won, I tell you!"

"This is *my* proxy fight," said the Old Man softly, his voice as final as doom. "I will not use it."

Will seized the front of Buck's jacket with both hands, pulling him behind the curtain.

"You son of a bitch! Now it's *your* fight and *your* decision. Whose was it when you begged me not to blow the whistle on your illness and to promise I wouldn't desert you once the fight started? In Miami a man was nearly killed to get you that information. I only had the shit kicked out of me last night for it."

He grabbed Buck's hand and forced it against the taped ribs.

"Feel that! See this bruise above my eye? I was pissing blood all night because four goons thought I had that information! You can't give up and turn coward on us." He was pleading now. "Girard himself has thugs as ruthless as any terrorist that ever lived. If any one person in the world would have no scruples about using this document, it's Girard. There's no dishonor in just *showing* it to him! I've got him, damn it! Just like I swore I would, I've got the son of a bitch by the balls!"

Buck pulled his hand from Will's side, shook his head no and walked back onto the stage.

A terrifying sadness flooded over Will. Retribution, finally in his hand like a stiletto, had been wrenched from him. He had committed himself to Buck's cause against all considered wisdom and had nearly yielded up his life in the process. All for naught. Perhaps Buck's timidity at the moment when only the final knife thrust was needed was the best proof of all that Ben Buck *had* grown too old and that Will himself had been a fool.

An aide who had arrived early and commandeered a block of seats close to the stage was signaling to the Faranco group.

Halfway down the center aisle, Marie Girard stopped still, as if noticing her surroundings for the first time. Her eyes locked on the man in the center of the stage. She grabbed her husband's arm.

"Why is General Benjamin here?"

"Who?"

"The man at the microphone. Why is he here?"

"This is his company we're about to take over."

"Oh," she said, as if orienting herself after suddenly being awakened. "I didn't know that. Does he want you to take it from him?"

"No."

"Then you can't."

Girard stared at his wife uncomprehendingly.

"You can't, Jamie."

Girard knew that if she was not pleased, for whatever reason, then it all meant nothing to him; the merest mention of the airline would turn acrid in his mouth. He led her to the back of the auditorium where they could speak in private.

The corporation's bylaws called for the chairman of the existing Board of Directors to serve as chairman of stockholders meetings. Ben Buck lifted the gavel, brought it down several times and called the meeting to order. The noise abated only slightly.

Will's seat was close to the rostrum so that he would be in position to help rule on sticky legal questions. As he made his way toward his chair, he noticed Lee Conway chatting with two of the outside directors. Conway appeared tired and on edge. Will had heard he had moved out of his house and was living at the Hilton temporarily. Conway seemed to be listening with only half his attention. His gaze was fixed on a section of the auditorium where his wife sat with Sally Emerson and one or two others of the "anti-female-discrimination" faction. Their stockholders' resolution requiring quotas for female-executive hiring and promotion had been submitted too late to print on management's ballot or to arouse much support at this meeting. The group was rumored to be planning nonetheless to propose the resolution from the floor as a way of gaining newspaper space. For maximum effect Helen Conway, who owned a hundred shares in her own name and was a director's wife, would submit it. Will noticed that although she responded to those around her, Helen's attention seemed to be on Lee. Both wife and husband wore similarly agitated expressions.

"The meeting will come to order." Buck rapped the gavel once more. "The first order of business will be the secretary's report."

All the seats were filled, many by reporters. Newcomers found they had to stand in the rear.

Natalie Harmon, the corporate secretary, replaced Buck at the rostrum. She presented proof that due notice of the meeting had been given to the stockholders and she produced an alphabetical list of them as of the record date. Buck then requested that all persons having proxies deliver them to the secretary.

Buck proceeded to give the president's report, and Bannister gave the financial report. Will was too sick at heart to listen. He watched the Girards speaking quietly in the rear, intent only on each other; and he watched the Conways, separated by half an auditorium, also intent only on each other. Will pondered the differences.

The agenda items dragged on like a slow-motion dream. Yet, strangely, instead of producing ennui, the languor engendered increasing anticipation of the conflict to come.

"The floor is now open to motions and resolutions," Buck declared.

Will's attention was drawn back to the proceedings.

Helen Conway's head lifted. This was the moment for her to rise and present her resolution. Those around her began to prod her. At last, almost unwillingly, she rose and was recognized. Her resolution was read, seconded by another in the group and then quickly and massively voted down. Helen regained her seat. Lee pivoted away, his eyes focused elsewhere.

Finally Buck announced, "The next item of business is the nomination of directors. The floor is now open for nominations."

Buck recognized a stockholder of record, who nominated management's slate. Another seconded.

Buck took a deep breath. "Any other nominations?"

Heads in the auditorium twisted toward the Faranco section. Some heads in that section turned toward the rear. The silence was total and electric. And then an undercurrent of murmuring began to rise up into it.

"Any other nominations?" Buck repeated.

Now all heads in the auditorium were facing the rear. All eyes were on J. Stephen Girard. The Faranco man who had been picked to nominate the opposing slate had just been given new instructions and remained silent, although he stood alertly in the aisle, watching Girard like all the rest in case the industrialist changed his mind yet again. Girard himself stared straight ahead, his face impassive, unreadable behind the dark glasses. Marie's face was radiant.

Grant Eckman raced to the back of the auditorium to confront Girard. Time was running out. Why hadn't his slate been nominated? Girard ignored him. Eckman demanded an answer.

In a tone so low only Eckman and Marie could hear, Girard replied, "It's over, Grant."

Buck spoke once more. "The chair will entertain a motion that nominations be closed."

A shareholder friendly to management stood up, was recognized and made the requested motion. It was seconded.

Less than a minute later the management slate had been overwhelmingly elected. The audience was bewildered, dissatisfied. They stood chattering in confused groups.

The final motion was made and seconded. Buck banged the gavel. The meeting was adjourned.

"Come on, Will," the Old Man said. "The drinks are on me."

Will followed Buck as he made his way out of the auditorium. The Old Man was oblivious to the reporters' frantic questions and to the backslapping and congratulations of well-wishers.

All the way up in the elevator Buck's eyes were cast down in thought. He progressed several steps into his office before he noticed the slim figure standing in the center of the room.

"Hello, General." Her voice was a strained whisper. "I hope you don't mind that I came up here."

"Hello, Marie."

She relaxed. "I was afraid you wouldn't remember. It's been so long."

"Men never forget beautiful women."

"You know, that night when my father was . . . was killed I was so shaken I never thanked you. Or for any of the other things."

"That's not so." Buck's tone was imbued with a tenderness Will had never heard from him. "The bank forwarded your letter every year."

"I didn't have any idea this was your airline. I want you to know that. Jamie was so young then and barely knew you, so he didn't make the connection, either. If he had, he never would have tried to buy your company. He told me to be sure and tell you that."

"He didn't come up himself."

"Oh, Ben, he just couldn't. Not when I reminded him who you were. He shuts that whole part of my life, all the men especially, out of his mind, as if he and I met for the first time the morning after that awful night."

"Have you shut them all out?"

"Not all." A shy smile lit her face, but then, her eyes going to Will in the doorway, her face registered a suspicion of recognition, and she reddened. "Do we know each other?"

Will shook his head. "I don't think so."

Her eyes moved back to Buck's, and the smile returned. At last she stepped up to him. One hand touched his face. She raised up on tiptoes and gave him a kiss as delicate as the fall of a flower petal.

"Thank you. For everything."

Neither Buck nor Will turned to follow her departure. Will closed the door, then went to the bar and poured drinks for them both. Buck was nearly at the bottom of his when he began to explain.

During World War II, he had spent a good deal of time in Miami, which the Air Transport Command was using as a jumping-off point for ferrying planes and airlifting supplies to Africa, South America and the Caribbean. In 1943 he met Marie Ivers there. Just eighteen, she was called Marie Logan then, and was working at one of the bordellos in town. She knew him as General Benjamin, the name he always used in such places. Buck, for his part, had no idea that Warren Ivers, who owned and ran the house, was her father.

Marie was totally devoted to Jamie Ivers, an unusually bright, quick youngster; they were inseparable. Buck knew that Jamie was Ivers's son. He did not know the boy was also Marie's younger brother. The boy was fourteen then and spent long nighttime hours in the bordello, playing poker and hanging out with men more than twice his age.

Buck became deeply attached to Marie. She was so young and fresh and gentle. He disliked thinking that she might be used by some of the rough types who frequented the place.

Late one night, after a bout of lovemaking with Marie, Buck was awakened by a horrible scream from the adjoining room. He threw on his pants and broke through the connecting door. He found young Jamie Ivers standing over his father's lifeless naked body. The boy had brought a metal lamp crashing down on the man's head. Marie, also naked, was crouching on the bed, terrified. It was then she stammered out that Warren Ivers was her father. After his wife's death, Ivers had forced his daughter first to submit to his own sexual desires, and then into prostitution. Marie had managed to keep from Jamie knowledge of the shameful acts committed with their father—until that night. Wanting to speak with his father, the boy had quietly entered Warren Ivers's bedroom. Seeing Ivers in bed with Marie, and the revulsion and hatred on his sister's face, in a terrible rage Jamie had slain his father.

Ben Buck never hesitated. He wrapped Ivers's body in a blanket, and he and Marie sneaked it out of the house and onto a small boat. Several miles out to sea, they dumped the weighted body into the ocean. By dawn a sign was posted announcing that the bordello had been closed down, and a rumor that Ivers had fled town to avoid gambling debts was being spread.

Marie had saved some money, managing to hide it from her father. Buck added enough to it for the sister and brother to move North. With a phone call, Buck arranged for an office job for Marie with the Navy in Norfolk, Virginia, where no one knew her. He also suggested Jamie be sent to a good private school. The boy was certainly smart enough to do well. Buck promised Marie a thousand dollars a year toward his education. Every year afterward, without fail, "General Benjamin's" bank sent her its check for a thousand dollars. And without fail until Jamie graduated college, Marie Logan sent Buck a thank-you note in care of the bank, the only address she had for "General Benjamin." The boy knew nothing about the arrangement. Buck was simply a customer who had helped them that night and passed out of their lives.

Then Buck and Marie lost contact. Buck did not know she and the boy had given up the names Ivers and Logan and had begun calling themselves Girard.

"Maybe they became husband and wife," Will conjectured, "because they feared no one else could ever love them after what they had done."

Buck shrugged. Marie had appeared happy. Condemnation, analysis, even regret, seemed superficial and self-indulgent in the face of that contentment.

Will offered another conjecture. "When Girard and Marie decided to marry, they created a phony Girard parentage with the help of their Virginia friend Dr. Johnson. He legitimized the Girard family tree with a stroke of his pen. That old friendship probably helped Jenabelle Draper, Johnson's wife, through the years—especially when the Administration began looking around for a new SEC chairman. That was a spot where Girard could use her to excellent advantage."

"At least we know who was knocking our heads in over there," observed Buck.

"When I met Johnson, he told me the car crash which was supposed to have killed Girard's parents happened on his property. That meant he and the policeman signing the death certificate could claim to be the only witnesses. Car skids off the road. Goes through a fence. Hurtles across a field till it's out of sight of the road. And only then hits a tree. No witnesses except the same two people who signed the death certificates. No bodies—Girard took them. If Johnson needed a coroner's okay or an undertaker's, no problem—he was a doctor. Why should people suspect there weren't even any bodies? The deal probably gave Johnson a nest egg the size of the Astrodome."

"Sounds perfect."

"Except for one thing. There never was a car accident—just two signatures on a death certificate after a stormy night—so the local newspaper never reported it, although Girard probably planted it in a few little papers well away from Crippville to add authenticity. Girard had to have that day's Crippville paper stolen out of the back-issue file. That made me suspect Girard had tried to hide some problem concerning his parents. It never occurred to me that they never existed at all."

Will fell silent and stared at the manila envelope in his hands. He spoke without taking his eyes from it. "What would you have done about Benke's memo if you hadn't seen Marie Girard walking into the auditorium?"

"I'll never really have to know the answer to that," Buck replied quietly.

"The police will bring charges against that hood in Miami, and maybe even track down one or two of the guys that took me apart last night. But they'll never find a link to Faranco or Girard without this."

"I can't stop you, Will. But you know I hope you won't use it. There's no longer anything to be gained."

"Benke may decide to spill it when the police question him about why he was attacked."

"Not if his client doesn't."

Will stared at the Old Man's tired eyes for several seconds, then down at the envelope again.

Finally, Will stood up, placed the envelope on Buck's desk and strode from the room and from the building.

It was time to move on.

Will's single ski swung lightly as the chairlift moved up the slope. The two outrigger poles with small skis were gripped in one hand. The day was vivid, the sky clear, the skiing good high in the Rockies, even so late in the spring. Donna sat beside him. Will had no idea how much of a future there was for him and Donna, but the happiness now was real.

He had been trying to decide whether to accept Ben Buck's offer to be his successor at Global Universal. Buck had told Will he had been picked because he was capable of grasping the totality of the problems confronting the company in the coming years without allowing any one factor to distort his judgment in solving them. Buck had made up his mind weeks before and had set up the new reorganization with Will's elevation in mind. The salary and the stock benefits would be huge, and Faranco would be out of the new president's hair—its stock would be sold gradually over the next three years. But some part of Will was still flirting with the idea of setting up a little law practice in some small Colorado town and seeing how it worked out. What was it that he really wanted to do, that would finally bring him satisfaction? He could not put off a decision much longer.

The lift halted for a moment. Will and Donna compared the skiers who cut and schussed below them. After a while Will looked up and noticed a vapor trail lengthening across the sky like a great white arrow. At the forward point was a silver fleck moving eastward at nearly the speed of sound, forty thousand feet above the earth.

He could not take his eyes off it.